D0872645

Qiu Xiaolong

Death of a Red Heroine

SCEPTRE

First published in the United States of America by Soho Press in 2000
First published in Great Britain in 2006 by Hodder and Stoughton
A division of Hodder Headline

A Sceptre Book

5

A CIP catalogue record for this title is available from the British Library

ISBN 0 340 89750 3

Typest in Giovanni Book
by Palimpsest Book Production Limited, Polmont, Stirlingshire

Printed and bound by Clays Ltd, St Ives plc

Hodder Headline's policy is to use papers that are natural, renewable and
recyclable products and made from wood grown in sustainable forests.
The logging and manufacturing processes are expected to conform to the
environmental regulations of the country of origin.

Hodder and Stoughton Ltd
A division of Hodder Headline
338 Euston Road
London NW1 3BH

For Lijun

I want to express my sincere thanks to my editor,
Laura Hruska, who discovered my manuscript and
helped me step by step, to shape this book.

Deep as the Peach Blossom Lake can be,
It is not so deep as the song you sing for me.

Li Bai

Chapter 1

The body was found at 4:40 P.M., on May 11, 1990, in Baili Canal, an out-of-the-way canal, about twenty miles to the west of Shanghai.

Standing beside the body, Gao Ziling, captain of the *Vanguard*, spat vigorously on the damp ground three times—a half-hearted effort to ward off the evil spirits of the day, a day that had begun with a long-anticipated reunion between two friends who had been separated for more than twenty years.

It was coincidental that the *Vanguard*, a patrol boat of the Shanghai River Security Department, should have ventured all the way into Baili around 1:30 P.M. Normally it did not go anywhere close to that area. The unusual trip had been suggested by Liu Guoliang, an old friend whom Gao had not seen for twenty years. They had been high-school buddies. After leaving school in the early sixties, Gao started to work in Shanghai, but Liu had gone to a college in Beijing, and afterward, to a nuclear test center in Qinghai Province. During the Cultural Revolution they had lost touch. Now Liu had a project under review by an American company in Shanghai, and he had taken a day off to meet with Gao. Their reunion after so long a time was a pleasant event, to which each of them had been looking forward.

It took place by the Waibaidu Bridge, where the Suzhou River and the Huangpu River met with a dividing line visible in the sunlight. The Suzhou, even more heavily polluted than the Huangpu, looked like a black tarpaulin in sharp contrast to the clear blue sky. The river stank despite the pleasant summer breeze. Gao kept apologizing; a better place should have been chosen for the occasion. The Mid-Lake Teahouse in Shanghai Old City, for instance. An afternoon over an exquisite set of teacups and saucers, where they would have so much to talk about, with lambent *pipa* and *sanxun* music in the background. However, Gao had been obliged to remain on board the *Vanguard* all day; no one had wanted to take over his shift.

Looking at the muddy water, with its burden of rubbish—plastic bottles, empty beer cans, flattened containers, and cigarette boxes—Liu suggested they go somewhere else in the boat to fish. The river had changed beyond the two old friends' recognition, but they themselves had not changed that much. Fishing was a passion they had shared in their high-school days.

"I've missed the taste of crucian carp in Qinghai," Liu confessed.

Gao jumped at the suggestion. He could easily explain going downstream as a routine trip. Also, it would display his power as captain. So he suggested Baili, a canal off the Suzhou River, about seventy miles south of the Waibaidu Bridge as a destination. It was yet untouched by Deng Xiaoping's economic reforms, far from any main road, with the nearest village a couple of miles away. But getting there by water was not easy. Once they passed the Oriental Refinery looming above Wusong the passage grew narrower, and at times it was so shallow it was hardly navigable. They had to push away trailing branches, but after an arduous struggle, they finally reached a dark stretch of water obscured by tall weeds and shrubs.

Fortunately, Baili turned out to be as wonderful as Gao had promised. It was small, but with no shortage of water thanks to the past month's heavy rain. The fish flourished there since it was relatively unpolluted. As soon as they flipped out the lures, they could feel bites. Soon they were busy retrieving their lines. Fish kept jumping out of the water, landing in the boat, jerking and gasping.

"Look at this one," Liu said, pointing out a fish twitching at his feet. "More than a pound."

"Great," Gao said. "You're bringing us luck today."

The next minute, Gao, too, dug the hook out of a half-pound bass with his thumbnail.

Happily, he recast his line with a practiced flick of his wrist. Before he had reeled it halfway back to the boat, something gave his line another terrific tug. The rod arched, and a huge carp exploded into the sunlight.

They did not have much time to talk. Time flashed backward as silver scales danced in the golden sun. Twenty minutes—or twenty years. They were back in the good old days. Two high-school students sitting side by side, talking, drinking, and angling, the whole world dangling on their lines.

"How much does a pound of crucian carp sell for?" Liu asked, holding another one in his hand. "One this size?"

"Thirty Yuan at least, I'd say."

"So I've already got more than four pounds. About a hundred Yuan worth, right?" Liu said. "We've been here only an hour, and I've hauled in more than a week's salary."

"You're kidding!" Gao said, pulling a bluegill off his hook. "A nuclear engineer with your reputation!"

"No, it's a fact. I should have been a fisherman, angling south of the Yangtze River," Liu said, shaking his head. "In Qinghai we often go for months without a taste of fish."

Liu had worked for twenty years in a desert area, where the local peasants observed a time-honored tradition of serving a fish carved from wood in celebration of the Spring Festival since the Chinese character for "fish" can also mean "surplus," a lucky sign for the coming year. Its taste might be forgotten, but not the tradition.

"I cannot believe it," Gao said indignantly. "The great scientist making nuclear bombs earns less than the petty peddlers making tea-leaf eggs. What a shame!"

"It's the market economy," Liu said. "The country is changing in the right direction. And the people have a better life."

"But that's unfair, I mean, for you."

"Well, I don't have too much to complain of nowadays. Can you guess why I did not write to you during the Cultural Revolution?"

"No. Why?"

"I was criticized as a bourgeois intellectual and locked up in a cell for a year. After I was released, I was still considered 'politically black,' so I did not want to incriminate you."

"I'm so sorry to hear that," Gao said, "but you should have let me know. My letters were returned. I should have guessed."

"It's all over," Liu said, "and here we are, together, fishing for our lost years."

"Tell you what," Gao said, eager to change the subject, "we've got enough to make an excellent soup."

"A wonderful soup—Wow, another!" Liu was reeling in a thrashing perch—well over a foot long.

"My old wife is no intellectual, but she's pretty good at making fish soup. Add a few slices of Jinhua bacon, throw in a pinch of black pepper and a handful of green onion. Oh, what a soup."

"I'm looking forward to meeting her."

"You're no stranger to her. I've shown your picture to her frequently."

"Yes, but it's twenty years old," Liu said. "How can she recognize me from a high-school picture? Remember He Zhizhang's famous line? *'My dialect is not changed, but my hair has turned gray.'*"

"Mine, too," Gao said.

They were ready to go back now.

Gao returned to the wheel. But the engine shuddered with a grinding sound. He tried full throttle. The exhaust at the rear spurted black fumes, but the boat did not move an inch. Scratching his head, Captain Gao turned to his friend with an apologetic gesture. He was unable to understand the problem. The canal was small but not shallow. The propeller, protected by the rudder, could not have scraped bottom. Something might have caught in it—a torn fishing net or a loose cable. The former was rather unlikely. The canal was too narrow for fishermen to cast nets there. But if the latter was the cause of the trouble, it would be hard to disentangle it to free the propeller.

He turned off the engine and jumped onto the shore. He still failed to see anything amiss, so he started feeling about in the muddy water with a long bamboo stick which he had bought for his wife to use as a clothesline on their balcony. After a few minutes, he touched something under the boat.

It felt like a soft object, rather large, heavy.

Taking off his shirt and pants, he stepped down into the water. He got hold of it in no time. It took him several minutes, however, to tug it through the water, and up onto the shore.

It was a huge black plastic bag.

There was a string tied around the neck of the bag. Untying it cautiously, he leaned down to look within.

"Holy—hell!" he cursed.

"What?"

"Look at this. Hair!"

Leaning over, Liu also gasped.

It was the hair of a dead, naked woman.

With Liu's help, Gao took the body out of the bag and laid it on its back on the ground.

She could not have been in the water too long. Her face, though slightly swollen, was recognizably young and good looking. A wisp of green rush was woven into her coil of black hair. Her body was ghastly white, with slack breasts and heavy thighs. Her pubic hair was black and wet.

Gao hurried back into the boat, took out a worn blanket, and threw it over her. That was all he could think of doing for the moment. He then broke the bamboo pole in two. It was a pity, but it would bring bad luck now. He could not bear the thought of his wife hanging their clothes over it, day in, day out.

"What shall we do?" Liu said.

"There's nothing we can do. Don't touch anything. Leave the body alone until the police come."

Gao took out his cellular phone. He hesitated before dialing the number of the Shanghai Police Bureau. He would have to write a report. It would have to describe the way he had found the body, but first of all, he would have to account for being there, at that time of day, with Liu on board. While supposedly working his shift, he was having a good time with his friend, fishing and drinking. But he would have to tell the truth. He had no choice, he concluded, dialing.

"Detective Yu Guangming, special case squad," a voice answered.

"I am Captain Gao Ziling, of the *Vanguard*, Shanghai River Security Department. I am reporting a homicide. A body was discovered in Baili Canal. A young female body."

"Where is Baili Canal?"

"West of Qingpu. Past Shanghai Number Two Paper Mill. About seven or eight miles from it."

"Hold on," Detective Yu said. "Let me see who is available."

Captain Gao grew nervous as the silence at the other end of the line was prolonged.

"Another murder case was reported after four thirty," Detective Yu finally said. "Everybody is out of the office now. Even Chief

Inspector Chen. But I'm on my way. You know enough not to mess things up, I assume. Wait there for me."

Gao glanced at his watch. It would take at least two hours for the detective to reach them. Not to mention the time he would have to spend with him after that. Both Liu and he would be required as witnesses, then probably would have to go to the police station to make their statements as well.

The weather was quite pleasant, the temperature mild, the white clouds moving idly across the sky. He saw a dark toad jumping into a crevice among the rocks, the gray spot contrasting with the bone-white rocks. A toad, too, could be an evil omen. He spat on the ground again. He had already forgotten how many times this made.

Even if they could manage to get back home for dinner, the fish would have been long dead. A huge difference for the soup.

"I'm so sorry," Gao apologized. "I should have chosen another place."

"As our ancient sage says, 'Eight or nine out of ten times, things will go wrong in this world of ours'," Liu replied with renewed equanimity. "It's nobody's fault."

As he spat again, Gao observed the dead woman's feet sticking out of the blanket. White, shapely feet, with arched soles, well-formed toes, scarlet-painted nails.

And then he saw the glassy eyes of a dead carp afloat on the surface of the bucket. For a second, he felt as if the fish were staring at him, unblinking; its belly appeared ghastly white, swollen.

"We won't forget the day of our reunion," Liu remarked.

Chapter 2

At four thirty that day, Chief Inspector Chen Cao, head of the special case squad, Homicide Division, Shanghai Police Bureau, did not know anything about the case.

It was a sweltering Friday afternoon. Occasionally cicadas could be heard chirping on a poplar tree outside the window of his new one-bedroom apartment on the second floor of a gray-brick building. From the window, he could look out to the busy traffic moving slowly along Huaihai Road, but at a desirable, noiseless distance. The building was conveniently located near the center of the Luwan district. It took him less than twenty minutes to walk to Nanjing Road in the north, or to the City God's Temple in the south, and on a clear summer night, he could smell the tangy breeze from the Huangpu River.

Chief Inspector Chen should have stayed at the office, but he found himself alone in his apartment, working on a problem. Reclining on a leather-covered couch, his outstretched legs propped on a gray swivel chair, he was studying a list on the first page of a small notepad. He scribbled a few words and then crossed them out, looking out the window. In the afternoon sunlight, he saw a towering crane silhouetted against another new building about a block away. The apartment complex had not been completed yet.

The problem confronting the chief inspector, who had just been assigned an apartment, was his housewarming party. Obtaining a new apartment in Shanghai was an occasion calling for a celebration. He himself was greatly pleased. On a moment's impulse, he had sent out invitations. Now he was considering how he would entertain his guests. It would not do to just have a homely meal, as Lu, nicknamed Overseas Chinese, had warned him. For such an occasion, there had to be a special banquet.

Once more he studied the names on the party list. Wang Feng, Lu Tonghao and his wife Ruru, Zhou Kejia and his wife Liping. The Zhous had telephoned earlier to say that they might not be able to come due to a meeting at East China Normal University. Still, he'd better prepare for all of them.

The telephone on the filing cabinet rang. He went over and picked up the receiver.

"Chen's residence."

"Congratulations, Comrade Chief Inspector Chen!" Lu said. "Ah, I can smell the wonderful smell in your new kitchen."

"You'd better not be calling to say you're delayed, Overseas Chinese Lu. I'm counting on you."

"Of course we are coming. It's only that the beggar's chicken needs a few more minutes in the oven. The best chicken in Shanghai, I guarantee. Nothing but Yellow Mountains pine needles used to cook it, so you'll savor its special flavor. Don't worry. We wouldn't miss your housewarming party for the world, you lucky fellow."

"Thank you."

"Don't forget to put some beer in your refrigerator. And glasses, too. It'll make a huge difference."

"I've put in half a dozen bottles already. Qingdao and Bud. And the Shaoxing rice wine will not be warmed until the moment of your arrival, right?"

"Now you may count yourself as half a gourmet. More than half, perhaps. You're certainly learning fast."

The comment was pure Lu. Even from the other end of line, Chen could hear in Lu's voice his characteristic excitement over the prospect of a dinner. Lu seldom talked for a couple of minutes without bringing the conversation around to his favorite subject—food.

"With Overseas Chinese Lu as my instructor, I should be making some progress."

"I'll give you a new recipe tonight, after the party," Lu said. "What a piece of luck, dear Comrade Chief Inspector! Your great ancestors must have been burning bundles of tall incense to the Fortune God. And to the Kitchen God, too."

"Well, my mother has been burning incense, but to what particular god, I don't know."

"Guanyin, I know. I once saw her kowtow to a clay image—it must be more than ten years ago—and I asked her about it."

In Lu's eyes, Chief Inspector Chen had fallen into Fortune's lap—or that of whatever god in Chinese mythology had brought him luck. Unlike most people of his generation, though an "educated youth" who had graduated from high school, Chen was not sent to the countryside "to be reeducated by poor and lower-middle peasants" in the early seventies. As an only child, he had been allowed to stay in the city, where he had studied English on his own. At the end of the Cultural Revolution, Chen entered Beijing Foreign Language College with a high English score on the entrance examination and then obtained a job at the Shanghai Police Bureau. And now there was another demonstration of Chen's good luck. In an overpopulated city like Shanghai, with more than thirteen million people, the housing shortage was acute. Still, he had been assigned a private apartment.

The housing problem had a long history in Shanghai. A small fishing village during the Ming dynasty, Shanghai had developed into one of the most prosperous cities in the Far East, with foreign companies and factories appearing like bamboo shoots after a spring rain, and people pouring in from everywhere. Residential housing failed to keep pace under the rule of the Northern warlords and Nationalist governments. When the Communists took power in 1949, the situation took an unexpected turn for the worse. Chairman Mao encouraged large families, even to the extent of providing food subsidies and free nurseries. It did not take long for the disastrous consequences to be felt. Families of two or three generations were squeezed into one single room of twelve square meters. Housing soon became a burning issue for people's "work units"—factories, companies, schools, hospitals, or the police bureau—which were assigned an annual housing quota directly from the city authorities. It was up to the work units to decide which employee would get an apartment. Chen's satisfaction came in part from the fact that he had obtained the apartment through his work unit's special intervention.

Preparing for the housewarming party, slicing a tomato for a side dish, he recalled singing a song while he stood beneath the portrait of Chairman Mao in his elementary school, a song that had been so popular in the sixties—"The Party's Concern Warms My Heart." There was no portrait of Chairman Mao in this apartment.

It was not luxurious. There was no real kitchen, only a narrow corridor containing a couple of gas burners tucked into the corner, with a small cabinet hanging on the wall above. No real bathroom either: a cubicle large enough for just a toilet seat and a cement square with a stainless-steel shower head. Hot water was out of the question. There was, however, a balcony that might serve as a storeroom for wicker trunks, repairable umbrellas, rusted brass spittoons, or whatever could not be decently squeezed inside the room. But he did not have such things, so he had put only a plastic folding chair and a few bookshelf boards on the balcony.

The apartment was good enough for him.

There had been some complaining in the bureau about his *privileges*. To those with longer years of service or larger families who remained on the waiting list, Chief Inspector Chen's recent acquisition was another instance of the unfair new cadre policy, he knew. But he decided not to think about those unpleasant complaints at the moment. He had to concentrate on the evening's menu.

He had only limited experience in preparing for a party. With a cookbook in his hand, he focused on those recipes designated easy-to-make. Even those took considerable time, but one colorful dish after another appeared on the table, adding a pleasant mixture of aromas to the room.

By ten to six he had finished setting the table. He rubbed his hands, quite pleased with the results of his efforts. For the main dishes, there were chunks of pork stomach on a bed of green *napa*, thin slices of smoked carp spread on fragile leaves of *jicai*, and steamed peeled shrimp with tomato sauce. There was also a platter of eels with scallions and ginger, which he had ordered from a restaurant. He had opened a can of Meiling steamed pork, and added some green vegetables to it to make another dish. On the side, he placed a small dish of sliced tomatoes, and another of cucumbers. When the guests arrived, a soup would be made from the juice of the canned pork and canned pickle.

He was selecting a pot in which to warm the Shaoxing wine when the doorbell rang.

Wang Feng, a young reporter from the *Wenhui Daily*, one of China's most influential newspapers, was the first to arrive. Attractive, young, and intelligent, she seemed to have all the makings of a successful reporter. But at the moment she did not have her black leather briefcase in her hand. Instead, she held a huge pine nut cake in her arms.

"Congratulations, Chief Inspector Chen," she said. "What a spacious apartment!"

"Thanks," he said, taking the cake from her.

He led her around for a five-minute tour. She seemed to like the apartment very much, looking into everything, opening the cupboard doors, and stepping into the bathroom, where she stood on her tiptoes, touching the overhead shower pipe and the new shower head.

"And a bathroom, too!"

"Well, like most Shanghai residents, I've always dreamed of having an apartment in this area," he said, giving her a glass of sparkling wine.

"And you have a wonderful view from the window, " she said, "almost like a picture."

Wang stood leaning against the newly painted window frame, her ankles crossed, holding the glass in her hand.

"*You* are turning it into a painting," he said.

In the afternoon light streaming through the plastic blinds, her complexion was matte porcelain. Her eyes were clear, almond-shaped, just long enough to be suggestive of a distinct character. Her black hair cascaded halfway down her back. She wore a white T-shirt and a pleated skirt, with a wide belt of alligator leather that cinched her "emancipated wasp" waist and accentuated her breasts.

Emancipated wasp. An image invented by Li Yu, the last emperor of the Southern Tang dynasty, also a brilliant poet, who depicted his favorite imperial concubine's ravishing beauty in several celebrated poems. The poet-emperor was afraid that he might break her in two by holding her too tightly. It was said that the custom of foot-binding also started in Li Yu's reign. There was no accounting for taste, Chen reflected.

"What do you mean?" she asked.

"'*Waist so slender, weightless she dances on my palm,*'" he said, changing the reference as he recalled the tragic end of the imperial concubine, who drowned herself in a well when the Southern Tang dynasty fell. "Du Mu's famous line fails to do justice to you."

"More of your bogus compliments copied from the Tang dynasty, my poetic chief inspector?"

This sounded more like the spirited woman he had first met in the Wenhui building, Chen was happy to note. It had taken quite a long while for her to get over the defection of her husband. A student in Japan, the man had decided not to return home when his visa expired. Wang had taken it hard, naturally.

"Poetically alone," he said.

"With this new apartment, you no longer have an excuse to remain celibate." She drained the glass with a toss of her long hair.

"Well, introduce some girls to me."

"You need my help?"

"Why not, if you are willing to help?" He tried to change the subject. "But how are things with you? About your own apartment, I mean. Soon you will get one for yourself, I bet."

"If only I were a chief inspector, a rising political star."

"Oh, sure," he said, raising his cup, "many thanks to you."

But it was true, or at least to a certain extent.

They had first met on a professional level. She had been assigned to write about the "people's policemen," and his name had been mentioned by Party Secretary Li of the Shanghai Police Bureau. As she talked with Chen in her office, she became more interested in how he spent his evenings than in how he did his day job. Chen had had several translations of Western mystery novels published. The reporter was not a fan of that particular genre, but she saw a fresh perspective for her article. And then the readers, too, responded favorably to the image of a young, well-educated police officer who "works late into night, translating books to enlarge the horizon of his professional expertise, when the city of Shanghai is peacefully asleep." The article caught the attention of a senior vice minister in Beijing, Comrade Zheng Zuoren, who believed he had discovered a new role model. It was in part due to Zheng's recommendation that Chen had been promoted to chief inspector.

It was only partially true, however, that Chen had chosen to translate mysteries to enrich his professional knowledge. It was more because he, an entry-level police officer at the time, needed extra cash. He had also translated a collection of American imagist poetry, but the publishing house offered him only two hundred copies in lieu of royalties for that work.

"You were so sure of the motive for my translations?" he said.

"Of course, as I declared in that article: a 'people's policeman's sense of dedication'." She laughed and tilted her glass in the sunlight.

At that moment, she was no longer the reporter who had talked to him seriously, sitting upright at the office desk, an open notebook in front of her. Nor was he a chief inspector. Just a man with a woman whose company he enjoyed, in his own room.

"It's been over a year since the day we first met in the hallway of the Wenhui office building," he said, refilling her wineglass.

"'*Time is a bird. / It perches, and it flies,*'" she said.

These were the lines from his short poem entitled "Parting." Nice of her to remember it.

"You must have been inspired by a parting you cannot forget," she said. "A parting from somebody very dear to you."

Her instinct was right, he thought. The poem was about his parting from a dear friend in Beijing years earlier, and it was still unforgotten. He had never talked to Wang about it. She was looking at him over the rim of her glass, taking a long slow sip, her eyes twinkling.

Did he catch a note of jealousy in her voice?

The poem had been written long ago, but its catalyst was not something he wanted to mention at the moment. "A poem does not have to be about something in the poet's life. Poetry is impersonal. As T. S. Eliot has said, it is not letting loose an emotional crisis—"

"What, an emotional crisis?" Overseas Chinese Lu's excited voice burst into their conversation. Lu barged through the doorway carrying an enormous beggar's chicken, his plump face and plump body all the more expansive in a fashionable heavily-shoulder-padded white suit and a bright red tie. Lu's wife

Ruru, thin as a bamboo shoot, and angular in a tight yellow dress, brought in a big purple ceramic pot.

"What are you two talking about?" Ruru asked.

Putting the food on the table, Lu threw himself down on the new leather sofa, looking at them with an exaggerated inquiry on his face.

Chen did not answer the question. He had a ready excuse in busily unwrapping the beggar's chicken. It smelled wonderful. The recipe had supposedly originated when a beggar baked a soil-and-lotus-leaf-wrapped chicken in a pile of ashes. The result was an astonishing success. It must have taken Lu a long time to cook.

Then he turned to the ceramic pot. "What's that?"

"Squid stew with pork," Ruru explained. "Your favorite in high school, Lu said."

"Comrade Chief Inspector," Lu went on, "emerging Party cadre, and romantic poet to boot, you do not need my help, not in this new apartment, not with a young girl as beautiful as a flower beside you."

"What are you talking about?" Wang said.

"Oh, it is just about the dinner—how delicious it smells. I'm going to have a fit if we don't start right away."

"He's just like that, he totally forgets himself with his old pal," Ruru explained to Wang whom she had met before. "Nowadays, only Chief Inspector Chen calls him 'Overseas Chinese.'"

"It's seven," Chen said. "If they're not here yet, Professor Zhou and his wife won't come. So let's start."

There was no dining room. With the Lus' help, Chen set up the folding table and chairs. When he was alone, Chen ate at the desk. But he had bought the space-saving set for occasions like this.

The dinner turned out to be a great success. Chen had worried about his capability as a chef, but the guests finished all the food rapidly. The improvised soup was especially popular. Lu even asked him for the recipe.

Rising from the table, Ruru offered to wash the dishes in the kitchen. Chen protested, but Lu intervened. "My old woman should not be deprived of the opportunity, Comrade Chief Inspector, to display her female domestic virtue."

"You chauvinistic men," Wang said, joining Ruru in the kitchen.

Lu helped him clear the table, put the leftovers away, and brew a pot of Oolong tea.

"I need to ask a favor of you, old pal," Lu said, holding a teacup in his hand.

"What is it?"

"I've always dreamed of starting a restaurant. For a restaurant, the heart of the matter is location. I have been looking around for a long time. Now here's the opportunity of a lifetime. You know Seafood City on Shanxi Road, don't you?"

"Yes, I've heard of it."

"Xin Gen, the owner of Seafood City, is a compulsive gambler—he plays day and night. He pays no attention to his business, and all his chefs are idiots. It's bankrupt."

"Then you should try your hand at it."

"For such an excellent location, the price Xin is asking is incredibly cheap. In fact, I don't have to pay the whole amount, he's so desperate. What he wants is a fifteen percent downpayment. So I just need a loan to start with. I've sold the few fur coats my old man left behind, but we're still several thousand short."

"You couldn't have chosen a better time, Overseas Chinese. I just got two checks from the Lijiang Publishing House," Chen said. "One's for the reprint of *The Riddle of the Chinese Coffin* and the other's an advance for *The Silent Step.*"

But it was not really a good time. Chen had been contemplating buying some more furniture for the new apartment. He had seen a mahogany desk in a thrift shop in Suzhou. Ming-style, perhaps of genuine Ming dynasty craftsmanship, for five thousand Yuan. It was expensive, but it could be the very desk on which he was going to write his future poems. Several critics had complained about his departure from the tradition of classical Chinese poetry, and the antique desk might convey a message from the past to him. So he had written a letter to Chief Editor Liu of the Lijiang Publishing House, asking for the advance.

Chen took out the two checks, signed the back of them, added a personal check, and gave all of them to Lu.

"Here they are," he said. "Treat me when your restaurant is a booming success."

"I'll pay you back," Lu said, "with interest."

"Interest? One more word about interest, and I will take them back."

"Then come and be my partner. I have to do something, old pal. Or I'll have a crisis with Ruru tonight."

"Now what are you two talking about—another crisis?"

Wang was returning to the living room, Ruru following her.

Lu did not reply. Instead he moved to the head of the table, clinked a chopstick against a glass, and started a speech: "I have an announcement to make. For several weeks, Ruru and I have been busy preparing for the opening of a restaurant. The only problem was our lack of the capital. Now, with a most generous loan from my buddy Comrade Chief Inspector Chen, the problem is solved. Moscow Suburb, the new restaurant, will be open soon—very soon indeed.

"From our newspapers, we learn that we're entering a new period in socialist China. Some old diehards are grumbling that China is becoming capitalist rather than socialist, but who cares? Labels. Nothing but labels. As long as people have a better life, that's all it is about. And we're going to have a better life.

"And my pal, too, is most prosperous. He has not only received promotion—a chief inspector in his early thirties—but also he has this wonderful new apartment. And a most beautiful reporter is attending the house-warming party.

"Now the party begins!"

Raising his glass, Lu put a cassette into the player, and a waltz began to flow into the room.

"It's almost nine." Ruru was looking at her watch. "I can't take the morning shift off."

"Don't worry," Lu said. "I will call in sick for you. A summer flu. And Comrade Chief inspector, not a single word about your police work either. Let me be an Overseas Chinese in truth just for one night."

"That's just like you." Chen smiled.

"An Overseas Chinese," Wang added, "drinking and dancing all night. "

Chief Inspector Chen was not good at dancing.

During the Cultural Revolution, the only thing close to dancing for the Chinese people was the Loyal Character Dance. People would stamp their feet in unison, to show their loyalty to Chairman Mao. But it was said that even in those years, many fancy balls were held within the high walls of the Forbidden City. Chairman Mao, a dexterous dancer, was said to have had "his legs still intertwined with his partner's even after the ball." Whether this tabloid tidbit was fictitious, no one could tell. It was true, however, that not until the mid-eighties could Chinese people dance without fear of being reported to the authorities.

"I'd better dance with my lioness," Lu said in mock frustration.

Lu's choice left Chen as the only partner for Wang.

Chen, not displeased, bowed as he took Wang's offered hands.

She was the more gifted dancer, leading him rather than being led in the limited space of the room. Turning, turning, and turning in her high heels, slightly taller than he was, her black hair streamed against the white walls. He had to look up at her as he held her in his arms.

A slow, dreamy ballad swelled into the night. Resting her hand on his shoulder, she slipped off her shoes. "We are making too much noise," she said, looking up at him with a radiant smile.

"What a considerate girl," Lu said.

"What a handsome couple," Ruru added.

It *was* considerate of her. Chen, too, had been concerned about the noise. He did not want his new neighbors to start protesting.

Some of the music called for slow two-steps. They did not have to exert themselves as the melody rose and fell like waves lapping around them. She was light on her bare feet, moving, wisps of her hair brushing against his nose.

When another melody started, he tried to take the initiative, and pulled her around—but a bit too suddenly. She fell against him. He felt her body all the length of his, soft and pliable.

"We have to go," Lu declared at the end of the tune.

"Our daughter will be worried," Ruru added, picking up the ceramic pot she had brought.

The Lus' decision was unexpected. It was hard to believe that half an hour earlier Lu had declared himself "Overseas Chinese" for the night.

"I'd better be leaving, too," Wang said, disengaging herself from him.

"No, you have to stay," Lu said, shaking his head vigorously. "For a housewarming party, it's not proper and right for the guests to leave all at once."

Chen understood why the Lus wanted to leave. Lu was a self-proclaimed schemer and seemed to derive a good deal of pleasure from playing a well-meant trick.

It was a pleasant surprise that Wang did not insist on leaving with them. She changed the cassette, to a piece he had not heard before. Their bodies pressed close. It was summer. He could feel her softness through her T-shirt, his cheek brushing against her hair. She was wearing a gardenia scent.

"You smell wonderful."

"Oh, it's the perfume Yang sent me from Japan."

The juxtaposed awareness of their dancing alone in the room, and her husband in Japan, added to his tension. He missed a step, treading on her bare toes.

"I'm so sorry, did I hurt you?"

"No," she said. "Actually, I'm glad you are inexperienced."

"I'll try to be a better partner next time."

"Just be yourself," she said, "the way—"

The wind languished. The floral curtain ceased flapping. The moonlight streamed through, lighting up her face. It was a young, animated face. At that moment, it touched a string, a peg, deep inside him.

"Shall we start over again?" he said.

Then the telephone rang. Startled, he looked at the clock on the wall. He put down her hand reluctantly, and picked up the phone.

"Chief Inspector Chen?"

He heard a familiar voice, somehow sounding as if it came from an unfamiliar world. He gave a resigned shrug of his shoulders. "Yes, it's Chen."

"It's Detective Yu Guangming, reporting a homicide case."

"What happened?"

"A young woman's naked body was found in a canal, west of Qingpu County."

"I—I will be on my way," he said, as Wang walked over to turn off the music.

"That may not be necessary. I've already examined the scene. The body will be moved into the mortuary soon. I just want to let you know that I went there because there was nobody else in the office. And I could not reach you."

"That's okay. Even though ours is a special case squad, we should respond when no one else is available."

"I'll make a more detailed report tomorrow morning." Detective Yu added, somewhat belatedly, "Please excuse me if I am disturbing you or your guests—in your new apartment."

Yu must have heard the music in the background. Chen thought he detected a sarcastic note in his assistant's voice.

"Don't mention it," Chen said. "Since you have checked out the crime scene, I think we can discuss it tomorrow."

"So, see you tomorrow. And enjoy your party in the new apartment."

There was certainly sarcasm in Yu's voice, Chen thought, but such a reaction was understandable from a colleague who, though senior in age, had no luck in the bureau's housing assignments.

"Thank you."

He turned from the phone to see Wang standing near the door. She had put on her shoes.

"You have more important things to occupy you, Comrade Chief Inspector."

"Just a new case, but it's been taken care of," he said. "You don't have to leave."

"I'd better," she said. "It's late."

The door was open.

They stood facing each other.

Behind her, the dark street, visible through the corridor window; behind him, the new apartment, aglow in the lily-white light.

They hugged before parting.

He went out to the balcony, but he failed to catch a glimpse of her slender figure retreating into the night. He heard only a violin from an open window above the curve of the street. Two lines from Li Shangyin's "Zither" came to his mind:

> The zither, for no reason, has half of its strings broken,
> One string, one peg, evoking the memory of the youthful years.

A difficult Tang dynasty poet, Li Shangyin was especially known for this elusive couplet. Certainly it was not about the ancient musical instrument. Why, all of a sudden, the lines came rushing to him, he did not know.

The murder case?

A young woman. A life in its prime wasted. All the broken strings. The lost sounds. Only half of its years lived.

Or was there something else?

Chapter 3

The Shanghai Police Bureau was housed in a sixty-year-old brown brick building located on Fuzhou Road. The gray iron gate was guarded by two armed soldiers, but, like the other police-men, Chen entered the bureau through a small door adjacent to a doorman's kiosk beside the gate. Occasionally, when the gates were opened wide for some important visitors, what could be seen from the outside was a curving driveway with a peaceful flowerbed in the middle of a spacious courtyard.

Acknowledging the stiff salute of the sentry, Chief Inspector Chen made his way up to his office on the third floor. His was just a cubicle within a large office which housed over thirty detectives of the homicide department. They all worked together, at communal desks, rubbing shoulders and sharing phones.

The brass name plaque on his cubicle door—CHIEF INSPECTOR CHEN CAO—shining proudly in the morning light, from time to time drew his gaze like a magnet. The enclosure was small. A brown oak desk with a brown swivel chair occu-pied much of the space. A couple of teacups had to stand on a dark green steel filing cabinet by the door, and a thermos bottle, by a bookshelf on the floor. There was nothing on the wall except a framed photograph of Comrade Deng Xiaoping standing on Huangpu Bridge under a black umbrella held by Shanghai's mayor. The only luxury in the office was a midget refrigerator, but Chen had made a point of letting all his staff members use it. Like the apartment, the cubicle had come with his promotion.

It was generally believed in the bureau that Chen's advance had resulted from Comrade Deng Xiaoping's new cadre policy. Prior to the mid-eighties, Chinese cadres usually rose in a slow process, step by step. Once they reached a certain high level, however, they could stay there for a long time, and some never retired, hanging on to their positions to the end. So a chief inspector in his mid-fifties would have considered himself lucky in his career. With the dramatic change Deng had introduced, high-ranking cadres, too, had to step down at retirement age. Being young and highly educated suddenly became the crucial criteria in the cadre promotion process. Chen happened to be qualified in both aspects, though his qualifications were not so warmly regarded by some officers. To them, educational background did not mean much. Especially Chen's since he had majored in English literature. They also felt that age signified experience in the field.

So Chen's status was a sort of compromise. As a rule, a chief inspector would serve as the head of the homicide department. The old department head had retired, but no successor had yet been announced. Chen's administrative position was just that of leader of a special case squad, consisting of only five people including Detective Yu Guangming, his assistant.

Detective Yu was not visible in the main office, but among the mass of papers on his desk, Chen found his report.

OFFICER AT THE SCENE: Detective Yu Guangming

DATE: 5/11/90

1. The body. A dead woman. Nameless. Naked. Her body found in a black plastic bag in the Baili Canal. Probably in her late twenties or early thirties, she had a healthy build, around 110 pounds in weight, 5′4″ in height. It was hard to imagine how she had actually looked when alive. Her face was a bit swollen, but unbruised, unscratched. She had thin, dark eyebrows and a straight nose. Her forehead was broad. She had long, well-shaped legs, small feet with long toes. Her toenails were painted scarlet. Her hands were small, too, no rings on her well-manicured fingers. No blood, dirt, or skin under her nails. Her hips were broad with copious, coal black pubic hair. It's possible that she had had sexual intercourse before her death. She didn't look beaten up. There was only a faint line of bruising around her neck, barely discernible, and a light scratch on her collarbone, but other than that, her skin was smooth, with no suggestion of bruises on her body. A general absence of contusions on the legs also showed that she had not struggled much before her death. The small spotty hemorrhages in the linings around her eyes could be presumptive evidence of death by asphyxiation.

2. The scene. Baili Canal, a small canal on the Suzhou River, about ten miles west of the Shanghai Paper Mill. It is, to be more exact, a dead creek overhung with shrubs and tall weeds. Some years ago it was chosen as a chemical plant site, but the state plan was abandoned. On one side is something of a graveyard with tombs scattered around. It's difficult to reach the canal, whether by water or by land. No bus comes there. According to the local people, few go there to fish.

3. The witnesses. Gao Ziling, captain of the *Vanguard*, Shanghai River Security Bureau. Liu Guoliang, Captain Gao's high-school friend, a senior engineer in the nuclear

science field in Qinghai. Both of them are Party members, with no criminal record.

Possible cause of death: Strangulation in combination with sexual assault.

When he finished reading the report, Chief Inspector Chen lit a cigarette and sat quietly for a while. Two possibilities arose with the curling rings of smoke. She had been raped and murdered on a boat, and then dumped into the canal. Or the crime had taken place somewhere else, and her body transported to the canal.

He was not inclined toward the first scenario. It would be extremely difficult, if not impossible, for the murderer to commit the crime with other passengers moving around on board. If it had been just the two of them in the boat, what was the point of covering her body up in a plastic bag? The canal was so out of the way, and most probably it had happened in the depth of night— there would have been no need to wrap the body. In the second scenario, the plastic bag might fit, but then the murder might have happened anywhere.

When he looked out into the large office again, Detective Yu was back at his desk, sipping a cup of tea. Mechanically Chen felt for the thermos bottle on the floor. There was still enough water. No need to go to the communal hot water boiler downstairs. He dialed Yu's extension.

"Detective Yu Guangming reporting." Yu appeared at the doorway in less than a minute, a tall man in his early forties, of medium build, with a rugged face and deep, penetrating eyes, holding a large manila folder in his hand.

"You must have worked quite late last night." Chen offered a cup of tea to his assistant. "A well-done job. I've just read your report."

"Thank you."

"Any new information about the case this morning?"

"No. Everything's in the report."

"What about the missing person's list?"

"No one on the list looks like her," Yu said, handing over the folder. "Some pictures have just been developed. She could not have been too long in the water. No more than twenty hours is my guess."

Chen started thumbing through photographs. Pictures of the dead woman lying on the bank, naked, or partially covered up, then several close-ups, the last one focusing on her face, her body concealed by a white covering, in the mortuary.

"What do you think?" Yu breathed slowly into his hot tea.

"A couple of possible scenarios. Nothing definite until Forensic finishes."

"Yes, the autopsy report will probably be here late this afternoon."

"You don't think she could be someone from the neighboring villages?"

"No, I don't. I have called the local county committee. There's no one reported missing there."

"But what about the murderer?"

"No, not likely, either. As the old saying goes, a rabbit does not browse near its lair. But he could be familiar with the canal."

"Two possibilities, then," Chen began.

Yu listened to Chen's analysis without interrupting. "As for the first scenario, I don't think it is so likely," he said.

"But it would be impossible for the murderer to get her body to the canal without some sort of transportation at his disposal," Chen said.

"He might be a taxi driver. We've had similar cases. Pan Wanren's case, remember? Raped and murdered. A lot of resemblance. Except the body was dumped in a rice paddy. The murderer confessed that he did not intend to kill her, but he panicked at the thought of the victim's being able to identify his car."

"Yes, I do remember. But if the murderer raped this one in a car, why should he have bothered to hide the body in the plastic bag afterward?"

"He had to drive all the way to canal."

"The trunk would have served his purpose."

"Maybe he just happened to have the bag in the car."

"Maybe you're right."

"Well, when a rape precedes homicide," Yu said, crossing his legs, "the motive comes down to concealing the rapist's identity. She could have identified him, or the car. So a taxi-driver hypothesis fits."

"But the murderer could also be the victim's acquaintance," Chen said, studying a picture in his hand. "With her body dumped in the canal, her disappearance would not be easily traced to him. That may account for the plastic bag, too. To conceal moving the body *into* the car."

"Well, not too many people have their own cars—except high cadres, and they would not have their chauffeurs drive them around on such an errand."

"It's true. There're not too many private cars in Shanghai, but the number is increasing rapidly. We cannot rule it out."

"If the murderer was the deceased's acquaintance, the first question we have to ask is why? A secret affair with a married man, we've had cases like that, but then the woman in such a case, almost without exception, is pregnant. I called Dr. Xia early this morning, and it was ruled out," Yu said, lighting a cigarette just for himself. "It's still possible, of course, I mean your theory. If so, there's probably nothing we can do until we find out her identity."

"So do you think we should start checking with the taxi bureau—in accordance with your theory?"

"We could, but it would not be easy. There weren't many taxis in Shanghai ten years ago—you could have waited on the street for hours without getting one. Now Heaven alone knows how many there are, running everywhere like locusts. Over ten thousand, I bet, not including the self-employed cab drivers. Maybe another three thousand."

"Yes, that's a lot."

"Another thing, we're not even sure that she was from Shanghai. What if she came from another province? If so, a long time will pass before we get information about her identity."

The air in the small office became thick with cigarette smoke.

"So what do you think we should do?" Chen asked, pushing open the window.

Detective Yu let a few seconds go by, and then asked a question of his own, "Do we have to take the case?"

"Well, that's a good question."

"I responded to the call because there was nobody else in the office and I couldn't find you. But we're only the special case squad."

It was true. Nominally their squad did not have to take a case until it was declared "special" by the bureau—sometimes at the request of another province, and sometimes by other squads, but more often than not, for an unstated political reason. To raid a private bookstore selling pirated hard-core CDs, for instance, would not be difficult or special for a cop, but it could get a lot of attention, providing material for newspaper headlines. "Special," in other words, was applied when the bureau had to adjust its focus to meet political needs. In the case of a nameless female body found in a small remote canal, they would ordinarily turn it over to the sex homicide group, to whom it apparently belonged.

That explained Detective Yu's lack of interest in the case though he had taken the phone call and examined the crime scene. Chen riffled through the pictures before he picked one up. "Let's have this picture cropped and enlarged. Someone may be able to recognize her."

"What if no one comes forward?"

"Well, then we must start canvassing—if we're going to take the case."

"Canvassing indeed," Yu picked a tiny tea leaf from his teeth. Most detectives disliked this drudgery.

"How many men can we call upon for the job?"

"Not too many, Comrade Chief Inspector," Yu said. "We're short. Qing Xiaotong's on his honeymoon, Li Dong's just resigned to open a fruit shop, and Liu Longxiang's in the hospital with a broken arm. In fact, it's just you and me on the so-called special case squad at the moment."

Chen was aware of Yu's acerbic undertone. His accelerated promotion was going to take some living down, not to mention his new apartment. A certain measure of antagonism was hardly surprising, especially from Detective Yu, who had entered the force earlier and had technical training and a police family background. But Chief Inspector Chen was anxious to be judged on what he could achieve in his position, not on the way he had risen to it. So he was tempted to take the case. A real homicide case. From the very beginning. But Detective Yu was right. They were short of men, and with many "special" cases on their hands, they could not afford to take on a case that just happened to come their way. A sexual murder case—with no clue or witness, already a cold case.

"I'll talk to Party Secretary Li about it, but in the meantime, we will have the picture copied and prints distributed to the branch offices. It's a necessary routine—whoever is going to take the case." Chen then added, "I'll go to the canal if I have some time in the afternoon. When you were there, it must have been quite dark."

"Well, it's a poetic scene there," Yu said, standing up, grinding out his cigarette, and making no attempt to conceal the sarcasm in his tone. "You may come up with a couple of wonderful lines."

"You never can tell."

After Yu left, Chen brooded at his desk for a while. He was rather upset with the antagonism shown by his assistant. His casual remark about Chen's passion for poetry was another jab. However, Yu's critique was true—to some extent.

Chen had not intended to be a cop—not in his college years. He had been a published poet as well as a top student at Beijing Foreign Language Institute. He had his mind set on literary pursuits. Just one month before graduation, he had applied to an M.A. program in English and American literature, a decision his mother had approved, since Chen's father had been a well-known professor of the Neo-Confucian school. He was informed, however, that a promising job was waiting for him in the Ministry of Foreign Affairs. In the early eighties, all graduates had their jobs assigned by the authorities, and as he was a student on the president's honor roll, his file had been requested by the ministry. A diplomatic career was not his own choice, even though such a position was generally considered fantastic for an English major. Then, at the last minute, there was another unexpected change. In the course of the family background check by the authorities, one of his uncles was found to have been a counterrevolutionary executed in the early 1950s. It was an uncle whom he had never seen, but such a family connection was politically unthinkable for an aspirant to a diplomatic position. So his name was removed from the ministry's list. He was then assigned to a job in the Shanghai Police Bureau, where, for the first few years, his work consisted of translating a police interrogation procedure handbook, which no one wanted to read, and of writing political reports for Party Secretary Li, which Chen himself did not want to write. So it was only in the last couple of years that Chen had actually worked as a cop, first at the entry level, now suddenly as a chief inspector, but responsible only for the "special cases" turned over to him by others. And Yu, like some people in the bureau, had his complaints fueled not only by Chen's rapid rise under Deng's cadre policy, but also by his continuing literary pursuits, which were conventionally—and conveniently—viewed as a deviation from his professional commitment.

Chen read through the case report for a second time, and then realized that it was lunchtime. As he stepped out, he found a message for him in the large office. It must have been left before his arrival that morning:

> Hi, it's Lu. I'm working at the restaurant. Our restaurant. Moscow Suburb. A gourmet paradise. It's important
> I talk to you. Give me a call at 638-0843.

Overseas Chinese Lu talked just like that—excited and ebullient. Chen dialed the number.

"Moscow Suburb."

"Lu, what's up?"

"Oh, you. How did it go last night?"

"Fine. We were together, weren't we?"

"No, I mean what happened after we left—between you and Wang?"

"Nothing. We danced a few more dances, and then she left."

"What a shame, old pal," Lu said. "You're a chief inspector for nothing. You cannot detect even the most obvious signal."

"What signal?"

"When we left, she agreed to stay on—alone with you. She really meant for the night. An absolutely unmistakable signal. She's crazy about you."

"Well, I'm not so sure," Chen said. "Let's talk about something else. How are things with you."

"Yes, Ruru wants me to thank you again. You're our lucky star. Everything is in good shape. All the documents are signed. I've already moved in. Our own restaurant. I just need to change its sign. A big neon sign in both Chinese and English."

"Hold on—Chinese and Russian, right?"

"Who speaks Russian nowadays? But in addition to our food, we will have something else genuinely Russian, I tell you, and you can eat them, too." Lu chuckled mysteriously. "With your generous loan, we'll celebrate the grand opening next Monday. A booming success."

"You're so sure about it."

"Well, I have a trump card. Everybody will be amazed."

"What is it?"

"Come and see for yourself. And eat to your heart's content."

"Sure. I won't miss your Russian cabbage soup for anything, Overseas Chinese."

"So you're a gourmet too. See you."

Other than that, however, they did not have too much in common, Chief Inspector Chen reflected with a smile, putting down the phone. It was in their high-school years that Lu had gotten his nickname. Not just because Lu wore a Western-style jacket during the Cultural Revolution. More because Lu's father had owned a fur store before 1949, and was thus a capitalist. That had made Lu a "black kid." In the late sixties, "Overseas Chinese" was by no means a positive term, for it could be used to depict somebody as politically unreliable, connected with the Western world, or associated with an extravagant bourgeois life style. But Lu took an obstinate pride in cultivating his "decadent" image—brewing coffee, baking apple pie, tossing fruit salad, and of course, wearing a Western-style suit at the dinner table. Lu befriended Chen, whose father was a "bourgeois professor," another "black kid." Birds of a feather, comforting each other. Lu made a habit of treating Chen whenever he made a successful cooking experiment at home. After graduating from high school, as an educated youth Lu had been sent to the countryside and spent ten years being reformed by the poor and lower-middle-class peasants. He only returned to Shanghai in the early eighties. When Chen, too, moved back from Beijing, they met with the realization that they were different, and yet all those years they had stayed friends, and they came to appreciate each other's differences while sharing their common delight in gourmet food.

Twenty years has passed like a dream.

It is a wonder that we are still here, together.

Two lines from Chen Yuyi, a Song dynasty poet, came to Chief Inspector Chen, but he was not sure whether he had omitted one or two words.

Chapter 4

After a nongourmet lunch in the bureau canteen, Chen went out to buy a collection of poems by Chen Yuyi.

Several new privately run bookstores had just appeared on Fuzhou Road, fairly close to the bureau. Small stores, but with excellent service. Around the corner of Shandong Road, Chen saw a tall apartment building, seemingly the first finished in a series of the new developments. On the other side of the street there was still a rambling cluster of low houses, remnants of the early twenties, showing no signs of change to come in the near future. It was there, in the mixture of the old and the new, that he stepped into a family bookstore. The shop was tiny but impressively stacked with old and new books. He heard a baby's babble just behind a bamboo-bead curtain at the back.

His search for Chen Yuyi was not successful. In the section of classical Chinese literature, there was an impressive array of martial arts novels by Hong Kong and Taiwan authors, but practically nothing else. When he was about to leave, he lighted on a copy of his late father's collection of Neo-Confucian studies, half hidden under a bikini-clad girlie poster marked "For Sale." He took the book to the counter.

"You have an eye for books," the owner said, holding a bowl of rice covered with green cabbage. "It's a hundred and twenty Yuan."

"What?" he gasped.

"It was once criticized as a rightist attack against the Party, out of print even in the fifties."

"Look," he said, grasping the book. "My father wrote this book, and the original price was less than two Yuan."

"Really," the owner studied him for a moment. "All right, fifty Yuan, with the poster free, for you."

Chen took the book without accepting the additional offer. There was a tiny scar on the poster girl's bare shoulder, which somehow reminded him of the picture of the dead girl pulled out of the plastic bag. There were one or two pictures of her in the mortuary, even less covered than the bikini-girl. He remembered having seen a scar somewhere on her body.

Or somebody else's. He was momentarily confused.

He started leafing through his father's book on his way back to the bureau, a reading habit his father had disapproved of, but the subject of the book made it difficult for him not to.

Back in the office, Chen tried to make himself a cup of Gongfu tea, another gourmet practice he had learned from Overseas Chinese Lu, so that he could read with more enhanced concentration. He had just put a pinch of tea leaves into a tiny cup when the phone started ringing.

It was Party Secretary Li Guohua. Li was not only the number-one Party official in the bureau, but also Chen's mentor. Li had introduced Chen to the Party, spared no pains showing him the ropes, and advanced him to his present position. Everybody in the bureau knew Li's legendary talent for political infighting—

an almost infallible instinct for picking the winner in inner-Party conflicts all those years. A young officer at the entrance level in the early fifties, Li had stepped his way through the debris of numerous political movements, rising finally to the top of the bureau. So most people saw it as another master stroke that Li had hand-picked Chen as his potential successor, though some called it a risky investment. Superintendent Zhao, for one, had recommended another candidate for the position of chief inspector.

"Is everything okay with your new apartment, Comrade Chief Inspector?"

"Thank you, Comrade Party Secretary Li. Everything's fine."

"That's good. And the work in the office?"

"Detective Yu got a case yesterday. A female body in a canal in Qingpu County. We're short of men, so I'm wondering if we should take it."

"Turn over the case to other people. Yours is a special case squad."

"But it was Detective Yu who went to examine the scene. We would like to handle a case from the beginning."

"You may have no time for it. There's some news I want to tell you. You're going to attend the seminar sponsored by the Central Party Institute in October."

"The seminar of the Central Party Institute!"

"Yes, it is a great opportunity, isn't it? I put your name on the recommendation list last month. A long shot, I thought, but today they informed us of their decision. I'll make a copy of the official admission letter for you. You have come a long way, Comrade Chief Inspector Chen."

"You have done so much for me, Party Secretary Li. How can I ever thank you enough?" He added after a pause, "Maybe that's another reason for us to take the case. I cannot be a chief inspector without solving some cases on my own."

"Well, it's up to you," Li said. "But you have to be prepared for the seminar. How much the seminar can mean for your future career, you don't need me to tell you. More important work is waiting for you, Comrade Chief Inspector Chen."

The talk with Party Secretary Li actually prompted Chen to do some investigation before making any decision about the case. He went down to the bureau's vehicle service group, took out a motorcycle, and borrowed a county map from the bureau library.

It was hot outside. The cicadas, napping in the languid trees, turned silent. Even the mailbox by the curb appeared drowsy. Chen took off his uniform and rode out in his short-sleeved T-shirt.

The trip to Baili Canal turned out to be rather difficult. Once past the Hongqiao Industrial Area, there were few road signs. He had to ask for directions at a ramshackle gas station, but the only worker there was taking a midday nap, his saliva dribbling onto the counter. Then the scenery became more rustic, with lines of hills visible here and there in the distance, and a solitary curl of white smoke rising like a string of notes from an invisible roof somewhere. According to the map, the canal should not be too far away. At a turn of the road, there appeared a winding path, like an entrance into a village, and he saw a girl selling big bowls of tea on a wooden bench. No more than thirteen or fourteen, she sat quietly on a low stool, wearing her ponytail tied with a girlish bow, reading a book. There were no customers. He wondered if there would be any all day. Only a few coins glittered in a cracked tin cup beside a bulging satchel at her feet. Apparently not a peddler, not one out there for profit, just a kid from the village, still small and innocent, reading against the idyllic background—perhaps a poetry collection in her hand, providing a convenience to thirsty travelers who might pass by.

Little things, but all of them seemed to be adding up into something like an image he had once come across in Tang and Song dynasty writings:

Slender, supple, she's just thirteen or so,
The tip of a cardamom bud, in early March.

"Excuse me," he said, pulling up his motorcycle by the road-side. "Do you know where Baili Canal is?"

"Baili Canal, oh yes, straight ahead, about five or six miles."

"Thank you."

He also asked for a big bowl of tea.

"Three cents," the girl said, without looking up from her book.

"What are you reading?"

"*Visual Basics.*"

The answer did not fit the picture in his mind. But it should not be surprising, he thought. He, too, had been taking an evening class on Windows applications. It was the age of the information highway.

"Oh, computer programming," he said. "Very interesting."

"Do you also study it?"

"Just a little."

"Need some CDs?"

"What?"

"Dirt cheap. A lot of advanced software on it. Chinese Star, TwinBridge, Dragon Dictionary, and all kinds of fonts, tradition-al and simplified . . ."

"No, thank you," he said, taking out a one-Yuan bill.

The CDs she offered might be incredibly cheap. He had heard people talking about pirated products, but he did not want to have anything to do with them, not as a chief inspector.

"I'm afraid I don't have enough change for you."

"Just give me all you have."

The little girl scooped out the coins to give him, and put the one Yuan bill in her purse, instead of into the tin cup at her feet. A cautious teenage profit-maker in her way. She then resumed her readings in cyberspace, the bow on her ponytail fluttering like a butterfly in a breath of air.

But his earlier mood was gone.

What irony. The wistful thoughts about the innocent tip of a cardamom bud, a solitary curl of white smoke, an unlost innocence in a rural background, a poetry collection . . . And a lapse in his professional perspective. Not until he had ridden another two or three miles did he realize that he should have done something about the CD business—as a chief inspector. Perhaps he had been too absent minded, in a "poetic trance," and then too surprised by the realities of the world. The episode came to him like an echo of his colleagues' criticism: Chief Inspector Chen was too "poetic" to be a cop.

It was past two o'clock when he reached the canal.

There was not a single cloud drifting overhead. The afternoon sun hung lonely in the blue sky, high over a most desolate scene, which was like a forgotten corner of the world. Not a soul was visible. The canal bank was overrun with tall weeds and scrubby growth. Chen stood still at the edge of the stagnant water, amid a scattering of wild bushes. Not too far away, however, he thought he could hear the hubbub of Shanghai.

Who was the victim? How had she lived? Whom had she met before her death?

He had not expected much from the scene. The heavy rains of the last few days would have washed away any trace of evidence. Being at the crime scene, he had thought, might help to establish a sort of communion between the living and the dead, but he failed to get any message. Instead, his mind wandered to bureau politics. There was nothing remarkable about the recovery of a body from a canal. Not for Homicide. They had encountered similar cases before, and would encounter them in the future. It did not take a chief inspector to tackle such a case, not at the moment, when he had to prepare himself for the important seminar.

Nor did it appear to be a case he could solve in a couple of days. There were no witnesses. Nor any traceable physical evidence, since the body had been lying in the water for some time. What had been found so far did not mean much for the investigation. Some old hands would have tried to avoid such a case. In fact, Detective Yu had implied as much, and as a special case squad, they were justified in not taking it on. The possibility of a failure to solve the case was not tempting. It would not help his status in the bureau.

He sat on a jutting slab of rock, dug out a half-crumpled cigarette, and lit it. Inhaling deeply, he closed his eyes for a second.

Across the canal, he then saw for the first time a tiny spangling of wildflowers, blue, white, violet in the hazy green weeds. Nothing else.

White puffs of cloud appeared, scuttling across the sky, when he started the trip back. The girl was no longer selling tea at the turn of the road. It was just as well. Perhaps she was no peddler of pirate CDs. She might just have an extra copy, and a couple of Yuan could mean a lot to a village kid.

When he got back to his office, the first thing he saw on the desk was a copy of the official admittance letter Party Secretary Li had referred to, but it did not give him the feeling of exaltation he had expected.

The preliminary autopsy report also came late in the afternoon. It produced little of interest. The time of death was estimated as between 1:00 A.M. and 2 A.M. on May 11. The victim had had sexual intercourse before her death. Acid-phosphate tests were positive for the presence of male ejaculate, but after the period of time the body had been immersed in the water, there was not enough left to isolate other positive or negative factors. It was difficult to tell whether the sexual intercourse had taken place against the victim's will, but she had been strangled. She was not pregnant. The report ended with the following wording: "Death by strangulation in conjunction with possible sexual assault."

The autopsy had been conducted by Doctor Xia Yulong.

Having read the report a second time, Chief Inspector Chen reached a decision: he would postpone making his decision. He did not have to take the case immediately, nor did he have to relinquish it to another squad. If some evidence appeared, he could declare his special case squad to be in charge. If the trail turned "deadly cold," as Detective Yu expected, it would not be too late for him to turn it over to others.

He believed that this was a correct decision. So he informed Yu, who readily agreed. Putting down the phone, however, he found his mood darkening, like the screen at the beginning of a movie, against which fragments of the scene he had just visited were displayed.

She had been lying there, abandoned, naked, her long dark hair in a coil across her throat, like a snake, in full view of two strangers, only to be carried away on a stretcher by a couple of white uniformed men, and, in time, opened up by an elderly medical man who examined her insides, mechanically, and sewed the body together again before it was finally sent to the mortuary. And all that time Chief Inspector Chen had been celebrating in his new apartment, having a housewarming party, drinking, dancing with a young woman reporter, talking about Tang dynasty poetry, and stepping on her bare toes.

He felt sorry for the dead woman. There was little he could do for her . . . but then he decided not to pursue this line of thought.

He made a call to his mother, telling her about the book he had bought during the lunch break. She was very pleased, as it happened to be the one she did not have in her attic collection.

"But you should have taken the poster as well, son."

"Why?"

"So that the girl could walk down from the poster," she said good-humoredly, "to keep you company at night."

"Oh, that!" he laughed. "The same old story you told me thirty years ago. I'm busy today, but I'll see you tomorrow. You can tell me the story again."

Chapter 5

Several days had passed since the housewarming party. At nine o'clock in the morning, grasping a *Shanghai Evening Post* in his hand, Chen had a feeling that he was being read by the news, rather than the other way round. What engaged him was the report of a *go* game between a Chinese and a Japanese player, with a miniature map of the *go* board showing all the movements of black and white pieces, each occupying a position full of meaning, and possibly of meanings beyond the surface meaning.

This was nothing but a last minute self-indulgence before the invariable bureau routine.

The phone on his desk rang. "Comrade Chief Inspector, you're such an important high official." It was Wang's satirical voice. "As the old Chinese saying goes, an important man has an impoverished memory."

"No, don't say that."

"You're so busy that you forget all your friends."

"Yes, I've been terribly busy, but how could I put you out of my mind? No. I'm just so busy with all the routine work plus the new case—you know, the one I got the night of the party—remember? I apologize for not having called you earlier."

"Never say sorry—" she changed the topic before finishing the sentence. "But I have some good news for you."

"Really?"

"First, your name is on the list of the fourteenth seminar sponsored by the Central Party Institute in Beijing."

"How did you learn that?"

"I've got my connections. So we will have to throw another party for your new promotion."

"It's too early for that. But what about having lunch with me next week?"

"It sounds like I am asking for an invitation to lunch."

"Well, I'll tell you what. Last night it rained, and I happened to be reading Li Shangyin—'When, when can we snuff the candle by the western window again, / And talk about the moment of Mount Ba in the rain?' And I missed you so much."

"Your poetic exaggeration again."

"No. Upon my word as a police officer, it's the truth."

"And a second piece of good news for a poetic chief inspector." She switched the subject again. "Xu Baoping, senior editor of our literature and art section, has decided to use your poem—'Miracle,' I believe that's the name of it."

"Yes, 'Miracle.' That is fantastic."

That was indeed a piece of exciting news. A poem in the *Wenhui Daily*, a nationally influential newspaper, could reach far more readers than one in some little magazine. "Miracle" was a poem about a policewoman's dedication to her work. The editor might have chosen it out of political considerations, but Chen was still overjoyed. "Well, at the Shanghai Writers' Association, few know that I'm a detective by profession. There's no point talking to them about it. They would probably say, 'What, a man who catches murderers should also try to catch muses?'"

"I'm not too surprised."

"Thanks for telling me the truth," he said. "What my true profession is, I've not decided yet!"

Chief Inspector Chen had tried not to overestimate his poet-

ic talent, though critics claimed to discover in his work a combination of classical Chinese and modern Western sensibility.
Occasionally he would wonder what kind of a poet he might
have become had he been able to dedicate all his time to creative writing. However, that was just a tantalizing fantasy. In the
last two or three weeks he had so much work to do during the
day that evenings had invariably found him too exhausted to
write.

"No, don't get me wrong. I believe in your poetic touch. That's
why I forwarded your 'Miracle' to Xu—'*The rain has washed your
shoulder length hair green—*' Sorry, that's about the only line I
remember. It just reminds me of a mermaid in a cartoon movie,
rather than a Shanghai policewoman."

"The poetic touch indeed—but I'll let you in on a secret. I have
turned you into several poems."

"What! You are really impossible," she said. "You never quit,
do you?"

"You mean washing my hands in the river?"

"Last time," she said laughingly, "you did not wash your
hands, I noticed, before the meal in your new apartment."

"That's just another reason I should treat you to a lunch," he
said. "To prove my innocence."

"You're always too innocently busy."

"But I will never be too busy to dine with you."

"I'm not so sure. Nothing is more important to you than a
case, not even whirling around with me."

"Oh—you're being impossible now."

"Well, see you next week."

He was pleased with the call from her. There was no denying
that he had been in her thoughts, too. Or why should she have
cared about the news of the seminar? She seemed to be quite
excited about it. As for the poem, it was possible she had put in
a word on his behalf.

Also, it was always pleasant to engage her in an exchange of wit. Casual, but intimate beneath the surface.

It was true that he had been terribly busy. Party Secretary Li had given him several topics for possible presentation at the seminar sponsored by the Central Party Institute. He had to finish all of them in two or three days, for the Party Secretary wanted to have someone in Beijing preview them. According to Li, the top Party leaders, including the ex-General Secretary of the Central Party Committee, had been invited to attend. A successful presentation there would get attention at the highest level. As result, Chief Inspector Chen had to leave most of the squad work to Detective Yu.

Wang's call, however, once more brought the image of the dead woman to his mind. Little had yet been done about the case. All their efforts to learn the identity of the young woman had yielded no clues. He decided to have another talk with Yu.

"Yes, it's been four days," Yu said. "We haven't made any progress. No evidence. No suspects. No theory."

"Still no one reported missing?"

"No one matching her description."

"Last time you ruled out the possibility of her being someone from the neighborhood. What about her being one of those provincial girls who come to Shanghai?" Chen said, "Since they have no family here, it would take a long time before a missing persons report came in."

With new construction going on everywhere, new companies being founded every day, the so-called "provincials" formed a cheap mobile labor force. Many were young girls who came to find jobs in the new restaurants and hotels.

"I thought about that, too," Yu said. "But have you noticed her fingernails? So professionally manicured, polished. And her toe-nails, too."

"But she might have worked in one of those fancy hotels."

"Let me tell you something, Comrade Chief Inspector. Last month, I saw a painting by Cheng Shifa," Yu said, shaking his head. "It shows a Dai girl walking along the rough Yuannan mountain path, her bare feet flashing white under her long green skirt. Well, one of my colleagues in Yuannan married a Dai girl. Afterward, he told me he was shocked to see how calloused and cracked her feet were in real life."

"You may have a point, Comrade Detective Yu," Chen said, not too pleased with the way Yu delivered his lecture, "but if she had stayed long enough in one of those foreign hotels, been totally transformed, so to speak, that would still be possible, right?"

"If so, we should have had a report already. Those foreign general managers have a way of running their business, and their people, too. And they keep in close contact with the police."

"True," he said, nodding, "but we have to do something."

"Yes, but what?"

The conversation left him disturbed. Was it true that they could not do anything but wait? Once more he took out the picture of the dead girl. The enlarged one. Though the image was not clear, he could see that she must have been an attractive woman. How could such a woman not be missed after almost a week? She should have had some people who cared for her. Friends, colleagues, parents, sisters and brothers, maybe lovers, who were anxious about her. No human being, particularly a young attractive woman, could be so alone that no one missed her when she disappeared for a week. He could not understand it.

But maybe she had said that she was going away on vacation or business. If so, it could take a long time before someone started wondering where she was.

He had a vague feeling that there was something about the case, something complicated, waiting for him. Something like a parallel to his writing experience . . .

A glimpse of a veiled face at the entrance of Beijing subway, a waft of the jasmine blossom fragrance from a blue teacup, or a particular rhythm in an attic with a train rumbling into the distant night, and he would have the feeling that he was on the verge of producing a wonderful poem. All this could turn out, however, to be a false lead, and he would end up crossing out fragments of unsatisfactory lines.

With this case, he did not even have such an evasive lead, nothing but an ineffable feeling. He pushed open the window. The early chorus of the cicadas assaulted him in hot waves.

"*Zhiliao, Zhiliao, Zhiliao . . . .*"

It was a homophone for "understanding" in Chinese.

Before he left for a meeting, he made a call to Dr. Xia, who had examined the victim's body.

"Dr. Xia, I have to ask a favor of you," Chen said.

"Anything I can do, Comrade Chief Inspector Chen."

"Remember the young woman found in the canal in a plastic bag—case number 736? The body has not yet been disposed of, I believe. Maybe the plastic bag is still there, too. Check it for me, and more importantly, write a description of the victim for me. Not a report but a detailed description. Not of a corpse but of a human being. Vivid. Concrete. Specific. What would she have looked like alive. I know you're busy, Dr. Xia. Please do it as a personal favor for me."

Doctor Xia, who loved classical Chinese poetry and was aware that Chen wrote poems in the so-called modernist style, said, "I know what you want, but I cannot promise my description will be as vivid as a modernist work, including every possible detail, ugly or not."

"Don't be too hard on me, Dr. Xia. I've been incorporating a streak of Li Shangyin's lyricism into my lines. I'll show some to you over our next lunch together. It will be my treat, of course."

Afterward, during the routine political meeting whose agenda was "Studies of *Comrade Deng Xiaoping's Selected Works*," Chen found his thoughts wandering, unable to concentrate on the book in his hands.

Dr. Xia's response however, came faster than he had expected. At two o'clock, there appeared a two-page fax in Dr. Xia's neat handwriting:

The following can be said about the woman who has been occupying your thoughts day and night:

1) She was thirty or thirty-one years old. She was five feet, four inches tall, and weighed about one hundred and ten pounds. She had a straight nose, small mouth, large eyes, and unplucked eyebrows. Her teeth were good too, even, white. She had an almost athletic build. Her breasts were small and slack, but her nipples large. With her slender waist, long, shapely legs, and round hips, she could have been a stunner—"so beautiful that the fish and the geese dive in shame."

2) She must have taken good care of herself. Her body skin was soft and resilient, probably resulting from extensive use of lotions and creams. Her hair was black and shiny. Not a single white hair. There were no calluses on her hands or feet. Not a mark or blemish. Both her fingers and toes had been well-cared-for.

3) In the record of the autopsy I emphasize the following: She had not had a child and never had an abortion. She had no scars from operations, nor any other marks on her body.

4) She had sexual intercourse shortly before death. She could have been raped, but there were hardly any bruises on her body except a light abrasion on her collarbone, which could have resulted from passionate love-making. No blood, dirt, or skin under her nails, and her hair mostly in place. At least she did not struggle much when her clothes were taken off . She was not wearing an IUD.

5) She had had a meal about forty minutes before she died: pork chops, mashed potatoes, green beans, and caviar.

After having read this memo, Chen worked out a new description, attached a photo, faxed it to a number of large work units, and had hundreds of copies ordered for delivery to Detective Yu, who was to post them in public places like store bulletin boards or bus stop signs where people might see them. That was all Chief Inspector Chen could think of.

The question was: How long would it take before he got a response?

Chapter 6

The response came before the end of the week.

Thursday afternoon, the same week the new notice was posted, a call came in from Shanghai First Department Store. A store security man had received a copy of the detailed description, which reminded him of a section manager who had not yet returned from vacation. Her colleagues had not been worried since it was common for people to spend a couple of extra days on vacation. When the security man showed the picture to the people who worked with her, she was immediately recognized.

"The picture is not clear, but they are all positive." According to the security man, this was because she was a well-known woman. "Her name is Guan Hongying. Guan, you know, for closing the door. Hong for the color red, and Ying for heroine."

"Red Heroine. What a revolutionary name! Guan Hongying," Chief Inspector Chen said. "It sounds familiar."

"She was a national model worker, thirty-one years old, single, who had worked in the store for more than ten years. A Party member, of course."

"What! A national model worker—Oh now I remember," Chen said. "Thank you. We appreciate your help, comrade. Contact us when you have any new information." In spite of his morning headache, Chen began to feel more hopeful than he had for a long time. Shanghai First was the largest department store in the city. A handful of security men in plainclothes were stationed there. While their main job was to deal with shoplifters, they knew how to gather information.

Sure enough, before lunchtime more information rolled in. The dead woman's identity was confirmed. Her dental records matched her medical history. Guan Hongying, thirty-one, unmarried, head of the cosmetics section, Party member for eleven years, national model worker and attendant at the Party's Ninth and Tenth Congresses. She had left home on May tenth for vacation and had since contacted no one.

At one o'clock, Chen got the first picture of Guan from a courier. Then the fax machine received a dozen more, as well as a huge amount of writing about her. Most of the pictures were clippings from newspapers and magazines. And all the writings were propaganda, about her commitment to her work, her noble spirit in serving the people, and her selfless dedication to the communist cause—all the familiar rhetoric of the Party's newspapers. As he read on, Chief Inspector Chen had second thoughts about taking the case. The rape and murder of a national model worker! Such a case, if solved, might still be hushed up for political considerations, but if it were not solved, political pressure could be expected from higher authorities. Still, he started to put some data together for a new case report.

NAME: Guan, Hongying
DATE OF BIRTH: December 11, 1958
RACE: Han
ADDRESS: Lane, Number 18, Lane 235, Hubei Rd.
　(Dormitory of the First Department Store)
STATUS: Single
OCCUPATION: Cadre (Head of cosmetics section, Party
　member, National Model Worker)
NEXT OF KIN: (mother, Alzheimer's patient in Ankang
　Nursing Home)
WORK HISTORY: From 1979 to 1990

At five thirty, an emergency meeting was called in the Number 3 Conference Room of the Shanghai Police Bureau. The meeting was presided over with exacting authority by Party Secretary Li, a stout man in his late fifties, whose face was dominated by the heavy bags under his eyes. He sat upright at the head of the long oak desk. Chen arrived first. Yu came to sit beside him. Sitting at the other end of the table, Commissar Zhang Zhiqiang made an unexpected appearance. A man of Zhang's high rank did not have to attend such a meeting. Nor was he a member of the special case squad.

"Thank you for coming, Commissar Zhang," Party Secretary Li said, paying his tribute to the old man before he started his speech.

Commissar Zhang had joined the Party in the early forties and received an 11th ranking in the system after 1949. Party Secretary Li, on the other hand, had become a Party member in the fifties, so his ranking was much lower. As always, Chen greeted Commissar Zhang respectfully. Zhang did not think too well of Chen, and on several occasions had come close to labeling him a liberal.

"This is a case of paramount political importance, comrades," Party Secretary Li began. "That's why we are having the meeting today. The mayor himself has just telephoned. He believes that it could be a serious political case. This is his instruction to us: 'Do your best, and solve the case as soon as possible. The city government is behind your work. Hold no press conferences. Do not reveal any details concerning her death'."

Chen was amazed. The dead woman had been somebody, her name frequently mentioned in newspapers, her image often seen on TV, but she had not been so important that the mayor himself should have made a call to the bureau, and so soon.

"But it's a homicide case," Detective Yu said.

The Party Secretary went on, "Comrades, we must realize, Comrade Guan could have been murdered out of political considerations. She was a well-known role model for the whole country—her tragic death is a significant loss to our Party, and a symbolic blow to the public security of our socialist society."

The Party Secretary was going too far, Chen reflected. As a party official, Li did not know much about homicide. But then, that might be the very reason Li, rather than anybody else, was the Party secretary; he was capable of seeing politics in everything.

"Besides, the way she was so brutally murdered could damage the pure image of our great Party."

That part was not difficult to accept. Chen nodded. The Party authorities would like very much to hush up the sensational details. The picture of National Model Worker Guan's naked body, violated and strangled, would contradict the hallowed image of a model worker fully dressed in a gray Mao suit.

Chen thought he saw an almost imperceptible smile on Yu's face.

"So, a special case group is to be formed. Chief Inspector Chen will be in charge of it. And Detective Yu is Chen's assistant. In addition, Commissar Zhang will be the adviser for the investigation."

"What if it is just a homicide case?" Yu asked doggedly.

"If it turns out to be no more than a homicide case, we'll solve it, too, of course. We just need to keep our minds open. The group will have a special budget. If more men are needed, Chief Inspector Chen can ask me."

That, Chen thought, was perhaps the secret of Li's success. Full of political nonsense, but not unaware of being so. So Li never forgot to add a few not-so-political words, words that made a little sense. That made Li somewhat different from other Party cadres.

Party Secretary Li was concluding his speech: "As you all know, this case has some sensitive aspects. It calls for a careful approach. So keep all information from the press. Anything that can lead to unnecessary speculation will not help our investigation."

"I've got your point, Comrade Party Secretary." Chen spoke for the first time. "With Comrade Commissar Zhang as our adviser, we will do our best and solve the case."

After the meeting, Chen stayed on with Li, alone.

"I want you to do a good job," Li said. "It may be a difficult case, but a successful conclusion will come to the attention of higher authorities."

"I understand, but Commissar Zhang—" Chen did not finish the sentence.

Zhang was generally considered the most orthodox Party commissar in the bureau, a political hard-liner of the older generation.

"Commissar Zhang has reached the age for retirement," Li said, "but what with inflation, and with the rising standard of living, it can be difficult for anyone to live on his pension alone. So the Party authorities have come up with a new regulation for the old comrades. They have to retire in accordance with the cadre retirement policy, no question about it, but as long as they remain in good health, they can do some secondary work appropriate to their age. In that way, they may still enjoy their full pay. 'Adviser' is an honorary position—he'll just give advice or suggestions. You have full authority as the head of the group."

"So what shall we do with him?"

"Just keep him informed about the investigation."

"Ah well, I see." Chen sighed.

Chen saw only too clearly what he was in for: four or five calls from the commissar as a daily routine, not to mention the necessity of listening to Zhang's long lectures larded with quotations from Mao, Deng, or *The People's Daily*, and the necessity of suppressing frequent yawns.

"It's not that bad. At least he is an incorruptible commissar."

Depending on one's perspective, that was a good point—or a bad one.

"It's in your interest, too, to work closely with a comrade of the older generation," the Party Secretary concluded in a lowered voice.

When Chen returned to the main office, he saw Detective Yu scanning a group of pictures at his desk. Chen took a seat opposite his assistant.

"Was Guan that important?" Yu asked.

"A national model worker is always important."

"But that was in the sixties and seventies, Comrade Lei Feng and all that propaganda."

"Yes, we have been brought up with these communist role model myths," Chen said. "In fact, such a concept is not without its root in Confucianism. Only Confucian models were called sages, whereas in the twentieth century, they are called model workers, model peasants, model soldiers. And even today, I can still sing the song, 'Learn from the Good Example of Comrade Lei Feng.'"

"So can I," Yu said. "There's another one. 'Be a Good Soldier to Chairman Mao.' I was humming the tune the other day, and my son was totally lost."

These songs had been very popular throughout the nation in the early sixties. Comrade Lei Feng was a model PLA soldier who served the people wholeheartedly, helped others in need, and never cared about his own interest. The Party lauded such mythical communist models to whom the people were expected to measure up, giving but not taking, contributing but not complaining, conforming but not making trouble. After the Cultural Revolution, and especially after the summer of 1989, however, few really believed in the orthodox propaganda.

"So," Chen said, "Comrade Lei Feng may be more needed than ever now."

"Why?"

"Contemporary social polarization. Nowadays, a handful of upstarts live in luxury beyond ordinary people's dreams, but so many workers are laid off—'waiting-for-retirement' or 'waiting-for-assignment.' Many people have a hard time making ends meet. So propaganda advocating a selfless communist model is all the more necessary."

"That's true." Yu nodded. "Those high cadres and their children, the HCC, have everything and take it for granted."

"That's why the propaganda ministry is trying very hard to come up with some contemporary role model. Guan was, at least, a pretty young woman. A considerable improvement—in the fashion-shop window of politics."

"So you don't believe in the political shit either."

"Well, so much for political myths," Chen said. "What do you think of the case?"

"It's anything but a political case."

"Yes, put politics aside."

"Guan was attacked that night on her way to a vacation. Forced to take off her clothes in a car, raped, and then strangled to death. Since she was not dating anyone at the time of her death—according to the department store—we can presume that the murderer was a stranger, probably the taxi driver."

"So what action do you suggest?"

"Inquire at the taxi bureau. Collect the drivers' receipts for that night, and check the records at the bureau. And of course, question those with suspicious pasts."

It was the same hypothesis, Guan as the victim of a taxi driver. Detective Yu had discussed it with Chen even before they had established the identity of the dead woman.

At least it explained how the body came to be found in that distant canal.

"Yes, that makes sense. Cover all the areas you think worth looking into."

"I'll do my best," Yu said, "but as I've mentioned, it won't be easy, with so many cars running around the city nowadays."

"In the meantime, let's do the regular checkup as well. I'll go to the dorm building where Guan lived, and you'll interview her colleagues in the department store."

"Fine," Yu said. "It's a special political case, I understand. But what about Commissar Zhang?"

"Well, keep him informed about our work. Whenever he wants to say something, just listen to him—as respectfully as possible," Chen said. "After all, Zhang's a veteran cadre, influential in his way."

Chapter 7

Detective Yu woke up early. Still sleepy, he took a look at the radio clock on the nightstand. It was barely six, but he knew a full day awaited him. He got up, moving carefully so as not to wake up his wife, Peiqin, who curled up against the towel-covered pillow, a striped blanket tucked down to her ankles, her bare feet exposed on the sheet.

As a rule, Yu got up at seven, jogged along Jinglin Road, read the morning newspaper, had his breakfast, sent his son Qinqin off to school, and left for the bureau. But that morning he decided to break this rule. He had to do some thinking. So he chose Renmin Road to do his jogging.

His mind was on Guan Hongying's case as he ran along at his customary pace, inhaling the fresh morning air. The street was quiet, with only a couple of old people doing Taiji on the sidewalk by the East Sea Furniture Store. A milkman was sitting in a corner, staring at a small crate of bottles at his feet, murmuring to himself, counting perhaps.

This was just another homicide case. Detective Yu would of course do his best to solve it. He had no objection to doing so, but he did not like the way the investigation was going. Politics. Nothing but damned politics. What was the difference between a model worker and non-model worker lying naked against the bare walls of an autopsy room?

According to the store's preliminary report Guan was not involved with anyone at the time of her death. In fact, all these years, Guan seemed not to have dated anybody. She had been too busy for an affair. So it could only be one of the common rape and murder cases, and the rapist, a total stranger to her, had assaulted her without knowing her identity, and killed her somewhere on her way to vacation on the night of May tenth. With neither evidence nor witnesses, the investigation would be difficult. Similar cases they had been assigned led nowhere despite all their efforts.

Detective Yu had a theory of his own concerning rapists. Most of them were repeaters who would never rest with one or two victims. So sooner or later they would be caught and convicted. The police could do little without clues or concrete evidence. It was a matter of time. Just waiting might seem too casual, considering what had been done to Guan. But what else could a cop possibly do? Detective Yu was conscientious. He took pride in being a good cop—one who could make a difference, but he knew what could be done and what could not. It was a matter of priorities.

As for any political factors being involved in this case, that was far-fetched.

Chinese people were complaining about a lot of things these days—corruption, unemployment, inflation, housing shortages, traffic congestion, and so on, but nothing related directly or indirectly to Guan. True, Guan was a national model worker and political celebrity, yet her death would leave no dent in China's socialist system. If so-called counterrevolutionaries had intended to sabotage the existing system, another far more symbolic target should have been chosen.

Yu was fed up with the Party Secretary's talk.

Still, he had to play his part. It could be crucial to his career goal, which was a simple one: to do better than his father, Yu Shenglin, usually known by his nickname, "Old Hunter." The old man, though an experienced and capable officer, was still a sergeant at retirement, with a meager pension, hardly enough to indulge himself with a pot of Dragon Well tea.

When Yu came back, panting and wiping his brow, Peiqin had already set a full breakfast on the table. a bowl of steaming beef noodle soup with a handful of green scallions.

"For you," she said. "It's still hot. I've had mine with Qinqin."

Wearing a fluffy robe, she sat hunched with her elbows on the table, supporting her chin with her hands, and looked at him over the soup. She was a few months older than he. As an ancient Chinese saying went, "An older wife knows how to take care of a husband." But with her long hair hanging down her back in ripples, she looked younger.

The noodles were good, the room clean, Qinqin already dressed for school, carrying a chicken sandwich with an apple in a sealed plastic bag. How could she have managed to do so many things in such a short while, he wondered.

And things were not easy for her, not just at home. She worked as an accountant in a small, plain restaurant called Four Seas, tucked far away in the Yangpu District. She had been assigned the job after coming back to Shanghai with him. In those days, the Office of Educated Youth assigned jobs, and decisions were made regardless of an applicant's education, intentions, or location. There was no use complaining since the office had a hard time dealing with the millions of ex-educated youths who'd returned to Shanghai. Any job opening was a blessing. But she had to make a fifty-five-minute bike ride from home to the restaurant. A tortuous journey, riding three or four bikes abreast in the rush-hour traffic. Last November she had fallen after a night's snow. She had needed seven or eight stitches, though the bike was hardly damaged, apart from a dent in the mudguard. And she was still riding the same old bike, rain or shine. She could have asked for a transfer to a closer restaurant. She didn't. Four Seas had been doing quite well, providing many perks and benefits. Some other state-run restaurants were so poorly managed that the profits were hardly enough even to maintain the employees' clinic.

"You ought to eat more," she said.

"I can't eat much in the morning, you know."

"Your job is tough. No time for lunch today again, I am afraid. Not like mine in the restaurant."

That was one disadvantage of being a cop, and an advantage of working at her restaurant job. She did not have to worry about her meals. Sometimes she even managed to bring home restaurant food—free, delicious, specially cooked by the chef.

He had not finished the noodles when the telephone started

ringing. She looked at him, and he let it ring for a while before picking it up.

"Hi, this is Chen. Sorry about calling so early."

"That's all right," he said. "Anything new—any change?"

"No," Chen said. "Nothing new. No change in our schedule either, except that Commissar Zhang wants to meet you sometime this afternoon. Say before four o'clock. Give him a call first."

"Why?"

"Commissar Zhang insists on doing something himself, he wants to conduct an interview. And then he would like to compare notes with you."

"It's no problem for me. I can set out earlier. But do we have to do this every day?"

"Perhaps I'll have to. Since it's the first day, you just do whatever the commissar wants you to."

Putting down the phone, Yu turned to Peiqin with a sigh.

"You've got to take Qinqin to school today, I'm afraid."

"No problem," she said, "but you are doing too much for too little."

"You think I don't know? A police officer makes four hundred and twenty Yuan a month, and a tea-leaf-egg vendor makes twice as much on the street."

"And that chief inspector of yours, what's his name—still single, but he's got an apartment."

"Perhaps I was born a mistake," Yu was trying to sound humorous. "A snake can never become a dragon. Not like the chief inspector."

"No, don't say that, Guangming," Peiqin said, starting to clear the table. "You're my dragon. Don't ever forget that."

But Yu felt increasingly disturbed as he stuffed the newspaper into his pants pocket, walking toward the bus stop on Jungkong Road. He had been born in the last month of the dragon year, according to the Chinese lunar calendar, supposedly a lucky year in the twelve animal cycle zodiac. According to the Gregorian calendar, however, the date was early in January of 1953, therefore the beginning of the snake year. A mistake. A snake's not a dragon, and it could never be as lucky. Not as lucky as Chief Inspector Chen. When the bus came, however, he was just lucky enough to get a seat by the window.

Detective Yu, who had entered the police force several years earlier than Chen and solved several cases, did not even dream of becoming a chief inspector. A position within his reasonable reach would be that of a squad leader. But that, too, had been taken away from him. In the special case squad, he was only the assistant to Chief Inspector Chen.

It was nothing but politics that Chen had been promoted because of his educational background. In the sixties, the more education one had, the more political unreliability one represented—in Chairman Mao's logic—as a result of being more exposed to Western ideas and ideologies. In the mid-eighties, under Comrade Deng's leadership, the Party's cadres-selecting policies had changed. That made sense, but not necessarily in the police bureau, not in Chief Inspector Chen's case. However, Chen got the position, and then the apartment.

Still, Yu was ready to admit that Chen, though not that experienced, was an honest and conscientious police officer, intelligent, well-connected, and dedicated to his job. That was a lot to say about someone in the bureau. He had been impressed by Chen's criticism of model myths the previous day.

He decided not to have a confrontation with Chen. A futile investigation would probably take two or three weeks. And if the case could be solved through their efforts, so much the better, of course.

The air grew more and more stuffy in the bus. Looking out the window, he realized that he was sitting there like a sentimental fool, feeling sorry for himself. When the bus arrived at Xizhuang

Road, Detective Yu was the first one out the door. He took a short-cut through the People's Park. One of its gates opened out to Nanjing Road, Shanghai's main thoroughfare, almost an extended shopping center in itself, stretching from the Bund to the Jian'an Temple area. The people were all in high spirits. Shoppers. Tourists. Peddlers. Messengers. A singing group was performing in front of the Helen Hotel, a young girl playing an ancient zither in the middle. A billboard in big Chinese characters exhorted Shanghai residents to promote good hygiene and preserve the environment by refraining from littering and spitting. Retired workers were waving red flags at corners, directing traffic and admonishing offenders. The sun was out, gleaming on the grated spittoons built into the sidewalks.

Detective Yu thought that he was merging with all of them. And he was their protector, too. But that, he admitted, was wishful thinking.

The First Department Store stood in the middle of Nanjing Road, facing the People's Park across Xizhuang Road. As always, the store was crowded, not only with local people, but also with people from other cities. Yu had to squeeze through the throng at the entrance. The cosmetics section was on the first floor. He stood close to it, with his back against a column, watching for a while. A lot of people flocked around the counters. Large pictures of beautiful models greeted the young shoppers, their varied body language all the more alluring under the bright lights. The youthful saleswomen were demonstrating the use of the cosmetics. They, too, looked quite attractive in green-and-white-striped uniforms, the ceaseless play of the neon lights shimmering around them.

He took the elevator up to General Manager Xiao Chi's office on the third floor.

General Manager Xiao greeted him in a spacious office, where the walls displayed an impressive assortment of awards and gold-framed pictures. One of them, Yu noticed, was Guan shaking hands with Comrade Deng Xiaoping at the Tenth Conference of the Party Central Committee.

"Comrade Guan was an important cadre of our department store. A loyal Party member," Xiao said. "A big loss to the Party, her tragic death. We will do whatever possible to assist your investigation."

"Thank you, Comrade General Manager," Yu said. "You may start by telling me what you know about her work in the store."

"She was a manager of the cosmetics section. She had worked at the store for twelve years. She did her job conscientiously, attended every Party group meeting, and helped other people in whatever way she could. A role model in every aspect of her life. Last year, for instance, she donated three hundred Yuan to Jiangshu flood victims. In response to the government's call, she also bought a large sum of government bonds every year."

"What about people's opinion of her work?"

"She was very efficient. A competent, methodical, and highly conscientious manager. People always had a high opinion of her work."

"A model worker indeed," Yu said, knowing that most of General Manager Xiao's information could have been obtained from her official file. "Well, I've got to ask you questions about something else."

"Yes, any question you want to ask."

"Was she popular—with the other staff?"

"I think so, but you'll have to ask them. I can't think of any reason why she should not be."

"And as far as you are aware, Guan had no enemies in the store?"

"Enemies? Now Comrade Detective Yu, that's a strong word. She might have had some people who didn't like her so much. So has everybody. You, too, perhaps. But you don't go in fear of being murdered, right? No, I wouldn't say she had enemies."

"What about the people in her private life?"

"That I don't know," the general manager said, slowly tracing the line of his left eyebrow with his middle finger. "She was a young woman, she never talked to me about her personal life. What we talked about was work, work, and work. She was very conscious of her position as manager, and as a national model worker. Sorry, I cannot help you."

"She had a lot of friends?"

"Well, she hadn't too many close friends in the store. No time, perhaps. All the Party activities and meetings."

"She had not discussed her vacation plans with you?"

"Not with me. It wouldn't have been a long vacation, so she did not have to. I have asked several of her colleagues; she had not talked with them either."

Detective Yu decided that it was time to interview the other employees.

A list of people had been prepared for him.

"They will tell you whatever they know. If there's anything else I can do, please contact me," Xiao said earnestly.

The interviews were to be held in a formal conference room, spacious enough to seat hundreds of people. The interviewees were waiting in an adjacent room, accessible through a glass door. Detective Yu was supposed to call them in one by one. Pan Xiaoxai, a close friend of Guan's, was the first. With two small children at home, one of them disabled, she had to hurry back home during the lunch break. She had been sobbing in the waiting room. He could tell that from her swollen eyes.

"It's awful—" she said bleakly, taking off her glasses and dabbing her eyes with a silk handkerchief. "I can't believe that Guan's dead . . . I mean—what a wonderful Party member. And to think, the last day Guan was in the store, I happened to have the day off."

"I understand your feelings, Comrade Pan," he said. "You were one of her closest friends, I've heard."

"Yes, we've worked together for years—six years." She wiped her eyes and sniffed loudly, as if anxious to prove the genuineness of their friendship. "I've been working here for ten years, but in the toy section first."

In reply to Yu's question about Guan's personal life, Pan admitted reluctantly, however, that the deceased had not been that close to her. In all those years, she had been to Guan's dorm only once. In fact, what they had been doing together was mostly window shopping during lunch break, comparing prices, or having curried beef noodles in Sheng's Restaurant across the street. That was about it.

"Did you ask her anything about her personal life?"

"No, I never did."

"How could that be? You were close friends, weren't you?"

"Um—she had a certain way about her. Difficult to define, but like a line was drawn. After all, she was a national celebrity."

At the end of the interview, Pan looked up through her tear-stained glasses, "You will find out who did it, won't you?"

"Of course we will."

Zhong Ailin, who worked with Guan on the morning of May tenth, was next. She started to offer her information immediately. "Comrade Detective Yu, I'm afraid I won't be helpful. On the morning of May tenth, we talked very little, two or three words at the most. To me, she seemed all right. She didn't tell me that she was leaving for a real vacation. As far as I can remember, she mentioned that she was going to take only a few days off. That's quite normal. As the department head, she sometimes worked extra hours. So she had earned a lot of days off."

"Did she say anything else to you during that day or that week?"

"She was a national model worker, always busy, working and serving people wholeheartedly, as Chairman Mao said long ago. So most of the talking she did was to her customers, not to us."

"Any idea who might have killed her?"

"No, none at all."

"Could it be somebody who worked with her?"

"I don't think so. She was not a difficult person to get along with, and she did her job well."

According to Zhong Ailin, some of her colleagues might have been envious of Guan, but it was undeniable that she knew the ropes at the store and was a decent and reliable woman—politics aside.

"As for her life outside of the store," Zhong concluded, "I don't know anything—except that she was not dating anyone—had probably never dated anyone."

Zhong was followed by Mrs. Weng, who had worked the afternoon shift on May tenth. Mrs. Weng started by declaring that the investigation was none of her business, and that she had not noticed anything unusual about Guan that last day.

"There was nothing different about her," she said. "She might have put a light touch of eye shadow on her eyelids. But it was nothing. We have a lot of free samples."

"What else?"

"She made a phone call."

"When?"

"It would be about six thirty, I think."

"Did she have to wait long before she started talking?"

"No. She started talking immediately."

"Anything you happened to overhear?"

"No. It was short," she said. "It was her business, not mine."

Mrs. Weng talked more than the first two, however, offering opinions even without being asked. And she went on speculating about some information which she believed might be of interest. Several weeks earlier, Mrs. Weng had gone with a Hong Kong friend to the Dynasty KTV Club. In the semi-dark corridor, she saw a woman emerging from a private room with a tall man, practically leaning on his shoulder—the woman's clothes in disarray, several buttons undone, her face flushed, and her steps reeling. A shameless karaoke girl, Mrs. Weng thought. A private karaoke room was an open secret, almost a synonym for indecent practices. But then it occurred to Mrs. Wen that the karaoke girl looked like someone she knew. As the image of the drunken slut was at such odds with the one flashing through her mind, recognition did not come until a few seconds later—Guan Hongying! Mrs. Weng could scarcely believe it, but she thought it was her.

"Did you take a closer look at her?"

"When recognition came to me, she had already walked past me. It wouldn't do for me to chase someone there."

"So you're not positive."

"No. But it was my impression."

Next on the list was Gu Chaoxi. Gu, though older than Guan by more than fifteen years, had been trained by Guan at the department store.

"Do you remember anything unusual about Guan before her death?" Detective Yu went directly to the point.

"Unusual—what do you mean?"

"Coming in late for work, for instance. Or leaving too early for home. Or any particular change you noticed about her."

"No, not that I'm aware of," Gu said, "but everything has been changing so fast. Our cosmetics section used to have only two counters. Now we have eight, with so many different products, and a lot of them made in the U.S.A. Of course, people are changing, too. Guan's no exception."

"Can you give me an example?"

"The first day I came to work here—that's seven years ago—she gave all of us a lecture I still remember, on the importance of adhering to the Party's hard-working and plain-living tradition. In fact, she had made a point of using no perfume and wearing no jewelry. But a few months ago, I saw her wearing a diamond necklace."

"Really," he said. "Do you think it was genuine?"

"I'm not sure," she said. "I'm not saying there was anything wrong with her wearing a necklace. It's just in the nineties people are changing. Another example, she went on a vacation half a year ago, last October, I think. And then in less than six months, she took a second one."

"Yes, that's something," he said. "Do you know where she went last October?"

"The Yellow Mountains. She showed me pictures from there."

"Did she travel alone?"

"I think she was alone. Nobody else was in the pictures."

"And this time?"

"I knew she was going on vacation, but she did not tell me where, or with whom," she said, looking at the door. "That's all I know, I'm afraid, Comrade Detective."

Despite the central air conditioning in the room, Detective Yu sweated profusely, watching Gu walk out. He recognized the familiar malaise that preceded a headache, but he had to proceed. There were five more names on the list. The next two hours, however, yielded even less information. He put all the notes together.

On May tenth, Guan had come to work as usual, around 8 A.M She was amiable as always, a true national model worker, toward her customers as well as her colleagues. She dined at the canteen at twelve o'clock, and she had a routine meeting with other Party members at the store late in the afternoon. She did not mention to her colleagues where she was going, though she said something about a vacation. At five, she could have left for home, but as usual, she stayed late. Around six thirty, she made a phone call, a short one, but no one knew to whom. After the phone call, she left the store, apparently for home. The last time she was seen by anyone there was around seven ten.

It was not much, and Detective Yu had a feeling that the people had been rather guarded talking about Guan, with Mrs. Weng the only exception. But then her information was not something he could count on.

It was long past lunchtime, but on his list there was still one person, who happened to have the day off. He left the department store at two forty. At a street corner minimarket, he bought a couple of pork-stuffed pancakes. Peiqin was right in her concern about his missing lunch, but there was no time for him to think about being nutritionally correct. The last person's name was Zhang Yaqing, and she lived on Yunnan Road. She was an assistant manager working in the cosmetics section, who had called in sick for the day. According to some employees, Zhang had been once regarded as a potential rival for Guan, but Zhang had then married and settled into a more prosaic life.

Detective Yu was familiar with that section of Yunnan Road. It was only fifteen minutes' walk from the store. North of Jinglin Road, Yunnan Road had turned into a prosperous "Delicacy Street" with a number of snack bars and restaurants, but to the south, the street remained largely unchanged, consisting of old, ramshackle houses built in the forties, with baskets, stoves, and common sinks still lined up on the sidewalk outside.

He arrived at a gray brick house, went up the stairs, and knocked on a door on the second floor. A woman opened the door immediately. She was in her early thirties, with ordinary but fine features, her short hair deep black. She wore blue jeans and a white blouse with the sleeves rolled up high. She was barefoot. She looked rather slender, and she was brandishing a huge cloth strip mop in her hand.

"Comrade Zhang Yaqing?"

"Yes?"

"I am Detective Yu Guangming, of the Shanghai Police Bureau."

"Hello, Detective Yu. Come on in. The general manager has called, telling me about your investigation."

They shook hands.

Her palm was cool, callused, like Peiqin's.

"Sorry, I was just cleaning up the room."

It was a cubicle of eight square meters, containing two beds and a white dresser. A folding table and chairs stood against the wall. There was an enlarged picture of her with a smiling big man and a smiling little boy. The Happy Family photo. She pulled out a chair, unfolded it, and gestured to him to sit down.

"Would you like a drink?"

"No, thanks."

"What do you want from me?"

"Just answer a few questions about Guan."

"Yes, of course," she said, settling into another chair.

She drew back her legs under it, as if intent on hiding her bare feet.

"How long have you worked with Guan?"

"About five years."

"What do you think of her?"

"She was a celebrated model worker, of course, and a loyal Party member, too."

"Could you be a bit more specific?"

"Well, politically, she was active—and correct—in every movement launched by the Party authorities. Earnest, loyal, passionate. As our department head, she was conscientious and thoroughgoing in her job: The first to arrive, and often the last to leave. I am not going to say that Comrade Guan was too easy to get along with, but how else could she have been, since she was such a political celebrity?"

"You have mentioned her political activities. Is it possible that through those activities she made some enemies? Did anyone hate her?"

"No, I don't think so. She was not responsible for the political movements. No one would blame her for the Cultural Revolution. And to be fair to her, she never pushed things too far. As for someone who might have hated her in her personal life, I'm afraid I don't know anything about it."

"Well—let me put it this way," Yu said. "What do you think of her as a woman?"

"It's difficult for me to say. She was very private. To a fault, I would say."

"What do you mean?"

"She never talked about her own life. Believe it or not, she did not have a boyfriend. Nor did she seem to have any close friends, for that matter. That's something beyond me. She was a national model worker, but that did not mean that she had to live her whole life for politics. Not for a woman. Only in one of those modern Beijing operas, maybe. You remember, like Madam A Qin?"

Yu nodded, smiling.

Madam A Qin was a well-known character in *Shajiabang*, a modern Beijing opera performed during the Cultural Revolution, when any romantic passion—even that between husband and wife—had been considered to detract from people's political commitment. Madam A Qin thus had the convenience of not living with her husband in the opera.

"She might have been too busy," he said.

"Well, I'm not saying that she did not have a personal life. Rather, she made a point of covering it up. We're women. We fall in love, get married, and have kids. There's nothing wrong with it."

"So you're not sure that she had never had an affair?"

"I'm telling you everything I know, but I don't like to gossip about the dead."

"Yes, I understand. Thank you so much for your information."

As he stood up, he took one more glance around the room, noticing a variety of perfumes, lipsticks, and nail polish on the dresser, some of the brands he had seen on glamorous movie stars in TV commercials. They were obviously beyond her means.

"There're all samples," she said, following his gaze, "from the First Department Store."

"Of course," Yu said, wondering whether Comrade Guan Hongying would have chosen to keep all her cosmetics more discreetly hidden in a drawer. "And good-bye."

Detective Yu was not happy about his day's work. There was not much to talk about with Commissar Zhang, but he had never had much to talk about with the commissar. He called from a public phone booth, but Commissar Zhang was not in the office. Yu did not have to listen to a political lecture delivered by the old commissar, so he went home.

No one was there. He saw a note on table, saying, "I'm with Qinqin at his school for a meeting. Warm the meal for yourself."

Holding a bowl of rice with strips of roast duck, he stepped into the courtyard, where he had a talk with his father, Old Hunter.

"A cold-blooded rape and murder case," Old Hunter said, frowning.

Yu remembered the frustration his father had suffered in the early sixties, dealing with a similar sex murder case, which had taken place in the Baoshan rice paddy. The girl's body had been found almost immediately. The police arrived on the scene in less than half an hour. One witness had glimpsed the suspect and gave a fairly recognizable description. There were some fresh footprints and a cigarette butt. Old Hunter worked late into the night, month after month, but all the work led to nothing. Several years later, the culprit was caught in the act of selling pictures of Madame Mao as a bewitching second-class actress in the early thirties—a wanton goddess in a low-cut gown. Such a crime at the time was more than enough cause to put him to death. During his examination, he admitted the murder years earlier in Baoshan. The case, as well as the unexpected solution—too late to be of any comfort—had left an indelible impact on Old Hunter.

Such a case was like a tunnel where one could move on and on and on without hope of seeing the light.

"Well, there could be a political angle, according to our Party secretary."

"Look, son," Old Hunter said, "you don't have to give me the crap about political significance. An old horse knows the way, as the saying goes. If such a homicide case isn't solved in the first two or three weeks, the solution probability drops off to zero. Politics or no."

"But we have to do something, you know, as a special case group."

"A special case group, indeed. If a serial killer were involved, the existence of your group would be more justified."

"That's what I figured, but the people high up won't give us a break, especially Commissar Zhang."

"Don't talk to me about your commissar either. A pain in the ass for thirty years. I've never gotten along with him. As for your chief inspector, I understand why he wants to go on with the investigation. Politics."

"He's so good at politics."

"Well, don't get me wrong," the old man said. "I'm not against your boss. On the contrary, I believe he is a conscientious young officer in his way. Heaven is above his head, the earth is under his feet—at least he knows that. I've spent all these years in the force, and I can judge a man."

After their talk, Yu stayed in the courtyard alone, smoking, tapping the ash into the empty rice bowl with roast duck bones forming a cross at the bottom.

He affixed a second cigarette to the butt of the first when it had been smoked down, and then added another, until it almost looked like an antenna, trembling in its effort to receive some imperceptible information from the evening sky.

Chapter 8

Chief Inspector Chen, too, had had a busy morning. At seven o'clock he'd met with Commissar Zhang in the bureau.

"It's a difficult case," Commissar Zhang said, nodding after Chen had briefed him. "But we mustn't be afraid of hardship or death."

Don't be afraid of hardship or death—one of Chairman Mao's quotations during the Cultural Revolution. Now it reminded Chen of a faded poster torn from the wall of a deserted building. Being a commissar for so many years had turned Zhang into something like an echoing machine. An old politician, out of touch with the times. The Commissar was, however, anything but a blockhead; it was said that he had been one of the most brilliant students at Southwest United University in the forties.

"Yes, you're right," Chen said. "I'm going to Guan's dorm this morning."

"That's important. There might be some evidence left in her room," Commissar Zhang said. "Keep me informed of anything you find there."

"I will."

"Have Detective Yu contact me, too."

"I will tell him."

"Now what about me?" Zhang said. "I also need to do something, not just be an advice-giving bystander."

"But we have every aspect of the initial investigation covered at present. Detective Yu's interviewing Guan's colleagues, and I'm going to check her room, talk to her neighbors, and afterward, if I have the time, I will visit her mother in the nursing home."

"Then I'll go to the nursing home. She's old, too. We may have things to talk about between us."

"But you really don't have to do anything. It is not suitable for a veteran cadre like you to undertake the routine investigations."

"Don't tell me that, Comrade Chief Inspector," Zhang said, getting up with a frown. "Just go to Guan's dorm now."

The dormitory, located on Hubei Road, was a building shared by several work units, including that of the First Department Store, which had a few rooms there for its employees. Considering Guan's political status, she could have gotten something better—a regular apartment like his, Chen thought. Maybe that was what made Guan a model worker.

Hubei was a small street tucked between Zhejiang Road and Fujian Road, not too far away from Fuzhou Road to the north, a main cultural street boasting several well-known bookstores. The location was convenient. The Number 71 bus was only ten minutes' walk away, on Yan'an Road, and it went directly to the First Department Store.

Chen got off the bus at Zhejiang Road. He decided to walk around the neighborhood, which could speak volumes about the people living there—as in Balzac's novels. In Shanghai, however, it was not up to the people to decide where they would get a room, but to their work units, Chen realized. Still, he strolled around the area, thinking.

The street was one of the few still covered with cobblestones. There were quite a number of small, squalid lanes and alleys on both sides. Children raced about like scraps of paper blowing in the wind, running out of one lane into another.

Chen took out his notebook. Guan Hongying's address read: Number 18, Lane 235, Hubei Road. But he was unable to find the lane.

He asked several people, showing them the address. No one seemed to have heard of the lane. Hubei was not a long street. In less than fifteen minutes, he had walked to the end and back. Still no success. So he stepped into a small grocery store on the corner, but the old grocer also shook his head. There were five or six hoodlums lounging by the grocery, young and shabby, with sparse whiskers and shining earrings, who looked at him challengingly.

The day was hot, without a breath of air. He wondered whether he had made a mistake, but a call to Commissar Zhang confirmed that the address was right. Then he dialed Comrade Xu Kexin, a senior librarian of the bureau—better known by his nickname of Mr. Walking Encyclopedia—who had worked in the bureau for over thirty years, and had a phenomenal knowledge of the city's history.

"I need to ask a favor of you," he said. "Right now I'm at Hubei Street, between Zhejiang and Fujian Road, looking for Lane 235. The address is correct, but I cannot find that lane."

"Hubei Street, hmm," Xu said. "It was known, before 1949, as a notorious quarter."

"What?" Chen asked, hearing Xu leafing through pages, "'Quarter'—what do you mean?"

"Ah yes, a brothel quarter."

"What's that got to do with the lane I cannot find?"

"A lot," Xu said. "These lanes used to have different names. Notorious names, in fact. After liberation in 1949, the government put an end to prostitution, and changed the names of the lanes, but the people there may still use the old names for convenience sake, I believe. Yes, Lane 235, I've got it here. This lane was called Qinghe Lane, one of the most infamous in the twenties and thirties, or even earlier. It was where the second-class prostitutes gathered."

"Qinghe Lane? Odd—the name does not sound so strange."

"Well, it was mentioned in the well-known biography of Chiang Kai-shek by Tang Ren, but that may well be fictional rather than factual. At that time, Fuzhou Road, still called Fourth Avenue, was a red-light district, and Fubei Street was part of it. According to some statistics, there were more than seventy thousand prostitutes in Shanghai. In addition to government-licensed prostitutes, there were also a large number of bar girls, hostesses, masseuses, and guides engaged in clandestine or casual prostitution."

"Yes, I have read that biography," Chen said, thinking it was time to close the "encyclopedia."

"All the brothels were closed in the 1951 campaign," Mr. Encyclopedia droned on. "Officially, at least, there're no prostitutes under China's sun. Those who refused to change were put into reform-through-labor institutes. Most of them turned over a new leaf. I doubt any of them would have chosen to stay in the same neighborhood."

"I doubt that, too."

"Some sexual case in the lane?"

"No. Just looking for somebody living there," Chen said. "Thank you so much for your information."

Qinghe Lane turned out to be the one next to the grocery store. The lane looked decayed and dismal, with a glass-and-concrete-fronted kiosk attached to the first building, which made the entrance even narrower. Droplets from laundry festooned over a network of bamboo poles overhead presented an Impressionist scene in the May sunlight. It was believed that walking under the women's lacy underwear like that streaming over the poles would bring bad luck for the day, but with the past associations of the lane in his mind, Chief Inspector Chen found it to be almost nostalgic.

Most of the houses had been built in the twenties or even earlier. Number 18 was actually the first building, the one with the kiosk attached. It had a walled-off courtyard, tiled roofs, and heavy carved beams, its balconies spilling over with laundry dripping on the piles of vegetables and used bicycle parts in the courtyard. On the door of the kiosk was a red plastic sign announcing in bold strokes: PUBLIC PHONE SERVICE. An old man was sitting inside, surrounded by several phones and phone books, working not only as a phone operator, but probably as a doorman as well.

"Morning," the old man said.

"Morning," Chen replied.

Even before the revolution, the house appeared to have been subdivided to accommodate more girls, each room containing one bed, of course, if not much else, with smaller alcoves for maidservants or pimps. That was probably why the house had been turned into a dorm building after 1949. Now each of these rooms was inhabited by a family. What might have originally served as a spacious dining room, where customers ordered banquets to please prostitutes, had been partitioned into several rooms, too. A closer examination revealed many signs of neglect characteristic of such dorm buildings: gaping windows, scaling cement, peeling paint, and the smell from the public bathroom permeating the corridor. Apparently each floor shared only one bathroom. And a quarter of the bathroom had been redesigned with makeshift plastic partitions into a concrete shower area.

Chen was not unfamiliar with this type of dorm. Dormitories in Shanghai could be classified into two kinds. One was conventional: each room contained nothing but beds or bunks, six or eight of them, each resident occupying no more than one bunk's space. For these residents, most likely bachelors or bachelor girls waiting for their work units to assign them rooms so that they could get married, such a dorm space was just a temporary solution. Chen, in the days before he had become a chief inspector, had thought about getting a dorm bunk for himself, for it could well be that such a gesture would bring pressure to bear upon the housing committee. He had even checked into it, but Party Secretary Li's promise had changed his mind. The second kind was an extension of the first. Due to the severe housing problem, those on the waiting list could find themselves reaching their mid-or-late thirties, still with no hope of having an apartment assigned to them. As a sort of compromise, a dorm room instead of a bunk space would be assigned to those who could not afford to wait any longer. They remained, theoretically, on the waiting list though their chances would be greatly reduced.

Guan's room, apparently of the second kind, was on the second floor, the last one at the end of the corridor, across from the public bathroom. It was not one of the most desirable locations, but easy access to the bathroom might count as a bonus. Guan, too, had to share it with other families on the same floor. Eleven of them in all. The corridor was lined with piles of coal, cabbages, pots and pans, and coal stoves outside the doors.

On one of the doors was a piece of cardboard with the character GUAN written on it. Outside the door stood a small dust-covered coal stove with a pile of pressed coal-cylinders beside it. Chen opened the door with a master key. The doormat inside was littered with mail—more than a week's newspapers, a postcard from Beijing signed by someone called Zhang Yonghua, and an electricity bill which, ironically, still bore the pre-1949 address—Qinghe Lane.

It was a tiny room.

The bed was made, the ashtray empty, and the window closed. There was nothing to indicate that Guan had entertained any guest before her death. Nor did it look like a place in which someone had been murdered. The room appeared too tidy, too clean. The furniture was presumably her parents', old and heavy, but still in usable condition, consisting of a single bed, a chest, a large wardrobe, a small bookshelf, a sofa with a faded red cover, and a stool that might have served as nightstand. A thirteen-inch TV stood on the wardrobe. On the bookshelf were dictionaries, a set of *Selected Works of Mao Zedong*, a set of *Selected Works of Deng Xiaoping*, and a variety of political pamphlets and magazines. The bed was not only old, it was narrow and shabby. Chen touched it. There was no squeak of bedsprings, no mattress under the sheet, just the hardboard. There was a pair of red slippers under the bed, as if anchoring the emptiness of the silent room.

On the wall above the headboard was a framed photograph of Guan making a presentation at the third National Model Workers Conference in the People's Great Conference Hall. In the background of the picture sat the First Secretary of the Central Committee of the Chinese Communist Party applauding with some other high ranking cadres. There was also a huge portrait of Comrade Deng Xiaoping on the other wall above the sofa.

In the wastebasket, he saw nothing but several balls of tissues. On top of the chest was a bottle of vitamin pills, the cap still unbroken. Several lipsticks. Bottles of imported perfumes. A tiny plastic-framed mirror. He checked the drawers of the chest. The top drawer contained cash receipts from stores, some blank envelopes, and a movie magazine. The second drawer held several photo albums. The contents of the third was more mixed. An imitation leather trinket box holding an assortment of costume jewelry. Some more expensive lotions and perfumes, perhaps samples from the store. He also found a gold choker with a crescent-shaped pendant, a Citizen watch with clear stones around the face, and a necklace made of some exotic animal bone.

In the cupboard fastened on the wall, he saw several glasses and mugs, but only a couple of black bowls with a small bunch of bamboo chopsticks. It was understandable, Chen reflected. It was not a place to which to invite people. She could have offered a cup of tea at the most.

He opened one door of the wardrobe, which revealed several shelves of tightly packed clothes: a dark-brown winter overcoat, several white blouses, wool sweaters, and three pairs of trousers hung in a corner, all of them demure and rather dull in color. They were not necessarily inexpensive but seemed conservative for a young woman. On the floor stood a pair of high-heeled black shoes, a pair of oxfords with rubber spikes, and a pair of galoshes.

When he opened the other door, however, it revealed a surprise. On the top shelf lay some new, well-made clothes, of fine material and popular design. Chief Inspector Chen did not know much about the fashion world, but he knew they were expensive from the well-known brands or the shop tags still attached to them. Underneath was a large collection of underwear that women's magazines would probably term "romantic," or even "erotic," some of the sexiest pieces he had ever seen, with the lace being a main ingredient rather than a trimming.

He was unable to reconcile the striking contrast between the two sides of the wardrobe.

She had been a single woman, not dating anyone at the time of her death.

Then he moved back to the chest, took the photo albums out of the drawer, and put them on the table, next to a tall glass of water containing a bouquet of wilted flowers, a pen holder, a small paper bag of black pepper, and a bottle of Crystal pure water. It seemed that the table had served as her dining table, desk, and kitchen counter—all in one.

There were four albums. In the first, most of the pictures were black-and-white. A few showed a chubby girl with a ponytail. A girl of seven or eight, grinning for the camera, or blowing out candles on a cake. In one, she stood between a man and woman on the Bund, the man's image blurred but the woman's fairly clear. Presumably her parents. It took four or five album pages for her to start wearing a Red Scarf—a Young Pioneer saluting the raising of the five-starred flag at her school. The pictures were arranged chronologically.

He snapped to attention when he turned to a small picture on the first page of the second album. It must have been taken in the early seventies. Sitting on a rock by a pool, one bare foot dabbling in the water, the other held up above the knee, Guan was piercing the blisters on her sole with a needle. The background showed several young people holding a banner with the words LONG MARCH on it, striding proudly toward the Yan'an pagoda in the distance. It was the *da chuanlian* period of the Cultural Revolution when Red Guards traveled all around the country, spreading Chairman Mao's ideas on "continuation of the revolution under the proletarian dictatorship." Yan'an, a county where Mao had stayed before 1949, became a sacred place, to which Red Guards made their pilgrimage. She must have been a kid, newly qualified as a Red Guard, but there she was, wearing a red armband, blistered, but eager to catch up.

In the middle of the second album, she had grown into a young girl with a fine, handsome face, big almond eyes, and thick eyelashes. There was more resemblance to National Model Worker Guan as shown in the newspapers.

The third album consisted of pictures from Guan's political life. There were a considerable number of them showing her together with various Party leaders at one conference or another. Ironically, these pictures could have served to trace the dramatic changes in China's politics, with some leaders vanishing, and some moving to the front, but Guan, unchanged, stood in her familiar pose, in the familiar limelight.

Then came the last album, the thickest: the pictures of Guan's personal life. There were so many of them, and they were all so different, Chen was impressed. Shots from various angles, in various outfits, and with various backgrounds: reclining in a canoe at dusk, wearing a striped camp shirt with a fitted skirt, her face calm and relaxed; standing on her toes by an imported limousine in sunlight; kneeling on the muddy plank of a little bridge, scratching her bare ankle, bending forward over the railing, the weight of her body resting on her right foot; gazing at the misty horizon through a window, her face framed by her tangled hair, a cloud of velvety cattail blurred in a distant field; perching on the steps of an ancient temple, a transparent plastic raincoat over her shoulders, a silk scarf drawn over her hair, her mouth half-open, as if she were on the verge of saying something . . . .

It was not just that the pictures formed a sharp contrast to her "model worker" image in the previous album. In these pictures, she struck Chief Inspector Chen as more than pretty or vivacious. She looked radiant, lit from within. It seemed there was a message in these pictures. What it was, however, Chen could not decipher.

There were also a couple of more surprising close-ups: in one, she was lying on a love seat, her round shoulders covered only with a white bath towel; in another, she was sitting on a marble table, wearing a terry robe, dangling her bare legs; in yet another, she was kneeling, in a bathing suit, its shoulder straps off, her hair tousled, looking breathless.

Chief Inspector Chen blinked, trying to break the momentary spell of Guan's image.

Who had taken these pictures, he wondered. Where had she had them developed? Especially the close-ups. State-run studios would have refused to take the order, for some of the pictures could be labeled as "bourgeois decadent." And at unscrupulous private studios, she might have run a serious risk, for those entrepreneurs could have sold such pictures for money. It could have been politically disastrous if she had been recognized as the national model worker.

An album page was large enough for four standard-sized pictures, but for several pages, each held only one or two. The last few pages were blank.

It was about noon when he returned the albums to the drawer. He did not feel hungry. Through the window he thought he could hear the distant roar of a bulldozer working at a construction site.

Chief Inspector Chen decided to talk to Guan's neighbors. He first went to the next door along the corridor, a door still decorated with a faded red paper couplet celebrating the Chinese Spring Festival. There was also a plastic *yin-yang* symbol dangling as a sort of decoration.

The woman who opened the door was small and fair, wearing slacks and a cotton-knit top, a white apron around her waist. She must have been busy cooking, for she wiped one hand on the apron as she held the door open with the other. He guessed she was in her mid-thirties. She had tiny lines around her mouth.

Chen introduced himself, showing his business card to her.

"Come in," she said, "my name is Yuan Peiyu."

Another efficiency room. Identical in size and shape to Guan's, it appeared smaller, with clothes and other diverse objects scattered round. In the middle of the room was a round table bearing row upon row of fresh-made dumplings, together with a pile of dumpling skins and a bowl of pork stuffing. A boy in an imitation army uniform came out from under the table. He was chewing a half-eaten bun, staring up at Chen. The little soldier stretched up a sticky fist and made a gesture of throwing the bun toward Chen like a grenade.

"Bang!"

"Stop! Don't you see he is a police officer?" said his mother.

"That's okay," Chen said. "I'm sorry to bother you, Comrade Yuan. You must have heard of your neighbor's death. I just want to ask you a few questions."

"Sorry," she said. "I cannot help you. I don't know anything about her."

"You've been neighbors for several years?"

"Yes, about five years."

"Then you must have had some contact with each other, cooking together on the corridor, or washing clothes in the common sink."

"Well, I'll tell you what. She left home at seven in the morning, and came back at seven—sometimes much later. The moment she got back, she shut the door tight. She never invited us in, nor visited us. She did her laundry in the store, with all the washing machines on display there. Free, and perhaps free detergent too. She ate at the store canteen. Once or twice a month, she would cook at home, a packet of instant noodles or something like that, though she kept her stove in the corridor all the time. Her sacred right to the public space."

"So you've never talked to her at all?"

"When we saw each other, she nodded to me. That's about all." Yuan added. "A celebrity. She would not mix with us. So what's the point of pressing our hot faces up to her cold ass?"

"Maybe she was just too busy."

"She was somebody, and we're nobody. She made great contributions to the Party! We can hardly make ends meet."

Surprised at the resentment shown by Guan's neighbor, Chen said, "No matter in what position we work, we're all working for our socialist China."

"Working for socialist China?" her voice rose querulously. "Last month I was laid off from the state-run factory. I need to feed my son; his father died several years ago. So making dumplings all day is what I do now, from seven to seven, if you want to call that working for socialist China. And I have to sell them at the food market at six in the morning."

"I'm sorry to hear that, Comrade Yuan," he said. "Right now China is in a transitional period, but things will get better."

"It's not your fault. Why should you feel sorry? Just spare me a political lecture about it. Comrade Guan Hongying did not want to make friends with us. Period."

"Well, she must have had some friends coming to visit her here."

"Maybe or maybe not, but that's her business, not mine."

"I understand, Comrade Yuan," he said, "but I still want to ask you some other questions. Did you notice anything unusual about Guan in the last couple of months?"

"I'm no detective, so I do not know what's usual or unusual."

"One more question," he said. "Did you see her on the evening of May tenth?"

"May tenth, let me think," she said. "I don't remember seeing her at all that day. I was at my son's school for a meeting in the evening. Then we went to bed early. As I've told you, I have to get up to sell the dumplings early in the morning."

"Perhaps you'd like to think about it. You can get in touch with me if anything comes to you," he said. "Again, I'm sorry about the situation in your factory, but let's hope for the best."

"Thank you." She added, as if apologizing in her turn now, "There may be one thing, now that I think about it. For the last couple of months, sometimes she came back quite late, at twelve o'clock or even later. Since I was laid off I have been worried too much to sleep soundly, so once or twice I heard her coming back at such hours. But then, she could have been really busy, such a national model worker."

"Yes, probably," he said, "but we will check into that."

"That's about all I know," she said.

Chief Inspector Chen thanked her and left.

He next approached Guan's neighbor across the corridor,

beside the public bathroom. He was raising his hand toward the tiny doorbell when the door was flung open. A young girl dashed out toward the stairs, and a middle-aged woman stood furiously in the doorway, with her hands firmly on her hips. "You, too, have to come and bully me. Little bitch. May Heaven let you die a thousand-stab death." Then she saw him, and stared at him with angry, pop-eyed intensity.

He immediately adopted the stance of a senior police officer with no time to waste, producing his official identity card and flashing it at her with a gesture often shown on TV.

It caused her to lose some of her animosity.

"I have to ask you some questions," he said. "Questions about Guan Hongying, your neighbor."

"She's dead, I know," she said. "My name is Su Nanhua. Sorry about the scene you have just witnessed. My daughter's seeing a young gangster and will not listen to me. It's really driving me crazy."

What Chen got after fifteen minutes' talk was almost the same version as Yuan's, except Su was even more biased. According to her, Guan had kept very much to herself all those years. That would have been odd in a young woman, though not for such a celebrity.

"You mean that she lived here all these years and you did not get a single chance to get acquainted?"

"Sounds ridiculous, doesn't it?" she said. "But it's true."

"And she never talked to you?"

"Well, she did and she didn't. 'It's fine today.' 'Have you had your dinner?' So on and so forth. Nothing but those meaningless words."

"Now what about the evening of May tenth, Comrade Su?" he said. "Did you see her or speak to her that evening?"

"Well, that evening, yes, I did notice something. I was reading the latest issue of *Family* quite late that evening. I would not have noticed her leaving the dorm, but for the sound of something heavy being dropped just outside my door. So I looked out. There she was, going to the stairs, with her back me, and I did not know what she had dropped. All I could see was that she had a heavy suitcase in one hand. So it could have been the suitcase. She was going downstairs. It was late. I was curious and looked out of the window, but I saw no taxi waiting for her at the curb."

"So you thought she was taking a trip."

"I guessed so."

"What time was it?"

"Around ten thirty."

"How did you know the time?"

"I watched *Hope* that evening on TV. Every Thursday evening, in fact. It finishes at ten thirty. Then I started reading the magazine. I had not read much before I heard the thump."

"Had she talked to you about the trip she was going to take?"

"No, not to me."

"Was there anything else about that night?"

"No, nothing else."

"Contact me if you think of anything," he said, standing up. "You have my number on the card."

Chen then climbed up to the third floor, to a room almost directly above Guan's. The door was opened by a white-haired man, probably in his mid-sixties, who had an intelligent face with shrewd eyes and deep-cut furrows around his mouth. Looking at the card Chen handed him, he said, "Comrade Chief Inspector, come in. My name is Qian Yizhi."

The door opened into a narrow strip of corridor, in which there were a gas stove and a cement sink, and then to another inner door. It was an improvement over his neighbors' apartments. Entering, Chen was surprised to see an impressive array of magazine photos of Hong Kong and of Taiwanese pop singers like Liu Dehua, Li Min, Zhang Xueyou, and Wang Fei on the walls.

"All my stepdaughter's favorite pictures," Qian said, removing a stack of newspapers from a decent-looking armchair. "Please sit down."

"I'm investigating Guan Hongying's case," Chen said. "Any information you can give about her will be appreciated."

"Not much, I'm afraid," Qian said. "As a neighbor, she hardly talked to me at all."

"Yes, I've spoken to her neighbors downstairs, and they also considered her too much of a big shot to talk to them."

"Some of her neighbors believed she put on airs, trying to appear head and shoulders above others, but I don't think that is true."

"Why?"

"Well, I'm retired now, but I've also been a model teacher for over twenty years. Of course, my model status was only at the district level, by no means as high as hers, but I know what it's like," Qian said, stroking his well-shaved chin. "Once you're a role model, you're model-shaped."

"That's a very original point," Chen said.

"People said, for instance, I was all patience with my students, but I was not—not all the time. But once you're a model teacher, you have to be."

"So it is like a magical mask. When you wear the mask, the mask becomes you."

"Exactly," Qian said, "except it's not necessarily a magic one."

"Still, she was supposed to be a model neighbor in the dorm, wasn't she?"

"Yes, but it can be so exhausting to live with your mask on all the time. No one can wear a mask all the time. You want to have a break. Back in the dorm, why should she continue to play her role and serve her neighbors the way she served her customers? She was just too tired to mix with her neighbors, I believe. That could have caused her unpopularity."

"That is very insightful," Chen said. "I was puzzled why her neighbors downstairs seemed so biased against her."

"They do not really have anything against her. They are just not in a good mood. And there's another important factor. Guan had a room for herself, while theirs was for the whole family."

"Yes, you're right again," he said. "But you have a room for yourself too."

"No, not really," Qian said. "My stepdaughter lives with her parents, but she has an eye on this room. That's why she put up all the Hong Kong star pictures."

"I see."

"People living in a dorm are a different lot. In theory, we are staying here just for a short transitional period. So we are not really concerned about relationships with our neighbors. We do not call this *home*."

"Yes, it must be so different, living in a dorm."

"Take the public bathroom for example. Each floor shares one. But if people believe they are going to move away tomorrow, who's going to take care of it?"

"You're really putting things into perspective for me, Comrade Qian."

"It has not been easy for Guan," Qian said. "A single young woman. Meetings and conferences all day, and back home alone at night—and not to someplace she could really call home."

"Can you be a bit more specific here?" Chen said. "Is there something particular you have noticed?"

"Well, it was several months ago. I was unable to fall asleep that night, so I got up and practiced my calligraphy for a couple of hours. But I remained wide awake afterward. Lying on my bed, I heard a strange sound coming from downstairs. The old dorm is hardly soundproof, and you can hear a lot. I listened more closely. It was Guan sobbing—heart-breakingly—at three A.M.. She was weeping inconsolably, alone."

"Alone?"

"I thought so," Qian said, "I did not hear another voice. She wept for more than half an hour."

"Did you observe anything else?"

"Not that I can think of—except that she was probably like me, and didn't sleep too well. Often I could see light coming up through the cracks in the floor."

"One of her neighbors mentioned that she came back quite late many nights," Chen said, "Could that be the reason?"

"I'm not sure. Sometimes I heard her footsteps late at night, but I had hardly any contact with her," Qian said, taking a sip at his cold tea. "I suggest you talk to Zuo Qing. She's a retired cadre, but keeps herself busy taking care of the utility fees for the building. She's also a member of the Neighborhood Security or something. She may be able to tell you more. And she also lives on Guan's floor, just on the other side of the corridor, close to the stairs."

Chief Inspector Chen went downstairs again.

An elderly woman wearing gold-rimmed glasses opened the door wide and said, "What do you want?"

"I'm sorry to bother you, Comrade Zuo, but I've come about Guan Hongying."

"She'd dead, I've heard," she said. "You'd better come in. I've got something on the stove."

"Thank you," he said, staring at the coal stove outside the door. There was nothing being cooked on it. As he stepped into the room, she closed the door behind him. His question was almost immediately answered. Inside the door was a gas tank with a flat pan on it, smelling very pleasant.

Zuo was wearing a black skirt and a silvery gray silk blouse with the top button open. Her high-heeled shoes were gray too. Gesturing to him to sit on a scarlet plush-covered sofa by the window, she continued her cooking.

"It's not easy to get a gas tank," she said, "and dangerous to put it in the corridor along with other people's coal stoves."

"I see," he said. "Comrade Zuo, I was told that you have done a lot for the dorm building."

"Well, I do volunteer work for the neighborhood. Someone has to do it."

"So you must have had a lot of contact with Guan Hongying."

"No, not a lot. She's a popular celebrity in her store, but here she was not."

"Why?"

"Too busy, I would say. The only time there was any conversation between us would be the occasion," she said, flipping the egg over in the pan, "when she paid her share of the utility bill on the first day of every month. She would hand over the cash in a white envelope, and say some polite phrase while her receipt was prepared."

"You never talked about anything else?"

"Well, she once mentioned that since she did not cook much in the dorm building, her equal share of the utility bill was not fair. But she did not really argue about it. Never mentioned it again. Whatever was on her mind, she kept to herself."

"She seemed to be quite secretive."

"Look, I don't mean to speak ill of her."

"I understand, Comrade Zuo," he said. "Now on the evening of May tenth, the night she was murdered, Guan left the building around ten thirty—according to one of her neighbors. Did you notice anything around the time?"

"As for that night," she said, "I don't think I saw or heard her go out. I usually go to bed at ten."

"Now, you're also a member of the Neighborhood Security Committee, Comrade Zuo. Did you notice anything suspicious in the dorm or in the lane, during the last few days in Guan's life?"

She took off her glasses, looked at them, rubbed them on her apron, put them on again, and then shook her head. "I don't think so, but there's one thing," she said. "I'm not sure whether you'd call it suspicious."

"What's that?" He took out his notebook.

"About a week ago, I was watching *Office Stories*. Everybody is watching it, it's hilarious. But my TV broke down, so I was thinking of going to Xiangxiang's place. And opening the door, I saw a stranger coming out of a room at the end of the corridor."

"Out of Guan's room?"

"I was not sure. There are only three rooms at the end of the corridor, including Guan's. The Sus happened to be out of town that night, I know. Of course, the stranger could have been Yuan's guest, but with only one dim light at the landing, and all the stuff stacked in disorder along the corridor, it's not that easy for a stranger to find his way. It's a matter of course for the host to accompany the guest to the stairs."

"A week ago. Then this was after Guan's death, wasn't it?"

"Yes, I did not even know that she was dead."

"But this could be an important lead if he was coming out of Guan's room, Comrade Zuo," he said, putting down a few words in his notebook.

"Thank you, Comrade Chief Inspector," she said, flattered by his attention. "I checked into it myself. At that time I did not think about it in connection with Guan's case. Just that it was suspicious, I thought, since it was after eleven o'clock. So I asked Yuan the next day, and she said that she had had no guests that night."

"Now what about the public bathroom at the end of the corridor," he said. "He could have been coming out of there, couldn't he?"

"That's not likely," she said. "His host would have to accompany him there, or he would not be able to find it."

"Yes, you have a point. What did this man look like?"

"Tall, decent looking. But the light's so dim I could not see clearly."

"How old do you think he was?"

"Well, mid-thirties, I should think, perhaps forty. Difficult to tell."

"Anything else about his appearance?"

"He seemed neatly dressed; I may have mentioned it."

"So you think he could have been coming out of Guan's room?"

"Yes," she said, "but I'm not sure."

"Thank you, Comrade Zuo. We'll investigate," he said. "If you can think of anything else, give me a call."

"Yes, I'll do that, Comrade Chief Inspector," she said. "Let us know when you solve the case."

"We will, and good-bye."

Walking down the stairs, Chen shrugged his shoulders slightly. He had been to the public bathroom himself without being accompanied by anybody.

At the bus stop on Zhejiang road, he stood for quite a long time. He was trying to sort out what he had accomplished in the day's work. There was not much. Nothing he had found so far presented a solid lead. If there was anything he had not expected, it would be Guan's fancy clothes and intimate pictures. But then—that was not too surprising, either. An attractive young woman, even if she was a national model worker, was entitled to some feminine indulgence—in her private life.

Guan's unpopularity among her neighbors was even less surprising. That a national model worker would be unpopular in the nineties was a sociological phenomenon, rather than anything else. So, too, in the dorm building. It would have been too difficult to be a model neighbor there, to be popular with her neighbors. Her life was not an ordinary one. So she did not fit into their circle, nor did she care for it.

There was only one thing he had confirmed: on the night of May tenth, Guan Hongying had left the dorm before eleven o'clock. She had a heavy suitcase in her hand; she'd been going somewhere.

Another thing not confirmed, but only a hypothesis: She could not have been romantically involved at the time of her death. There was no privacy possible in such a dorm building, no way of secretly dating someone. If there had been anything going on behind her closed door, her dorm neighbors would have known it, and in less than five minutes, the news would have spread like wildfire.

It would also have taken a lot of courage for a man to come to her room. To the hardboard bed.

The bus was nowhere in sight yet. It could be very slow during this time of the day. He crossed to the small restaurant opposite the lane entrance. Despite its unsightly appearance, a lot of people were there, both inside the restaurant and outside it. A fat man in a brown corduroy jacket was rising from a table outside on the pavement. Chief Inspector Chen took his seat and ordered a portion of fried buns. It was a perfect place from which to keep his eyes out for a bus arriving, and at the same time, he could watch the lane entrance. He had to wait for quite a few minutes. When the buns came, they were delicious, but hot. Putting down the chopsticks, he had to blow on them repeatedly. Then the bus rolled into sight. He rushed across the street and boarded it with the last bun in his hand. It then occurred to him that he should have made inquiries at the restaurant. Guan might have sat there with somebody.

"Keep your oily hand away from me," a woman standing next to him said indignantly.

"Some people can be so unethical," another passenger commented, "despite an impressive uniform."

"Sorry," he said, aware of his unpopularity in his police uniform. There was no point in picking a quarrel. To hold a pork-stuffed bun in an overcrowded bus was a lousy idea, he admitted to himself.

At the next stop, he got off. He did not mind walking for a

short distance. At least he didn't have to overhear the other passengers' negative comments. There was no way to prevent people from making such comments about one.

Guan, a national model worker, was by no means an exception. Not so far as her neighbors' comments went.

Who can control stories, the stories after one's life?

The whole village is jumping at the romantic tale of General Cai.

In this poem by Lu You, the "romantic tale" refers to a totally fictitious romance between General Cai and Zhao Wuniang of the late Han dynasty. The village audience would have been interested in hearing the story, regardless of its historical authenticity.

There is no helping what other people will say, Chief Inspector Chen thought.

Chapter 9

It was Wednesday, five days after the formation of the special case group, and there had been hardly any progress. Chief Inspector Chen arrived at the bureau, greeted his colleagues, and repeated polite but meaningless words. The case weighed heavily on his mind.

At the insistence of Commissar Zhang, Chen had extended his investigation into Guan's neighborhood by enlisting assistance from the local police branch office and the neighborhood committee. They came up with tons of information about possible suspects, assuming this was a political case. Chen was red-eyed from poring over all the material, pursuing the leads provided by the committee about some ex-counter revolutionaries with "deep hatred against the socialist society." All this was routine, and Chen did it diligently, but there was a persistent doubt in his mind about the direction of the investigation.

In fact, the choice of their number-one suspect exemplified Commissar Zhang's ossified way of thinking. This suspect was a distant relative of Guan's with a long-standing personal grudge, which had originated from Guan's refusal to acknowledge him, a black Rightist, during the Cultural Revolution. The rehabilitated Rightist had said that he would never forgive her, but was too busy writing a book about his wasted years to be aware of her death. Chief Inspector Chen ruled him out even before he went to interview him.

It was *not* a political case. Yet he was expecting another of Commissar Zhang's morning lectures about "carrying out the investigation by relying on the people." That morning, however, he had a pleasant surprise.

"This is for you, Comrade Chief Inspector," Detective Yu said standing at the door, holding a fax he had picked up in the main office.

It was from Wang Feng, with a cover page bearing the *Wenhui Daily* letterhead. Her neat handwriting said "Congratulations," on the margin of a photocopied section of the newspaper, in which his poem "Miracle" appeared. The poem was in a conspicuous position, with the editor's note underneath saying, "The poet is a young chief inspector, Shanghai Police Bureau."

The comment made sense since the poem was about a young policewoman providing relief to storm-damaged homes in the pouring rain. Still holding the fax in his hand, he received his first call from Party Secretary Li.

"Congratulations, Comrade Chief Inspector. A poem published in the *Wenhui Daily*. Quite an achievement."

"Thank you," he said. "It's just a poem about our police work."

"It's a good one. Politically, I mean," Li said. "Next time, if there's something in such an influential newspaper, tell us beforehand."

"Okay, but why?"

"There are a lot of people reading your work."

"Don't worry, Party Secretary Li, I'll make sure that it is politically correct."

"Yes, that's the spirit. You are not an ordinary police officer, you know," Li said. "Now, anything new in the investigation?"

"We're going all out. But unfortunately there's not much progress."

"Don't worry. Just try your best," Li said before putting down the phone, "And don't forget your seminar in Beijing."

Then Dr. Xia called. "This one is not that bad, this 'Miracle' of yours."

"Thank you, Dr. Xia," he said, "your approval always means such a lot to me."

"I especially like the beginning—'The rain has soaked the hair / Falling to your shoulders / Light green in your policewoman's / Uniform, like the spring / White blossom bursting / From your arms reaching / Into the gaping windows— / 'Here you are!'"

"It's a true experience. She persisted in sending out relief to the victims, despite the pouring rain. I was there, too, and was touched at the sight."

"But you must have stolen the image from Li He's 'Watching a Beauty Comb Her Hair.' The image about the green comb in her long hair."

"No, I didn't, but I'll let you in on a secret. It's from another two classical lines—With the green skirt of yours in my mind, everywhere, / Everywhere I step over the grass ever so lightly." Our policewoman's uniform is green, and so, too, the spring, and the package. Looking out in the rain, I had the impression of her long hair being washed green, too."

"No wonder you've made such an improvement," Dr. Xia said.

"I'm glad you are acknowledging your debt to classical poetry."

"Of course I do. But so much for the poetics," Chen said. "Actually, I was thinking of calling you, too. About the black plastic bag in the Guan case."

"There's nothing to recover from the plastic bag. I made some inquiries about it. I was told that it is normally used for fallen leaves in people's backyards."

"Indeed! Imagine a taxi driver worrying about the fallen leaves in his backyard!"

"What did you say?"

"Oh, nothing," he said. "But thank you so much, Dr. Xia."

"Don't mention it, Comrade Chief Inspector Chen, also Chinese imagist poet."

Out of the black plastic bag, her white bare feet, and her red polished toenails like fallen petals in the night. It could be a modernist image.

Chen then dialed Detective Yu.

Entering his office, Yu, too, offered his congratulations, "What a surprise, Comrade Chief Inspector Chen. A terrific breakthrough."

"Well, if only we could say that about our case."

Indeed they needed a "miracle" in their investigation.

Detective Yu had come up empty-handed. Following his theory, Lu had made inquiry at the taxi bureau. To his dismay, he found that obtaining anything close to reliable information for the night was impossible. There was no point in checking the taxi drivers' receipts. Most drivers—whether the taxi company was state-run or private—kept a considerable portion of their money by not giving receipts to customers, he was told, so it was possible for a driver to claim to have driven around for the night without being able to pick up one single passenger—thus avoiding taxation.

In addition, Yu had checked all the customer lists of Shanghai travel agencies during May. Guan's name had not been on any of them.

And Yu's research with respect to the last phone call Guan had made from the department store was not successful either. Many people had used the phone that evening. And Mrs. Weng's recollection of the time was not accurate. After spending hours to rule out other calls made roughly around the same time, the one most likely made by Guan was to weather information. It made sense, for Guan had been planning her trip, but that only confirmed something they had known.

So like Chen, Yu had not gotten anything, not even a tip worthy of a follow-up.

And the more time that elapsed, the colder the trail became.

They were under pressure, not just from the bureau and the city government. The case was being buzzed about among people in general, in spite of the low-profile treatment it had been given by the local media. And the longer the case remained unsolved, the more negative impact it would have on the bureau.

"It is *becoming* political," Chen said.

"Our Party Secretary Li is always right."

"Let's put something in the newspaper. A reward for information."

"That's worth trying. The *Wenhui Daily* can run the request for help. But what shall it say? This is so sensitive, as Party Secretary Li has told us."

"Well, we don't have to mention the case directly. Just ask for information about anything suspicious around the Baili Canal area on the night of May tenth."

"Yes, we can do that," Chen said. "And we'll use some of our special case group funds for the reward. We have left no stone unturned, haven't we?"

Detective Yu shrugged his shoulders before leaving the cubicle.

Except one, Chief Inspector Chen thought. Guan Hongying's mother. He had refrained from discussing this with Yu, who did not get along well with the commissar.

The old lady had been visited by Commissar Zhang, who had gotten nothing from her. A late-stage Alzheimer's patient, she was totally deranged, unable to provide any information. It was not the commissar's fault. But an Alzheimer's patient might not be deranged all the time. There were days when the light could miraculously break through the clouds of her mind.

Chen decided to try his luck.

After lunch, he dialed Wang Feng. She was not in the office, so he left a message expressing his thanks to her. Then he left. On his way to the bus stop he bought several copies of the *Wenhui Daily* at the post office on Sichuan Road. Somehow he liked the editor's note even more than the poem itself. He had not told many of his friends about his promotion to chief inspectorship, so the newspaper would do the job for him. Among those friends he wanted to mail the newspaper to, there was one in Beijing. He felt that he had to say something about his being in this position, an explanation to a dear friend who had not envisioned such a career for him. He thought for a moment, but he ended up scribbling only a sentence underneath the poem. Somewhat ironically self-defensive, and ambiguous, too. It could be about the poem as well as about his work: *If you work hard enough at something, it begins to make itself part of you, even though you do not really like it and know that part isn't real.*

He cut out the section of the newspaper, put it into an envelope, addressed it, and dropped it into a mailbox.

Then he took a bus to Ankang, the nursing home on Huashan Road.

The nursing home arrangement was not common. It was not culturally correct to keep one's aged parent in such an institution. Not even in the nineties. Besides, with only two or three nursing homes in Shanghai, few could have managed to move in there, especially in the case of an Alzheimer's patient.

Undoubtedly her mother's admission had been due to Guan's social and Party status.

He introduced himself at the front desk of the nursing home, A young nurse told him to wait in the reception room. To be a bad news bearer was anything but pleasant, he reflected, as he waited. The only cold comfort he could find was that Guan's mother, suffering from Alzheimer's, might be spared the shock of her daughter's violent death. The old woman's life had been a tough one, as he had learned from the file. An arranged marriage in her childhood, and then for years her husband had worked as a high-school teacher in Chengdu, while she was a worker in Shanghai Number 6 Textile Mill. The distance between the two required more than two days' travel by train. Once a year was all he could have afforded to visit her. In the fifties, job relocation was out of the question for either of them. Jobs, like everything else, were assigned once and for all by the local authorities. So all those years she had been a "single mother," taking care of Guan Hongying in the dorm of Number 6 Textile Mill. Her husband passed away before his retirement. When her daughter got her job and her Party membership, the old woman broke down. Shortly afterward she had been admitted to the nursing home.

At last, the old woman appeared, shuffling, with a striking array of pins in her gray hair. She was thin, sullen-faced, perhaps in her early sixties. Her felt slippers made a strange sound on the floor.

"What do you want?"

Chen exchanged glances with the nurse standing beside the old woman.

"She is not clear here," the nurse said, pointing at her own head.

"Your daughter wants me to say hi to you," Chen said.

"I have no daughter. No room for a daughter. My husband lives in the dorm in Chengdu."

"You have one, aunt. She works in Shanghai First Department Store."

"First Department Store. Oh yes, I bought a couple of pins there early this morning. Aren't they beautiful?"

Clearly the old woman was living in another world. She had nothing in her hand, but she was making a gesture of showing something to him.

Whatever might happen, she did not have to accept the disasters of this world. Or was she merely such a scared woman, anticipating such dreadful news, that she had shut herself up?

"Yes, they are beautiful," he said.

She might have been attractive in her day. Now everything about her was shrunken. Motionless, she sat there, staring vacantly ahead, waiting for him to go. The look of apathy was not unmixed, he reflected, with a touch of apprehension. There was no point trying to gather any information from the old woman.

A worm safe and secure inside its cocoon.

He insisted on helping her back to her room. The room, holding a dozen iron beds, appeared congested. The aisle between them was so narrow that one could only stand sideways. There was a rattan rocker at the foot of her bed, a radio on the nightstand. No air conditioning, though a single ceiling fan for the whole room was working. The last thing he noticed was a dried bun, partly chewed, shriveled, on the windowsill above her bed. A period to a life story. One of the ordinary Chinese people, working hard, getting little, not complaining, and suffering a lot.

What influence could such a life have exerted on Guan?

The daughter had taken a different road.

There was something about the case, Chief Inspector Chen felt vaguely, something mystifying him, challenging him, and drawing him in an unknown direction. He decided to walk home. Sometimes he thought better while walking.

He stopped at a traditional Chinese pharmacy and bought a

box of Jinsheng pills. A halfhearted believer in Chinese herbal medicine, he assumed that frustration had somehow eroded the balance of his essence. And he needed something extra to bolster his whole system. Chewing at a bitter Jinsheng pill, he thought that a possible alternative approach to the case would be to find out how Guan had become a national model worker. In the literary criticism he had studied, it would be termed the biographical approach. Only its result might not be so reliable, either. Who could have expected that *he* would have become a chief inspector of police?

It was almost seven when he reached home. He turned on the TV and watched for a while. Several Beijing opera players were doing a series of somersaults, flourishing sabers and swords in the dark. *The Cross Road*, a traditional Beijing opera, he recollected, about fighting at night without knowing who's who.

He dialed Commissar Zhang. A formality, since Chen did not have anything to report.

"Believe in the people. Our strength comes from our close connection to them," Commissar Zhang concluded their conversation. It was inevitable: Commissar Zhang had to give such an instruction.

Chen got up and went into the kitchen. There was half a pot of steamed rice left in the refrigerator. He took the rice out, added some water, and put it on the gas stove. The kitchen wall no longer appeared immaculately white. It would not take too many weeks to turn it into an oil-and-smoke-stained map. An exhaust fan could solve the problem, but he could not afford one. He looked for some leftovers. There were none. Finally, he dug out a tiny plastic bag of dried mustard, a present from his aunt in Ningbo. He put a few pieces on the rice, and swallowed the watery meal trying not to taste too much of it.

"Chef Kang's Instant Noodles." A TV commercial flashed through his mind as he stood by the gas stove. The plastic-bowl-contained-noodles might be a solution, he reflected, putting the dried mustard back. Again, the problem was his tight budget. After the loan to Overseas Chinese Lu, Chief Inspector Chen had to live like Comrade Lei Feng in the early sixties.

At the level of a chief inspector, his monthly pay was 560 Yuan, plus all his bonuses under various titles, which added up to 250 more. His rent was fairly inexpensive. Together with utilities, it was less than 100 Yuan, but he had to spend half of his income on food. As a bachelor, he did not cook much at home; he ate at the bureau canteen.

A great help in the last few years had been the advances he earned from his translations, but at this moment he was not working on anything. He had not had the time, nor the energy— nor even the interest—since he had taken over the Guan case. The case did not make sense, not the sense he found in the mysteries he had been translating. Still, getting another advance was possible. He could promise the editor that he would complete the job by October. He needed such a deadline for himself, too.

Instead he started to summarize on a piece of paper beside the bowl what he had learned so far about the case. All the odds and ends of information he had been collecting and storing during the week, without having them sorted out and pieced together to consider where they could possibly lead, filled a sheet of paper. In the end, however, he tore up the paper in frustration. Perhaps Detective Yu was right. Possibly it was just one of those "insoluble" sexual murder cases. The bureau had had enough of them.

He knew he could not fall asleep. Often insomnia was the effect of little things coming together. A poem rejected without a rejection slip, a crazy woman cursing in a crowded bus, or a new shirt missing from the wardrobe. This night, something about the Guan case vanquished sleep.

The night was long.

What might have crowded into Guan's mind during such a long night? He thought of a poem by the mid-Tang dynasty poet Wang Changling:

> Boudoir-sheltered, the young lady knows no worries,
> Fashionably dressed, she looks out of the window in spring.
> What a view of green willow shoots—all of a sudden:
> She regrets having sent her love away fighting for fame.

So after the flashlight along the corridor, after the shadows shifting on the sleepless wall, after the cold sweat in the dark, solitary dorm room, Guan, too, could have been thinking of the price paid for fame.

What's the difference?

In the Tang dynasty, more than a thousand years earlier, the girl had been unable to console herself because she had sent her lover far away in pursuit of fame, and in the nineties, Guan couldn't because she had kept herself too busy pursuing fame.

What about Chief Inspector Chen himself?

There was a bitter taste in his mouth.

Sometime after two, when he had slid into that floating area between sleep and waking, he felt hungry again. The image of the dried bun on the window came back to his mind.

And another image with it.

Caviar.

Only once had he tasted caviar. It was years earlier, at the International Friendship Club in Beijing, where at the time only foreign visitors were admitted and served. He was there with a drunken English professor who insisted on treating him to caviar. Chen had read about it in Russian novels. Actually he did not like it too much, though afterward the fact he had tasted caviar took Overseas Chinese Lu down a peg or two.

Things had been changing. Nowadays anybody could go to the International Friendship Club. A few new luxurious hotels also served caviar. Guan could have had it in one of those hotels, though not too many people could have afforded to order it—on that particular night.

It would not be difficult to find out.

Caviar—he jotted the word on the back of a matchbox.

Then he felt ready to fall asleep.

Chapter 10

It was a humid Friday morning for May.

Detective Yu had slept fitfully, tossing and turning half of the night. As a result, he was feeling more tired than the night before, with patches of partially forgotten dreams hovering in his mind.

Peiqin was concerned. She made a bowl of sticky rice dumplings, a favorite breakfast for him, and sat with him at the table. Yu finished the dumplings in silence.

Finally, as he was ready to leave for the bureau, she said, "You're burning yourself out, Guangming."

"No, it's just I've not slept well," he said. "Don't worry about me."

When Yu stepped into the bureau meeting room, the restless feeling surged up again. The topic of the meeting, which had been requested by Commissar Zhang, was the progress of the investigation.

A week had passed since the special case group had taken the case. The team, formed with such a fanfare of political jargon, had made little progress. Detective Yu had been working long hours, making numerous phone calls, interviewing a number of people, discussing all the possible scenarios with Chief Inspector Chen, and making quite a few reports to Commissar Zhang, too. Yet there was no breakthrough in sight. In routine police work when a case went beyond a week without a solid lead, it might as well be thrown into the "open" file. Yu had learned from experience. In other words, it was the time to close the case as unsolved.

It was not the first time in the bureau's history that this had happened, nor would it be the last.

Yu sat beside the window, smoking a cigarette. The streets of Shanghai were spread out beneath his gaze, gray and black roofs with curls of peaceful white smoke undulating into the distance. Yet he seemed to smell crime smoldering in the heart of the city. Skimming a copy of the bureau newsletter, he read of several robberies, each bigger than the other, and seven reports of rape in the last night alone. And then new cases of prostitution, even in the upper area of the city.

As the other divisions were so short of manpower, a number of cases had been designated as "special" and pushed over to their squad, but they were in no better shape. Qing Xiaotong had come back from his honeymoon, but with that dreamy look in his eyes, not really back to work, and Liu Longxiang was still recovering from his injury. With Chief Inspector Chen's increasingly busy schedule of meetings and other activities, Detective Yu had to take on the main responsibility for the squad.

Why should they spend so much time on one case?

Political priority, of course—Yu knew the answer. To hell with politics. It's a homicide case.

But others did not think so. Commissar Zhang, for one, sitting straight at the head of the table, wearing the neat but nondescript Mao suit, high buttoned as always, holding a pen in his hand, and leafing through a leather notebook. The commissar had never discussed anything with him, as far as Yu could remember, except politics. What could possibly be up that grizzled, skinny commissar's sleeve, Yu wondered.

Looking at Chief Inspector Chen, who nodded at him, Detective Yu was the first to take the floor, "We have already put a lot of hours into the investigation. For my part, I've talked to the general manager of the First Department Store as well as Guan's colleagues. In addition, I have checked with the Shanghai Taxi Bureau and a number of travel agencies. I'd like to sum up some important aspects of my work.

"A national model worker, Guan lived a model life, too, dedicated to the Communist cause, way too busy with all her Party activities for anything else. She seemed never to have dated anyone, nor was she involved with anyone at the time of her death. Needless to say, she did an excellent job at the store. With her position there, she might have been the envy of some people, but there's no reason to suspect that this made her a murderer's target.

"As for her activities on the day she was murdered, according to her colleagues, there was nothing unusual about her during that day. All routine work. Lunch at the canteen around twelve o'clock, and a Party meeting in the afternoon. She mentioned to a colleague that she was going to take some vacation time, but did not say where. Not too far away, not for long, it was assumed. Otherwise she should have submitted a written request to the general manager. She didn't. The last time she was seen in the store was around seven ten, after her shift, which was not unusual for her. She went back to the dorm, where she was last seen at about ten thirty or a bit later, carrying a suitcase, alone, presumably leaving for her vacation.

"Now comes the difficult part. Where was she going? There are so many tourist groups nowadays. I've checked all of the local travel agencies, but Guan's name was not registered with any of them. Of course, she could have chosen to travel by herself. To travel by air would have been out of the question. Guan's name was not registered with any of the airlines. She might have gone to the railway station. In her neighborhood, no bus goes directly to the station. She might have walked to Xizhuang Road for Bus Number Sixty-four. The last scheduled bus arrives there at eleven thirty-five; after that there's one every hour. Again it's rather unusual for a young woman alone to carry a heavy suitcase along the street, when she might easily miss the last bus.

"So whether she was going to travel with a group or by herself, there's reason to assume that she got into a taxi after leaving the dorm. But she did not finish the trip. Somewhere along the way, she was attacked and murdered by someone, who could be no one other than the driver. That also explains how her body came to be found in the canal. A taxi driver would have the means of transporting the body to dump it into a distant canal. That's my hypothesis, and that's why I have been conducting my investigation at the taxi bureau.

"My original plan was to check copies of all drivers' receipts for the night to focus on those who failed to show any transaction during those few hours of the night. But according to the bureau, taxi drivers do not always give receipts, so there is no way to account for their activities. In fact, a considerable number of the drivers showed no business for the whole night—for tax avoidance reasons."

"Hold on, Comrade Detective Yu," Commissar Zhang interrupted. "Have you done any investigation into the political aspects of the case?"

"Well, as for the political aspects, I don't think I have seen any. The murderer would have been a stranger to her. For her part, there would have been no reason for her to reveal her identity to a taxi driver. So it's possible that he might not know her identity yet."

"So what's your suggestion for the next stage of the investigation?" Zhang continued, without changing his position in the chair, or the expression on his face.

"At present, with no evidence, and no witness," Yu said,

"there's not much we can do. Let the case run its natural course. A rapist is a repeater, so sooner or later he will strike again. In the meantime, we will keep in close touch with the taxi bureau and travel agencies; hopefully, some new information will turn up. In fact, the taxi bureau has promised to give me a list of possible suspects, those drivers with something suspicious in their history. I have not gotten it yet."

"So basically we're not going to do anything until the criminal strikes again?"

"No, we are not going to close the case as unsolved. What I'm saying is—um, it's not realistic to expect a quick solution. Eventually, we should be able to find the murderer, but that takes time."

"How long?" Zhang asked, sitting even more upright.

"I don't know."

"It's an important political case, comrade. That's something we should all be well aware of."

"Well—" Yu paused.

There was a lot more Yu wanted to say, but he knew it was not the moment. Chief Inspector Chen had not yet made any comment. As for the commissar's position, Yu thought he understood it well; this might well be the old man's last case. So naturally the commissar wanted to make a big deal out of it. Full of political significance. A finishing touch to his life-long career. It was easy for Zhang to talk about politics, of course, since he did not have to attend to the daily work of the squad.

"There may be something in Comrade Yu's analysis." Zhang stood up, opening his notebook, and cleared his throat before he began his formal speech. "It is a difficult case. We may spend hours and hours before seeing any real progress. But it's not an ordinary case, comrades. Guan was a model worker of national renown. She dedicated her life to the cause of communism. Her tragic death has already had a very negative impact. I'm a retired old man, but here I am, working together with you. Why? It's a special case assigned by the Party. People are watching our work. We cannot fail. So we have to find a new approach."

Yu enjoyed a reputation as a detail man: patient, meticulous, sometimes even plodding. It was possible to waste time, he knew, on ninety-nine leads and to break the case on the hundredth. That was the way of almost all homicide investigations. He had no objection to that. They just had too many cases on their hands. But there was no "new approach"—as Commissar Zhang called it—except the ones in those mysteries Chief Inspector Chen translated.

"Rely on the people," Zhang was continuing. "That's where our strength lies. Chairman Mao told us that long ago. Once we get the people's help, there's no difficulty we cannot overcome . . ."

Yu had had it. It was more and more difficult for him to concentrate on the commissar's lecture filled with such political rhetoric. At the bureau political education sessions, Yu sometimes could choose to sit in the back of the room and let the speaker's voice lull him while doing meditation exercises. But that morning he could not.

Then Chief Inspector Chen took the floor. "Commissar Zhang's instruction is very important. And Comrade Yu Guangming's analysis makes a lot of sense, too. It is tough, especially when we've got so many other cases on our hands. Comrade Yu has done a lot of work. Most of it, I would say. If we have so far made little progress, it's my responsibility. There is one point, however, that has just come to my attention. In fact, Comrade Yu's analysis is bringing it into focus.

"According to the autopsy report, Guan had a meal between one and two hours before her death. The food she had consumed included, among other things, a small portion of caviar. Caviar. Expensive Russian sturgeon caviar. Now there are only three or four top-class Shanghai restaurants serving caviar. I've done some research. It's hard to believe that she would have chosen to dine at one of those expensive restaurants by herself, with a heavy suitcase at her feet. Think about the timing, too. She left home around ten thirty; she died between one and two. So the meal would have to have been eaten around midnight. Now, according to my investigation, not a single restaurant served caviar to a Chinese customer on that particular night. If this information is accurate, it means she had caviar somewhere else. With somebody who kept caviar at home."

"That's something indeed," Yu said.

"Hold on," Zhang raised his hand to interrupt Chen. "So you are suggesting the murderer could be somebody Guan knew?"

"Yes, that's a possible scenario: perhaps the murderer's no stranger to Guan. After she left home, they met somewhere and had a midnight meal together. Possibly at his home. Afterward they had sex—remember, there were no real bruises on her body. Then he murdered her, moved her body into his car, and dumped it in the canal. The plastic bag would make sense, too, if the crime was committed at the murderer's home. He was afraid of being seen in the act of moving the body—by his neighbors or other people. Furthermore, that also explains the choice of that far-away canal, where he hoped that the body would never be found, or at least not for a long time. By then no one might be able to recognize her, or remember with whom she was involved."

"So you don't think it's a political case either," Zhang said, "though you are offering a different theory."

"Whether it is a political case or not, I cannot say, but I think there are some things worth further investigation."

Yu was even more surprised than Zhang by Chen's speech.

The plastic bag was not something new, but the caviar was something they had not discussed. Whether Chen had purposely saved it for the meeting, Yu was not sure. It appeared to be a master stroke, like in those of western mysteries Chen had been translating, perhaps.

Was Chen doing this to impress Commissar Zhang?

Yu did not think so, for Chen did not like the old man either. It was nonetheless a crucial detail Yu had overlooked, that portion of caviar.

"But according to the information at the department store," Yu said, "Guan was not seeing anyone at the time of her death."

"That puzzles me," Chen said, "but that's where we should be digging more deeply."

"Well, do it your way," Zhang said, standing up to leave. "At least, that's preferable to waiting for the criminal to act again."

So Detective Yu was placed in an unfavorable light. A cop too lazy to attend to the important details. Yu could read the negative message in the old man's knitted brows.

"I overlooked the caviar," Yu said to Chen.

"It just occurred to me last night. So I have not had time to discuss it with you."

"Caviar. Honestly, I have no idea what it is."

Afterward he made a phone call to Peiqin. "Do you know what caviar is?"

"Yes, I've read about it in nineteenth-century Russian novels," she said, "but I have never tasted it."

"Has your restaurant ever served caviar?"

"You're kidding, Guangming. Ours is such a shabby place. Only five-star hotels like the Jinjiang might have it."

"Is it very expensive?"

"A tiny dish would cost you several hundred Yuan, I think," she added. "Why your sudden interest?"

"Oh, just something about the case."

Chapter 11

Chief Inspector Chen woke with a slight suggestion of headache. A shower did not help much. It would be difficult to shake off the feeling during the day. And it happened to be a day in which he had so much work cut out for him.

He was no workaholic, not in the way some of his colleagues claimed. It was true, however, that often it was only after he had successfully forced himself into working like a devil, that he felt the most energetic.

He had just received a rare collection of Yan Shu's poems—a hand-bound rice paper edition, in a deep blue cloth case. An unexpected present from Beijing, in return for the copy of the *Wenhui Daily* he had sent.

There was a short note inside the cloth case.

> *Chief Inspector Chen:*
>
> *Thanks for your poem. I like it very much. Sorry I cannot send you anything of my own in return. I alighted on a collection of Yan Shu's poems in Liulichang Antique Fair a couple of weeks ago, and I thought you would like it. Also, congratulations on your promotion.*
>
> *Ling*

Of course he liked it. He recalled his days of wandering around in the Liulichang Antique Fair, then a poor student from Beijing Foreign Language Institute, examining old books without being able to buy any of them. He had seen something like it only once—in the rare book section of the Beijing Library where Ling had compared his ecstatic sampling to that of the silverfish lost in the pages of the ancient volumes. Such a hand-bound collection could be very expensive, but it was worth it. The feel of the white rice paper was exquisite. It almost conveyed a message from antiquity. Like his, Ling's note did not say much. The choice of such a book spoke for itself. Ling had not changed. She was still fond of poetry—or of his poetry.

He should have told Ling about the seminar in October, but he did not want her to think that he had thrown himself into politics. For the moment, however, he did not have to think too much about it. There was nothing like spending a late May morning wandering about in the green ivy-covered world of the celebrated Song dynasty poet.

He flipped through the pages.

Helpless the flowers fall,
The swallows return, seemingly no strangers.

A brilliant couplet. Often people see something for the first time, but with the feeling of having seen it before, of déjà vu. Such a phenomenon had been attributed to the effects of half-remembered dreams or else to misfiring neurons in the brain. Whatever the interpretation, Chen, too, had a feeling—both strange and familiar—like the swallows in Yan's lines, of having visited Guan's world. As he held the book in his hand, the feeling was mixed with the elusive memories of his college years in Beijing. . . .

It was disturbing. Guan no longer represented an esoteric character. The case had somehow become a personal challenge. People had seen Guan as a national model worker, ever politically correct, an embodiment of the Party's much propagandized myth. But he did not. There must have been something else, something different in her. Just what it was, he could not say yet, but until he was able to explain it to himself, he would continue to be oppressed by an indefinable uneasiness.

It was not just because of the caviar.

He had talked to a lot of people who seemed to have thought well of her. Politically, of course. Personally, they knew practically nothing. It seemed that she had so committed herself to her political role that she could play no other part, personal or otherwise. A point Detective Yu had made.

She had no time, perhaps. Eight hours a day, six days a week, she had to be busy living up to what was expected of her. She had to attend numerous meetings and to make all the presentations at Party conferences, in addition to the long working hours she put in at the store. Everything was possible, of course, according to Communist Party propaganda. Comrade Lei Feng had represented just such a selfless miracle. There was no mention at all of his personal life in *The Diary of Comrade Lei Feng*, which had sold millions of copies. It was revealed in the late eighties, however, that the diary was a pure fabrication by a professional writing team commissioned by the Central Party Committee.

Political correctness was a shell. It should not, could not, spell an absence of personal life. And that could have been said of himself as well, Chief Inspector Chen thought.

He suspected he needed a respite from the case, at least for a short while. And at once it came to him that what he wanted most—one of his first thoughts on awakening—was to be with Wang Feng. He put his hand on the phone, but he hesitated. It might not be the right time. Then he remembered her call earlier in the week. A ready excuse. A breakfast invitation would commit him to no more than a pleasant morning. A hard-working chief inspector was entitled to the company of a reporter who had written about him.

"How are you this morning, Wang?"

"I'm fine. But it's early, not even seven o'clock."

"Well, I woke up thinking of you."

"Thank you for telling me this. So you could have called earlier—three o'clock if you happened to roll out of your bed then."

"I've just come up with an idea. The Peach Blossom Restaurant is serving morning tea again. It's quite close to your home. What about having a cup of tea with me?"

"Only a cup of tea?"

"You know it's more than that—*dimson* or Guangdong-style

morning tea, along with a wide variety of delicacies."

"There's a deadline I've got to meet today. I'll feel drowsy after a full meal, even at ten o'clock in the morning. But you can meet me on the Bund, close to Number Seven dock, opposite the Peace Hotel. I'll be practicing Taiji."

"The Bund, Number Seven dock. I know where it is," he said. "Can you make it there in fifteen minutes?"

"I'm still in bed. You really want me to come running to you barefoot?"

"Why not? See you in half an hour then." He put down the phone.

It was an intimate allusion between them. Arising from their first meeting. He was pleased with the way she had said it over the phone.

He had met Wang about a year earlier. On a Friday afternoon, Party Secretary Li told him to go to the office of the *Wenhui Daily*, saying that a reporter named Wang Feng would like to interview him there. Why a *Wenhui* reporter should be interested in seeing a junior police officer, Chen could not figure out.

The *Wenhui* building was a twelve-story sandstone edifice located on Tiantong Road, commanding a magnificent view over the Bund. Chen arrived there about two hours late, having been delayed with a traffic violation case. At the entrance, there was an old man sitting at something like a front desk. When Chen handed over his name card, he was told Wang was not in her office. The doorman was positive, however, that she was somewhere in the building. So Chen took a seat in the lobby, waited, and started to read a paperback mystery, *The Fallen Curtain*. It was not much of a lobby, just a small space for a couple of chairs in front of an old-fashioned elevator. There were not too many people coming and going at the moment. Soon he was lost in Ruth Rendell's world until a clatter of footsteps caught his attention.

A tall, slender girl was walking out of the elevator with a pink plastic pail over her bare arm. *Wenhui* must have a shower room for its staff, he thought. She was in her early twenties, wearing a low-cut T-shirt and shorts. Her wet hair was tied up with a sky-blue kerchief. Her wooden slippers clapped crisply against the floor. Probably a college student doing an internship, he thought. She certainly scampered like one. And then she stumbled, pitching forward.

Throwing away the book, he jumped up and caught her in his arms.

Standing on one slipper, her hand on his shoulder for balance, she reached one bare foot out to the other slipper which had been flung into the corner. She blushed, disengaging herself from his embrace. It took her only a second to regain her balance, but she remained deeply embarrassed.

She did not have to be, Chen thought with a wry humor, feeling her wet hair brushing against his face, her body smelling of some pleasant soap.

In traditional Chinese society, however, such physical contact would have been enough to result in a wedding contract. "Once in a man's arms, always in his arms."

"Wang Feng," the doorman said. "The police officer has been waiting for you."

She was the reporter who had summoned him there. And the interview afterward led to something he had not expected.

Afterward, he had joked about her coming barefoot to him. "Coming barefoot" was an allusion to a story in classical Chinese literature. In 800 B.C., the Duke of Zhou, anxious to meet a wise man who would help him unify the county, ran barefoot out of the hall to greet him. The phrase was later used to exaggerate one's eagerness to meet a guest.

It did not apply to them. She had happened to fall, walking out of the bathroom, and he had happened to be there, catching her in his arms. That was all. Now a year later, he was walking toward her again. At the intersection of the Bund and Nanjing road, the top of the *Wenhui* office building shimmered behind the Peace Hotel.

The morning's in the arms of the Bund, her hair dew-sparkled . . .

The Bund was alive with people, sitting on the concrete benches, standing by the bank, watching the dark yellow tide rolling in, singing snatches of Beijing operas along with the birds in the cages hung on the trees. A light haze of May heat trembled over the colored-stone walk. A long line of tourists stretched out, leading to the cruise ticket offices, near the Bridge Park. At the Lujiazhui ferry, he saw a swarthy sailor coiling the hawsers as a small group of students looked on curiously. The boat appeared crowded, as always, and as the bell rang urgently, men and women hurried to their destination, and then to new destinations. A tunnel project was said to be under construction beneath the river, so people would soon have alternative ways to get across the water. Several petrels glided over the waves, their wings glistening white in the sunlight, as if flying out of a calendar illustration. The river, though still polluted, showed some signs of improvement.

Exhilaration quickened his steps.

There were groups of people doing Taiji along the Bund, and he saw Wang in one of them.

History does not repeat itself.

One of the first things he noticed was the long green skirt covering her feet. She was striking a sequence of Taiji poses: a white crane flashing its wings, a master strumming the lute, a wild horse shaking its mane, a hunter grasping a bird's tail. All the poses were in imitation of nature—the essence of Taiji.

A mixed feeling came over him as he stood gazing at her. Nothing was wrong with Taiji itself. It was an ancient cultural heritage following the Taoist philosophy of subduing the hard by being soft, the *yin-yang* principle. As a means to keep fit, Chen himself had practiced it, but he was troubled by the fact that she was the only young woman in the group, her black hair held back by a blue cotton scarf.

"Hi," he greeted her.

"What are you staring at?" Wang said, walking toward him. She was wearing white casual shoes.

"For a second, you were walking to me out of a Tang poem."

"Oh, here you go again with your quotations and interpretations. Am I seeing a poetry critic or a police officer this morning?"

"Well, it is not we who make the interpretation," Chen said, "but the interpretation makes us—a critic or a cop."

"Let me see," she said, breaking into a smile. "It's just like Tuishou practice, isn't it? It's not that we push Tuishou, but the practice pushes us."

"You're no stranger to deconstruction."

"And you're good at spouting poetically deconstructive nonsense."

That was just another reason her company was always so enjoyable. She was not bookish, but she had read across a wide range of subjects, even the latest ones.

"Well, I used to be quite good at Taiji. At Tuishou too."

"No kidding?"

"It's years ago. I may have forgotten some techniques, but try me."

Tuishou—or push-hand sparring exercise—was a special form of Taiji. Two people standing opposite each other, palms to palms, pushing and being pushed in a slow, spontaneous flow of rhythmic harmony. There were several people doing that near the Taiji group.

"It's easy. Just keep your arms in constant contact," she said, taking up his hands, pedantically, "and make sure that you push neither too little nor too much. Harmonious, natural, spontaneous. Tuishou values dissolving an oncoming force before striking a blow."

She was a good instructor, but it did not take her long to find out that he was actually the more experienced. He could have pushed her off balance in the first few rounds, but he found this experience, with his palms pressed against hers, their bodies moving together in an effortless effort, too intimate to bring to a quick stop.

And it was really intimate—her face, her arms, her body, her gestures, the way she moved and was moved, her eyes shining into his eyes.

He did not want to push her too hard. But she was getting impatient, throwing more force into it. He rotated his left forearm to ward off her attack by turning his body slightly to the side. With a subtle technique of neutralizing her force, he drew in his chest, shifting his weight onto his right leg and pressing her left arm downward. She leaned forward too much.

He took the opportunity of pushing her back. She lost her balance, staggering forward. He reached out to take her in his arms. She was blushing deeply, trying to disengage herself.

Since their first meeting, he had been resisting the temptation to hold her in his arms again—this time not by accident. Initially he was not sure what she might think of him. Perhaps he had a touch of an inferiority complex. What reason was there for him to believe that a pretty, promising reporter, almost ten years younger, would be interested in an entry-level cop? Then he learned that she had been married, a fact he had since been trying to overlook, for she had been married—he had kept telling himself—only nominally. Two or three months before their first meeting, her boyfriend, Yang Kejia, was about to leave for an approved study program in Japan. His father, lying in the hospital, gasped out his last wish to the two young people: that they would go to the city hall for a marriage license, even though the wedding could be postponed until after Yang's return from Japan. It was a matter of Confucian significance that he leave this world with the satisfaction of seeing his only son married. Wang did not have the heart to say no, so she agreed. In a couple of weeks her father-in-law passed away, and then her husband defected in Japan, refusing to return to China. That was a terrible blow to her. As a wife, she was supposed to know everything about Yang's movements, but she was totally in the dark. Chen believed the defector would not have discussed it with her in long-distance calls which could be tapped. But some Internal Security officers did not credit this, and she was questioned several times.

According to a colleague of hers, it would serve Yang right if, having left her in such a situation, she divorced him. But Chen had not discussed this with her. There was no hurry. He knew he liked her, but he had not made up his mind yet. In the meantime, he was happy to be with her whenever he could find the time.

"You know how to push," she said, her hand still in his.

"No, I'll never push you. It's just the natural flow. But on second thought," he said, gazing at her flushed face, "I do want to push you a little. What about a cup of coffee in the Riverside Café?"

"In full view of the *Wenhui* Building?"

"What's wrong with that?" He could sense her hesitation. There was the possibility of their being seen together by her colleagues passing along the Bund. He himself had heard of gossip about them in the bureau. "Come on, this is the nineties."

"You don't have to push for that," she said.

The Riverside Café consisted of several chairs and tables on a large cedar deck jutting out above the river. They climbed a silver-gray wrought-iron spiral staircase and chose a white plastic table under a large flowered umbrella that offered a wonderful view of the river and the colorful vessels coming and going slowly along its eastern bank. A waitress brought them coffee, juice, and a glass bowl of assorted fruit.

The coffee smelled fresh. So did the juice. She picked up the bottle and raised it to her mouth. Loosening the kerchief that secured her hair, she looked relaxed, her foot hooked over the horizontal bar of the chair.

He could not help wondering at the change in her face in the sunlight. Every time he met her, he would seem to perceive something different in her. One moment she appeared to be a bluestocking, nibbling at the top of a fountain pen, mature and pensive, with the weight of fast-developing world news on her shoulders; the next moment she would come to him, a young girl in wooden sandals, scampering down the corridor. But on this May morning, she appeared to be a typical Shanghai girl, soft, casual, at ease in the company of the man she liked.

There was even a light green jade charm dangling on a thin red string over her bosom. Like most Shanghai girls, she, too, wore those small, superstitious trinkets. Then she began chewing a stick of gum, her head leaned back, blowing a bubble into the sunlight.

He did not feel the need to speak at the moment. Her breath, only inches away, was cool from the minty gum. He had intended to take her hand across the table, but instead, he tapped his finger on the paper napkin in front of her.

A sense of being up and above the Bund filled him.

"What're you thinking about?" he said.

"What mask are you wearing at this moment—policeman or poet?"

"You've asked that for the second time. Are the two so contradictory?"

"Or a prosperous businessman from abroad?" she said, giggling. "You're certainly dressed like one."

He was wearing his dark suit, a white shirt, and one of his few ties that looked exotic, a gift from a former schoolmate, an owner of several high-tech companies in Toronto who had told him that the design on the tie represented a romantic scene in a modern Canadian play. There was no point in sitting with her in his police uniform.

"Or just a lover," he said impulsively, "head over heels." He met her gaze, guessing he had made himself as transparent as water. Not the water in the Huangpu River.

"You're being impossible," she said, smiling, "even in the middle of your murder investigation."

It did slightly disturb him that he could be so sensitive to her attractiveness when he should have been concentrating on solving the case. When she was alive, Guan Hongying might have been as attractive. Especially in those pictures in the cloud-wrapped mountains, Guan posing in a variety of elegant attire, young, lively, vivacious. All in such a sharp contrast to that naked, swollen body pulled out of a black plastic garbage bag.

They sat at the table, not speaking for a couple of minutes, watching an antique-looking sampan swaying in the tide. A wave shook the sampan near the parrot wall, bringing down a cloth diaper from a clothesline stretched across the deck.

"A family sampan, the couple working down in the cabin," he said, "and living there too."

"A torn sail married to a broken oar," she said, still chewing the gum.

A bubble of metaphor iridescent in the sun.

A half-naked baby was crawling out of the cabin under the tarpaulin, as if to satisfy their expectation, grinning at them like a Wuxi earthen doll.

For the moment, they felt they had the river to themselves.

Not the river, but the moment it starts rippling in your eyes . . .

He was on the track of a poem.

"Your mind is on the case again?"

"No, but now that you mention it," he said, "there is something puzzling about it."

"I'm no investigator," she said, "but talking about it may help."

Chief Inspector Chen had learned that verbalizing a case to an attentive listener *was* helpful. Even if the listener did not offer any constructive suggestions, sometimes questions alone from an untrained—or simply a new—perspective could open fresh paths of inquiry. So he started talking about the case. He was not worried about sharing information with her, even though she was a *Wenhui* reporter. She listened intently, her cheek lightly resting on her hand, then leaned forward across the table, gazing at him, the morning light of the city in her eyes.

"So here we are," Chen said, having recapitulated the points he had discussed in the special group meeting the previous day, "with a number of unanswered questions. And the only fact we have established is that Guan left the dorm for a vacation around ten thirty on May tenth. As for what happened to her afterward, we have discovered nothing—except the caviar."

"Nothing else suspicious?"

"Well, there is something else. Not really suspicious, but it just does not make sense to me. She was going somewhere on vacation, but no one knew where. People are usually so excited about their vacation that they will talk a lot about it."

"That's true," she said, "but in her case, couldn't her reserve result from a need for privacy?"

"That's what we suspect, but the whole thing seemed to be just too secretive. Detective Yu has checked with all the travel agencies, and there's no record with her name registered either."

"Well, she might have traveled by herself."

"That's possible, but I doubt that a single young woman would travel all by herself. Unless she had some other people, or one man as her companion, I think it unlikely. That's my hypothesis, and the caviar fits. What's more, last October she had made another trip. We know where she went that time—the Yellow Mountains. But whether she went there by herself, with someone, or with a group, we don't know. Yu has researched that, too, but we have no leads."

"That's strange," she said, her eyes half closing in thought. "No train goes there. You have to change to a bus in Wuhu, and to get from the bus terminal to the mountains, you have to walk quite a distance. And then to find a hotel for yourself in the mountains can be a headache. It saves you a lot of money, and energy, too, to go with a tourist group. I've been there, I know."

"Yes, and another thing. According to the records at the department store, her vacation in the mountains lasted about ten days, from the end of September through the first week in October. Detective Yu has contacted all the hotels there. But her name did not appear on any of their records."

"Are you sure that she went there?"

"Positive. She showed her colleagues some pictures from the mountains. In fact, I've seen quite a few in her album."

"She must have a lot of pictures."

"For a young pretty woman, not too many," he said, "but some are really good."

Indeed, some of the pictures appeared highly professional. Still vivid in his mind, for instance, was the one of Guan leaning against the famous mountain pine, with white clouds woven into her streaming black hair. It would do for the cover of a travel brochure.

"Are there pictures of her with other people?"

"A lot of them, of course. One with Comrade Deng Xiaoping himself."

"Pictures from that mountain trip?" Wang said, picking up a grape with her slender fingers.

"Well, I'm not sure," Chen said, "but I don't think so. That's something—"

Something worth looking into.

"Supposing Guan made the trip all by herself," she was peeling the grape. "She could have met some people in the mountains staying in the same hotel, talked about the scenery, taken pictures for each other—"

"And taken pictures together. You're absolutely right," he said. "And some of the tourists would have worn their name tags."

"Name tags—yes, that's possible," she said, "if they were traveling in a group."

"I have looked through all the albums," he said, stealing a glance at his wristwatch, "but I may do it all over again."

"And as soon as possible," she was putting the peeled grape into his saucer.

The grape appeared greenish, almost transparent against her lovely fingers.

He reached across to take her hands on the table. They had a sort of mutual understanding that he appreciated: Chief Inspector Chen had to investigate.

She shook her head, looking as though she was about to say something, but changed her mind.

"What is it?"

"I'm concerned about you." She withdrew her hand with a small frown.

"Why?"

"Your obsession with the case," she said softly, standing up from the chair. "An ambitious man is not necessarily obnoxious, but you are going a bit too far, Comrade Chief Inspector."

"No, I'm not that obsessed with the case," he said. "In fact, you are just reminding me of two lines—'With the green skirt of yours in my mind, everywhere, / Everywhere I step over the grass ever so lightly'."

"You don't have to cover yourself by quoting those lines," she said, starting to move toward the staircase. "I know how much your work means to you."

"Not as much as you think," he said, imitating the way she shook her head, "certainly not as much as you."

"How is your mother?" she was changing the subject again.

"Fine. Still waiting for me to grow up, get hitched, make her a grandma."

"Work on growing up first."

Wang could be sarcastic at times, but it might just be a defense mechanism. So he laughed.

"I am wondering," he said, "if we can get together again—this weekend."

"To talk more about the investigation?" she teased him good-humoredly.

"If you like," he said. "I also want to have dinner with you at my place."

"Fine, I'd like that, but not this weekend," she said. "I'll check my calendar. I'm not a gourmet cook like your 'Overseas Chinese' pal, but I can work up a pretty good Sichuan pickle. How does that sound?"

"It sounds terrific."

She turned to him with an enigmatic smile, "You don't have to accompany me to my office."

So he stood, lit a cigarette, and watched her crossing the street, coming to a stop at the central safety island. There she looked back, the green skirt trailing across the long curve of her legs, and her smile filled him with a surprising sense of completeness. She waved to him before she turned into the side street leading to the *Wenhui* building.

Of late, he had been giving some thought to the future of their relationship.

Politically she would not make an ideal choice. Her future would be affected by her so-called husband's defection. Even after her divorce, the stain in her file would remain. It would not have mattered that much if Chen had not been a chief inspector.

As an "emerging Party member cadre," he knew the Party authorities were aware of every step he was making. So were some of his colleagues, who would be pleased to see his career tarnished by such a union.

A married woman, though no more than nominally married, was not "culturally desirable," either.

But what was the point of being a chief inspector if he could not care for a woman he liked?

He threw away his cigarette. One decision he had made: he was walking to Qinghe Lane instead of taking a bus. He wanted to do some thinking.

Crossing the safety island, he stepped over the green grass lightly.

Chapter 12

This May morning was bright and despite the early heat the air was fresh.

The traffic wound itself into a terrible snarl along Henan Road. Chief Inspector Chen cut his way through the long line of cars, congratulating himself on his decision to walk. New construction was under way everywhere, and detour signs popped up like mushrooms after a spring rain, adding to the traffic problem. Near the Eastern Bookstore, he noticed another old building being pulled down. In its place, a five-star hotel would soon arise. An imported red convertible rolled by. A young girl sitting by the driver waved her hand at a postman late on his round.

Shanghai was changing rapidly.

So were the people.

So was he, seeing more and more meaning in his police work, though he stepped into a bookstore, and spent several minutes looking for a poetry collection. Chief Inspector Chen was not that obsessed with the case, nor with its political significance for his career.

There was, perhaps, one side of him that had always been bookish, nostalgic, or introspective. Sentimental, or even somewhat sensual in a classic Chinese version—*"fragrance from the red sleeves imbues your reading at night."* But there was also another side to him. Not so much antiromantic as realistic, though not as ambitious as Wang had accused him of being at the Riverfront Café. A line memorized in his college years came back to him: *"The most useless being is a poor bookworm."* It was by Gao Shi, a well-known general, successful in the mid-Tang dynasty, and a first-class poet at the same time.

General Gao had lived in an era when the once prosperous Tang dynasty was torn by famine, corruption, and wars, so the talented poet-general had taken it upon himself to make a difference—through his political commitment—for the country.

Today, China was once more witnessing a profound change, with significant challenges to the established systems and views. At such a historical juncture, Chen was also inclined to think that he could make a more realistic difference as a chief inspector than just as a poet. A difference, even if not as substantial as General Gao's, which would be felt in the lives of the people around him. For example, by his investigation of this crime.

In China, and perhaps anywhere else, making such a difference would be more possible from a position of power, Chief Inspector Chen thought, as he inserted the key into the lock of Guan's dorm room door.

To his dismay, the hopes that led him to make a second visit to Guan's room were evaporating fast. He stood there under the framed portrait of Comrade Deng Xiaoping, musing. Nothing seemed to have changed in the room. And he could find nothing new in the photos, either, though there were several showing Guan in the mountains. He took these out and arranged them in a line on the table. Vivid images. Sharp colors. Standing by the famous welcoming pine, she smiled into the camera. Looking up at the peak, she lifted up her arms to the white clouds. Sitting on a jutting rock, she dabbled her bare feet in the mountain stream.

There was also one in a hotel room. Perching on the window sill, she was dressed rather scantily, her long, shapely bare legs dangling gracefully beneath a short cotton skirt. The morning sun shone through her thin cotton tunic, rendering it almost transparent, the swell of her breasts, visible beneath the material, suggesting the ellipse of her abdomen. Behind her, the window framed the verdant mountain range.

No mistaking her presence in the mountains. There was not a single picture, however, of her together with somebody else. Could she have been that narcissistic?

The idea that she'd made the trip by herself did not make sense, as Wang had pointed out at the café. But supposing she had, there was another question—Who had taken all the pictures of her? For her? Some had been taken at difficult angles, or from a considerable distance. It was hard to believe that she could have managed to have taken them by herself. There was not even a camera left among her few belongings. Nor a single roll of film, used or unused, in the drawers.

Comrade Deng Xiaoping himself appeared to be leaning down out of the picture frame, beneath which he stood, frustrated at Chen's frustration.

One metaphor Chen had translated in a mystery came to his mind. Policemen were like wind-up toy soldiers, hustling here and bustling there, gesticulating, and chasing around in circles, for days, months, and even years, without getting anything done, and then suddenly they found themselves put aside, shelved, only to be wound up for another time.

Something about this case had been winding him up. It was a nameless impulse, which he suspected might not totally be a policeman's.

Suddenly he felt hungry. He had had only a cup of black coffee at the Riverside Café. So he headed out to the shabby restaurant across the street. Choosing a rickety wooden table on the sidewalk, he once more ordered a portion of fried buns plus a bowl of beef soup. The soup came first with chopped green onion floating on the surface, but like the last time, he had to wait for the buns. The place had only one big flat wok for frying them.

There's no breakthrough every day for a cop, he thought, and lit a cigarette, inhaling the fragrance of Peony mixed with the fresh air. Looking across the street, he became fascinated by the sight of an old woman standing close to the entrance of the lane. Almost statuesque on her bound feet, she was hawking ices from an ancient wheelbarrow, her shrunken face as weatherbeaten as the Great Wall in a postcard. Sweating, she was swathed in black homespun, like an opaque piece of smoke-darkened glass for watching a summer sun eclipse. She wore a red armband with *Best Socialist Mobile Service Woman* in Chairman Mao's calligraphy. Perhaps she was not in her right mind, or she would not have worn that antique armband. Fifty or sixty years earlier, however, she could have been one of those pretty girls, standing there, smiling, her bare shoulders shining against the bare wall, soliciting customers under the alluring gas lights, launching a thousand ships into the silent night.

And in time, Guan might have become as old, shrivelled, ravenlike as the peddler, out of touch with the time and tide, unstrung, unnoticed.

Then Chen noticed that there were, indeed, several young people hanging around the dorm building. They seemed to be doing nothing in particular—crossing their arms, whistling off key, looking at the passersby along the road. As his glance fell on the wood-and-glass kiosk attached to the dorm, he realized that they must be waiting for phone calls. Looking into the cubicle, Chen could see the white-haired old man picking up a phone, handing it to a middle-aged woman outside, and putting coins into a small box. Before the woman finished speaking, the old man was picking up another phone, but this time he wrote something down on a slip of paper. He moved out of his cubicle toward the staircase, shouting upwards, a loudspeaker in one hand and the slip of paper in the other. Possibly he'd called the name of some resident upstairs. That must have been an incoming call. Due to the severe shortage of private phones in Shanghai, such public telephone service remained the norm. Most people had to make phone calls in this way.

Guan, too.

Chen stood up without waiting for the arrival of the fried buns and strode across the street to the dorm.

The old man was in his late sixties, well-preserved, well-dressed, speaking with an air of serene responsibility. Against a different office background, he might have looked like a high-ranking cadre. Lying on the table amid the phones was a copy of the *Romance of the Three Kingdoms* with a bamboo bookmark. He looked up at Chen.

Chief Inspector Chen produced his I.D.

"Yes, you're doing the investigation here," the old man said. "My name is Bao Guozhang. Folks here just call me Uncle Bao."

"Uncle Bao, I would like to ask you a few question about Comrade Guan Hongying," Chen remained standing outside the cubicle, which could hardly seat two people. "Your help will be greatly appreciated."

"Comrade Guan was a fine member of the Party. It's my

responsibility to help your work as a member of the Residents' Committee," Uncle Bao said seriously. "I'll do my best."

The Residents' Committee was, in one sense, an extension of the local district police office, working partially, though not officially, under its supervision. The organization was responsible for everything happening outside people's work units—arranging weekly political studies, checking the number of the people living there, running daycare centers, distributing ration coupons, allocating birth quotas, arbitrating disputes among neighbors or family members, and most important, keeping a close watch over the neighborhood. The committee was authorized to report on every individual, and the report was included as confidential in the police dossier. Thus the institution of the Residents' Committee enabled the local police to remain in the background while maintaining effective surveillance. In some instances, the Residents' Committee had actually helped the police solve crimes and capture criminals.

"Sorry, I did not know that you're a member of the committee," Chen said. "I should have consulted you earlier."

"Well, I retired three years ago from Shanghai Number Four Steel Factory, but my old bones would have rusted if I did nothing all day. So I started working here. Besides, the committee pays a little, too."

While a few officials of the committee were full-time cadres, most members were retired workers on pensions, receiving a little extra pay in return for their community service. In view of the high inflation in the early nineties, an additional stipend was most welcome.

"You're doing something important for the neighborhood," Chen said.

"Well, in addition to the public telephone services here, I also keep an eye on the dorm building security," Uncle Bao said, "and on the whole lane, too. People cannot be too careful these days."

"Yes, you're right," Chen said, noticing two phones ringing at the same time. "And it keeps you pretty busy."

There were four phones on a wooden shelf behind the small windows. One phone was labeled "FOR INCOMING CALLS ONLY." According to Uncle Bao, the public phone service had been originally put in for the convenience of the dorm residents only, but now people in the lane could also use the phones for just ten cents.

"When a call comes in, I write down the name and call-back number on a pad, tear off that page, and give the message to the intended recipient. If it happens to be a dorm resident, I just need to shout the name at the foot of the stairs with a loudspeaker."

"What about the people who don't live in the building?"

"I've got an assistant. She goes out to inform them, shouting with her loudspeaker under their windows."

"So they come here to return the call, right?"

"Yes," Uncle Bao said. "By the time everyone gets a phone at home, I will really be retired."

"Uncle Bao." A young girl burst into the cubicle with a gray loudspeaker in her hand.

"This is the assistant I'm talking about," Uncle Bao said. "She's responsible for delivering the messages to the lane residents."

"I see."

"Xiuxiu, this is Comrade Chief Inspector Chen," Uncle Bao said. "Chief Inspector Chen and I need to talk about something. So take care of things here for a while, will you?"

"Sure, no problem."

"It's not much of a job for her," Uncle Bao sighed, moving across the street to the table where Chen had been waiting. "But that's all she can find nowadays."

The fried buns had not arrived yet, but the soup was already cold. Chen ordered another bowl for Uncle Bao.

"So, any progress with your investigation?"

"Not much. Your help may be really important to us."

"You're welcome to whatever I know."

"Since you're here every day, you probably know who has a lot of visitors. What about Comrade Guan?"

"Some friends or colleagues might have visited, but not too many. On one or two occasions I noticed her with people. That's about all I saw—during my three years here."

"What kind of people were they?"

"I cannot really remember. Sorry."

"Did she make a lot of calls?"

"Well, yes, more than other residents here."

"And received a lot?"

"Yes, quite a lot, too, I would say," Uncle Bao said reflectively. "But then it's little wonder, for a national model worker, with her meetings and conferences."

"Anything unusual about those phone calls?"

"No, nothing that I noticed. There're so many calls, and I am always busy."

"Anything you happened to have overheard?"

"It's not proper and right, Comrade Chief Inspector," Uncle Bao said, "for me to listen to what other people say."

"You're right, Uncle Bao. Forgive me for this improper question. It's just because the case is so important to us."

The arrival of the fried buns interrupted their discussion.

"But—as for anything unusual—now that you mention it, there might be something, I think," Uncle Bao said, nibbling at a tiny bun. "The working hours for a public phone service station are, generally, from seven A.M. to seven P.M. For the benefit of the residents here, several of whom work the night shift, we extend our service hours— from seven A.M. to eleven P.M. Guan made quite a number of calls, I remember, after nine or ten P.M. Especially during the last half year."

"Was that wrong?"

"Not wrong, but unusual. The First Department Store closes at eight o'clock."

"Yes?"

"The people she called must have had private phones at home."

"Well, she might have talked to her boss."

"But I wouldn't call my boss after ten o'clock. Would a young single woman?"

"Yes, you're very observant."

The R.C. member had ears, Chen nodded, and brains, too.

"It's my responsibility."

"So you think that she was seeing somebody before her death?"

"It's possible," Uncle Bao said after a pause. "As far as I can remember, it was a man who made most of the phone calls to her. He spoke with a strong Beijing accent."

"Is there any way to trace the phone numbers, Uncle Bao?"

"Not with the phone calls she made. There's no way of knowing the number she dialed out. But for the calls she got, we may recover some from our record stubs. You see, we put down the number both on the slip and the stub attached to it. So if people lose their slips, we can still recover the numbers."

"Really! Have you kept all the stubs?"

"Not all of them. Most are useless after several days. But for the past few weeks, I may be able to dig out some for you. It will take some time."

"That will be great," Chen said. "Thank you so much, Uncle Bao. Your information is throwing new light on our investigation."

"You're most welcome, Comrade Chief Inspector."

"Another thing. Did she get a phone call on May tenth? That is, the night she was murdered."

"May tenth was—a Thursday, let me see. I'll have to check the stubs. The phone station drawer's too small, so I keep most of the stubs at home."

"Call me immediately if you find anything," Chen said. "I don't know how to express our appreciation."

"Don't mention it, Comrade Chief Inspector," Uncle Bao said. "What's an R.C. member for?"

At the bus station, Chen turned back and glimpsed the old man busy working in the cubicle again, cradling a phone on his shoulder, nodding, writing on a piece of paper, his other hand holding another piece out the window. A conscientious R.C. member. Most likely a Party member, too.

It was an unexpected lead: Guan might have been seeing somebody before her death.

Why she should have made such a secret of it, he did not know yet. He no longer had any conviction about its being a political case. It was Wang, with the green jade charm dangling from a thin red string round her neck, who had inspired him to pursue this line of investigation. But the moment he squeezed into the bus, he ran out of luck. Wedged among the passengers at the door, he pressed forward only to be crushed against a middle-aged fat woman, her florid blouse soaked in sweat, wet, nearly transparent. He tried his best to keep some distance, but to no avail. What was even worse, with new construction under way everywhere, the condition of the road was not smooth. The incessant bumps made the ordeal almost unbearable. More than once the bus came to an emergency halt, and his fleshy neighbor was thrown off balance, colliding with him. It was no Tuishou. He heard her cursing under her breath, though it was not anybody's fault.

Finally he gave up. Before the bus reached the bureau, he got off at Shandong Road.

The fresh breeze was heavenly.

Bus Number 71. Possibly the very bus Guan used to take to the department store, and back, day after day.

Not until Chief Inspector Chen returned home, took off his uniform, and lay down on his bed, did he think of something that could have been a cold comfort—for Guan. Though single, Guan had not been too lonely—at least not toward the end of her life. She had someone to call after 10 P.M. He had never tried to call Wang so late in the evening. She lived with her parents. He had only visited her home once. Old, prudish, traditional, her parents were not too friendly because they were aware of his attentions to their married daughter.

What was Wang doing at the moment? He wished he could call her, tell her that success in his career, gratifying as it appeared, was no more than a consolation prize for the absence of personal happiness.

It was a serene summer night. The moonlight was lambent among the shimmering leaves, and a lonely street lamp cast a yellow flickering light on the ground. A violin could be heard from an open window across the street. The melody was familiar, but he could not recall its name. Sleepless, he lit a cigarette.

A young woman, Guan must also have experienced her moments of surging loneliness—sudden sleeplessness, in that small dorm room of hers.

The ending of a poem by Matthew Arnold came swelling to him in the night-air:

> *Ah, love, let us be true*
> *To one another! for the world, which seems*
> *To lie before us like a land of dreams,*
> *So various, so beautiful, so new,*
> *Hath really neither joy, nor love, nor light,*
> *Nor certitude, nor peace, nor help for pain.*
> *And we are here as on a darkling plain*
> *Swept with confused alarms of struggle and flight,*
> *Where ignorant armies clash by night.*

It was a poem he had translated years earlier. The broken and uneven lines, as well as the abrupt, almost surrealist transitions and juxtapositions, had appealed to him. The translation had appeared in *Reading and Understanding,* along with a short critical essay by him, claiming it as the saddest Victorian love poem. Whether it was really an echo of the disillusioned Western world, as he had maintained in the essay, however, he was no longer so sure. Any reading, according to Derrida, could be a misreading. Even Chief Inspector Chen could be read in one way or another.

Chapter 13

Saturday in late May was once again clear and fine.

The Yus were visiting the Grand View Garden in Qingpu, Shanghai.

Peiqin was in her element, carrying a copy of *The Dream of the Red Chamber*. It was a dream come true to her.

"Look, that's the bamboo grove where Xiangyuan takes her nap on the stone bench, and Baoyu stands watching her," she said, turning the pages to that part of the story.

Qinqin was in high spirits, too, running about, losing and finding himself in a traditional Chinese garden maze.

"Take a picture of me by the vermilion pavilion," she said.

Yu had the blues, but he was making a gallant effort to conceal his mood. He held up the camera, knowing how much the garden meant to Peiqin. A group of tourists also came to a stop in front of the pavilion, and the guide began elaborating on the ancient architectural wonder. Peiqin listened intently, oblivious to him for the moment. He stood among the crowd, nodding, but pursuing his own thoughts.

He had been under a lot of pressure in the bureau. Commissar Zhang was unpleasant to work with, all the more so after the last group meeting. Chief Inspector Chen was not intolerable, but he obviously had something up his sleeve. The Party Secretary, while gracious to Chen and Zhang, brought all the pressure to bear upon Yu, who was not even the lead investigator for the case. Not to mention the fact that Yu actually had the main responsibility for the other cases in the squad.

Little had come out of his renewed focus on the taxi bureau and travel agencies. The reward offered for information about any suspicious driver seen that night near the canal was a long shot. No response came, as Yu had expected.

There was no progress from Chen either, with respect to his theory about the caviar.

"The garden is a twentieth-century construction of the archetypal idea exhibited in *The Dream of the Red Chamber*, the classical Chinese novel most celebrated since the mid-nineteenth century." The guide was speaking glibly, holding a cigarette with a long filter tip as he delivered his introduction. "Not only are the lattice windows, doors, or wood pillars exactly of the same design, the furniture also reflects the conventions of the time. Just look at the bamboo bridge. And the asparagus fern grotto, too. We're truly living in the novel here."

Indeed, the garden was a draw to fans of the novel. Peiqin had talked about visiting it five or six times. There had been no putting off this visit.

A moss-covered winding path led into a spacious hall with oblong windows of stained glass, through which the "inner garden" appeared cool and inviting, but Yu was in no mood for any further expedition. He felt stupid and out-of-place, as he stood by Peiqin in the crowd, though he pretended to be interested like everybody else. Some people were taking pictures. By a strange-shaped grotto stood a makeshift photography booth where tourists could rent so-called Ming dynasty costumes and jewelry. A young girl was posing in a heavy antique golden headdress, and her boyfriend was changing into a dragon-embroidered silk gown. And Peiqin, too, was being transformed by the splendor of the garden, as she busily compared the chambers, stone pavilions, and moon-shaped gates with the pictures in her mind. Looking at her, he almost believed that she belonged there, expecting Baoyu—the young, handsome hero of the novel—to walk out of the bamboo grove any minute.

She also seized the opportunity to share her knowledge of classical Chinese culture with Qinqin. "When Baoyu was your age, he had already memorized the four Confucian classics."

"The four Confucian classics?" Qinqin said. "Never heard of them in school."

Having failed to elicit the expected response from her son, she turned to her husband. "Look, this must be the stream where Daiyu buries the fallen flower," she exclaimed.

"Daiyu buries her flower?" he said, at a total loss.

"Remember the poem by Daiyu—'*I'm burying the flower today, but who's going to bury me tomorrow?*'"

"Oh, that sentimental poem."

"Guangming," she said, "your thoughts are not in the garden."

"No, I am enjoying every minute of it," he assured her. "But I read the novel such a long time ago. We were still in Yunnan, you remember."

"Where are we going now?"

"To be honest, I'm a bit tired," he said. "What about you and Qinqin going ahead to the inner garden? I'll sit here for a few minutes, finish my cigarette, and then I'll join you there."

"That's fine, but don't smoke too much."

He watched Peiqin leading Qinqin into the quaint inner garden through the gourd-shaped gate, effortlessly, as if she were moving back into her own home.

He was no Baoyu, and never meant to be. He was a cop's son. And a cop himself. Yu ground out his cigarette under his foot. He was trying to be a good cop, but he was finding it more and more difficult.

Peiqin was different. It was not that she complained. In fact, she was contented. As a restaurant accountant, she earned decent money, about five hundred Yuan a month with perks. Enjoying a nice little niche, she did not have to work with the customers. And at home, small as it was, things were smooth and satisfactory, too, she had often said.

But her life could have been different, he knew. A Daiyu or a Baochai, just like one of those beautiful, talented girls in the romantic novel.

In the beginning of *The Dream of the Red Chamber*, there were twelve lovely girls who lived out their romantic karma as preordained in Fate's heavenly register. According to the author, a love affair is predestined for lovers sauntering under the moon in the Grand View Garden. Of course that's fiction. In real life, however, things might be stranger even than in fiction.

He tried to extract another cigarette, but the pack was empty. A crumpled Peony box. The monthly ration coupons allowed him only five quality-brand packs, such as Peony and Great Wall, which he had already finished. He reached into his jacket pocket for a metal cigarette case, in which he kept some cigarettes he had rolled himself, a secret from Peiqin, who was worried about his heavy smoking.

They had known each other since their early childhood. *"Playmates on stilted bamboo horses, / Chasing each other, plucking green plum blossoms."* Doctor Xia had copied the couplet from Li Bai's "Zhanggan Song" on two red silk streamers for Yu and Peiqin's wedding.

But that innocently romantic childhood had not been exactly true for them. It was just that her family had happened to move into the same neighborhood in the early sixties. So they became schoolmates in grade school, and then in high-school, too.

Instead of seeking each other's company, however, they'd kept their distance. The sixties was a revolutionary puritan period in China. It was out of the question for boys and girls to mix together at school.

Another factor was her bourgeois family background. Peiqin's father, a perfume company owner before 1949, had been sent to a labor-reform camp in the late sixties, sentenced to a number of years for something unexplained, and died there. Her family, driven out of their Jingan District mansion, had to move to an attic room in Yu's neighborhood. A thin, sallow girl with a tiny ponytail secured with a rubber band, she was anything but a proud princess. Though a top student in their class, she was often bullied by other kids of working-class family background. One morning, several Little Red Guards were trying to cut off her ponytail. It went too far, and Yu stepped forward to stop them. He exerted a sort of authority over the neighborhood kids as the son of a police officer.

It was only in the last year of their junior high-school that something occurred to bring them together. The early seventies witnessed a dramatic turn of the Cultural Revolution as Chairman Mao came to see the Red Guards, once his ardent young supporters, standing in the way of his consolidation of power. So Mao said it was necessary for the Red Guards—then called "educated youths"—to go to the countryside to "be reeducated by the lower and middle-poor peasants," so that the young people would be gone from the cities, unable to make trouble. A nationwide campaign was carried on with drums and gongs sounding everywhere. In their naive response to Mao's call, millions of young people went to the far-away countryside. To Anhui Province, to Jiangxi Province, to Helongjiang Province, to Inner Mongolia, to the northern border, to the southern border . . .

Yu Guangming and Jing Peiqin, though too young to be Red Guards, found themselves labeled as educated youths, despite the fact that they had received little education, with copies of the shining red *Quotations of Chairman Mao* as their textbook. As educated youths, they, too, had to leave Shanghai to "receive education in the countryside." They were to go to an army farm in Yunnan province, on the southern China / Burma border.

On the eve of their leaving home, Peiqin's mother came to see Yu's parents. The two families had a long talk that night. The next morning Peiqin came to his place, and her brother, a truck driver at Shanghai Number 1 Steel Mill, took both of them to the North Railway Station. They sat in the truck, facing each other, staring at the cheering crowds, holding on to two trunks—all their belongings—and singing a Chairman Mao quotation song: *Go to the countryside, go to the frontier, go to where our motherland needs us the most....*

It was a sort of arranged engagement, Yu guessed, but he accepted it without too much thought. The parents of the two families wanted them, two sixteen-year-olds sent thousands of miles away, to take care of each other. And she had grown into a pretty girl, slender, almost as tall as he. They sat shyly beside each other in the train. They did take care of each other there. There was no alternative for them.

The army farm was tucked into a faraway region called Jinghong, Xishuangbanna, in the depths of southern Yunnan Province. Most of the poor and lower-middle peasants there were of the Dai minority; they spoke their own language and held to their own cultural traditions. To keep themselves above the dank and humid earth, the result of frequent tropical rains, the Dais lived in bamboo shelters raised off the ground on solid stilts, with pigs and chickens moving around below. In contrast, the educated youth stayed in the damp and stuffy army barracks. It was out of the question for the young people to receive reeducation from the Dais. A few things they did learn, but not what Chairman Mao might have wanted. The Dai convention of romantic love, for instance. On the fifteenth of the fourth month in the Chinese lunar calendar year came the Water Splashing Festival, which was supposed to wash away the dirt, death, and demons of the previous year, but it was also an occasion when a Dai girl would declare her affection by pouring water on her beau. The beau then came to sing and dance beneath her windows at night. If she opened the door, he would be her bed partner for the night.

Yu and Peiqin were shocked upon first arrival, but they learned fast. It was not a matter of choice. They needed each other's company during those years, for there were no movies, no library, no restaurant: no recreation of any kind. At the end of long working days, they had only each other. They had long nights. Like so many educated youths, they began to live together. They did not get married. It was not because they had not grown affectionate towards one another, but because there might still be a chance, while their status was still recorded as single, for them to move back to Shanghai. According to the government policy, the educated youth, once married, had to settle down in the countryside.

They missed Shanghai.

The end of the Cultural Revolution changed everything again. They could return home. The movement of educated youths going to the countryside was discontinued, if not officially denounced. Once back in Shanghai, they did marry. Yu "inherited" his police position as a result of his father's early retirement, and Peiqin was assigned the restaurant accountant job. It was not what she wanted, but it proved fairly lucrative. One year after the birth of their son Qinqin, their marriage had slipped into a smooth routine. There was little he could complain about.

Sometimes, however, he could not help missing these years in Yunnan. Those dreams of coming back to Shanghai, getting a job in a state company, starting a new career, having a family, and leading a different life. Now he had reached a stage where he could no longer afford to have impractical dreams. A low-level cop, he would probably remain one all his life. He was not giving up on himself, but he was becoming more realistic.

The fact was, with his poor educational background, and with few connections, Detective Yu was in no position to dream of a future in the force. His father had served twenty-six years, but ended up a cop at the entry level. That would probably be his lot, too. In his day, Old Hunter had at least enjoyed a proud sense of being part of the Proletarian Dictatorship. In the nineties, the term "Proletarian Dictatorship" had disappeared from the newspapers. Yu was just an insignificant cop at the bottom, making the minimum wage, having little say at the bureau.

This case served only to highlight his insignificance.

"Guangming."

He was startled from his reveries.

Peiqin had come back to his side, alone.

"Where is Qinqin?"

"He's having a good time in the electronic game room. He won't come looking for us until he spends all his coins."

"Good for him," he said. "You don't need to worry about him."

"You've something on your mind," she said, perching on a slab of rock beside him.

"No, nothing really. I have just been thinking about our days in Yunnan."

"Because of the garden?"

"Yes," he said. "Don't you remember Xishuangbanna is also called a garden?"

"Yes, but you don't have to say that to me, Guangming. I've been your wife for all these years. Something is wrong at work, right?" she said. "I should not have dragged you here."

"It's okay." He touched her hair gently.

She was silent for a while.

"Are you in trouble?"

"A difficult case, that's all," he said. "I'm just preoccupied."

"You're good at solving difficult cases. Everybody says so."

"I don't know."

She stretched out her hand and placed it over his.

"I know I shouldn't say this, but I'm going to. If you're not happy doing what you're doing, why not quit?"

He stared at her in surprise.

She did not look away.

"Yes, but—" he did not know what else to say.

But he would think about her question, he knew, for a long time.

"No progress with the case?" she was changing the subject.

"Not much."

Yu had mentioned the Guan case to her, although he rarely brought up police work at home. Running criminals down could be difficult and dangerous. There was no point in dwelling on it with his family. Besides, Chen had emphasized the sensitivity of the case. It wasn't a matter of trust, but more of professionalism. But he had been so frustrated.

"Talk to me, Guangming. As your detective father often says," she said, "talk always helps."

So he started to summarize what had been puzzling him, focusing on his failure to get any information regarding Guan's personal life. "She was like a hermit crab. Politics had formed her shell."

"I don't know anything about criminal investigation, but don't tell me an attractive woman—thirty or thirty-one, right—could have lived like that."

"What do you mean?"

"She never had affairs?"

"She was too busy with Party activities and meetings. Too difficult—in her position—for her to find someone, and difficult, too, for someone to find her."

"Laugh at me, Guangming, but I cannot believe it—as a woman.

The thing between a man and a woman, I mean. It's the nineties."

"You have a point," he said. "But I have talked to most of Guan's colleagues again since Chen raised the issue about the caviar, and they've just confirmed our earlier information. They say she was not dating anyone at the time of her death, and as far as they could remember, she had not had a boyfriend. They would have noticed it."

"But it's against human nature. Like Miaoyu in *The Dream of the Red Chamber*."

"Who's Miaoyu?" he asked.

"Miaoyu, a beautiful young nun, lives a life devoted to the abstract ideal of Buddhism. Proud of her religious cultivation, she considered herself above romantic entanglement of the red dust."

"Sorry for interruption again, what is the red dust?"

"Just this mundane world, where the ordinary folk like us live."

"Then it is not too bad."

"Toward the end of the novel, while Miaoyu's meditating one lonely night, she falls prey to her own sexual fantasy. Unable even to speak in the throes of passion, she's easily approached and attacked by a group of bandits. She's not a virgin when she dies. According to literary critics, it's a metaphor: Only the demon in her heart could lure the demon to her body. She's a victim of her long sexual repression."

"So what is the point?"

"Could ideals be enough to sustain a human being, especially a female human being, to the end? During the final moments of her consciousness, I believe, Miaoyu must be full of regret for her wasted life. She should have devoted hers to cleaning her house, going to bed with her husband, fixing school lunches for her children."

"But Miaoyu is just a character in the novel."

"But it is so true. The novel shows brilliant insight into the nature of human beings. What is true for Miaoyu, should also be true for Guan."

"I see," he said. "You're full of insight, too."

Indeed, politics seemed to have been Guan's whole life, but was that really enough? What Guan read in *People's Daily* would not love her back.

"So I cannot imagine," she said, "that Guan could have lived only for politics—unless she had suffered some traumatic experience earlier in her life."

"That's possible, but none of her colleagues ever mentioned it."

"Well, most of her colleagues have not worked too many years with her—haven't you told me that?"

"Yes, that's also true."

Guan had been at the store for eleven years, but none of the interviewees had worked there for so long a time. General Manager Xiao had been transferred from another company just a couple of years earlier.

"Women do not want to talk about their past, especially a single woman to younger women."

"You're certainly right, Peiqin. I should have interviewed some retired employees as well."

"By the way, what about your chief inspector?"

"Well, he has his ideas," he said, "but no breakthrough, either."

"No, I mean his personal life."

"I don't know anything about it."

"He's in his mid-thirties, isn't he? A chief inspector at his age must be a most eligible bachelor."

"Yes. Some people say a woman reporter from the *Wenhui Daily* has been seeing him. For an article about him, he says."

"Do you think that he would tell people if it were for something else?"

"Well, he's somebody in the bureau. Everybody is watching. Of course he will not say anything."

"Just like Guan," she said.

"There may be one difference."

"What's that?"

"She was more well-known."

"All the more reason she would not say anything to others."

"Peiqin, you're extraordinary."

"No, I'm an ordinary girl. Just lucky with an extraordinary husband."

A light breeze had sprung up.

"Sure," he said ruefully, "an extraordinary husband."

"Oh, Guangming, I still remember so clearly those days in Xishuangbanna. Lying alone at night, I thought of you coming to my rescue in elementary school, and it was almost unbearable. I have told you that, haven't I?"

"You never stop amazing me," he said, squeezing her hand.

"Your hand in my hand," she said with twinkle in her eyes, "that is all I ask for in the Grand View Garden. I'm so happy sitting here with you and thinking of those poor girls in the novel."

A soft mist drifted away outside the antique chamber.

"Look at the couplet on the moon-shaped door," Peiqin said.

Hill upon hill, the road seems to be lost,
Willows and flowers, another village appears.

Chapter 14

Saturday morning, Chief Inspector Chen had arrived at the bureau earlier than usual, when the old doorman, Comrade Liang, called out of his cubicle by the iron gate, "Something for you, Chief Inspector Chen."

It was an electronic money order, 3,000 Yuan, a substantial advance for his translation from Lijiang Publishing House. After the loan to Overseas Chinese Lu, Chen had written to Su Liang, the editor in chief, mentioning his new position and apartment as causing him extra expense, but 3,000 Yuan was still a surprise. Enclosed was also a short note from Su:

> *Congratulations.*
>
> *With the current inflation, we believe it is fair to give an author the largest advance possible. Especially you.*
>
> *As for your new position, don't worry about it. If you don't take it, those turtle eggs would jump at it. Which is the worse scenario? That's what I told myself when I took my job.*
>
> *I like your poem in the* Wenhui Daily. *You are enjoying the "fragrance from the red sleeves that imbues your reading at night," I have heard.*
>
> *Su Liang*

Su was not only a senior editor who had helped him, but also an old friend who had known him well in the past.

He phoned Wang, but she was not in her office. After he put down the phone, he realized that he did not have any specific topic. He'd just had an impulse to speak to her after he had read the note. The reference to "the fragrance of the red sleeves" could have caused it, though he would probably not talk about it. Wang would guess his mind was on the case again. But that was not true.

Detective Yu was having the day off. Chen was resolved to do something about the routine work of the squad. He had been giving too much time to Guan. Now he found it necessary to make a wholehearted effort, at least for half a day, to clear off the arrears of paperwork piling up on his desk before he gave the case another thought. He took a perverse delight in shutting himself up, polishing off a mass of boring administrative work, signing his name on Party documents without reading them, and going through all the mail accumulated during the week.

The effort lasted for only a couple of hours. He did not have his heart in it. It was a beautiful, sunny morning outside. Chen went to Guan's dorm again. He had not yet received a phone call from Uncle Bao, but he was eager to know if there was anything new for him.

The early summer heat, with no air conditioning, dictated a sidewalk life. At the lane entrance, several retired old men were playing a game of mahjongg on a bamboo table. Kids were gathered around a small earthen pot that contained two crickets fighting each other, the crickets chirping, the children cheering. Close to the dorm building, a middle-aged woman was leaning over a public sink, scrubbing a pan.

In the phone booth, a young girl was serving as the operator. Chen recognized her, Xiuxiu. Uncle Bao was not there. He thought about asking for Uncle Bao's address, but reconsidered. The old man deserved a Saturday off with his grandchildren. So he decided to take yet another look at Guan's room.

Once more he went through all the albums. This time he discovered something else tucked inside the backcover of the most recent one. It was not the picture of Guan in the mountains, but a Polaroid of a gray-haired lady standing underneath the famous Guest-Welcome pine.

He took out the picture, and turned it over. On the back he saw a small line: *To Comrade Zhaodi, Wei Hong October 1989.*

Comrade Zhaodi. Who was that?

Could Zhaodi be another name for Guan?

Zhaodi was a sort of common pet name, meaning "to bring a young brother into the world." A likely wish to have been cherished by Guan's parents, who had only one daughter. Some Chinese parents believed in such a superstitious name-giving practice. As Confucius once said, *"Naming is the most important thing in the world."*

The date seemed to fit. It was the very month that Guan had made the trip to the mountains. Also fitting was the unmistakable Guest-Welcoming pine in the background. If it had been meant for somebody else, why should Guan have kept the picture in her album?

He lit a cigarette under the portrait of Comrade Deng Xiaoping before he put the photo into his briefcase. Downstairs, he looked into the small window of the phone station again. Still no Uncle Bao.

"Is Uncle Bao off today?" he asked.

"You must be Comrade Chief Inspector," the girl said, eyeing his uniform. "Comrade Bao has been waiting for you. He wants me to tell him as soon as you are here."

In less than three minutes, Uncle Bao came trotting in with a big envelope in his hand.

"I have something for you, Comrade Chief Inspector."

"Thank you, Uncle Bao."

"I've called you a couple of times, but the line was busy."

"Sorry, I should have given you my home phone number."

"Let's have a talk. My place is quite close, you know, but it's a bit small."

"Well, we may talk over a pot of tea in the restaurant across the street."

"Good idea."

The restaurant was not crowded on Saturday morning. They chose a table inside. The waiter seemed to know Uncle Bao well, and he brought over a pot of Dragon Well tea immediately.

The old man produced several stub books, which covered the period from February to early May. Altogether, there were more than thirty stubs showing that Guan had received calls from the number 867-831, quite a few of them after nine o'clock. The caller's surname was Wu.

"So all are from the same number," Chen said.

"And from the same man, too," Uncle Bao said. "I'm positive."

"Do you know anything about the number, or the man?"

"No, I don't know anything about the number. As for the man, I think I told you already, he's middle-aged, speaking with a clear Beijing accent, but he is not from Beijing. More likely a Shanghainer who speaks the Beijing dialect a lot. He's rather polite, too, calling me Old Uncle. That's why I remember that the most calls came from him, and the records prove it."

"You're doing a great job for us, Uncle Bao. We'll check the number today."

"Another thing. I don't know who Guan called, but that person did not use the public phone service. Most likely it was a home phone. Every time she dialed, she got through immediately. And she made a number of calls after nine or ten o'clock at night."

"Yes, that is another important point," he said. "Now what about the night of May tenth?"

"I've found something."

Uncle Bao produced a small envelope, which contained just one stub.

It was just a simple message: *We'll meet as scheduled.* And it was from a caller surnamed Wu, though with no phone number written underneath it.

"These may not be his words exactly," Uncle Bao said, "but they were to that effect."

So a couple of hours before her trip, Guan had received a call from a man surnamed Wu, evidently the same one who had called more than thirty times in the period from February to May.

"Why is no phone number recorded on the stub of May tenth?"

"Because the caller did not request a call back," Uncle Bao explained. "In such cases, we just put down the message for the recipient."

"Do you remember anything else he said that evening?"

"No, I'm sorry."

"Well, you've already helped us such a lot," he said. "It is definitely a lead for our investigation. I don't know how we can ever thank you enough."

"When the case is solved," Uncle Bao said, "give a me call."

"I will. And a long call, you bet."

"And we'll have another pot of tea. At Mid-Lake Teahouse, my treat."

"Yes, we will. So see you soon—" Chen said, standing up, "at Mid-Lake Teahouse."

Chapter 15

Chief Inspector Chen hurried back to his office.

The first thing he did was to call the Shanghai Telephone Bureau. He told the operator that he wanted to check out the owner of the number 867-831.

"That is not a listed residential phone," the operator said. "I'm not authorized to reveal the owner's name."

"It is crucial for our investigation."

"Sorry. You need to come with an official letter from your bureau, proving that you're engaged in a criminal investigation. Otherwise we are not supposed to tell you anything."

"No problem. I'll be over with an official letter."

But there was a problem. Pan Huizhen, the bureau assistant clerk in charge of the official seal, happened to have the day off. Chen had to wait until Monday.

Then he thought about the photo of the gray-haired lady tucked into Guan's album. Was she Wei Hong?

At least that was something he could do.

Detective Yu had compiled a detailed list of travel agencies with phone numbers and addresses. Chen had a copy of it. It just needed some narrowing down.

Chen called the Shanghai Tourism Bureau. He had to wait about ten minutes before anyone answered. But he got the information. There were five travel agencies that sponsored Yellow Mountains trips.

So he dialed these agencies. All the agents were busy, and it was out of the question for them to provide offhand the information he requested. Some promised to call back, but he suspected that it would take them days. The manager of East Wind Travel did call back, however, within twenty minutes. She had found the name Wei Hong in her computer.

"I'm not sure if she's the one you are looking for," she said, "but you can come and take a look."

"Thank you," he said. "I'm on my way."

East Wind Travel Agency occupied a single office suite on the second floor of a colonial-style building on Chengdu Road. In front of the reception desk were gathered a group of people with various pieces of baggage, which made the office appear even more congested. All of them had plastic name tags on their lapels. It looked like a group that had just arrived and was waiting for a guide. Several people were smoking. The air in the office was bad.

The manager threw up her arms in an apologetic gesture to Chen, but she lost no time in giving him a computer printout. "We have the name, date, and address here. We do not store photos in our database. So we cannot say if this Wei Hong is the one you're looking for."

"Thank you so much for your information. Also, I'm looking for another person." He showed the manager Guan's photograph, "Guan Hongying."

"A couple of weeks ago, somebody else in your bureau

inquired about her, but we do not have the name in our records," she said, shaking her head. "The national model worker—we should have recognized her. You think she traveled together with Wei Hong?"

"That's possible."

"Little Xie was the escort for that group. She may be able to tell you whether Guan was one of the tourists. But Little Xie no longer works with us."

"What about Zhaodi?" he asked. "Was there someone named Zhaodi traveling in the group?"

"I'm afraid you have to check for yourself." She pounded several times on the keyboard, gesturing for him to sit down. "I've got so many people waiting here, you see."

"That's all right, I understand."

The agency did a good job of storing data. He started searching by date. After pulling up that October's records, he found the name of Zheng Zhaodi listed for a trip to the Yellow Mountains. The information was not complete, however. There was no entry for her address or occupation. But there were also a few others with missing addresses, too. To key in all the data in Chinese was a time-consuming job.

Wei Hong was listed for the same trip.

Before he took his leave, Chen also asked for Little Xie's address. The address was Number 36 Jianguo Road, 303, and her full name was Xie Rong. Since she lived not too far away, he decided to go there first.

His destination was at the end of a small apartment complex built in the style of the mid-fifties. The staircase was dark, damp, difficult. There should have been a light on even during the day. He failed to detect the switch. He knocked at the door, which was opened a little, though still secured with a chain from inside. A white-haired woman wearing a pair of gold-rimmed glasses peeked out.

He told her who he was, showing her his card through the door. She took it and studied it carefully before admitting him. She was in her early sixties, and she wore a pearl-colored blouse with a high pleated neckline, a full skirt, stockings and oxford shoes, and carried a foreign-language book in her hand.

The room had little in the way of furniture, but he was impressed by the tall bookshelves lining the otherwise bare walls.

"What can I do for you, Comrade Chief inspector?"

"I am looking for Xie Rong."

"She's not here."

"When will she be back?"

"I don't know. She's left for Guangzhou."

"For a trip?"

"No, a job."

"Oh? What kind?"

"I don't know."

"You're her mother, right?"

"Yes."

"Then you must know where she is in Guangzhou."

"What do you want with her?"

"I want to ask her a few questions. About a homicide case."

"What—how could she be involved in a homicide case?"

"No, she's a witness, but an important one."

"Sorry, I don't have her address for you," she said. "I received only one letter from her when she first arrived there, just the address of the hotel where she was staying. She said that she was going to move out, and that she would send me her new address. Since then I've heard nothing from her."

"So you do not know what your daughter is doing there?"

"It's hard to believe, isn't it?" She shook her head. "She's my only daughter."

"I'm sorry."

"You don't have to be, Comrade Chief Inspector," she said.

"It's the Modern Age, isn't it? 'Things fall apart; the center cannot hold'."

"Well, that's true," he said, surprised at the old woman's literary quotation, "from one perspective. But it is not necessarily that anarchy is loosed upon the world. It is just a transitional period."

"Historically, a transitional period is short," she said, in her turn surprised, but animated for the first time in the course of their conversation, "but existentially, not so short for the individual."

"Yes, you're right. So our choice is all the more important," he said. "By the way, where do you work?"

"Fudan University, comparative literature department," she added, "but the department is practically gone. And I'm retired. No one wants to study the subject in today's market."

"So you are no other than Professor Xie Kun?"

"Yes, retired Professor Xie Kun."

"Oh, what an honor to meet you today! I have read *The Modernist Muse*."

"Have you?" she said. "I had not expected that a high-ranking police officer would be interested in it."

"Oh, yes, in fact, I have read it two or three times."

"Then I hope you did not buy it when it first came out. I came across it the other day on a broken rickshaw, marked on sale for twenty-five cents."

"Well, you never know. *'Green, green grass spreading out everywhere,'*" he said, pleased to make another quick-witted allusion which suggested that she had readers and students everywhere who appreciated her work.

"Not everywhere," she said, "not even at home. Xie Rong, for one, has not read it."

"How can that possibly be?"

"I used to hope that she, too, would study literature, but after graduating from high school, she started working at Shanghai Sheldon Hotel. From the very beginning, she earned three times my salary, not to mention all the free cosmetics and tips she got there."

"I'm so sorry, Professor Xie. I don't know what to say." He sighed. "But as the economy improves, people may change their minds about literature. Well, let us hope so."

He decided not to tell her about his own literary pursuits.

"Have you heard that popular saying—'The poorest is a Ph.D., and the dumbest is a professor.' I happen to be both. So it is understandable that she chose a different road."

"But why did she quit the hotel job to work for a travel agency?" he said, anxious to change the subject. "And then why did she quit the travel agency to go to Guangzhou?"

"I asked her about that, but she said I was too old fashioned. According to her, young people nowadays change jobs like clothes. That is not a bad metaphor, though. The bottom line is money, of course."

"But why Guangzhou?"

"Um, that's what worries me. For a young girl to be there—all alone."

"Has she talked to you about a trip to the Yellow Mountains last October?"

"She did not talk to me much about her work. But as for that trip, I do remember. She brought back some green tea. The Cloud and Mist tea of the mountains. She seemed a bit upset when she got back."

"Did you know why?"

"No."

"Could that be the reason she changed her job?"

"I don't know, but soon afterward she left for Guangzhou."

"Can you give me a recent picture of her?"

"Certainly." She took a picture out of an album, and handed it to him.

It was of a young slim girl standing by the Bund, wearing a

tight white T-shirt and a very short pleated skirt rather ahead of current Shanghai fashion.

"If you find her in Guangzhou, please tell her that I'm praying for her to come back. It can't be easy for her, all alone there. And I'm alone here, an old woman."

"I will," he said, taking the picture. "I'll do my best."

As he left Professor Xie's home, the earlier excitement he had felt about the new development was fading. It was not just that Xie Rong's having moved to Guangzhou—without leaving an address—added to the difficulty of the investigation. It was the talk with the retired professor that had left him depressed.

China was changing rapidly, but with honest intellectuals now viewed as "the poorest and dumbest," the situation was worrisome.

Wei Hong's address was Number 60, Hetian Road, a new apartment complex. He pushed the doorbell for several seconds, but no one answered. Finally he had to bang on the door with his fist.

An elderly woman opened it and looked at him with suspicious eyes. "What's the problem?"

He immediately recognized her from the photo.

"You must be Comrade Wei Hong. My name is Chen Cao," he said, producing his I.D., "from the Shanghai Police Bureau."

"Old Hua, there is a police officer here." Wei turned round, speaking loudly into the room before she nodded to him. "Come on in then."

The room was a tightly packed efficiency. He was not so surprised to see a portable gas tank stove inside the doorway, for it was the same arrangement as he had seen in Qian Yizhi's dorm room. There was a pot boiling above the gas jet. Then he saw a white-haired old man rising from an oyster-colored leather sofa. There was a half-played game of solitaire on the low coffee table in front of him.

"So what can we do for Comrade Chief Inspector today?" the old man said, studying the card Wei had handed him.

"I'm sorry to bother you at your home, but I have to ask you a few questions."

"Us?"

"It's not about you, but about somebody you knew."

"Oh, go ahead."

"You went to the Yellow Mountains several months ago, didn't you?"

"Yes, we went there," Wei said. "My husband and I like traveling."

"Is this a picture you took in the mountains?" Chen took a Polaroid picture out of his briefcase. "Last October?"

"Yes," Wei said, her voice containing a slight note of exasperation, "I can surely recognize myself."

"Now what about the name at the back—" he turned over the picture. "Who is Zhaodi?"

"A young woman we met during the trip. She took some pictures for us."

He took out another picture of Guan making a presentation at an important Party meeting in the People's Great Hall.

"Is she the woman named Zhaodi?"

"Yes, that's her. Though she looks different, you see, in different clothes. What has she done?" Wei looked inquisitive, as he took out his notebook and pen. "At our parting in the mountains, she promised to call us. She never has."

"She's dead."

"What!"

The astonishment on the old woman's face was genuine.

"And her name's Guan Hongying."

"Really!" Hua cut in. "The national model worker?"

"But that Xiansheng of hers," Wei said, "he called her Zhaodi too."

"What!" It was Chen's turn to be astonished. "Xiansheng"—a term rediscovered in China's nineties—was ambiguous in its meaning, referring to husband, lover, or friend. Whatever it might have meant in Guan's case, she'd had a companion traveling with her in the mountains. "Do you mean her boyfriend or husband?"

"We don't know," Wei said.

"They traveled together," Hua added, "and shared their hotel room."

"So they registered as a couple?"

"I think so, otherwise they could not have had the same room."

"Did she introduce the man to you as her husband?"

"Well, she just said something like 'This is my mister.' People do not make formal introductions in the mountains."

"Did you notice anything suspicious in their relationship?"

"What do you mean?"

"She was not married."

"Sorry, we didn't notice anything," Wei said. "We are not in the habit of spying on others."

"Come on, Wei," Hua intervened. "The chief inspector is just doing his job."

"Thank you," he said. "Do you know that man's name?"

"We were not formally introduced to one another, but I think she called him Little Tiger. It could be his nickname."

"What was he like?"

"Tall, well-dressed. He had a fine foreign camera, too."

"He did not speak much, but he was polite to us."

"Did he speak with any accent?"

"A Beijing accent."

"Can you give a detailed description of him?"

"Sorry, that's about all we can—" Wei stopped suddenly, "The gas—"

"What?"

"The gas is running out."

"The gas tank," Hua said. "We're too old to replace it."

"Our only son was criticized as a counter revolutionary during the Cultural Revolution, and sentenced to a labor camp in Qinghai," Wei said. "Nowadays he's rehabilitated, but he chose to stay there with his own family."

"I'm so sorry. My father was also put into jail during those years. It's a nationwide disaster," Chen said, wondering if he was in any position to apologize for the Party, but he understood the old couple's antagonism. "By the way, where is the gas tank station?"

"Two blocks away."

"Do you have a cart?"

"Yes, we have one. But why?"

"Let me go there to fetch a new gas tank for you."

"No, thank you. Our nephew will come over tomorrow. You are here to question us, Comrade Chief Inspector."

"But I can be of some service, too. There's no bureau rule against it."

"All the same, no," Wei said. "Thank you."

"Anything else you want to ask?" Hua added.

"No, if that's all you can remember, our interview is finished. Thank you for all your information."

"Sorry, we have not helped you much. If there are some questions—"

"I'll contact you again," he said.

Out on the street, Chief Inspector Chen's mind was full of the man in Guan's company in the mountains.

The man spoke with a clear Beijing accent.

So did the man with an unmistakable Beijing accent in Uncle Bao's description.

The man was tall, polite, well dressed.

Could it also be the same tall gentleman that Guan's neighbor had seen in the dorm corridor?

The man had an expensive camera in the mountains.

There were many high-quality pictures in Guan's album.

Chief Inspector Chen could not wait any longer. Instead of going back to his office, he turned in the direction of the Shanghai Telephone Bureau. Luckily, he had carried in his briefcase stationery with an official letterhead. It took him no time to pen an introduction on it.

"Nice to meet you, Comrade Chief inspector," a clerk in his fifties said. "My name is Jia. Just call me Old Jia."

"I hope that's enough," he said, showing his I.D. and the letter of introduction.

"Yes, quite enough." Jia was cooperative, keying in the numbers on a computer immediately.

"The owner's name is—Wu Bing."

"Wu Bing?"

"Yes, the numbers starting with 867 belong to the Jin'an district, and—"The clerk started fidgeting. "It's the high-ranking cadre residential area, you know."

"Oh, *Wu Bing*. Now I see."

Wu Bing, the Shanghai Minister of Propaganda, had been in the hospital for most of the last few years. Wu Bing was out of the question, but somebody in his family. . . . Chen thanked Jia and left in a hurry.

To find information about Wu's family was not difficult. A special folder was kept for every high cadre, along with his family, in the Shanghai Archive Bureau where Chen happened to have a special connection. Comrade Song Longxiang was a friend he had made in his first year in the police force. Chen dialed Song's number from a street corner phone booth. Song did not even ask why Chen wanted the information.

Wu Bing had a son whose name was Wu Xiaoming.

Wu Xiaoming, a name Chen had already run across in the investigation.

It was in a list Detective Yu had compiled of the people he had interviewed or contacted for possible information. Wu Xiaoming was a photographer for *Red Star* magazine; he had taken some pictures of Guan for the *People's Daily*.

"Do you have a picture of Wu Xiaoming?"

"Yes, I do."

"Can you fax one to my office? I'll be there in half an hour, waiting by the fax machine."

"Sure. You don't need a cover letter, do you? Just a picture."

"Yes, I'll call you as soon as I get it."

"Fine."

Chen decided to take a taxi.

He soon had a faxed copy of Wu Xiaoming's picture. It might have been taken a few years ago. But clearly Wu Xiaoming was a tall man.

It was urgent for Chief Inspector Chen to move forward.

He did two more things that late afternoon. He made a phone call to the *Red Star* editorial office. A secretary said that Wu was not in.

"We're compiling a dictionary of contemporary artists, including young photographers," Chen said. "Any information about Comrade Wu Xiaoming's work would be helpful."

The tactic worked. A list of Wu Xiaoming's publications was faxed to him in less than one hour.

And Chen went to visit the old couple again. The second visit turned out to be less difficult than the chief inspector had expected.

"That's him," Wei said, pointing at the fax copy in Chen's hand, "a nice young man, always with a camera in his hand."

"I'm not sure if he's nice or not," Hua said, "but he was good to her in the mountains."

"I've got another picture," Chen said, taking out Xie Rong's picture. "She was your guide in the mountains, wasn't she?"

"Yes, actually—" Wei said with an inscrutable smile, "she may be able to tell you more about them, much more."

"How?"

"Guan had a big fight with Xie in the mountains. You know what, Guan called Xie a whore."

Chapter 16

Sunday morning, Chief Inspector Chen took more time than usual brushing his teeth, but it was a futile attempt to get rid of the bitter taste in his mouth.

He did not like the development of the investigation. Nor his plan for the day: to do a day's research in the Shanghai Library.

It was evident that Guan Hongying had had an affair with Wu Xiaoming. Though a national model worker, Guan had led a double life under a different name in the mountains. So had Wu. This was far from proving, however, that her death came about as a result of the clandestine affair.

Whatever complications might be involved, Chen was determined to solve the case. He could not be a chief inspector without taking up the challenge. So he planned to learn more about Wu Xiaoming by examining his work. The approach could be misleading; according to T. S. Eliot's "impersonal theory," Chen recollected, what could be learned from a creative artist's work was nothing but his craftsmanship. Nonetheless, he would give it a shot.

In the reading room of the Shanghai Library, Chen soon found that there was a lot more for him to do. The list he had received the previous day included only the work published in the *Red Star* magazine; as for Wu's publications elsewhere, the list gave only the total number with abbreviated magazine names minus dates. As most of the magazines had no year-end index for photographs, Chen had to go through them issue by issue. The back issues were in the basement of the library, which meant a long wait before he could get what he ordered.

The librarian was a nice woman, moving about briskly in her high heels, but a stickler for library rules. All she could give him at one time were the issues of one particular magazine for a year. For anything more, he had to write out a new order slip and to wait for another half an hour.

He sat in the lobby, feeling idle on a supposedly busy day. Every time the librarian came out of the elevator with a bundle of books on a small cart, he would stand up expectantly. But they were other peoples' books. Waiting there, he felt disturbed, distantly . . .

How long ago it was—the fragments of the time still book-marked—another summer, another library, another sense of waiting with expectations, different expectations, and the pigeons' whistles fading in the high, clear Beijing sky. . . . He closed his eyes, trying not to conjure up the past.

Chief Inspector Chen had to pull himself back to the work of the present.

At eleven thirty, he concluded that he had accomplished little for a morning; he packed up all his notes and went out for lunch. The Shanghai Library was located on the corner of Nanjing Road and Huangpi Road. There were a number of fancy restaurants in the neighborhood. He walked to the north gate of the People's Park, where there was a young vendor selling hot dogs and sandwiches from a cart on the sidewalk sporting a

Budweiser umbrella, an imported coffee maker, and a radio playing loud rock-and-roll music. The chicken sandwich he bought was not cheap. He washed it down with a paper cup of reheated, lukewarm coffee, not at all like what he had enjoyed with Wang at the River Café.

When he returned to the library, he phoned Wang at *Wenhui*. He could hear a couple of phones ringing at the same time in the background as he chatted a little about her heavy responsibility on Sunday as a *Wenhui* reporter before he switched topics.

"Wang, I have to ask a favor of you."

"People never go to a Buddhist temple without asking for help."

"They do not grab Buddha's legs unless in desperation," he said, knowing she enjoyed his repartee. A cliché for a cliché.

"Grab or pull Buddha's legs?" She giggled.

He explained the problem he had with his library research.

"With your connections, maybe you can help. Of course, only as long as you are not too busy at the moment."

"I'll look into it," she said. "I'm busy, but not that busy."

"Not too busy for me, I know."

"When do you need it?"

"Well . . . as soon as possible."

"I'll call you."

"I'm in the library. Beep me."

He resumed his reading. For the next twenty minutes, however, he did not come across a single issue containing Wu's work, and he had to wait again. So he started reading something else. A collection of Bian Zilin's poems. A brilliant Chinese modernist, Bian should have enjoyed much more recognition. There was a short one entitled "Fragment" Chen especially liked—"*Looking at the scene from the window above, / You become somebody else's scene. / The moon decorating your window, / you decorate somebody's dream.*" He had first read it in the Beijing Library, together with a friend. Supposedly it was a love poem, but it could mean much more: the relativity of the things in the world.

Suddenly his beeper sounded. Several other readers stared at him. He hurried out into the corridor to return the call. "Have you got something for me already, Wang?"

"Yes, I contacted the Association of Photographers. As a member, Wu Xiaoming has to fill in a report every time he publishes something."

"I should have thought of that," he said. "You're so clever."

"Too bad I'm not a detective," she said, "like that cute little girl in the French movie. What's her name—Mimi or something? Now, how can I give the list to you?"

"I can come to your office," he said.

"You don't have to do that. I'm on my way to a separator factory in the Yangpu District. I'll change to Bus Number Sixty-one on Beijing Road. If the traffic's not too bad, I'll be there in about forty-five minutes. Just meet me at the bus stop."

"How far is the factory from there?'

"Another fifty minutes, I think."

"Well, see you at the bus stop."

Chen then dialed the bureau's car service—a privilege he was going to enjoy for the first time in the investigation.

It was Little Zhou who answered the call. "Comrade Chief Inspector Chen," Little Zhou said, "you have hardly used our service at all. If everybody were like you, we'd all be out of a job."

Little Zhou, a former colleague of Overseas Chinese Lu, had applied for a position in the bureau at the beginning of the year. Chief Inspector Chen had put in a word for his friend's friend. That was not the reason, however, Chen hesitated to use the bureau car. All the bureau cars were used—theoretically—only for the official business of high cadres. As a chief inspector, Chen was entitled to a car. With the snarl of traffic everywhere, and buses moving at almost a snail's pace, it could be a necessary privilege. He was aware, however, that people were complaining about high cadres using the cars for all kinds of private purposes. But for once, Chen felt justified in requesting a car.

"You're so busy, I know. I hate to bother your people."

"Don't mention it, Chief Inspector Chen. I'll make sure you have the most luxurious car today."

Sure enough, it was a Mercedes 550 that arrived at the entrance of the library.

"Superintendent Zhao is attending a meeting in Beijing," Little Zhou said, opening the door. "So why not?"

As the car pulled up at the bus stop on Beijing Road, he saw a surprised smile on Wang's face. She moved out of the line of passengers waiting there, some squatting on their heels, some eying her with undisguised envy.

"Come on in," he said, reaching out of the window. "We'll drive you there."

"So you're really somebody nowadays." She stepped in, stretching her long legs out comfortably in the spacious car. "A Mercedes at your disposal."

"You don't have to say that to me." He turned around to Little Zhou, "Comrade Wang Feng is a reporter for the *Wenhui* newspaper. She has just compiled an important list for us. So let's give her a ride."

"Of course, we should help each other."

"You're going out of your way," she said.

"No, you're going out of your way for us," he said, taking the list from her. "There are—let's see—four pages in the list. All typed so neatly."

"The fax is not that clear, with all the magazine names in abbreviation, and things added here and there in pen or pencil. So I had to type them out for you."

"It must have taken you a lot of time."

"To tell you the truth, I have not had my lunch yet."

"Really! I, too, have had only a sandwich for the day."

"You should learn to take care of yourself, Comrade Chief Inspector."

"That's right, Comrade Wang," Little Zhou cut in, turning over his shoulder with a broad grin. "Our chief inspector is a maniac for work. He definitely needs somebody to take good care of him."

"Well," he said smiling, "there's a small noodle restaurant around the corner at Xizhuang Road. Small Family, I think that's the name. The noodles there are okay, and the place is not too noisy. We may discuss the list over there."

"It's fine with me."

"Little Zhou, you can join us."

"No, thank you," Little Zhou said, shaking his head vigorously, "I've just had my lunch. I'll wait for you outside—taking a good nap in the car. We had a mahjongg game until three this morning. So enjoy yourselves."

The noodle restaurant had changed. He remembered it as a homely place with only four or five tables. Now it appeared more traditionally fashionable. The walls were paneled with oak, against which hung long silk scrolls of classical Chinese painting and calligraphy. There was also an oblong mahogany service counter embellished with a huge brass tea urn and an impressive array of purple sand teapots and cups.

A young, fine-featured waitress appeared immediately, slender and light-footed, in a shining scarlet silk Qi skirt with its long slits revealing her olive-colored thighs. She led the way to a table in the corner.

He ordered chicken noodles with plenty of chopped green onion. She decided on a side dish of fried eel with plain noodles. She also had a bottle of Lao Mountain spring water. She slipped her blazer from her shoulders, put it on the chair back, and unbuttoned the collar button of her silk blouse.

There was no ring on her left hand, he observed.

"Thank you so much," he said.

He did not open the list in his hand. Enough time for him to read it in the library. Instead, he put it down and patted her hand across the table.

"You know who Wu Xiaoming is," she said, without taking back her hand.

"Yes, I do."

"And you're still going on with the investigation."

"I'm a cop, aren't I?"

"An impossibly romantic cop who believes in justice," she said. "You cannot be too careful with this case."

"I'll be careful," he said. "You're concerned for me, I know."

Her eyes met his, not denying his message.

At that hour, they were the only customers, sitting in the corner as if enclosed in a capsule of privacy.

"They should have put candles on the table," she said, "to match your mood."

"What about dinner at my place tomorrow night?" he said. "I'll have candles."

"A dinner to celebrate your enrollment in the seminar?"

"No, that's in October."

"Well—a lot of people may wonder what our chief inspector is doing—over a candlelit dinner."

She was right, he admitted to himself. An affair with her was not in his best interest at the moment.

"What's the point of being a chief inspector," he said, "if I cannot have a candlelit dinner with a friend?"

"But you have a most promising career, Comrade Chief Inspector. Not everybody has your opportunity."

"I'll try to be discreet."

"Coming to a restaurant in a bureau Mercedes," she said, "is not the best way of exercising discretion, I'm afraid."

The arrival of the noodles forestalled any reply he was going to make.

The noodles were as good as he had remembered. The green onion in the soup smelled wonderful. She liked it too, wiping the sweat from her brow with a pink paper napkin.

Afterward, he bought a pack of Kents at the counter.

"Not for me," he said to her.

He handed the cigarettes to Little Zhou.

"Thanks, but you don't have to, Comrade Chief Inspector," Little Zhou said. "By the way, Superintendent Zhao is going to retire toward the end of year. Haven't you heard?"

"No, but thanks for your information."

In the backseat, they were sitting close to each other. Feeling her nearness, he was content with a light brushing of her shoulder as the car bumped along. They did not talk much. She let him take her hand. The car passed the black dome of the new city stadium, then swung around Peace Park. Little Zhou explained why he had to make such a detour. Several streets had just been declared one-way.

It would take them much longer to get there, but Chief Inspector Chen had no cause for complaint.

But she was already telling Little Zhou to pull up. In front of them was the separator factory, about which she was going to write a report.

"Thank you," she said, "for the lift."

"Thank you," he said, "for the opportunity of giving you a lift."

When he got back to the library, it was already three thirty. He sent Little Zhou back to the bureau. He had no idea how long it would take him to work on the new list.

An impressive list it was, including most of the influential journals and newspapers, containing detailed information with dates and page numbers. In addition, it noted a number of awards Wu had won.

The late afternoon research was much more effective. Three hours of reading produced quite a revelation. Wu Xiaoming was apparently a productive photographer who had published widely, from the top magazines to the second or even the third-class ones. Wu's photographs also showed a broad range of subjects, but could be classified into two major categories.

The first was the political. With his family background, Wu had obtained access to a number of powerful people who had no objection to seeing the publication of their pictures, which could be symbolic of their stay in power, and, in turn, contribute to Wu's career.

The second consisted of what might be called the artistic, which showed remarkable professional expertise. One feature in this category was Wu's characteristic arrangement: a group of pictures with the same subject taken from different perspectives. Wu seemed to enjoy producing so-called "subject sequences."

A group of Guan's pictures in the *Xingming Evening Post*, for instance, could be seen as such a thematic sequence. These were pictures of Guan at work, at meetings, and at home. There was one of her cooking in the kitchen. Wearing an embroidered apron around her waist and scarlet slippers, Guan was frying fish, with beads of sweat visible on her brow. The kitchen apparently was somebody else's: bright, spacious, sporting a dainty half round window above the sink. The picture focused on the soft, feminine side of a national model worker, balancing the other pictures in the group.

Most of Wu Xiaoming's subjects were also well known in their respective fields. Chen particularly liked the group of Huang Xiaobai, a celebrated calligrapher. The pictures showed Huang in the act of brush-penning the different strokes in the formation of the Chinese character *cheng*—a horizontal stroke, a dot, a slant stroke, a vertical stroke—as if each stroke represented a different phase in his life, culminating in the character meaning "truthful."

What came as a surprise was a sequence about Jiang Weihe, an emerging young artist, whom Chen had met on several occasions. In one of the photographs Jiang was working on a statue. Wearing short overalls, standing bare legged, she was absorbed in the effect. The statue portrayed a nude photographer, having nothing but a camera held in front of him, focusing at her. The title was "Creation." The composition was original.

In addition to these pictures, there were also some pieces for fashion magazines. Most of the subjects were young beautiful girls. Semi-nude or even nude photos were no longer censored in China, but still they were controversial. Chen was surprised at Wu's extraordinary journey into the field.

In a small provincial magazine called *Flower City*, Chen saw a sleeping nude on her side. Melting into the background of the white sheet and white wall was her soft body with all its soft curves. A black mole on the back of her neck was the only accent, enhancing the effect. Somehow the woman in the picture struck him as familiar, though he could not see her face. Then he remembered. Frowning, he put down the magazine.

Chen had not finished his research at the library's closing time. He borrowed the copy of *Flower City*. The librarian was gracious, offering to put all the other magazines on hold, so that Chen could resume his work without waiting the next day. He thanked her, wondering if he could afford to spend another day in the library. Besides, he found it hard to concentrate there. Something subtle in the atmosphere disturbed him. Or in his subconscious? Chief Inspector Chen did not want to analyze himself—not in the middle of the case.

It could be the first important breakthrough in the investigation, but he was not lighthearted. Wu Xiaoming's involvement was leading to something more than Chen had expected.

It meant a confrontation with Wu.

And quite possibly, with Wu as a representative of the HCC—high cadres' children.

Back in his office, he made a call to Wang. Luckily she was still there.

"Thank you so much for your help."

"Don't mention it." Wang's clear voice sounded close. "Any progress?"

"Some," he said. "Are you alone in the office?"

"Yes, I have to meet a deadline," she said. "I've also done some additional research on your suspect, but you may already know a lot about him."

"Tell me."

"In terms of his position, Wu's just a member of the staff of *Red Star* in Shanghai, but he may be far more important. As everybody knows, the magazine is the mouthpiece of the Party Central Committee, which means he has direct contact with some people at the very top. What is more, the publication of these people's pictures puts him in close relationship with them."

"That much I suspected."

"Also, there is some talk about him being promoted to a new position—acting cultural minister of Shanghai."

"What?"

"Yes. People say Wu is both 'red and expert'—young, talented, with a degree from an evening college. He is also on the list for the same seminar you're going to attend."

"Well—as an ancient saying goes," Chen said, "'foes must meet in a narrow path.' I'm not worried about that, only—"

"Only—what is the problem?" She was quick to catch him.

"Well, let me put it this way. In an investigation, one important link is motive. There must be one reason or another for people to do something, but I cannot find it."

"So without the motive, you cannot go forward in the investigation?"

"Yes, that's it," he said. "Circumstantial evidence may point to Wu, but there's no convincing theory explaining why he would act in such a way."

"Maybe we should have another cup at the Riverfront Café," she said, "to talk more about the case."

"At my place, tomorrow evening," he said. "You haven't said no to my invitation, have you?"

"Another party?"

"No, just you and me."

"With romantic candlelight?"

"If there's a power failure."

"You never know," she said, "but I'll see you."

Chapter 17

Monday morning Chief Inspector Chen had a meeting at the city hall.

On his way back to the bureau, he bought a piece of transparent rice cake from a street vendor and ate it without really tasting it.

Detective Yu was not in the large office. Chen picked up a manila envelope delivered that morning containing a cassette tape that bore the following label: *Examination of Lai Guojun held at Shanghai Police Bureau, 3:00 P.M., June 2, 1990. Examining Officer Detective Yu Guangming. Also present at examination, Sergeant Yin Wei.*

Chen popped the tape in the recorder. Detective Yu, too, had a lot to do, dealing with all the routine work of the squad, even on Sunday. The tape was probably made about the time when he and Wang talked in the noodle restaurant. The tape started with

Yu's voice making the introduction, and then came another voice marked with an unmistakable Ningbo accent. Chen began listening as he propped up his legs on the desk, but after no more than a minute, he jumped up and rewound the tape to the very beginning:

YU: You are Lai Guojun, thirty-four years old, living at Number Seventy-two Henan Street, Huangpu District, Shanghai. You are an engineer, having worked for ten years at People's Chemical Company. You are married, with a daughter of five. Is that correct?

LAI: Yes, that's correct.

YU: I want you to know that you are helping with our inquiry. We appreciate your help.

LAI: Please go ahead.

YU: We're going to ask you some questions about Guan Hongying. She was murdered last month. You have heard of that?

LAI: Yes, I've read about it in the newspaper. So I guessed your people would come to me—sooner or later.

YU: Some of the questions may involve the intimate details of your life, but nothing you say in this room will be used against you. Whatever it is, it will be confidential. I have talked to your boss, and he, too, believes that you will cooperate. He suggested that he himself be present at the interview. I told him No.

LAI: What choice do I have? He has talked to me, too. I will answer any question you have for me.

YU: You can make an important contribution to the case, so the person or persons responsible for the murder will be captured and punished.

LAI: That's what I want. I'll do my best.

YU: When did you get to know Guan?

LAI: It was about ten years ago.

Yu: The summer of 1980?

Lai: Yes, in June.

Yu: Under what circumstances did you meet each other?

Lai: We met at the apartment of my cousin, Lai Weiqing.

Yu: At a party?

Lai: No. Not exactly a party. A colleague of Weiqing's knew Guan, so they had arranged for us to meet there.

Yu: In other words, Lai Weiqing and her colleague acted as matchmakers. They introduced you to each other.

Lai: Well, you could say that. But not so formally.

Yu: How was your first meeting?

Lai: Guan sort of surprised me. With arranged introductions, you can hardly expect to meet a pretty young girl. More often than not, those you get introduced to are plain, over thirty, and without education. Guan was only twenty-two and quite attractive. A model worker, and taking college correspondence courses at the time. You know all that, I believe. I have never figured out why she consented to such an arrangement. She could have had a lot of men dancing around her.

Yu: What other impressions did you have of her that day?

Lai: A moving awkwardness. Innocent, almost naive. Obviously she was not used to such meetings.

Yu: Was it her first date?

Lai: I was not sure about it, but she had no idea how to express herself in my company. She was literally tongue-tied when we were left alone.

Yu: Then how did things work out between you?

Lai: Well, we clicked, as some people would say, without talking much to each other. We did not stay long the first time, but we did go to a movie the next week, and then had dinner in Meilong Zheng.

Yu: She was still tongue-tied the second time?

LAI: No, we talked a lot, about our families, the lost years in the Cultural Revolution, and the common interests we had. A few days later, I went to one of her presentations at the Youth Palace without her knowledge. She seemed to be a totally different person on the stage.

YU: Interesting. How different?

LAI: Well, she seldom talked about politics in my company. Once or twice, maybe, I tried to bring the topic up, but she seemed unwilling to talk about it. On the stage, she appeared so confident, speaking with genuine conviction. I was glad that she did not talk politics to me, for we soon became lovers.

YU: Lovers—in what sense?

LAI: What do you mean?

YU: Physically?

LAI: Yes.

YU: How soon?

LAI: After four or five weeks.

YU: That was quick.

LAI: It was sooner than I had expected.

YU: Was it you who took the initiative?

LAI: I see what you mean. Do I have to answer questions like that?

YU: I cannot force you, Comrade Lai. But if you do, it may help our investigation. And it may also save me another trip to your boss.

LAI: Well, it was a Friday night, I remember. We went to a dancing party in the western hall of the Shanghai Writers' Association. It was the first year when social dancing was publicly allowed in Shanghai. A friend of mine had obtained the tickets for us. While we were dancing, I noticed that she was getting excited.

YU: Excited—in which way?

LAI: It was obvious. It was in the summer. Her body was pressed against me. Her breasts—I noticed—you know, I really can't be more precise.

YU: And you? Were you also excited?

LAI: Yes.

YU: What happened afterwards?

LAI: We went back to my place with a group of friends. We talked and had some drinks.

YU: Did you drink a lot that night?

LAI: No, only a cup of Qingdao beer. In fact, I shared the cup with her. I remember that because later—later we kissed. It was our first time, and she said we smelled of each other—from the same cup.

YU: That sounds really romantic.

LAI: Yes, it was.

YU: And then?

LAI: People were leaving. She could have left with them. It was already twelve thirty, but she stayed on. It was a terrific gesture. She wanted to help me clean up, she declared.

YU: So you must have been terribly pleased with her offer?

LAI: Well, I told her to leave everything alone. It was not a night to worry about dirty dishes and leftovers.

YU: I guess you would say that.

LAI: She would not listen to me. Instead, she started hustling and bustling in the kitchen. She did everything, washing the dishes, sweeping the floor, wrapping up the leftovers, and putting them in a bamboo basket on the balcony. She said that the food wouldn't go bad that way; I did not have a refrigerator at the time.

YU: Very domestic, very considerate.

LI: Yes, that's exactly what a wife would choose to do. So I kissed her for the first time.

YU: So you stayed in the kitchen with her all the time?

LAI: Yes, I did, watching in amazement. But after she finished, we moved back into the room

YU: Go on.

LAI: Well, we were alone. She did not show any intention of leaving. So I suggested I take a few pictures of her. I had just got a new camera, a Nikon 300. My brother had bought it for me in Japan.

YU: That's a fancy one.

LAI: She was reclining on the bed, saying something about the transience of a woman's beauty. I agreed. She wanted to have some pictures that would capture her youth. After a few shots, I proposed to have a picture of her wrapped in a white towel. To my surprise, she nodded and told me just to turn around. She started taking off her clothes there and then.

YU: She undressed herself in your presence?

LAI: I did not see. I did, of course, afterward.

YU: Afterward, of course. So what happened afterward?

LAI: Well . . . I guess you don't have to ask.

YU: Yes, I have to. You'd better give us an account, as detailed as possible, of what happened between you and her that night.

LAI: Is it necessary, Comrade Detective Yu?

YU: I understand your feelings, but the details may be important to our investigation. It's a sexual murder case, you know.

LAI: Fine, if you think that can really help.

YU: Did you have sexual intercourse with her then?

LAI: She made herself really clear. It was she who gave the unmistakable signal. So that was the only natural thing for me to do. You are a man, aren't you? Why should I say any more?

YU: I understand, but I still have to press for some details.

LAI: More details. Heavens!

YU: Was it the first time for her, or for you?

LAI: Not for me, but for her.

YU: You were sure about that?

LAI: Yes, though she was not too shy.

YU: How long did she stay that night?

LAI: The whole night. Well, more than that. Early next morning, she phoned the department store, asking for sick leave. So we had practically all the next morning in the room. We made love again. We did some shopping in the afternoon. I chose for her a white wool sweater with a red azalea on the right breast.

YU: Did she accept it?

LAI: Yes, she did. And I started talking about marriage.

YU: And how did she react?

LAI: Well, she seemed unwilling to talk about it that day.

YU: You talked about it again, I believe.

LAI: I was head over heels—laugh at me if you want—so I did mention it a couple of times. She seemed to avoid the subject every time. Finally, when I tried to discuss it with her seriously, she left me.

YU: Why?

LAI: I did not know. I was confounded. And terribly hurt, you can imagine.

YU: Did you quarrel with her?

LAI: No. I didn't.

YU: So it was all of a sudden? That's really something. Did you notice any sign of it before she said anything about it?

LAI: No, it happened three or four weeks after that night— that night we slept together. Actually, she had come to my place a number of times during the period. Eleven in all, including the first night. I can tell you how I remember. Every time we stayed together, I drew a star above the date on my calendar. We never quarreled. Then, out of the blue, she dumped me—for no reason at all.

YU: That's strange indeed. Did you ask her for an explanation?

LAI: Yes, but she would not say anything about it. She kept saying that it was her fault, and she was really sorry.

YU: Normally, when a young girl, especially a virgin, has slept with you, she will surely insist on your marrying her. To make a chaste woman of her, so to speak. But she didn't, saying it was her fault. What fault?

LAI: I did not know. I demanded an explanation, but she would not give any details.

YU: Could there be another man involved?

Lai: No, I did not think so. She was not that kind of woman. In fact, I inquired about it through my cousin, and she said not. Guan simply left without giving a reason. I tried to find out, and at first I even thought that she might be a nymphomaniac.

YU: Why? Was there anything abnormal about her sexual behavior?

LAI: No. She was just a bit—uninhibited. She wept and cried the first time she came. In fact, after that she came every time, biting and screaming, and I believed that she was satisfied. But now she's dead, I really should not say anything against her.

YU: It must have been hard for you when you broke up?

LAI: Yes, I was devastated. But I gradually came to terms with it. It was a losing game for me anyway. She was not the type of woman I could afford to make happy in the long run. Failing that, I myself would not be happy. But she was a wonderful woman in her way.

YU: Did she say anything else at your parting?

LAI: No, she kept saying that it was her fault, and she

actually offered to stay that night with me if I wanted. I said No.

Yu: Why? I'm just curious.

Lai: If her heart's going to leave you forever, what's the point of having her body for one more night?

Yu: I see, and I'd say that you're right. Have you tried to contact her again since then?

Lai: No, not after we parted.

Yu: Any form of contact—letters, postcards, phone calls?

Lai: It was she who dumped me. So why should I? Besides, she became more and more of a national celebrity, with big pictures in all the newspapers, so I couldn't avoid her national model worker image.

Yu: Male pride and ego, I understand. It has been a difficult subject for you, Comrade Lai, but you have been most helpful. Thank you.

Lai: You will keep it confidential, won't you? I am married now. I've never told my wife anything about it.

Yu: Of course. I said so in the beginning.

Lai: When I think of the affair, I am still confused. I hope you will catch the criminal. I don't think I will ever forget her.

There was a long silence. Apparently the conversation came to an end. Then he heard Yu's voice again:

Comrade Chief Inspector Chen, I found Engineer Lai Goujun through Huang Weizhong, the retired Party Secretary of the First Department Store. According to Huang, Guan had made a report to the Party committee when they first started dating. The Party committee had looked into Lai's family background and discovered that Lai had an uncle who had been executed as a counterrevolutionary during the Land Reform movement. So the Party committee wanted her to end the affair. It was politically incorrect for her, an emerging model worker and Party member, to get involved with a man of such a family background. She agreed, but she did not make a report to Huang about her parting with Lai until two months later, and she did not give any details about it.

I'm collecting more information about Lai, but I don't think he is a suspect. It was so many years ago, after all. Sorry I cannot stay in the office this morning; Qinqin is sick. I have to take him to the hospital, but I'll be home after two or two thirty. Call me if there's anything you need.

Chen punched the off button. He slumped back in his seat, wiping the sweat from his forehead. It was getting hot again. He took a cola out of the little refrigerator, tapped on the top, but put it back. There was a small fly buzzing in the room. He poured himself a cup of cold water instead.

That was not what he had expected.

Chief Inspector Chen had never believed in such a mythical embodiment of the Communist Party selfless spirit as Comrade Lei Feng. A sudden wave of sadness washed over the chief inspector. It was absurd, Chen thought, that politics could have so shaped a life. If she had married Lai, Guan would not have been so successful in her political life. She would not have been a national model worker, but an ordinary wife—knitting a sweater for her husband, pulling a propane gas tank on her bike rack, bargaining for a penny or two when she bought food in the market, nagging like a broken gramophone, playing with a lovely child sitting on her lap—but she would have been alive.

If Guan's decision appeared absurd in the early nineties, it would have been most understandable in the early eighties. At that time, someone like Lai who had a counterrevolutionary relative was out of the question. Lai would have brought trouble to the people close to him. Chen thought of his own "uncle," a distant relative he had never seen, but it was that uncle who had determined his profession.

So it could be said that the decision of the First Department Store Party committee, however hard, was made in her interest. As a national model worker, Guan had had to live up to her status. That the Party should have interfered in her private life was by no means surprising, but her reaction was astonishing. She gave herself to Lai, then parted with him without having revealed the true reason. Her act was intolerably "liberal" according to the codes of the Party. But Chen thought he could understand. Guan had been a more complicated human than he had supposed. All that had happened, however, ten years earlier. Could it have anything to do with Guan's recent life?

It might have been a traumatic experience for her, which would explain why she'd had no lover for years until she crossed Wu Xiaoming's path.

Also, Guan had been one who dared to act—despite the shadow of politics.

Or was there something else?

Chen dialed Yu's home.

"Qinqin is much better," Yu said. "I'll come back to the office soon."

"You don't have to. Nothing particular is going on here. Take good care of your son at home." He added, "I've got your tape. A great job."

"I've checked Lai's alibi. On the night of the murder, he was in Nanning with a group of engineers at a conference."

"Has Lai's company confirmed that?"

"Yes. I've also talked to a colleague of his who shared the hotel room for the night. According to that colleague, Lai was there all the time. So his alibi is solid."

"Did Lai contact Guan in the last half year—via phone calls or whatever?"

"No, he said not. In fact, Lai's just got back from America. He's worked at a university lab there for a whole year." Yu added, "I don't think we can get anywhere in that direction."

"I think you are right," he said. "It's been so many years. If Lai had wanted to do anything, he would not have waited for such a long time."

"Yes, Lai nowadays works with American universities once or twice a year, earning a lot of U.S. dollars, enjoying a reputation in his field, living happily with his family. In today's market society, Guan, rather than Lai, should have been the one who rued what happened ten years ago."

"And in our society, Lai can be seen as the one who got the advantage from the affair—a gainer rather than a loser. In retrospect, Lai might not be too unhappy about his long-ago affair."

"Exactly. There was something surprising about Guan."

"Yes, what a shame!"

"What do you mean?"

"Well, it was politics for her then, and politics for us now."

"Oh, you're right, boss."

"Call me if you find anything new about Lai."

Chen then decided to make a routine report to Commissar Zhang, whom he had not briefed of late.

Commissar Zhang was reading a movie magazine when Chen entered his office.

"What wind has brought you in here today, Comrade Chief Inspector Chen?" Zhang put down the magazine.

"A sick wind, I'm afraid."

"What wind?"

"Detective Yu's son is sick, so he has to take him to the hospital."

"Oh, that. So Yu cannot come to the office today."

"Well, Yu has been working hard."

"Any new leads?"

"Guan had a boyfriend nine or ten years ago, but, following the Party's instruction, she parted with him. Yu has talked to retired Party Secretary Huang of the First Department Store, who was her boss then, and also to Engineer Lai, her ex-boyfriend."

"That's no news. I have also talked to that retired Party Secretary. He told me the story. She did the right thing."

"Do you know she—" he cut himself short, not sure what Zhang's reaction to Lai's version might be. "She was very upset when she had to part with him."

"That's understandable. She was young, and perhaps a little romantic at the time, but she did the right thing by following the Party's decision."

"But it could have been traumatic to her."

"Another of your Western modernist terms?" Zhang said irritably. "Remember, as a Party member, she had to live for the interests of the Party."

"No, I was just trying to see its impact on Guan's personal life."

"So Detective Yu is still working on this angle?"

"No, Detective Yu doesn't think Mr. Lai is involved with the case. It was such a long time ago."

"That's what I thought."

"You're right, Commissar Zhang," he said, wondering why Zhang had not shared this information with him earlier. Was Zhang so anxious to maintain the communist puritan image of Guan?

"I don't think that's the right direction. Nor is your theory involving caviar," Zhang concluded. "It's a political case, as I have said a number of times."

"Everything can be seen in terms of politics," Chen got up, pausing in the doorway, "but politics is not everything."

Such talk was possible now, though hardly regarded as in good taste politically. There had been opposition to Chen's attaining promotion—something expressed by his political enemies when they praised him as "open," and by his political friends when they wondered if he was too open.

Chapter 18

As soon as Chief Inspector Chen got back in his own office, the phone started ringing.

It was Overseas Chinese Lu. Once more Lu declared that he had successfully started his own business—Moscow Suburb, a Russian-style restaurant on Huaihai Road, with caviar, potage, and vodka on the menu, and a couple of Russian waitresses walking around in scanty dresses. Lu sounded complacent and confident on the phone. It was beyond Chen to comprehend how Lu could have done so much at such short notice.

"So business is not bad?"

"It's booming, buddy. People come swarming in all day to look at our menu, at our vodka cabinet, and at our tall, buxom Russian girls in their see-through blouses and skirts."

"You really have an eye for business."

"Well, as Confucius said thousands of years ago, 'Beauty makes you hungry.'"

"No. 'She is so beautiful that you could devour her,'" Chen said. "That's what Confucius said. How were you able to dig up these Russian girls?"

"They just came to me. A friend of mine runs a network of international applicants. Nice girls. They earn four or five times more than at home. Nowadays China is doing much better than Russia."

"That is true." Chen was impressed by the pride in Lu's voice.

"Remember the days when we used to call the Russians our Big Brothers? The wheel of fortune has turned. Now I call them my Little Sisters. In a way they really are. They depend on me for everything. For one thing, they've got nowhere to stay, and the hotels are way too expensive. I've bought several folding beds, so they can sleep in back of the restaurant and save a lot of money. For their convenience, I've also put in a hot water shower."

"So you are taking good care of them."

"Exactly. And I'll let you into a secret, buddy. They have hairs on their legs, these Russian girls. Don't fall for their smooth and shining appearance. A week without razor and soap, those terrific legs could be really hairy."

"You are being Eliotic, Overseas Chinese Lu."

"What do you mean?"

"Oh, nothing, it just reminds me of something by T. S. Eliot."

Something about bare, white, braceleted legs which suddenly appear in the light to be downy.

Or was it by John Donne?

"Eliot or not, that's none of my business. But it's true. I saw it with my own eyes—a bathtub full of golden and brown hair."

"You're kidding."

"Come and see for yourself. Not just the legs, the business, of course. This weekend, okay? I'll assign you one of the blondes. The sexiest. Special service. So special that you want to devour her, too. Confucius' satisfaction guaranteed."

"That will be too much for my wallet, I'm afraid."

"What do you mean? You're my greatest friend, and part of my success, too. All on me, of course."

"I will come," Chen said, "if I can spare one evening next week."

Chief Inspector Chen wondered if he would go there even if

he could spare the time. He had read a report about the so-called special service in some notorious restaurants.

He looked at his watch. Three thirty. There would probably be nothing left in the bureau canteen. The conversation with Overseas Chinese Lu had made him feel hungry.

Then he thought of something he had almost forgotten. Dinner with Wang Feng. In his apartment.

Suddenly everything else could wait until tomorrow. The thought of having her over for a candlelit dinner was making his pulse race. He left the bureau in a hurry, heading for a food market on Ninghai Road, which was about fifteen minutes' walk from his apartment.

As always, the market presented a scene of crowds milling about with bamboo baskets on their arms, plastic bags in their hands. He had consumed his ration of pork and eggs for the month. He hoped he could get some fish and vegetables. Wang liked seafood. A long line stretched back from a fish stall. Aside from the people standing there, there was also a collection of baskets, broken cardboard boxes, stools, and even bricks—all of them placed before or after the people in line. At every slow forward step, the people would move these objects a step farther. Placing an object in line was symbolic, he realized, of the owner's presence. When a basket drew near to the stall, the owner would assume his or her position. Consequently, a line of fifteen people might really mean fifty people were ahead of him. At the speed the line was moving, he judged, it would probably take him more than an hour to be waited on.

So he decided to try his luck at the free market, which was just one block beyond the state-run Ninghai food market. The free market remained nameless in the early nineties, but its existence was known to everybody. The service there was better; so was the quality. The only difference was the price, usually two or three times more than the Ninghai.

A peaceful coexistence: the state-run and the private-run markets. Socialism and capitalism, side by side. Some veteran Party cadres were worried about the inevitable clashing of the two systems, but the people in the market were not, Chen observed, as he came to a stop at the colorful display of green onions and ginger under a Hangzhou umbrella. He picked up a handful of fresh green onions. The peddler added a small piece of ginger without charging for it.

Chen spent some time choosing what else he thought necessary for the dinner. Thanks to the advance from the Lijiang publishing house, he could well afford to buy two pounds of lamb, a pile of oysters, and a small bag of spinach. Then, on an impulse, he left the market for the new jewelry store at Longmen Road.

The shop assistant came up to him with a surprised expression. He was an unlikely customer, Chen realized, a cop in his uniform, with a plastic bag of food in his hand. But he turned out to be a good customer. He did not spend much time choosing among the dazzling items on display. He was immediately attracted by a choker of pearls placed on silver satin in a purple velvet box. The jewelry cost him more than eight hundred Yuan, but it would suit Wang well, he thought. Ruth Rendell would probably be pleased, too, with the way he spent the money earned by his translation of her work. Besides, he had to give himself some additional motivation to complete his next translation, *Speaker of Mandarin*.

Back in his apartment, he realized for the first time—to his astonishment—how unpresentable a bachelor's room could be. Bowls and dishes in the sink, a pair of jeans on the floor beside the sofa, books everywhere, gray streaks on the windowsills. Even the brick-and-board bookcase flanking the desk struck him as unsightly. He threw himself into the task of cleaning up.

It was the first time she had accepted his invitation to dine with him—alone, at his place. Since the night of the house-

warming party, there had been some real progress in their relationship. In the course of the investigation, he seemed to have
been finding more and more things about her, too. She was not
only attractive and vivacious, but intelligent—intuitively percep-
tive, even more so than Chen himself.

But it was more than that. In the course of this investigation,
he had raised more questions about his own life. It was time for
him to make up his mind—as Guan should have made up her
mind, years earlier.

Wang arrived a few minutes before six o'clock. She was wearing a white silk blazer over a simple black dress with two narrow
shoulder straps that looked more like a slip. He helped her take
off the blazer; her shoulders were dazzlingly white under the fluorescent light.

She brought a bottle of white wine with her. A perfect gift for
the occasion. He had a set of glasses in the cabinet.

"What a spick-and-span room for a busy chief inspector!"

"I had the right motive. It's rewarding to keep the place neat,"
he said, "when a friend is coming over."

The table was set with a white tablecloth, folded pink napkins,
mahogany chopsticks, and long-handled silver spoons. The dinner was simple. A small pot of water boiling over a portable gas
burner. Around it, paper thin sliced lamb, a bowl of green
spinach, and a dozen oysters were laid out on a platter decked
with lemon wedges. There were also vinegar-marinated cucum-
ber and pickled garlic in little side dishes. Each of them had a
small dish of sauce.

They dipped the slices of lamb into the boiling water, took
them out after just a second or two, and dipped them into the
sauce, a special recipe he had learned from Overseas Chinese Lu,
a mixture of soy sauce, sesame butter, fermented bean curd, and
ground pepper strewn with a pinch of parsley. The lamb, still
pinkish, was tender and delicious.

He opened her bottle of wine. They touched glasses before sipping the sparkling white wine under the soft light.

"To you," he said.

"To us."

"For what?" he asked, turning the lamb over in the sauce.

"For tonight."

She was peeling an oyster with a small knife. Her fingers, small, delicate, maneuvered the knife and cut loose the hinge muscle. She lifted the oyster to her mouth. A wisp of green seaweed still clung to its shell. He saw the glistening inside of the shell, its matchless whiteness against her lips.

"That's good," she sighed with satisfaction, putting down the shell.

He gazed at her over the rim of his cup, thinking of the way her lips touched the oyster, and then the cup. She sipped at her wine, dabbed at her mouth with the paper napkin, and picked up another oyster. To his surprise, she dipped it in the sauce, leaned across and offered to him. The gesture was terribly intimate.. Almost that of a newly married wife. He let her insert the chopsticks into his mouth. The oyster immediately melted on his tongue. A strange, satisfying sensation.

That was a new experience to him, being alone with a woman he liked, in a room he called his own. They spoke, but he didn't feel that he had to make conversation. Nor did she. They could afford to gaze at each other without speaking.

It had started drizzling, but the city at night also seemed more intimate, peaceful, its veil of lights glistening into the infinite.

After dinner, she murmured that she wanted to help him clean up.

"I really enjoy washing dishes after a good meal."

"No, you don't have to do anything."

But she had already stood up, kicked off her sandals, and taken over his apron that hung on the doorknob. It was pleasant to see her breezing around effortlessly, as if she had been living here for years. She appeared intensely domestic with the white apron tied tight around her slender waist.

"You are my guest today," he insisted.

"I can't just watch you doing everything in the kitchen."

It was not really a kitchen, but a narrow strip of space with the gas burner and the sink squeezed together, barely large enough for the two to move around in. They stood close to each other, their shoulders touching. He pushed open the small window above the sink. His feeling of well-being—in addition to the effects of the good food and wine—came from a sense of being, not just in a scantily furnished apartment, but at home.

"Oh, let's just leave everything here," he said, untying the apron. "That's good enough."

"Soon you will have roaches crawling all about in your new apartment," she warned him with a smile.

"I already have." He led her back into the living room. "Let's have another drink—a nightcap."

"Whatever you say."

When he came back with glasses, she was rocking back and forth in the rattan chair near the couch. As she sank deep into the chair, her short dress revealed a glimpse of her thighs.

He leaned against the cabinet, his hand touching the top drawer, which contained the choker of pearls.

She seemed to be absorbed in the changing color of the wine in her hand.

"Would you mind sitting by me for one minute?"

"Easier to look at you this way," he said, smelling the intoxicating scent from her hair.

He remained standing with his glass of wine. A "nightcap." To translate it into Chinese was difficult. He had learned its romantic connotation in an American movie, in which a couple sipped the last cup of wine before going to bed. He was intoxicated with the atmosphere of intimacy that had sprung up between them.

"Oh, you've forgotten candlelight," she said, sipping at the wine.

"Yes, I could use it now," he said, "and *Bolero* on a CD player, too, would be great."

That was also in the movie. The lovers, while making love, put on their favorite record: the rhythm of ever-approaching climax.

She held a slender finger against her cheek, scrutinizing him intently, as if for the first time. She reached up, taking the elastic band from her ponytail, and shook the black hair loose. It tumbled freely down her back. She looked relaxed, comfortable, at home.

Then he kneeled down on the floor at her feet.

"What's that?"

"What?"

His finger touched her bare foot. There was a sauce stain on her small toe. He rubbed it off with his fingers.

Her hand slid down and grasped his. He glanced at her hand, at her ring finger. There was a lighter band of flesh below the joint where she'd once worn a wedding band.

They remained like that, holding hands.

Gazing at her flushed face, he felt he was looking into an open, inviting book. Or was he reading too much?

"Everything's so wonderful tonight," she said. "Thank you."

"The best is yet to be," he said, echoing a half-forgotten poem.

He had been waiting for this moment a long time.

The soft light silhouetted her curves against the sheer fabric of her dress. She looked like another woman, mature, feminine, and seductive.

How many different women could there be inside her, he wondered.

She rocked back, away from him, and touched his cheek with the palm of her hand. Her palm was light as cloud.

"Is your mind on the case again?"

"No. Not at this moment."

It was a true answer, but he wondered why he had been so occupied with the case. Was it because of the raw human emotions involved? Perhaps his own personal life was so prosaic that he needed to share the passion of others. Or perhaps he had been yearning for a dramatic change in his own life.

"I have to ask you a favor," she said.

"Anything," he said.

"I don't want you to misunderstand." She took a deep breath, then paused for a moment. "There's something between us, isn't there?"

"What do you think?"

"I knew it when we first met."

"So did I."

"I had been engaged to Yang, you know, before I met you, but you have never asked me about it."

"Nor have you ever asked about me, have you?" he said, gripping her palm. "It's not that important."

"But you have a promising career," she said, with the emotion visibly washing over her fine features. "That is so important to you, and to me, too."

"Promising career—I don't know—" Those words sounded like a prelude, he could tell. "But why start talking about my career now?"

"I've had all the words ready to say, but it's harder than I thought. With you here, being so nice to me, it's more difficult . . . a lot more difficult."

"Just tell me, Wang."

"Well, I went to the Shanghai Foreign Language Institute this afternoon, and the school demands compensation for what they have done for him, for Yang, you know—compensation for his education, salary, and medical benefits during his college years. Or I won't be able to get the document for my passport. It's a large sum, twenty thousand Yuan. I wonder whether you could say something to the passport department of your bureau. So I could get one without the document from the Foreign Language Institute."

"You want to get a passport—to go to Japan?"

That was not at all what he had expected.

"Yes, I've been applying for it for several weeks."

To leave China, she needed a passport. So she had to present an authorized application with her work unit's approval. And her marriage to Yang, even though only a nominal one, necessitated some document from Yang's work unit, too.

It might be difficult, but not impossible. Passports had been issued without work unit authorization before. Chief Inspector Chen was in a position to help.

"So you are going to him." He stood.

"Yes."

"Why?"

"He has obtained all the necessary documents for me to join him. Even a job for me at a Chinese TV station in Tokyo. A small station, nothing like here, but still something in my line. There's not much between him and me, but it's an opportunity I cannot afford to miss."

"But you also have a promising career here."

"A promising career here—" Wang said, a bitter smile upon her lips, "in which I have to pile lies upon lies."

It was true, depending on how one chose to perceive a reporter's job in China. As a reporter for the Party's newspaper, she would have to report in the Party's interest. First and foremost, the Party's interest. She was paid to do that. No question about it.

"Still, things are improving here," Chen said, feeling obliged to say something.

"At this slow pace, in twenty years, I might be able to write what I want to, and I will be old and gray."

"No, I don't think so." He wanted to say that she would never be old and gray, not in his eyes, but he chose not to.

"You're different, Chen," she said. "You really can do something here."

"Thank you for telling me this."

"A candidate for the seminar of the Central Party Institute, you can go a long way in China, and I don't think I can be of any help to you here." She added after a pause. "For your career, I mean. And even worse—"

"The bottom line is—" he said slowly, "you're going to Japan."

"Yes, I'm going there, but there will be some time—at least a couple of months—before I can get the passport and visa. And we'll be together—just like tonight." She raised her head, putting a hand up to her bare shoulder, lightly, as if to pull one strap down. "And some day, when you're no longer interested in your political career here, you may want to join me there."

He turned to look out of the window.

The street was now alive with a surf of colorful umbrellas. People hurrying along in different directions, to their destinations, and then, perhaps, to new ones. He had been telling himself that Wang's marriage had failed. No one could break up a marriage unless it was already on the rocks. That a man had left this woman in the lurch was a proof of it. But she still wanted to go to that man. Not to him.

Even though it might not be so for tonight and, perhaps, for a couple of months more.

That was not what he had expected, not at all.

Chen's father, a prominent professor of Neo-Confucianism, had instilled into his son all the ethical doctrines; it had not been a useless effort.

He had not been a Party member all these years for nothing.

She was somebody's wife—and still going to be.

That clinched it. There was a line he could not step over.

"Since you are going to join your husband," he said, turning to look at her, "I don't think it's a good idea for us to see each other—this way, I mean, in the future. We will stay friends, of course. As for what you asked me to do, I'll do my best."

She seemed stunned. Speechless, she clenched her fists, and then buried her head in her hands.

He shook a cigarette from a crumpled flip-top pack and lit it.

"It's not easy for me," she murmured "And it's not just for me either."

"I understand."

"No, you don't. I've thought about it. It is not right—for you."

"I don't know," he said. "But I will do my best to get your passport, I promise."

That was the only thing he could think of saying.

"I know how much I owe you."

"What's a friend for?" he said, as if an invisible record of clichés had dropped onto the turntable of his mind.

"Then I'm leaving."

"Yes, it's late. Let me call a taxi for you."

She lifted her face, showing glistening tears in her eyes. Her pallor made her features sharper.

Was she even more beautiful at this moment?

She bent to pull on her shoes. He helped her to her feet. They looked at each other without speaking. Presently a taxi arrived. They heard the driver honking his horn in the rain.

He insisted that she wear his raincoat. An ungainly black police raincoat with a ghostly hood.

At the doorway, she halted, turning back to him, her face almost lost under the hood. He could not see her eyes. Then she turned away. Nearly his height, she could have been taken for him in the black police raincoat. He watched the tall raincoat-wrapped figure disappearing in the mist of the rain.

Zhang Ji, a Tang dynasty poet, had written a well-known couplet: Whistling to himself, Chen opened the top drawer of his file cabinet. He had not even had a chance to take out the pearls, which shone beautifully under the light. *"Returning your lustrous pearls with tears in my eyes, / Lord, I should've met you before I married."*

According to some critics, the poem was written at the moment when Zhang decided to decline an offer from Prime Minister Li Yuan, during the reign of Emperor Dezhong in the early eighth century. Hence there was a political analogy.

There's nothing but interpretation, Chen thought, rubbing his nose. He did not like what he had done. She had made herself clear. It could have been the first night that he had longed for, and there would have been more. And he would not have placed himself under any obligation.

But he had said no.

Maybe he would never be able to rationalize his reaction, not even to himself.

A bicycle bell spilled into the silence of the night.

He could be logical about other people's lives, but not about his own.

Was it possible that his decision was precipitated by the report he had read in the afternoon? There seemed to be a parallel working in his subconscious mind. He thought of Guan's willingness to give herself to Lai before parting with him, now of Wang's offer before leaving to join her husband in Japan.

Chief Inspector Chen had made many mistakes. Tonight's decision might be another he would come to rue.

After all, a man is only what he has decided to do, or not to do.

Some things a man will do; some things a man will not do. It was another Confucian truism his father had taught him. Maybe deep inside, he was conservative, traditional, even old-fashioned—or politically correct. The bottom line was no.

Whatever he was going to do, whatever kind of man he was

going to be, he made a pledge to himself: He was going to solve the case. That was the only way he, Chief Inspector Chen, could redeem himself.

Chapter 19

Finally Detective Yu arrived home for dinner.

Peiqin had already finished cooking several main dishes in the public kitchen area.

"Can I help?"

"No, just go inside. Qinqin is much better today, so you may assist him with his homework."

"Yes, it's been two days since I took him to the hospital. He must have missed a number of classes."

But Yu did not move immediately. He felt guilty at the sight of Peiqin busy working there, her white short-sleeved shirt molded to her sweating body. Squatting at the foot of a concrete sink, she was binding a live crab with a straw. Several Yangchen crabs were crawling noisily on the sesame-covered bottom of a wooden pail.

"You have to bind them, or the crab will shed its legs in the steaming pot," Peiqin explained, noticing his puzzled look.

"Then why is all the sesame in the pail?"

"To keep the crabs from losing weight. Nutritious food for them. We got the crabs early in the morning."

"So special nowadays."

"Yes, Chief Inspector Chen is your special guest."

The decision to invite Chen over for dinner had been Peiqin's, but Yu had seconded it, of course. She had made it for his sake, since it was she who had to prepare everything in their single room of eleven square meters. Still, she had insisted.

Last night, he had told Peiqin about the bureau Party Committee meeting the previous day. Commissar Zhang had grumbled about his lackluster attitude, which was not something new. At the meeting, however, Zhang went so far as to suggest to the Party Committee that Yu be replaced. Zhang's suggestion was discussed in earnest. Yu was not a committee member, so not in the position to defend himself. With the investigation bogged down, switching horses might help, or at least shift responsibility. Party Secretary Li seemed ready to agree. Yu did not have his heart in the case, but his removal would have caused a domino effect. His fate would have been sealed— according to Lieutenant Lao, who had attended the meeting— but for Chief Inspector Chen's intervention. Chen surprised the committee members by making a speech on Yu's behalf, arguing that different opinions regarding a case were normal, reflecting the democracy of our Party, and that it did not detract at all from Detective Yu's worth as a capable police officer. "If people are not happy with the way the investigation is going," Chen had concluded, "I'm the one to take responsibility. Fire me." So it had been due to Chen's emotional plea that Yu remained in the special case group.

Lao's information came as a surprise to Yu, who had not expected such staunch support from his superior.

"Your chief inspector knows how to speak the Party language," Peiqin said quietly.

"Yes, he does. Luckily, this time on my behalf," he said.

"What about inviting him to dinner? The restaurant is going to have two bushels of live crabs, Yangchen Lake crabs, at the state price. I can bring a dozen home, and I will just need to add several side dishes."

"That's a good idea. But it will be too much work for you."

"No. It's fun to have a guest once in a while. I'll make a meal that your chief inspector won't forget."

And more or less to his surprise, Chen had accepted his invitation readily, adding that he would like to discuss something with Yu afterward.

It was really turning out to be too much work for Peiqin, Yu stood there thinking somberly, watching her moving busily around in the confined space. Their portion of the public kitchen area contained no more than a coal stove and a small table with a makeshift bamboo cabinet hung on the wall. There was hardly room for her to put down all the bowls and plates.

"Go into our room," she repeated. "Don't stand here watching me."

The table in their room, set for dinner, presented an impressive sight. Chopsticks, spoons, and small plates were aligned with folded paper napkins. A tiny brass hammer and a glass bowl of water stood in the middle. It was not exactly a dining table though, for it was also the table on which Peiqin made clothes for the family, where Qinqin did his homework, and where Yu examined bureau files.

He made himself a cup of green tea, perched on the arm of the sofa, and took a small sip.

They lived in an old-fashioned two storied *shikumen* house—an architectural style popular in the early thirties, when such a house had been built for one family. Now, sixty years later, it was inhabited by more than a dozen, with all the rooms subdivided to accommodate more and more people. Only the black-painted front door remained the same, opening into a small courtyard littered with odds and ends, a sort of common junk yard, which led to a high-ceilinged hall flanked by the eastern and western wings. This once spacious hall had long since been converted to a public kitchen and storage area. The two rows of coal stoves with piles of coal briquettes indicated that seven families lived on the first floor.

Yu's room was on the southern end of the eastern wing on the first floor. Old Hunter had been assigned to that wing in the early fifties with the luxury of having one extra room as a guest room. Now in the nineties, the four rooms accommodated no fewer than four families: Old Hunter with his wife; his two daughters, one married, living with her husband and daughter; the other thirty-five, still single; and his son, Detective Yu living with Peiqin and Qinqin. As a result, each room functioned as bedroom, dining room, living room, and bathroom.

Yu's room had originally been the dining room, about eleven square meters in size. It had not been ideal since the northern wall had only a window no bigger than a paper lantern, but it was worse as an all-purpose room, and especially inconvenient for visitors, for the room next to it was Old Hunter's, which had originally served as a living room, with the door opening into the hall. Thus a visitor had to walk through Old Hunter's room first. That was why the Yus had seldom had a guest.

Chen arrived at six thirty, carrying in one hand a small urn of Shaoxing sticky rice wine—Maiden Red. The perfect wine for crabs. Chen had his black leather briefcase, as usual, in his other hand.

"Welcome, Chief Inspector," Peiqin said, a perfect Shanghai hostess, wiping her wet hands on her apron. "As an old Chinese saying goes, 'Your company lights up our shabby room.'"

"We have to squeeze a bit," Yu added. "Please take your seat at the table."

"Any crab banquet room is a great room," Chen said. "I really appreciate your kindness."

The room was hardly large enough to hold four chairs around the table. So they were seated on three sides, and on the fourth side, their son Qinqin sat quietly on the bed.

Qinqin had long legs, large eyes, and a plump face, which he hid behind a picture book on Chen's arrival. But he was not shy when the crabs appeared on the table.

"Where is your father, Old Hunter?" Chen asked, setting his chopsticks on the table. "I haven't greeted him yet."

"Oh, he's out patrolling the market."

"Still there?"

"Yes, it's a long story," Yu said, shaking his head.

Since his retirement, Old Hunter had served as a neighborhood patroller. In the early eighties, when private market peddlers were still considered illegal, or at least "capitalistic" in political terminology, the old man made himself responsible for safeguarding the holiness of the state-run market. Soon, however, the private market became legal, and was even declared a necessary supplement to the socialist market. The government no longer interfered with private businessmen as long as they were willing to pay their taxes, but the retired old cop still went there, patrolling without any specific purpose, just to enjoy a sense of being useful to the socialist system.

"Let's talk over our meal," Peiqin cut in. "The crabs cannot wait."

It was an excellent meal, a crab banquet. On the cloth-covered table the crabs appeared rounded, red and white, in small bamboo steamers. The small brass hammer shone among the blue and white saucers. The rice wine was nicely warmed, displaying an amber color under the light. On the windowsill, a bouquet of chrysanthemums stood in a glass vase, perhaps two or three days old, thinner, but still exquisite.

"I should have brought my Canon to photograph the table, the crabs, and the chrysanthemums," Chen said, rubbing his hands. "It could be an illustration torn from *The Dream of the Red Chamber*."

"You're talking about Chapter Twenty-eight, aren't you? Baoyu and his 'sisters' composing poems over a crab banquet," Peiqin said, squeezing out the leg meat for Qinqin. "Alas, this is not a room in the Grand View Garden."

Yu was pleased that they had just visited the garden. So he knew the reference. "But our Chief Inspector Chen is a poet in his own right. He will read us his poems."

"Don't ask me to read anything," Chen said. "My mouth's full of crab. A crab beats a couplet."

"The crab is not really in season yet," Peiqin apologized.

"No, it's the best."

Apparently Chen enjoyed Peiqin's excellent cooking, relishing the Zhisu sauce particularly, using up a small saucer of it in no time. When he finished eating the golden digestive glands of a female crab, Chen was sighing with pleasure.

"Su Dongbo, the Song dynasty poet, said on one occasion, 'O that I could have crabs without a wine-supervisor sitting beside me.'"

"A wine-supervisor of the Song dynasty?" Qinqin spoke for the first time during the meal, showing his interest in history.

"A wine-supervisor was a low-ranking officer in the fifteenth century," Chen said, "like a medium-rank police officer nowadays, responsible only for other officials' behavior at formal feasts and festivals."

"Well, you don't have to worry about that, Chief Inspector Chen. Drink to your heart's content," Peiqin said. "Our meal is informal and you are Yu's supervisor."

"I'm really overwhelmed by your dinner, Mrs. Yu. A crab feast is something I have been missing for a long, long time."

"It's all to Peiqin's credit," Yu said. "She managed to get all the crabs at the state price."

It was a well-acknowledged fact that no one could be so lucky as to buy live crabs at a state-run market. Or at the official price. The so-called state price still existed, but merely in newspapers or government statistics. People paid seven or eight times more in the free markets. However, a state-run restaurant could still obtain one or two baskets of crabs at the state price during the season. Only the crabs never appeared on the restaurant's tables. The moment they were shipped in, they were divided and taken home by the restaurant staff.

"To finish off today's meal, we'll have a bowl of noodles." Peiqin was holding a huge bowl of soup with slices of pink Jinghua ham floating on the surface.

"What's that?"

"The across-the-bridge noodles," Yu said, helping Peiqin place a big platter of transparent rice noodles on the table, along with several side dishes of pork slivers, fish fillets, and green vegetables arranged around the steaming hot soup.

"Nothing fancy," Peiqin said, "just something we have learned to make as educated youths in Yunnan Province."

"Across-the-bridge-noodles—I think I've heard of that unusual dish." Chen showed a gourmet's curiosity. "Or I have read about it somewhere. Very special, but I have never tasted it."

"Well, here's the story about it." Yu found himself explaining. "In the Qing Dynasty, a bookish husband studied in an isolated island cottage, preparing for the civil service examination. His wife made one of his favorite dishes, chicken soup with noodles. To bring the noodles there, his wife had to cross a long wooden bridge. When she got there, the noodles were cold, and had lost their fresh, crisp taste. So the next time she carried two separate bowls, one bowl of hot soup with surface layer of oil to keep the heat in, and one bowl of rinsed noodles. She did not mix the noodles with the soup until she was in the cottage. Sure enough, it tasted wonderful, and the husband, feeling energetic after finishing the noodles, did a good job of preparation, and succeeded in the examination."

"What a lucky husband," Chen said.

"And Peiqin's an even better chef," Yu chuckled.

Yu, too, had enjoyed the noodles, the soup rippling with the memories of their days in Yunnan.

Afterward, Peiqin served tea from a purple sand pot on a black-lacquered tray. The cups were as dainty as lichee. It was the very set for the special Dark Dragon tea. Everything was as wonderful as Peiqin had promised.

Over the tea, Yu did not say anything to his guest about the Party committee meeting. Nor did Peiqin make any reference to their work. They just talked about trivial things. Chief Inspector Chen did not seem to be a status-conscious boss.

The tea leaves were unfolding like satisfaction in his small purple sand cup.

"What a wonderful meal!" Chen declared. "I almost forget I'm a cop."

It was time to talk about something else—a subtle signal—Detective Yu got it. That was probably why Chief Inspector Chen had come. But it might be inconvenient to have the subject brought up in the presence of Peiqin.

"I left quite early yesterday," Yu said. "Did something come up at the office?"

"Oh, I've just received some information—about the case."

"Peiqin, can you excuse us for a minute?"

"That's all right. I'm going out with Qinqin. He needs to buy a pencil sharpener."

"No, I'm sorry, Mrs. Yu," Chen said. "Yu and I can take a walk outside. It may not be a bad idea—after a full meal."

"How can you think of it, Chief Inspector? You're our guest for the first time. Have a few more cups of wine, and talk with Yu here. I'll be back in about an hour—to serve you our home-made dessert."

She put on a blue denim vest, and walked out with Qinqin.

"So what's up?" Yu said after he heard the door close after Peiqin.

"You talked to Wu Xiaoming," Chen said, "didn't you?"

"Wu Xiaoming—yes, I remember, the photographer of the *Red Star*. Just one of the people who had known Guan. A routine checkup at the time." Yu took out a notebook, thumbing through a few pages. "I made two phone calls to him. He said he had taken a few pictures of Guan. The pictures appeared in the *People's Daily*. A political assignment. Anything suspicious about him?"

"Quite a lot," Chen sipped at his tea, while summing up the new development in his investigation.

"That's really something!" Yu said. "Wu lied to me. Let's get hold of him."

"Do you know anything about Wu's family background?"

"Family background?"

"His father is Wu Bing."

"What are you saying?"

"Yes, no other than Wu Bing, the Shanghai Minister of Propaganda. Wu Xiaoming is his only son. Also the son-in-law of Liang Guoren, former governor of Jiangsu Province. That's why I want to talk to you here."

"That bastard of an HCC!" Yu burst out, his fist banging on the table.

"What?" Chen seemed surprised at his reaction.

"These HCC." Yu was making an effort to calm himself down. "They think they can get away with anything. Not this time. Let's issue a warrant."

"At present, we only know there was a close relationship between Guan and Wu. That isn't enough."

"No, I don't agree. So many things fit. Let's see," Yu said, draining his tea, "Wu had a car, his father's car. So he was capable of dumping her body in the canal. The plastic bag makes sense, too. Not to mention the caviar. And as a married man, Wu had to keep their affair a secret, and for the same reason, so did

Guan. That's why Guan made such a point of concealing her personal life."

"But all this is not legally sufficient proof that Wu Xiaoming committed the murder. What we have so far is just circumstantial evidence."

"But Wu has been withholding information. That's enough for us to interrogate him."

"That's exactly what I'm worried about. A lot of politics will be involved if we are going to confront Wu Bing's son."

"Have you discussed it with Party Secretary Li?"

"No, not yet," Chen said. "Li's still in Beijing."

"Then we can go ahead without having to report to him."

"Yes, we can, but we have to move carefully."

"Is there anything else you know about Wu?"

"Just these official files." Chen produced a folder out of his brief case. "Not much, general background information. If you want, you can read it tomorrow."

"I would like to read a few pages now if you don't mind," Yu said, lighting a cigarette for Chen and then one for himself.

So Yu began to read the documents enclosed in the folder. The most comprehensive one was an official dossier Chen had obtained from the Shanghai Archives Bureau. The dossier did not offer much of immediate interest, but it was more thoroughly compiled than what Yu had been used to seeing in ordinary bureau files. Wu Xiaoming was born in 1949. Born with a silver spoon in his mouth. His father Wu Bing was a high cadre in charge of the Party's ideological work, living in one of the most luxurious mansions in Shanghai. Wu Xiaoming grew to be a "three good" student in his elementary school. A proud Young Pioneer with the streaming red scarf and then a Communist Youth League member with a golden badge shining in the sunlight of the early sixties. The Cultural Revolution changed everything. Wu Bing's political rival, Zhang Chunqiao, a Party politburo member, was merciless toward his opponents. Wu Xiaoming saw his parents dragged out of the mansion, hand-cuffed, and thrown into prison, where his mother died a miser-able death. Homeless, Wu and his sister were left struggling on the streets. No one dared to take care of them. For six or seven years he labored as an educated youth in Jiangxi Province. In 1974 he was allowed to move back to Qingpu County, Shanghai, on the grounds of his father's poor health. In the late seventies, the old man was let out of jail, and rehabilitated—more or less symbolically, since he no longer had the strength for his office. Wu Xiaoming, too, had been assigned a good position. As a pho-tographer for *Red Star*, he had access to the top Party leaders and made several trips abroad. With praiseworthy diligence, the report went on in some detail about Wu Xiaoming's own family. Wu was married in Jiangxi province in his educated youth years. His wife, Liang Ju, was also from a high cadre family. They came back to Shanghai together. Liang had a job in the city govern-ment, but suffering from some serious neurosis, she stayed at home for several years. They had no children. As Wu Xiaoming had to take care of his father, he and his wife lived in his father's mansion.

In the part about Wu's work, Yu found several pages of more recent date, the "cadre promotion background checkup" filled out by Wu's current boss, Yang Ying. Wu was described as the magazine's photo editor and "ace photographer," who had pro-duced several pictures of Comrade Deng Xiaoping in Shanghai. The report highlighted Wu's dedication to his work. Wu had demonstrated his political commitment by giving up holidays to carry out special assignments. At the end of the report, Yang Ying gave his "full recommendation for a new important position."

When Yu finished reading, he found his cigarette totally burnt out in the ashtray.

"Not much, eh?" Chen said.

"Not much for us," he said. "What will his new position be?"

"I don't know yet."

"So how shall we proceed with our investigation?"

"A difficult investigation, even dangerous," Chen said, "with Wu's family connections. If we make one mistake, we'll be in serious trouble. Politics."

"Politics or no politics. Do you have a choice?"

"No, not as a cop."

"Then neither have I," Yu said, standing up. "I am your assistant."

"Thank you, Comrade Detective Yu Guangming."

"You don't have to say that." Yu moved over to the cabinet and returned with a bottle of Yanghe. "We're a team, aren't we? Drink up. It's a bottle I've saved for several years."

Yu and Chen drained their cups.

In *The Romance of Three Kingdoms*, Yu remembered, the heroes would drink wine when vowing to share wealth and woe.

"So we have to interview him," Chen said, "as soon as possible."

"It may not be too good an idea to startle a snake by stirring the weeds. And possibly a poisonous snake," Yu said, pouring himself another cup.

"But it's the route we must follow, if we make him our main suspect," Chen said slowly. "Besides, Wu Xiaoming will get wind of our investigation one way or another."

"You're right," Yu said. "I'm not afraid of the snake's bite, but I want to finish it at one blow."

"I know," Chen said. "So when do you think we should act?"

"Tomorrow," Yu said. "We may be able to take him by surprise."

By the time Peiqin returned with Qinqin, Yu and Chen had finished the bottle of Yanghe and agreed on the steps they would take the following day.

The dessert Peiqin had promised was an almond cake.

Afterward, Yu and Peiqin accompanied Chen to the bus stop.

Chen thanked them profusely before he boarded.

"Was everything okay this evening?" Peiqin said, taking Yu's arm.

"Yes," he said absentmindedly. "Everything."

But not quite everything.

Once back, Peiqin started cleaning up the kitchen area. Yu moved out into the small courtyard, lighting another cigarette. Qinqin was already asleep. He did not like smoking in the room. The yard presented an unlovely sight—like a battlefield with each family trying to occupy the maximum space. He stared at the mound of coal briquettes, twenty at the bottom, fifteen above, and then seven at the top, confronting him like a large letter A.

Another achievement of Peiqin's.

She had to carry all of them from a neighborhood coal store, to store them in the yard, and then, every day, to carry a briquette in her hands to the stove. In *The Dream of the Red Chamber*, Daiyu carried in her hand a white basket full of fallen petals.

And he turned to find Peiqin scrubbing the pots over the sink under the glaring light. It was hotter there. He could see the perspiration on her brow. Humming a tune, though off-key, she stood on tiptoe to put the dishes back in the makeshift wall cabinet. He hurried over to help. After closing the cabinet door, he remained standing close behind her, slipping his arms round her waist. She nestled back against him and made no attempt to stop him as he slid his hands up her back.

"Strange, isn't it," he said, "to think Chief Inspector Chen should come to envy me."

"What?" she murmured.

"He told me what a lucky husband I am."

"He told you that!"

He kissed the nape of her neck, feeling grateful for the evening.

"Go to bed now," she said smiling. "I'll join you soon."

He did, but he did not want to fall asleep before she came to bed. He lay there for a while without turning off the light. Out in the lane, all sorts of vehicles could be heard moving along Jingling Road, but once in a while came a rare minute when all the traffic faded into the night. A blackbird twittered nostalgically in the maple tree. His neighbor's door slammed closed across the kitchen area. Somebody gargled at the concrete common sink, and he heard another indistinct sound like swatting a mosquito on the window screen.

Then he heard Peiqin snapping off the kitchen lights, and stepping lightly into the room. She changed into an old robe of shot silk that rustled. Her earrings clinked into a dish on the dresser. She pulled a plastic spittoon from under the bed and put it in the corner partially sheltered by the cabinet. There was a gurgling sound. Finally she came over to the bed and slid under the towel blanket.

He was not surprised when she pressed herself against him. He felt her moving the pillow to a more comfortable position. Her robe fell open. Tentatively, he touched the smooth skin on her belly, feeling the warmth of her body, and pulling her knees against his thighs. She looked up at him.

Her eyes mirrored the response he had expected.

They did not want to wake up Qinqin.

Holding his breath, he tried to move with as little noise as possible; she cooperated.

Afterward, they held each other for a long time.

Normally he would feel sleepy afterward, but that night he found his mind working with intense clarity.

They were ordinary Chinese people, he and Peiqin, hard-working and easily contented. A crab dinner like tonight's could make them happy, excited. In fact, little things went a long way for them: a movie on the weekend, a visit to the Grand View Garden, a song on a new cassette, or a Mickey Mouse sweater for Qinqin. Sometimes he complained like other folks, but he counted himself as a lucky guy. A marvelous wife. A wonderful son. What else mattered that much on this earth?

"Heaven or hell is in one's mind, not in the material things one has in the world," Old Hunter had once told him.

There were a few things, however, Detective Yu would like to have. A two bedroom apartment with a bathroom, for instance. Qinqin was already a big boy who needed a room of his own. He and Peiqin would not have to hold their breath making love. A propane gas tank for cooking instead of coal briquettes. And a computer for Qinqin. His own school years were wasted, but Qinqin should have a different future . . .

The list was quite long, but it would be nice to have just a few of the items at the top.

All of these, it had said in *People's Daily*, would come in the near future. *"Bread we will have, and milk, too."* So said a loyal Bolshevik in a movie about the Russian Revolution, predicting to his wife the marvelous future of the young Soviet Union. It was a movie seen many times in his high-school years—the only foreign movie available at the time. Now the Soviet Union was practically gone, but Detective Yu still believed in China's economic reform. In a few years, maybe, a lot would improve for the ordinary Chinese people.

He dug out the ashtray from under a heap of magazines.

But those HCC! That was one of the things making life so hard for the ordinary Chinese. With their family connections, HCC could do what other people could not dream of doing, and rocketed up in their political careers.

A typical HCC, Wu must have thought the world was like a watermelon, which he could cut to pieces as he pleased, spitting other people's lives away like seeds.

Life's not fair to everybody, a fact Detective Yu had long accepted. Family background, for one thing, made a huge difference everywhere, though nowhere so much as in China in the nineties.

But now Wu Xiaoming had committed a murder. Of that, Yu was convinced

Staring up at the ceiling, Yu thought he could see exactly what had happened on the night of May tenth: Wu made the phone call, Guan came to his house, they had caviar and sex, then Wu strangled her, put her body in a plastic garbage bag, took it to the canal, and dumped it there . . .

"Your chief inspector has a lot on his mind," Peiqin said, cuddling against him.

"Oh, you're still awake?" he said, startled. "Yes, he does. The case is tough, involving some important people."

"Perhaps something else."

"How do you know?"

"I'm a woman," she said, her lips curving into a suggestion of smile. "You men do not notice things written on each other's faces. A handsome chief inspector, and a well-published poet, too—he must be a highly eligible bachelor, but he looks lonely."

"You, too, have a soft spot for him?"

"No. I already have such a wonderful husband."

He hugged her again.

Before he fell asleep, he heard a faint sound near the door. He lay listening for a moment, and he remembered that several live crabs remained unsteamed in the pail there. They were no longer crawling on the sesame-covered bottom of the wooden pail. What he heard was the bubbles of crab froth, bubbles with which they moistened each other in the dark.

Chapter 20

Early the following morning, Detective Yu and Chief Inspector Chen arrived at the Shanghai office of *Red Star*. The magazine was housed in a Victorian building at the intersection between Wulumuqi and Huaihai Roads, one of the best locations in Shanghai. No wonder, Yu thought, considering its political influence. *Red Star* was the voice of the Central Committee of the Chinese Communist Party. Every staff member working there seemed highly conscious of the prestige of his position.

Sitting at a marble reception desk was a young girl in a neat polka-dot dress. Intent on her laptop, she did not stop vigorously punching at the keys on their arrival. The two police officers' introductions made little impression on her. She told them that Wu was not in the office, without asking why they wanted to see him.

"You must know where the Zhou Mansion is—the Wu Mansion nowadays, needless to say," she said. "Wu is working at home today."

"Working at home?" Yu said.

"At our magazine, it is not unusual."

"Everything at *Red Star* is unusual."

"Better call him first," she said. "If you want, you can use our phone here."

"No, thanks," Yu said. "We have our car phone."

Outside, there was no car waiting for them, let alone a car phone.

"I could not stand it," Yu grumbled. "She gave herself such airs."

"You're right," Chen said, "Better not to call Wu beforehand, so we can take him by surprise."

"Well, a surprised snake will bite back," Yu said. "The Wu mansion on Henshan Road is not too far away. We can walk there."

They soon came to the midsection of Henshan Road, where the Wu Mansion stood looming behind high walls. Originally it had been owned by a tycoon surnamed Zhou. When the Communists took over in 1949, the Zhou family fled to Taiwan, and Wu Bing's family moved in.

The mansion and the area of Henshan Road around it was in a part of Shanghai Yu had never come to know, even though he had lived in the city for so long. Yu had been born and brought up in the lower end of Huangpu District, an area mainly inhabited by mid- and low-income families. When Old Hunter moved there in the early fifties, an era of communist egalitarianism, it was a district considered as good as any other in Shanghai. Like the other kids there, running in and out of those small lanes, playing games on the narrow cobblestone paths, Yu believed that he had everything possible in his neighborhood, though he knew that there were other better ones in Shanghai, where the streets were broader and the houses larger.

In his high-school years, often after a day's class of *Chairman Mao's Quotations*, Yu would join a group of his schoolmates in their campaigns—roaming the various areas of the city. Sometimes they would also venture into stores, though they did not shop for anything. Occasionally they would end their excursion by treating themselves at some cheap snack bar. Most of the time, however, they just wandered through one street after another, walking aimlessly, talking energetically, and basking in their friendships. So they had become familiar with various parts of the city.

Except one area. That was the one around Henshan Road, which they had seen only in the movies before 1949—movies about the fabulous rich capitalists, imported cars, and uniformed chauffeurs, young maids in black dresses with white aprons and starched caps. Once they actually ventured into the area, but they felt out of their element immediately. Visible behind high walls, the mansions appeared the same as in the old movies, so impressive, but so impersonal. In front of them, Henshan Road stretched out silent, solemn, and almost soulless—except for some armed PLA soldiers standing still at the iron gates. It was a residential area for high cadres, they knew, a level of existence way above theirs. Still it came as a shock to them that in such a large mansion, there lived only one family, while in their own neighborhood, a much smaller house could be partitioned out to accommodate a dozen families. The environment struck them as the setting of an unfriendly fairy tale. Perhaps they lingered, wondering a bit too long. An armed soldier came over, asking them to leave; it was not an area they belonged in. The realization dampened their interest in going there again.

Now on an early June morning, Detective Yu found himself there again. He was no longer a school kid, but the atmosphere of the area was still oppressive. A PLA soldier raised his hand in salute as they passed through. Not the same soldiers as so many years ago, of course. But these people now living behind the high walls were not entirely different.

The white wall enclosing the Wu mansion appeared unchanged too, except here and there it was ivy-mantled. Out on the street, people barely glimpsed the red-tiled roof shining among treetops. The lot on which the house stood was immense. Now there was no soldier standing at the wrought-iron gate embellished with spiraling pinnacles, but it seemed to correspond all the more closely to the impressions of Shanghai seen in old movies.

Detective Yu placed his hand on the bell at the side of the gate and rang.

Presently a woman opened the gate a couple of inches. She was probably in her mid-thirties, dressed in a black-and-white top with a brief matching skirt. Her eyelids were adorned with false eyelashes and powder-blue eyeshadow, and she stared at them questioningly. "Who are you?"

"We are from the Shanghai Police Bureau," Yu said, flashing his I.D. "We need to talk to Wu Xiaoming."

"Does he expect your visit?"

"No, we don't think so. We are investigating a murder."

"Come with me. I'm his younger sister."

She led them through the gate.

So Detective Yu saw the mansion in its entirety for the first time. A magnificent three-story building, it looked like a modernized castle, with the pinnacles and towers of its original design, and the porches and glass verandahs added in recent renovations. The lawn was immense and well-kept, sporting several flowerbeds. In the middle, a shell-shaped swimming pool of clear blue water shimmered against light blue tiles.

Following her up a flight of steps, they crossed a large hall and came to a colossal living room with a staircase curving up to the left. Opposite a green marble fireplace, there was a black leather sectional sofa, and a coffee table with a thick plate-glass top.

"Please sit down," she said. "Would you like anything to drink?"

"No, thanks."

Yu was vaguely aware of the flower arrangement on the mantelpiece, of the carpet gleaming against polished wood, of the subdued ticking of a mahogany grandfather clock, as he looked around, sinking deep into the sofa.

"I'll tell Xiaoming that you are here," she said, disappearing through another door.

Wu Xiaoming came out immediately. A man in his early forties, Wu was tall, broad-chested, but surprisingly ordinary-looking. His eyes were keen and wary under heavy lids, just like his sister's, with deep creases around the corners. He had none of the artistic airs of professional photographers portrayed on TV. It was difficult for Detective Yu to associate the man before him with the HCC who had taken pictures of nude models, slept with Guan, and perhaps a lot of other women, too. But then Yu sensed something else in Wu's presence—not so much in his appearance, but something emanating from him. Wu looked so successful, confident in his talk and gestures; he emitted a physical glow characteristic of those enjoying and exercising power at a higher level.

Could it be the glow that had drawn so many moths?

"Let's talk in the study," Wu said when they had finished their introductions to one another.

Wu led the way across the hall into a spacious room, austerely furnished except for a single gold-framed picture on the wall suggestive of the owner's taste. Behind a mahogany desk, the French window displayed a view of a lawn and blossoming trees.

"This is my father's study," Wu said. "He's in the hospital, you know."

Yu had seen the old man's picture in the newspapers, a lined face, sensitive, with a high-bridged nose.

Tapping his fingers lightly on the desk, Wu sat comfortably in the leather swivel chair that had belonged to his father. "What can I do for you, comrades?"

"We're here to ask you a few questions," Yu said, taking out a mini-recorder. "Our conversation will be recorded."

"We've just been to your office," Chen added. "The secretary told us that you're working at home. We're engaged in a serious investigation. That's why we came here directly."

"Guan Hongying's case, right?" Wu asked.

"Yes," Chen said. "You appear to be aware of it."

"This officer, Comrade Detective Yu, has made several phone calls to me about it."

"Yes, I did," Yu said. "Last time you told me that your relationship with Guan was one hundred percent professional. You took some pictures of her for the newspaper. That's about it, right?"

"Yes, for the *People's Daily*. If you want to see those pictures, I've kept some in the office. And for another magazine, too, a whole sequence, but I'm not sure I can find them here."

"You met her just a couple of times for the photo sessions?"

"Well, in my profession, you sometimes need to take hundreds of pictures before getting a good one. I'm not so sure about the exact time we worked together."

"No other contact?"

"Come on, Comrade Detective Yu. You could not shoot, shoot, shoot, and do nothing else all the time, could you? As a photographer, you have to know your model well, tune her up, so to speak, before you can capture the soul."

"Yes, the body and soul," Chen said, "for your exploration."

"Last October," Yu said, "you made a trip to the Yellow Mountains."

"Yes. I did."

"You went there by yourself?"

"No. It was in a tourist group sponsored by a travel agency. So I went there with a number of people."

"According to the record at East Wind Travel Agency, you bought tickets for two. Who's the other one you booked the ticket for?"

"Er—now you mention it," Wu said. "Yes, I did buy a ticket for another person."

"Who was it?"

"Guan Hongying. I happened to mention the trip. She, too, was interested in it. So she asked me to buy a ticket for her."

"But why was the ticket not booked in her own name?"

"Well, she was such a celebrity. And she did not want to be treated as such in a tourist group. Privacy was the very thing she craved. Also, she was afraid that the travel agency might put her picture up in its windows."

"What about you?" Yu asked. "You did not use your own name either."

"I did it for the same reason, my family background and all that," Wu said with a smile, "though I am not such a celebrity."

"According to the rules, you must show your I.D. to register with a travel agency."

"Well, people travel under different names. It is not something uncommon even if they show their true I.D.s. The travel agency is not too strict about it."

"I've never heard of that," Yu said. "Not as a cop."

"As a professional photographer," Wu said, "I have traveled a lot. I know the ropes, believe me."

"There's something else, Mr. Professional Photographer for the *Red Star*." Yu could barely control the mounting sarcasm in his voice. "You not only registered under the assumed names, but also as a couple."

"Oh, that. I see why you're here today. Let me explain, Comrade Detective Yu," Wu said, taking a cigarette out of a pack of Kents on the desk, and lighting one for himself. "When you travel with a group of people, you have to share rooms. Now, some tourists are so talkative, they would never give you a break all night. What is worse, some snore thunderously. So instead of sharing the room with a stranger, Guan and I decided it might be a good idea to share a room between ourselves."

"So the two of you stayed in the same hotel room during the trip?"

"Yes, we did."

"So you knew her inside out," Chen cut in, "knowing that she would keep her mouth shut when you were in no mood to listen, and that she slept sweetly, never snoring or tossing about in bed. Vice versa, of course."

"No, Comrade Chief Inspector," Wu said, tapping his cigarette lightly over the ashtray. "It's not what you might think."

"What do we think?" Yu detected the first slight sign of discomfort in Wu's voice. "Tell me, Comrade Wu Xiaoming."

"Well, it was all Guan's idea," Wu said. "To be honest, there's a more important reason why she wanted us to register as a couple. It was to save money. The travel agency gave a huge discount to couples. A promotional gimmick. Buy one and get the second at half price."

"But the fact was that you shared the room," Yu said, "as man and woman."

"Yes, as man and woman, but not as what you are implying."

"You stayed with a young, pretty woman in the same hotel room for a whole week," Yu said, "without having sex with her. Is that what you're telling us?"

"It surely reminds me of Liu Xiawei," Chen cut in. "Oh, what a perfect gentleman!"

"Who is Mr. Liu Xiawei?" Yu said.

"A legendary figure during the Spring and Autumn War Period, about two thousand years ago. Liu once held a naked woman in his arms for a night, it is said, without having sex with her. Confucius had a very high opinion of Liu, for it's against Confucian rules to have sex with any woman except one's wife."

"You don't have to tell me these stories," Wu said. "Believe it or not, what I'm telling you is the truth. Nothing but the truth."

"How could the travel agency have permitted you to share a room?" Yu said. "They are very strict about that. You must show your marriage license, I mean. Or they will lose their own business license."

"Guan insisted on it, so I managed to get some identification materials for us."

"How did you manage that?"

"I took a piece of paper with the company's letterhead on it. I typed a short statement to the effect that we were married. That's all. We did not have to show a marriage license. Those travel agencies are after profits, so such a statement is enough for them."

"It is a crime to fabricate a legal document."

"Come on, Comrade Detective Yu. Just a few words on an office letterhead, and you call it a legal document? A lot of people do it every day."

"It's nonetheless illegal," Chen said.

"You can talk to my boss if you want. I did play a little trick, using a piece of paper with the official letterhead. It's wrong, I admit. But you cannot arrest me for that, can you?"

"Guan was a national model worker, a Party member with high political consciousness, and an attendant at our Party's Tenth National Congress," Yu said. "And you want us to believe she did it just to save a couple of hundred Yuan?"

"And at the cost of sharing herself, an unmarried woman," Chen added, "with a married man for a whole week."

"I've been trying my best to cooperate with you, comrades," Wu said, "but if all you want is to bluff, show me your warrant. You can take me to the bureau."

"It's an important case, Comrade Wu Xiaoming," Chen said, "We have to investigate everyone related to Guan."

"But that's all I can tell you. I took a trip to the mountains in her company. It did not mean anything. Not in the nineties."

"It's definitely more than that," Yu said. "Now, what is your explanation for your phone call to her on the night she was murdered?"

"The night she was murdered?"

"Yes, May tenth."

"May tenth, uh, let me think. Sorry, I cannot remember anything about the phone call. Every day I make a lot of calls, sometimes more than twenty or thirty. I cannot remember a particular call on a particular day."

"We've checked with the Shanghai Telecommunications Bureau. The record shows that the last call Guan got was from your number. At nine thirty P.M. on May tenth."

"Well, it's possible, I think. We did talk about taking another set of pictures. So I might have called her."

"What about the message you left for her?"

"What message?"

"'We'll meet as scheduled.'"

"I don't remember," Wu said, "but it could refer to the photo session we had discussed."

"A photo session after nine o'clock in the evening?"

"I see what you are driving at," Wu said, flicking cigarette ash at the desk.

"We are not driving at anything," Chen said. "We're just waiting for your explanation."

"I forget the exact time we scheduled, but it could be the following day, or the day after that."

"You seem to have an explanation for everything," Yu said. "A ready explanation."

"Isn't that what you want?

"Now where were you on the night of May tenth?"

"May tenth, let me think. Ah, I remember. Yes, I was at Guo Qiang's place."

"Who is Guo Qiang?"

"A friend of mine. He works at the People's Bank in Pudong New District. His father used to be the deputy director there."

"Another HCC."

"I don't like people to use that term," Wu said, "but I do not want to argue with you. For the record, I just want to say that I stayed at his place for the night."

"Why?"

"Something was wrong with my darkroom. I had to develop some films that night. I had a deadline to meet. So I went there to use his study instead."

"Haven't you got enough rooms here?"

"Guo likes photography, too. He dabbles in it. So he has some equipment. It would be too much of a hassle to move things around here."

"A convenient answer. So you were with your buddy for the whole night. A solid alibi."

"That's where I was on May tenth. Period. And I hope it satisfies you."

"Don't worry about that," Yu said. "We will be satisfied when we bring the murderer to justice."

"Why should I have killed her, comrades?"

"That's what we'll find out," Chen said.

"Everybody's equal before the law, HCC or not," Yu said. "Give us Guo's address. We need to check with him."

"All right, here it is. Guo's address and phone number," Wu said, scribbling a few words on a scrap of paper. "You're wasting my time and yours."

"Well," Yu said, standing up, "we'll see each other soon."

"Next time, please give me a call beforehand," Wu said, rising up from his father's leather swivel chair. "You won't have any problem finding the way out, I believe?"

"What do you mean?"

"The Wu mansion is huge. Some people have lost their way here."

"Thank you for your important information," Yu said, looking at Wu squarely. "We're cops."

They had no problem finding the way out.

Outside the gate, Yu turned back for another look at the mansion still partially visible behind the tall walls, and set off without saying anything. Chen walked beside him, trying not to break the silence. There appeared to be an unspoken understanding between them: The case was too complicated to talk about on the street. They continued to plod in silence for several more minutes.

They were supposed to take Bus Number 26 back to the bureau, but Chief Inspector Chen was not familiar with this area either. At Chen's suggestion, they attempted to take a shortcut to Huaihai Road, but found themselves turning into one side street after another, and then to the beginning of Ouqi Road. Huaihai Road was not visible. Ouqi Road could not be far from Henshan

Road, but it appeared so different. Most of the houses there were the cheap-material apartment buildings from the early fifties, now discolored, dirty, and dwarfed. It was there, however, Detective Yu was finally able to shake off his feeling of oppression.

The weather was splendid. The blue sky above seemed to transform the sordid look of the back street through which they were passing in silence. A middle-aged woman was preparing a bucket of rice field eels by a moss-covered public sink. Chen slowed his step, and Yu stopped to take a look, too. Having slapped an eel hard like a whip against the concrete ground, the woman was fixing its head on a thick nail sticking out of a bench, pulling it tight, cutting through its belly, deboning it, pulling out its insides, chopping off its head, and slicing its body delicately. She might be an eel woman for some nearby market, making a little money. Her hands and arms were covered with eel blood, and her bare feet too. The chopped-off heads of the eels lay scattered at her bare feet, like scarlet-painted toes.

"No question about it." Yu came to an abrupt halt. "That bastard's the murderer."

"You handled him quite well," Chen said, "Comrade Young Hunter."

"Thank you, chief," Yu said, pleased with the compliment, and even more so with the invention of this nickname by his boss.

At the end of the side street, they caught sight of a dingy snack bar.

"Can you smell curry?" Chen sniffed the air appreciatively. "Oh, I'm hungry."

Yu nodded his agreement.

So they made their way into the bar. Pushing aside the bamboo bead curtain over the entrance, they found the interior surprisingly clean. There were no more than three plastic-topped tables covered with white tablecloths. Each table exhibited a bamboo beaker of chopsticks, a stainless steel container of toothpicks, and a soy sauce dispenser. A hand-written streamer on the wall limited the menu to cold noodles, cold dumplings, and a couple of cold dishes, but the curry beef soup was steaming hot in a big pot. It was two fifteen, late for lunch customers, so they had the place to themselves. A young woman emerged from the back-room kitchen at their footsteps, wiping her flour-covered hands on a jasmine-embroidered white apron, leaving a smudge on her smiling cheek. She was probably the proprietress, but also the waitress and chef in one. Leading them to a table, she recommended the special dishes of the day. She brought them a complimentary quart of iced beer.

After unwrapping the paper covers from their bamboo chopsticks, and placing a generous helping of curry sauce in their soup, the proprietress withdrew to the kitchen.

"A surprising place for this area," Chen said, chewing at the aniseed-flavored peas, as he filled Yu's beer glass.

Yu took a deep draught and nodded in agreement. The beer was cold enough. The smoked fish head was also tasty. The squid had a special texture.

Shanghai was indeed a city full of wonderful surprises, whether in the prosperous thoroughfares or on small side streets. It was a city in which people from all walks of life could find something enjoyable, even at such a shabby-looking, inexpensive place.

"What do you think?"

"Wu killed her," Yu repeated. "I'm positive."

"Perhaps, but why?"

"It's so obvious, the way he answered our questions."

"You mean the way he lied to our faces?"

"No question about it. So many holes in his story. But it's not just that. Wu had a prompt answer for everything, way too prompt—didn't your notice? It echoed of research and rehearsal. Just a simple clandestine affair would not have been worth all that effort."

"You're right." Chen said, sipping at his beer. "But what could Wu's motive be?"

"Somebody else had entered the picture? Another man? And Wu got insanely jealous."

"That's possible, but according to the phone records, almost all the calls Guan got in the last few months came from Wu," Chen said. "Besides, Wu is an ambitious HCC, with a most promising career, and a number of pretty women around him— not only at work, I would say. So why should Wu have played the jealous Othello?"

"Othello or not, I don't know, but possibly it's the other way around. Maybe Wu had another woman or women—all those models, naked, from his work to his bed—and Guan could not take it, and made an ugly scene about it."

"Even so, I still cannot see why Wu had to kill her. He could have broken off with her. After all, Guan was not his wife, not in a position to force him into doing anything."

"Yes, that's something," Yu said. "If Guan had been found to be pregnant, we might suppose she was threatening him. I've had a case like that. The pregnant woman wanted the man to divorce his wife for her. The man couldn't, so he got rid of her. But Guan's autopsy report said she was not pregnant."

"Yes, I've also checked that with Dr. Xia."

"So what will be our next step?"

"To confirm Wu's alibi."

"Okay, I'll take care of Guo Qiang. But Wu will have arranged things with him, I bet."

"Yes, I doubt if Guo will tell us anything."

"What else can we do?"

"Interview some other people."

"Where are they?"

Chen produced a copy of the *Flower City* from his briefcase, and turned to a full page picture of a nude female reclining on her side. She showed only her back to the camera, but all her lines and curves were soft, suggestive, her round buttocks moon-like. A black mole on her nape accentuated the whiteness of her body melting into the background.

"Wow, what a body," Yu said. "Did Wu take the picture?"

"Yes, it was published under his pseudonym."

"That S.O.B. surely has had his share of peach blossom luck!"

"Peach blossom luck?" Chen went on without waiting for an answer. "Oh, I see what you mean. Luck with women. Yes, you can say that again, but this picture is a sort of artwork."

"Now what's that to us?"

"I happen to know who the model is."

"How?" Yu then added, "Through the magazine?"

"She's a celebrity, too. It is not surprising that Wu, a profes-sional photographer, uses nude models, but why she chose to pose for him, I cannot figure out."

"Who is she?"

"Jiang Weihe, a rising young artist."

"Never heard of her," Yu said, putting down the cup. "Do you know her well?"

"No, not really. I've just met her a couple of times at the Writers and Artists Association."

"So you're going to interview her?"

"Well, perhaps you're a more appropriate officer for the job. At our previous meetings, we discussed nothing but literature and art. It would be out of place for me to knock on her door as a cop. And I would not be able to exercise the necessary authority, psy-chologically, I mean, in cross-examination. So I suggest you go to see her."

"Fine, I'll go there, but what do you think she will tell us?"

"It's a long shot. Maybe there is nothing. Jiang's an artist herself, so it's no big deal for her to pose without a shred on. It's just her back, and she thought no one would recognize her. But if people know that it is her naked body, it will not be too pleasant for her."

"Got you," Yu said. "So what are you going to do?"

"I'll make a trip to Guangzhou."

"To look for Xie Rong, the tour guide?"

"Yes, one thing in Wei Hong's statement intrigues me. Guan called Xie a whore. It's really something unusual for Guan, a national model worker, to have used such language. Xie, too, might be involved in some way, or at least she knows something about the relationship between Wu and Guan."

"When are you leaving?"

"As soon as I can get a train ticket." Chen added, "Party Secretary Li will be back in two or three days."

"I see. A general can do whatever he wants if the emperor is not beside him."

"You surely know a lot of old sayings."

"I got them from Old Hunter," Yu said with a laugh. "Now what about our old Commissar Zhang?"

"Let's have a meeting tomorrow morning."

"Fine." Yu held up his brimming cup. "To our success."

"To our success!"

Afterward, Chief Inspector Chen was quick to grab the bill from the small tray on which it was presented, and to pay for them both. The proprietress stood smiling beside them. Yu did not like the idea of arguing in front of her. As soon as they got outside, Yu started explaining that the total bill amounted to some forty-five Yuan, so he insisted paying his share. Chen waved away the proffered twenty.

"Don't say anything more about it," Chen said. "I've just received a check from the *Wenhui Daily*. Fifty Yuan, for that short poem about our police work. So it's proper and right that we use the money for our lunch."

"Yes, I saw it on the fax sent you by the *Wenhui* reporter— what's her name—it is really a good one."

"Oh, Wang Feng." Chen then said. "By the way, when you talked about peach blossom luck, it reminded me of a Tang dynasty poem."

"A Tang dynasty poem?"

"This door, this day / —Last year, your blushing face, / And the blushing faces / Of the peach blossoms reflecting / Yours. This door, this day/—this year, where are you, / You, in the peach blossoms? / The peach blossoms still/here, giggling / At the spring breeze."

"Does the expression come from this poem?"

"I'm not sure, but the poem is said to be based upon the poet's true experience. The Tang poet, Cui Hu, was broken-hearted when he failed to see his love after his successful civil service examination in the capital."

That was just like Chief Inspector Chen, rhapsodizing about a Tang dynasty poem in the middle of a murder investigation. Perhaps Chen had had too much beer. A month earlier, Detective Yu would have taken it as an instance of his boss's romantic eccentricity. But he found it acceptable today.

Chapter 21

Commissar Zhang had had a totally rotten day.

Early in the morning, he had gone to the Shanghai Number One Old Cadre Club to choose a gift for a comrade-in-arms' birthday.

The club had come into being as a byproduct of the cadre retirement policy—an embodiment of the Party's continuing concern for the revolutionaries of the older generation. The old cadres, though retired, were reassured that they did not have to worry about changes in their living standards. Not every cadre could go there, of course. Only those of a certain rank.

At first, Zhang was quite proud of holding a membership card, which earned him immediate respect, and also a number of privileges then unavailable elsewhere. It had enabled him to buy much-in-demand products at the state price, to book vacations in resorts closed to the general public, to eat in restricted restaurants with security men guarding the entrance, and to enjoy swimming, ball games, and golf at the huge club complex. There was also a small meandering creek where old people could angle away an afternoon, reminiscing about their glory years.

Of late, however, Zhang had not made many visits to the club. There were more and more restrictions on the bureau's car service. As a retired cadre, he had to submit a written request for a car. The club was quite a distance away, and he was not enthusiastic about being squeezed and bumped all the way there in a bus. That morning he took a taxi.

At the club shop, Zhang searched for a presentable gift at a reasonable price. Everything was too expensive.

"What about a bottle of Maotai in a wooden box?" the club shop assistant suggested.

"How much is it?" Zhang asked.

"Two hundred Yuan."

"Is that the state price? Last year, I bought one for thirty-five Yuan."

"There's no state price anymore, Comrade Commissar. Everything's at the market price. It's a market economy for the whole country," the assistant added, "like it or not."

It was not the price, or not just the price. It was the assistant's indifferent attitude that upset Zhang more than anything else. It seemed as if the club had turned into an ordinary grocery store which everybody could visit and Commissar Zhang found himself to be no more than an ordinary old man with little money in his pocket. But then, it should not be too surprising, Zhang thought. Nowadays people valued nothing but money. The economic reforms launched by Comrade Deng Xiaoping had created a world Zhang failed to recognize.

Leaving the shop empty-handed, Zhang ran across Shao Ping, a retired old cadre from the Shanghai Academy of Social Sciences. They grumbled about market prices.

"Now, Comrade Shao, you used to be the Party Secretary of the Economics Institute. Give me a lecture on the current economic reform."

"I'm confused, too," Shao said. "Everything's changing so fast."

"Is it good to have all this emphasis on money?" Zhang said.

"No, not so good," Shao said. "But we have to reform our old system, and according to the *People's Daily*, a market economy is the direction to go in."

"But people no longer care about the Party leadership."

"Or maybe we are just getting too old."

On the bus, Zhang got an idea that somewhat comforted him. He had been taking a class in traditional Chinese landscape painting since his retirement. He could choose one of his paintings, have it presentably framed, and make a surprising, meaningful gift to his old comrade-in-arms.

However, the special case group meeting turned out to be very unpleasant.

Chief Inspector Chen presided. In spite of Commissar Zhang's superior cadre rank, it was Chen who had the most important say in the group. And Chen did not seek his advice frequently—not as much as he had promised. Nor had Chen adequately informed him of the developments in the investigation.

Detective Yu's presence in the meeting room troubled him, too. It was nothing personal, but Zhang believed that the political dimension of the case required a more enthusiastic officer. To his chagrin, Yu had remained in the group, thanks to the unexpected intervention of Chief Inspector Chen. It was an outcome which served to highlight, more than anything else, Commissar Zhang's insignificance.

The alliance between Chen and Yu put him in a disadvantageous position. But what really worried Zhang was Chief Inspector Chen's ideological ambiguity. Chen appeared to be a bright young officer, Zhang admitted. Whether he would prove to be a reliable upholder of the cause the old cadres had fought for, however, Zhang was far from certain. He had attempted to read several of Chen's poems. He did not understand a single line. He had heard people describing Chen as an avant-gardist—influenced by Western modernism. He had also heard that Chen was romantically involved with a young reporter whose husband had defected to Japan.

While Zhang was still musing, Chief Inspector Chen finished his introductory remarks, saying in a serious voice, "It's an important new direction. We have to go on with our investigation, as Commissar Zhang has told us, unafraid of hardship and death."

"Hold on, Comrade Chief Inspector," Zhang said. "Let's start from the very beginning."

So Chen had to start all over again, beginning with his second search of Guan's dorm room, his attention to those photographs of hers, to the phone records, and then to the trip she had made to the mountains—all those leading to Wu Xiaoming, who was not only the frequent caller, but also Guan's companion during the trip. After Chen's speech, Yu briefed them on the interview they had had with Wu Xiaoming the previous day. Neither Chen nor Yu pushed for conclusion, but the direction of the investigation was obvious, and they seemed to take it for granted.

Zhang was astonished. "Wu Xiaoming!"

"Yes, Comrade Wu Bing's son."

"You should have shown me the pictures earlier," Zhang said.

"I thought about it," Chen explained, "but they might have turned out to be another false lead."

"So Wu is now your main suspect, I presume?"

"Yes, that's why I suggested the meeting today."

"Why didn't you discuss your interview with me earlier, I mean, before you went to Wu's residence?"

"We tried to contact you, Comrade Commissar, early yesterday morning," Yu said, "around seven o'clock."

"Oh, I was doing my Taiji practice," Zhang said. "Couldn't you have waited for a couple of hours?"

"For such an important case?"

"What will be your next step?"

"Detective Yu will go and interview some people connected with Wu," Chen said. "I am leaving for Guangzhou."

"For what?"

"To find the tourist guide, Xie Rong—a witness who may know more about what happened between Guan and Wu."

"What led you to the guide?"

"The travel agency gave her name to me, and then Wei Hong told me about the fight between Xie and Guan in the mountains."

"Couldn't that have been just a squabble between a tourist and a guide?"

"Possibly, but not probably. Why did Guan, a national model worker, call another woman a whore?"

"So you think that the trip will lead to a breakthrough?"

"At this point, there are no other clues, so we have to pursue this one."

"Well, supposing Wu had had an affair with Guan," Zhang said, "What have you got to connect him with the murder? Nothing. What could Wu Xiaoming's motive be?"

"What are we detectives for?" Yu said.

"That's exactly what I want to find out in Guangzhou," Chen said.

"What about Wu's alibi for the night of May tenth?" Zhang said.

"Guo Qiang, one of Wu's friends, provided Wu's alibi. Guo told Yu that Wu was with him that night, developing film at Guo's home."

"So an alibi isn't an alibi, comrades?"

"Guo's just trying to cover up for Wu Xiaoming." Chen added, "Wu has all the equipment at home. Why should he have chosen that night to be with somebody?"

"Come on, Commissar Zhang," Yu cut in. "Guo is just another HCC, though his father's not that high, no more than thirteenth level, and retired, too. That could be the very reason that he has to curry favor with Wu. Those HCC are capable of anything."

"HCC—" Zhang burst out, his temples throbbing and his throat hurting, "high cadres' children—that's what you mean, I know, but what's wrong with these young people?"

"There're so many stories about those HCC." Yu was not ready to give in. "Haven't you heard any of them?"

"A few HCC, as you call them, may have done some things improperly, but it is an outrageous lie that there are so many corrupt HCC, or a whole group of them, in our socialist China. It is utterly irresponsible to base the case upon your own concept of HCC, Comrade Detective Yu."

"Comrade Commissar Zhang," Chen said, "I would like to make one point for myself and Comrade Detective Yu. We have nothing but respect for our old high cadres. There is no prejudice whatsoever against the HCC involved in the investigation."

"But you're still going to search for your witness in Guangzhou?" Zhang said.

"That is the direction to go in."

"Now if it proves to be a wrong direction," Zhang said, "have you considered the possible consequences?"

"We are not issuing a search warrant or arresting anybody right now."

"Political consequences, I mean. If the word gets around that Wu Bing's son is a homicide suspect, what will people's reaction be?"

"Everybody's equal before the law," Chen said. "I see nothing wrong with it."

"If there's no further evidence, I don't think your trip to Guangzhou is called for," Zhang said, standing up. "The budget of our special case group does not allow for it."

"As for the budget," Chen said, also rising from the table, "I can draw on my Chief Inspector's Fund for an annual amount up to three hundred fifty Yuan."

"Have you discussed your plan with Party Secretary Li?"

"Li is still in Beijing."

"Why not wait until Li comes back?"

"The case cannot wait. As the head of the special case group, I assume full responsibility."

"So you must have it your way?"

"I have to go there because there're no other leads for us. We cannot afford to ignore a single one."

Afterward, Zhang sat brooding for a while in his own office. It was lunchtime, but he did not feel hungry. He went through the contents of a large envelope marked with the date. In addition to notices for several conventional old cadre meetings, there was also an invitation to a restricted *neibu* or inside movie at the auditorium of the Shanghai Movie Bureau. He was in no mood for a movie, but he needed something to take his mind off the investigation.

At the ticket window, he turned in his special old cadre pass with the invitation. Tickets had been reserved for old high cadres like him, one of the few privileges he still enjoyed.

But he saw several young men approaching him near the entrance.

"Do you want a ticket? R-rated."

"Nudity. Explicit sex. Fifty Yuan."

"A boost to an old man's bedroom energy."

It was not supposed to happen, Zhang thought, that those young rascals, too, held tickets in their hands. The movie was not supposed to be accessible to ordinary people. The bureau should have put some cops at the ticket window.

Zhang hurried in and found himself a seat at the rear, close to the exit. To his surprise, there were not as many people as he had expected, especially in the last few rows. There were only a couple of young people sitting in front of him, whispering and nestling against each other. It was a postmodernist French movie with an inexperienced interpreter doing a miserable simultaneous translation, but with one graphic scene after another, it was not too difficult to guess what was happening to the people in the movie.

He noticed the young couple continuously adjusting their bodies, too, in front of him. It was not difficult for him to guess what they were doing either. Soon Zhang heard the woman moaning, and saw her head sliding down the man's shoulder, and disappearing out of sight. Or was this a scene from the movie? There were explicit images being juxtaposed on the screen . . .

When the movie was finally over, the woman got up languidly from the man's arms, her hair tousled, and buttoned up her silk blouse, her white shoulder flashing in the semi-darkness of the theater.

Commissar Zhang strode out of the theater, indignant. It was hot outside. There were several cars waiting on the street—imported cars, luxury models, shining in the afternoon sun. But not for him. A retired old cadre. Marching along Chengdu Road, Zhang sensed the cars rushing past him like stampeding animals.

Back home, he was exhausted and famished. He had had only a bowl of green onion instant noodles in the morning. There was nothing but half a dry loaf left in the refrigerator. He took it out and brewed himself a pot of coffee, using three spoonfuls. That was his dinner: bread that tasted like cardboard and coffee strong enough to dye his hair. Then he took out the case file, though he had already read it several times. After a futile attempt to find something new, he took out the magazines he had borrowed from the club in the morning. To his surprise, there was a poem by Chief Inspector Chen in *Qinghai Lake*. It was entitled "Night Talk."

> *Creamy coffee, cold;*
> *Toy bricks of sugar cubes*
> *Crumbling, a butter blossom still*
> *Reminiscent of natural freedom*
> *On the mutilated cake,*
> *The knife aside, like a footnote.*
> *It is said that people can tell the time*
> *By the change of color*
> *In a cat's eyes—*
> *But you can't. Doubt, a heap*
> *Of ancient dregs*
> *From the bottle of Great Wall*
> *Rests in the sparkling wine.*

Zhang could not understand it. He just knew that some images were vaguely disturbing. So he skipped a couple of stanzas toward the end, to reach the last one.

> *Nothing appears more accidental*
> *Than the world in words.*
> *A rubric turns by chance*

In your hands, and the result,
Like any result, is called history . . .
Through the window we see no star.
Mind's square deserted, not a pennant
Left. Only a rag picker of the ages
Passes by, dropping scraps
Of every minute into her basket.

The words "mind's square" suddenly caught his attention. Could that possibly be an allusion to Tiananmen Square? "Deserted" on a summer night of 1989, with no "pennant" left there. If so, the poem was politically incorrect. And the issue about "history," too. Chairman Mao had said that people, people alone make the history. How could Chen talk about history as the result of a rubric?

Zhang was not sure of his interpretation. So he started to read all over again. Before long, however, his eyesight grew bleary. He had to give up. There was nothing else for him to do. So he took a shower before going to bed. Standing under the shower head, he still thought that Chen had gone too far.

Zhang decided to sleep on his misgivings, but his brain kept churning. Around eleven thirty, he got out of bed, turned on the lights, and donned his reading glasses.

The apartment was so quiet. His wife had passed away at the beginning of the Cultural Revolution. Ten years, the living, the not living. It's more than ten years. Then the telephone on the nightstand rang.

It was a long distance phone call from his daughter in Anhui. "Dad, I'm calling from the local county hospital. Kangkang, our second son, is sick, his temperature is 104. The doctor says that it is pneumonia. Guolian has been laid off. We've got no money left."

"How much?"

"We need a thousand Yuan as a deposit, or they won't treat him."

"Give them what you have. Tell the doctors to go ahead. I'll express mail it to you the first thing tomorrow morning."

"Thank you, Dad. Sorry to touch you like this."

"You don't have to say that." He added after a pause, "I'm the one to blame for all this—all these years."

So Zhang believed. For whatever had happened to his daughter, he held himself responsible. Often, with unbearable bitterness, at night he would recollect the distant moments of taking her to school, hand in hand, back in the early sixties. A proud child of a revolutionary cadre family, a bright student at school, her future in socialist China was rosy. In 1966, however, all that changed. The Cultural Revolution turned him into a counterrevolutionary, and her into a child of a black capitalist roader family, a target of the Red Guards' revolutionary criticism. As a politically discriminated-against educable educated youth, she was sent to the poor countryside in Anhui Province, where she worked for no more than ten cents a day. He could never imagine what had happened to her there. Other educated youths received money from their families in Shanghai, or came back for family reunions at the Spring Festival, but she couldn't. She had no family; he was still in jail. When he was finally released and rehabilitated in the mid-seventies, he could hardly recognize his child, now a sallow, deeply wrinkled woman in black homespun with a baby on her back. She had married a local mine worker—a survivor's choice, perhaps. In those years, a mine worker's monthly salary of sixty Yuan could have made a world of difference. There she soon became the mother of three. In the late seventies, she passed up the opportunity to return to Shanghai, for Party policy forbade any ex-educated youth like her from bringing her husband and children to the city with her.

Sometimes he felt that, by torturing herself, she was torturing him.

"Dad, you shouldn't blame yourself."

"What else can I do? I have not taken good care of you. Now I'm too old."

"You don't sound well. Have you overworked?"

"No, it's just the last task before my retirement."

"Then take care."

"I will."

"Next time I come to Shanghai, I'll bring a couple of Luhua hens for you."

"Don't bother."

"The folks here say Luhua hens are good for an old man's health. I'm raising half a dozen. Genuine Luhua."

Now she was sounding more and more like her poor and lower-middle-class peasant self again.

A click. He heard her putting down the phone. And the empty silence. She was thousands of miles away. So many years had passed since he talked to the daughter in his heart.

Slowly he moved back to the desk. The file was still lying there, and he turned to the notes he had made during the meeting, going over everything again. Stretching out across the desk to get a cigarette, he found only an empty pack beside the pen holder. He reached into his pocket. The only thing he found, however, was something he did not immediately recognize.

It was a number on a piece of paper crumpled into a small ball. He must have put it there himself—it was in his own handwriting. Why? He was lost. For a moment, he felt he was much closer to Wu Bing, alone, lying unconscious on a hospital bed. All his life, Comrade Wu Bing had fought for the cause of communism. And what then? A vegetable, unable to do anything to protect his son from being targeted as a suspect. His opposition to the direction of the investigation, Zhang hastened to tell himself, did not stem from the kinship he was feeling with Wu Bing. Nor was it the young people coming to the fore, upstarts making tons of money, or Chief Inspector Chen challenging his authority. To build the investigation on such a biased concept about

HCC was part of a social trend questioning the correct leadership of the Party.

What if Wu Xiaoming had committed the murder? Whoever had committed the crime should be punished, of course. But then, would that be in the interests of the Party? With such a social trend, news of the investigation would certainly add fuel to the fire.

Zhang could not find an answer.

It had never been difficult, however, for him to find an answer in the early years when he had first joined the Party. In 1944, a promising college student, he went to Yan'an without finishing his studies, experiencing all the hardships of a donkey-back trip. Life there was harsh—sharing a Yan'an cave with four other comrades, working twelve hours a day, and reading by candlelight. After three months, he could barely recognize his reflection in the river. Gaunt, unshaven, undernourished, scarcely any trace left of a young intellectual from the big city. But he believed he had a satisfactory answer in the changed reflection. He knew he was doing the right thing for the country, for the people, for the Party. And for himself, too. Those were the happy years.

In the following years, though Commissar Zhang's career had not been too smooth, he had never doubted the answer.

But now—

Finally he decided.

He would write a report to Jiang Zhong, an old comrade-in-arms who still held an influential position in Internal Security, thus leaving the question to the higher Party authorities. They should know how to handle a sensitive case like this, whether Wu Xiaoming was guilty—or not. In the best interests of the Party.

He also enclosed a copy of "Night Talk," underlining some words in the poem. He felt it was his responsibility to share with the higher authorities his concern about Chief Inspector Chen's ideological ambiguity. In spite of his efforts, he was not sure what

Chen had tried to say in the poem, but what really mattered would be the interpretation of the reader. If anyone could associate the "square" in the poem with the one in contemporary politics, then it should not have been written at all. So with the investigation, people's responses would be a matter of crucial concern for the Party.

Commissar Zhang was not unaware of the possible impact his report might bring to bear on Chief Inspector Chen. But then, it need not necessarily mean the end of the world for a young man.

Chapter 22

Guangzhou.

Chief Inspector Chen stood under the sign at the railroad station, which was swarming with travelers from all over the country. The economic and cultural center of South China, Guangzhou was fast becoming a second Hong Kong.

Ironically, Guangzhou had a much longer history according to a travel guide in Chen's hand. It had come into contact with Western barbarian businessmen when Hong Kong was still a fishing village. For thirty years after 1949, however, since Guangzhou was so near to Hong Kong, it had been put under special ideological surveillance, and as a result, its cultural and economic development lagged. It was not until Comrade Deng Xiaoping toured the southern provinces in the early eighties, pushing forward the Open Door Policy, that things began to change. With the rapid rise of free markets and private business, an economic revolution transformed Guangzhou and its surrounding cities.

Guangzhou, like Shenzhen, a neighboring special zone city of commercial skyscrapers, became "special"—in the sense that most of the orthodox socialist codes were not applied to it. Now the advantages of socialism were redefined in terms of a better, more prosperous life for the people. Foreign capitalists and investors swarmed in. Its close connection to Hong Kong was further accentuated by a newly built railway.

That explained why so many people came to Guangzhou, including Xie Rong, Chen reflected. At one end of the station, travelers were lining up along the platform, waiting for the new Guangzhou-Hong Kong express train. The local newspapers were full of discussions about a country with two systems. Peddlers were shouting "Hong Kong roast goose" and "Hong Kong barbecue pork," as if everything, once labeled "Hong Kong," immediately became more desirable.

The issue that Chen was musing over was not, however, how to get to Hong Kong like those excited people on the platform. After 1997 when Hong Kong came under Chinese rule, he would probably visit there, and Hong Kong would still be capitalist in theory. At this moment, he had to find a place to stay in Guangzhou—a place within the bureau's socialist budget.

His budget plight had been further complicated by Commissar Zhang in the special case group meeting, where Chen had given a number of reasons for making the trip. Actually, there was one he had not mentioned. Maybe it was not that important, but it was there. He had intended to keep himself busy working on the case, so busy that he had no time to think about his own personal problem. And for that, an investigative trip away from Shanghai for a few days was just the thing. But in Guangzhou Chen found the budget situation worse than he had expected. Owing to price reforms, a small, shabby hotel room in a not-too-inconvenient location would cost forty Yuan per day. Chen had already used one hundred fifty Yuan for the round-trip train ticket. The remaining two hundred Yuan was inadequate even for five days. As a chief inspector, he got a maximum of five Yuan for his standard meal allowance, but a tiny bowl of shrimp dumplings and noodles eaten at a sidewalk stand would cost him more. The only solution was to find a cheap guesthouse with a small canteen.

After spending twenty minutes at the station hotel service desk, he decided to make a phone call to Ms. Yang Ke, the head of the Guangzhou Writers' Association.

"Comrade Yang, it's Chen Cao speaking."

"Little Chen, I'm so pleased that you're calling me," Yang said. "I recognized your Shanghai accent."

"So you still remember me?"

"Of course, and the article you wrote about the movie, too. So where are you?"

"I'm here in Guangzhou. And I want to say hi to you, a greeting to the well-known established writer from an unknown young writer."

"Thank you, but you're not that unknown. And it is not common nowadays for the young to be respectful to the old."

A novelist in her mid-sixties, Yang had written a bestseller, *The Song of Revolution*, in the early sixties that was later made into a popular movie, showing Daojin, a revolutionary goddess, as a young heroine. Chen was too young to see the movie when it was first released, but he kept clippings from several movie magazines. Both the novel and the film were banned during the Cultural Revolution. When the movie was re-released afterward, Chen hastened to see it. To his great dismay, it was not at all the movie he had dreamed of. The story struck him as a stereotyped propaganda, the colors of the movie unreal, the heroine too serious, stiff, moving about with gestures familiar from revolutionary posters. Still, Chen wrote an essay arguing for the historical merit of the novel.

"What has brought you here?"

"Nothing particular. People are all saying that Guangzhou has changed a lot. So I want to see for myself, and hopefully find something to write about."

"Exactly, that's why so many writers are coming here. So where are you staying, Chen?"

"I've not decided yet. In fact, you're the first one I'm calling in Guangzhou. The hotels seem quite expensive."

"Well, that is just what our Writers' Home is for. You've heard of it, haven't you? Let me make a call for you. Just go there. The location is excellent, and you will receive a huge discount."

"Oh yes, now that you remind me."

A guesthouse had been made from the original building of the Guangzhou Writers' Association, a virtue made out of necessity. Nominally an unofficial organization, the Writers' Association had always been funded with government money to support professional writers and activities. In recent years, however, the funding had undergone huge cuts. As a last resort, Yang had turned the office building into a guesthouse, using the profit to support the association.

"You know, that's the very argument I made to the local authorities to get approval. Since Guangzhou's changing so fast, writers will come here to experience life, and they have to stay somewhere. The hotels are too expensive, and our Writers' Home charges about only one-third their price for the members of the Writers' Association. It's in the interest of socialist spiritual civilization."

"What a wonderful idea!" he said. "The Writers' Home must be a great success."

"See for yourself," Yang said, "but I won't be able to meet you there today. I'm leaving for a PEN conference in Hong Kong. Next week I'll arrange a welcome meal on behalf of the association, Guangzhou branch."

"Don't bother, Chairman Yang, but I certainly would love to meet you and other writers."

"You joined the National Writers' Association a long time ago. I voted for you, I remember. Bring your membership card with you. The people there need to see that, for the discount."

"Thank you."

Though he had been a member of the National Writers' Association for several years, Chen still could not figure out how he had been enrolled in the first place. He had not even applied for membership. His poems were not popular among some critics, nor was he such an ambitious writer as to look forward to seeing his name in print every month. Perhaps he had been selected for membership in part because of his position as a police officer. It was in accordance with part of the Party authorities' favorite propaganda: Writers in socialist China came from all walks of life.

It did not take him long to arrive at the Writers' Home, which was not exactly a dream house as it had been described in some newspapers. Located at the end of a winding road, it displayed a classical colonial facade, but its surface was broken and pockmarked. In contrast to the other new or recently refurbished buildings on the slope, it looked modest, even a bit shabby. Still, its position on a hillside provided a splendid view of the Pearl River.

"My name is Chen Cao," he said to the front desk clerk, producing his card. "Comrade Yang Ke suggested I come here."

On the card, beneath his name, was his title, POET, in golden characters. The card, originally designed by the Writers' Association, did not indicate his professional title as CHIEF INSPECTOR—an omission he had insisted on.

The front desk clerk looked at Chen's membership card and said, "So you are the well-known poet. General Manager Yang has just called. A very quiet room is reserved for you. Full of light, too, so you can concentrate on your writing."

"General Manager Yang?" Chen was amused at the new title of the elderly novelist. He was also pleased that, for once, his poet's card would stand him in good stead.

"Number Fourteen." Chen looked at the receipt. "That's my room number?"

"No, that's your bed number. It's a double room, but right now you are the only one there. So you can have the room to yourself. All the single rooms are full."

"Thank you."

Chen crossed the lobby to the gift shop for a copy of the Guangzhou paper. Tucking it under his arm, he made for his room.

It was a corner room at the end of the corridor, quiet, and peaceful, as the clerk had promised. And reasonably clean. There were a couple of narrow beds, nightstands, and a small desk, the top covered with cigarette burns—reminders of a writer's hard work. The room smelled of laundry soap—like new shirts that have been hung in old closets. The bathroom was the smallest he had ever seen. The toilet flushed with a tarnished brass chain hanging from an overhead tank. There was no air conditioner. No TV either. Only an old-fashioned electric fan stood at the foot of the bed, but it worked.

He walked over to the bed assigned to him. A pair of plastic slippers stood underneath it. An iron-hard bed covered with a thin sheet, which somehow reminded him of a *go* board.

Despite the fatigue of the journey, he was not ready for a nap. So he decided to shower. It was a suddenly-hot-and-cold one, due to the vagaries of the electric water heater, but it refreshed him. Afterward, with a bath towel wrapped around his waist, he propped himself up on the bed with a couple of pillows and closed his eyes for just a few minutes. Then he called the front desk, asking how to get to Guangzhou Police Bureau. The clerk seemed a bit surprised, but Chen explained that he wanted to visit a friend there. So he got directions, dressed, and left.

Inspector Hua Guojun received him in a bright, spacious office. Hua was a man in his late forties, with a broad smile constantly on his face. Chen had faxed Hua some information before he left Shanghai.

"Comrade Chief Inspector Chen, I welcome you on behalf of my colleagues here."

"Comrade Inspector Hua, I appreciate your cooperation. It's my first trip to Guangzhou. As a total stranger here, I cannot do anything in Guangzhou without your help. Here is the official letter from our bureau."

Chen explained the situation without mentioning Wu Xiaoming's family background. Leafing through the file folder, he produced a picture. "That's the girl we are looking for, Xie Rong."

"We have made some inquiries," Hua said, "but with no success yet. You are taking this very seriously, to come all the way from Shanghai, Comrade Chief Inspector Chen."

It was true. Normally a fax to the Guangzhou police bureau would have been enough. The local officers would do the job in their way. If it was important, a few more phone calls could be made. But no more than that. A chief inspector's presence was uncalled for.

"At present, she is our only lead," Chen said, "and it's such a political case."

"I see, but it is a difficult search. Heaven knows how many people have come to Guangzhou in the last few years. And only about one-fourth of them, or even fewer, have showed their identification cards or other documents to local neighborhood committees. Here is a list of the people we've checked, but your potential witness is not included."

"So she could be among the others," Chen said, taking over the list. "But why don't they report themselves?"

"They come with no intention of showing their identification cards. It's not illegal for them to come, but some of the professions they're engaged in are illegal. They just want to make money. As long as they can find someplace to stay, they will not bother to report themselves to the local authorities."

"So where can we look for her?"

"Since your witness is a young girl, she may have landed a job in a small hotel or restaurant," Hua said. "Or maybe in a karaoke club, massage salon, or something like that. These are fashionable professions for these gold-diggers."

"Can we check those places?"

"Since the case is so important to you, we'll send a couple of people around to check. It may take weeks, and it will probably be futile."

"Why?"

"Well, the employer and employee are both trying to avoid taxes. So why should they tell you who works there? Especially those karaoke clubs and massage salons, they will shun you like plague."

"What else can we do?"

"That's all we can do right now. Patience pays."

"And what can I do—in addition to being patient?"

"It's your first trip to Guangzhou, so just relax and enjoy yourself here. Special zones like Shengzhen and Shekou are close by. A lot of tourists go there," Hua said. "Check with us every day if you want. But if you want to look around yourself, why not?"

Perhaps Chen had been taking the case too seriously, as Inspector Hua had implied. Outside the Guangzhou Police Bureau, Chen made a call to Huang Yiding, an editor at a local literary magazine that had published some of his poems. Huang had quit to run a bar called Nightless Bay in the Gourmet Street, a young woman who answered the phone said. It was not too far away. So he took a taxi there.

The so-called Gourmet Street was a living menu. Underneath

a multitude of signs, a variety of exotic animals were exhibited in cages of different sizes outside the restaurants along the street. Guangdong cuisine was well-known for its wild imagination. Snake soup, dog stew, monkey brain dip, wildcat, or bamboo-rat dishes. With the live animals exhibited in the cages, customers would have no doubt about the freshness of the fare.

Nightless Bay was there, but he was told that Huang had left for a new career in Australia. That meant the end of Chen's connections in Guangzhou. Strolling along the street, Chen saw people eating and drinking, inside as well as outside the restaurants. Some of the wildlife delicacies might have come from endangered species, he suspected. The *People's Daily* had recently reported that, in spite of government policies, a large number of restaurants were still serving them to their customers.

He turned around, aimlessly, walking toward the river, and then to a landing stage. Along the shore stood a row of wooden benches, and several couples were waiting there for their turns in the boats. He was not in the mood to row alone. After sitting on a bench for a few minutes, he left for the hotel.

A mass of black clouds was gathering along the horizon. The hotel room was sultry. He made himself a cup of green tea from the lukewarm water in the thermos flask. After he had a second cup of tea, it started to rain, with thunder rumbling in the distance. Outside, the streets were covered with muck. There was no point in trying to go out. He decided to have something in the hotel canteen. The dining room was clean, the tables set with starched cloths and shining glasses. There were few choices on the menu. He had a portion of rubbery fish with steamed rice. The food was not the greatest, but it was edible. More important for him, it was inexpensive. Soon, however, he found the lingering aftertaste of fish not so agreeable. He poured himself another cup of tea, hoping that it would quiet his stomach, but the lukewarm water did not help. There were still two or three hours to kill before bedtime.

Leaning against the bed, he turned on his portable radio. The local news was broadcast in the Guangdong dialect, which he could hardly understand. He turned it off. Then he heard footsteps moving down the corridor and coming to his door. There was a light knock, but before he could say anything, the door was pushed open. In came a man in his early forties, tall, gaunt, prematurely bald, wearing an expensive gray suit with an imported label still attached to the sleeve—a sign of his wealth—and an embroidered silk tie. He had no luggage except for a leather briefcase.

A popular novelist with one or two books on the bestseller list, Chen guessed.

"Hi, I'm not disturbing your writing?"

"No, not at all," Chen said. "You are also staying in the hotel?"

"Yes, and in the same room too. My name is Ouyang."

"Chen Cao." He handed over his card. "It's nice to meet you."

"So you are a poet—and whoa—a member of the Association!"

"Well, not exactly." Chen was going to explain, but he thought better of it. There was no point revealing his identity as a police chief inspector. "I've written just a couple of poems."

"Wonderful!" Ouyang extended his hand to him. "Fancy meeting a poet today."

"You are a novelist, then?"

"No, I am not—um, as a matter of fact, I'm a businessman." Ouyang fumbled in his vest pocket and came out with an impressive card. His name was printed in gold beside a long list of companies. "Every time I come to Guangzhou, I choose to stay here. The Writers' Home is not just open to writers. You know why? I come in the hope of meeting writers. And my dream has come true tonight! Oh, by the way, have you had your dinner?"

"Yes, down in the cafeteria."

"What? That cafeteria's an insult to writers."

"I did not eat much."

"Good," Ouyang said. "There's a sidewalk restaurant just a few two blocks away. A small family business, but the food there is not too bad. The rain has ceased. So let us go then, you and I."

The evening was spreading out against the sky, Chen observed, as he followed Ouyang to a street lined with red-and-black-lettered food booths illuminated by paper lanterns. Pots were broiling over small coal stoves, several labeled with signs advertising "stamina" or "hormone" or "male essence" in Guangdong style. These food booths, like other private enterprises, had mushroomed in Guangzhou's streets since Deng Xiaoping's visit to the south.

The booth Ouyang took him to was rather simple: several wooden tables with seven or eight benches. A big coal-burning stove and two small ones comprised the open kitchen. Its only sign was a red paper lantern with the traditional-style character "happiness" embossed on it. Beneath it were live eels, frogs, clams, and fish squirming and swimming in water-filled wooden basins and buckets. There was also an impressive glass cage with several snakes of various sizes and shapes. Customers could choose, and have their choice cooked in a specified way.

A middle-aged woman was peeling a water snake by the cage. With its head chopped off, the snake was still twitching in a wooden basin, but in a couple of minutes, a coil of white meat would be steamed in a brown earthware pot. An old man wearing a white hat was flourishing a ladle and frying a carp in a sizzling wok. A young girl was serving the customers, bustling about with several platters placed on her slender bare arm, her wooden sandals clacking on the sidewalk. She called the white-hatted cook Grandpa. A family business.

More diners were arriving; soon every table was occupied. The place obviously had a reputation. Chen had seen the booth earlier in the afternoon, but he had guessed that the cost was beyond his standard meal allowance.

"Hi, Old Ouyang. What favorable wind has brought you here today?" The young girl coming over to their table appeared to know Ouyang well.

"Well, today's favorable wind is our distinguished poet, Chen Cao. It's really a great honor for me. As usual, your special dishes. And your best wine, too. The very best."

Ouyang took out his wallet and put it on the table.

"The best, of course," the girl echoed, walking away.

In less than fifteen minutes, an impressive array of bowls, dishes, pots, saucers, and platters appeared on the rough, unpainted table.

The paper lantern cast a ruddy light on their faces and the tiny cups in their hands. In Guangzhou, Chen had heard, there was nothing with four legs that people had not found a way to turn into a delicacy. And he was witnessing such a miracle: Omelet with river clams, meatballs of four happiness, fried rice field eel, peeled shrimp in tomato containers, eight-treasure rice, shark's fin soup, a whole turtle with brown sauce, and bean curd stuffed with crabmeat.

"Just a few simple dishes, sidestreet cooking," Ouyang said, raising his chopsticks, and shaking his head in apology. "Not enough respect to a great poet. We'll go to another place tomorrow. It's too late today. Please try the turtle soup. It's good for *yin*, you know, for us men."

It was a huge softshell turtle. No less than two pounds. At about eighty Yuan per pound in the Guangzhou market, the dish must have cost more than a hundred Yuan. The exorbitant price arose from the medical folklore. Turtles, stubborn survivors in water or on land, were considered to be beneficial to *yin*, hence a possible boost to human longevity. That it was nutritious Chen could accept, but why it was good for *yin*, in terms of the *yin* and *yang* system in the human body, was totally beyond him.

But Chen didn't have time to muse. An eager host, Ouyang kept putting what he believed were culinary delights on Chen's plate. After the second round of the Maotai wine, Chen, too, felt a sense of elation rising in him. Excellent food, mellow wine, the young waitress serving, light-footed, radiant as a new moon. The aromatic breath of the Guangzhou night was intoxicating.

Perhaps more than anything else, Chief Inspector Chen was intoxicated with his new identity. A well-established poet being worshipped by his devotee.

"'By the wine urn, the girl is the moon, / Her bare arms frost-white.'" Chen quoted a couplet from Wei Zhuang's "Reminiscence of the South." "I'm tempted to think that Wei was describing a scene in Guangzhou, not too far from this booth."

"I have to put down those lines in my notebook," Ouyang said, swallowing a spoonful of shark fin soup. "That is poetry."

"The image of a street tavern is quite popular in classical Chinese poetry. It could have originated from the Han dynasty love story of Zhuo Wenjun and Sima Xiangru. At the lowest point of their life, the lovers had to support themselves by selling wine in a side street tavern."

"Wenjun and Xiangru," Ouyang exclaimed. "Oh yes, I have seen a Guangzhou opera about their romance. Xiangru was a great poet, and Wenjun eloped with him."

The dinner turned out to be superb, accompanied by a second bottle of Maotai that Ouyang insisted on ordering toward the end. Chen was becoming effusive, talking poetry shop. In the office, his literary pursuit was regarded as a distraction from his profession, so he seized the chance to discuss the world of words with such an eager listener.

The young waitress kept pouring wine for them, her white wrists flashing around the table, her wooden sandals making pleasant sounds in the night air, the same sights and the sounds that Wei Zhaung had been intoxicated by thousands of years earlier.

Over the cups and chopsticks, Chen also pieced together parts of Ouyang's life story.

"Twenty years ago, it's just like yesterday—" Ouyang said, "as fast as a snapping of your fingers."

Twenty years earlier, a high-school student in Guangzhou, Ouyang had set his mind on becoming a poet, but the Cultural Revolution had smashed his dream as well as his classroom windows. His school was closed. Then, as one of the educated youths, he was sent down to the countryside. After a total waste of eight years, he was allowed to come back to Guangzhou, an unemployed returned youth. He failed the college entrance examination, but succeeded in launching his private enterprise, a plastic-toy factory in Shekou, about fifty miles south of Guangzhou. A prosperous entrepreneur, Ouyang had everything now but time for poetry. More than once he had thought about quitting the business, but his memory of working ten hours a day for seventy cents as an educated youth was too fresh. He decided to make enough money first, and in the meantime tried various ways to keep his literary dream alive. This trip to Guangzhou, for instance, was made for business, but also for a creative writing seminar sponsored by the Guangzhou Writers' Association.

"The Writers' Home is worth it," Ouyang said, "for I have finally met a real poet like you."

Not really, Chen reflected, tearing the turtle leg off with his chopsticks. But sitting beside Ouyang, he felt he was a poet, a "pro." It did not take him long to discover Ouyang to be an amateur, seeing poetry as no more than an outpouring of personal sentimentality. The few lines Ouyang showed him presented a spontaneous flow, but suffered from a lack of formal control.

Ouyang obviously wanted to spend more time discussing poetry. The next morning Ouyang brought up the topic again over their morning tea—*dimson* in the Golden Phoenix Restaurant.

A waitress came to a stop at their table with a stainless-steel cart presenting an amazing display of appetizers and snacks. They could choose whatever they wanted in addition to a pot of tea.

"What would you like to have today, Mr. Ouyang?" the waitress said.

"Steamed ribs with bean sauce, chicken with sticky rice, steamed beef tripe, mini-bun of pork, and a pot of chrysanthemum tea with sugar," Ouyang said, turning to Chen with a smile. "These are my favorites here, but choose for yourself."

"We're having too much, I'm afraid," he said. "It's just morning tea."

"According to my research, morning tea originated in Guangzhou, where people used to have a cup of good tea the first thing in the morning," Ouyang said. "'Better to have something that goes along with the tea,' somebody must have thought. Not a full meal, but a delicious bite. So these tiny appetizers were invented. Soon people became more interested in the variety of the small dishes. Tea's secondary now."

The room was abuzz with people talking, drinking tea, discussing business, and eating appetizers, carts of which were continuously wheeled around. Young waitresses kept introducing the new dishes. It was not an ideal place for a poetry discussion.

"People are so busy in Guangzhou," Chen said, "so how can they afford the time for the morning tea?"

"Morning tea is a must." Ouyang smiled expansively. "It's easier for people to talk business over their tea. To cultivate the feeling before they cut the deal. But we can just talk poetry to our hearts' content."

Chen was a bit disturbed, however, when he was not allowed to pay. Ouyang stopped him with a passionate speech: "I have made some money. But what then? In twenty or thirty years, what will be left? Nothing. My money will be somebody else's. Dog-eared, worn-out, and torn in half. What did our dear Old Master Du Fu say? 'Nothing but your writing lasts forever.' Yes, you are a nationally known poet, so let me be your student for a couple of days, Chen, if you do not consider me below your standard. In ancient times, a student was also supposed to offer a whole Jinhua ham to his teacher."

"I'm not a teacher, nor a well-known poet."

"Well, let me tell you something. Last night I did a little research in the library of the Writers' Home—that's one of the advantages there, open shelf, all night. You know what? I've found no less than six essays about you, all praising your poems highly."

"Six! I did not know there were so many."

"Indeed, I was so excited, as it says in the *Book of Songs*, 'Turning and turning in bed, I cannot fall asleep'."

Ouyang's allusion to the *Book of Songs* was not exactly right. It was actually a love poem. Still, there was no doubting his sincerity.

After morning tea, Chen went to the hotel where Xie had stayed. The hotel had a run-down façade, a likely choice for job-hunting girls. The desk clerk looked stoically through the register until he found the name. He pushed the book across the desk so that Chen could read it himself. Xie had left there on July 2. Where she went, no one knew.

"So she left no forwarding addresses?"

"No. Those young girls don't leave any forwarding address."

So Chen had to resort to his door-knocking technique, going from one hotel to another, holding a picture in one hand and a city map in another. In an unfamiliar and fast-changing city, it was a much tougher job than he had expected, even though he had a list of the names of the possible hotels.

The answer came, invariably, with a head-shaking.

"No, we don't really remember . . ."

"No, you should try the Metropolitan Security Bureau . . . ."

"No, I am sorry, we have so many guests here . . ."

In short, no one recognized her.

In the afternoon, Chen went into a small snack bar tucked away in a side street and asked for a bowl of shrimp dumplings with several steamed buns. Sitting there, he became more aware of something characteristic of Guangzhou. It was not one of the main streets in the city, but business was good. People were moving in and out all the time, picking up plastic boxes of various lunch combinations, and starting to eat with disposable chopsticks on their way out. Chen was the only one sitting there, waiting. Time seemed to be more important here. Whatever might be said about the changes in the city, Guangzhou was alive with a spirit that could hardly be called socialist, in spite of the slogan "Build a socialist new Guangzhou" seen everywhere, even on the gray wall of the small restaurant.

Guangzhou was indeed turning into a second Hong Kong. Money was pouring in. From Hong Kong, and from other countries, too. So young girls came there. Some came to find jobs, but some came to walk the streets. It was not easy for the local authorities to keep close control of them. They became part of the attraction of the city for the people from Hong Kong or abroad.

So what could Xie Rong be doing in this city, a young girl all by herself? He understood why Professor Xie was so worried.

He called the Guangzhou Bureau, but there was no new information. The local police were none too enthusiastic in their cooperation. They had their problems, Inspector Hua explained, with insufficient manpower to take care of their own cases.

At the end of the third futile day, Chen went back to the Writers' Home, totally exhausted, and Ouyang offered to take him to the Snake King Restaurant for a "special dinner." Chen had almost despaired of completing his mission in Guangzhou. The last few days had been too frustrating. Holding a picture in his hand and asking the same question, like a displaced Don Quixote, moving from one hotel to another, attempting the impossible, knowing it, but still going on. So he thought, not without a touch of self-deprecatory irony, that a great meal might be able to bolster up a battered chief inspector.

They were led into a private room with white walls and a flight of cherubim painted in blue tones across the high ceiling, which struck him as a direct import from Hong Kong. The delicacies printed in the menu included roast suckling pig and bear paws, but the chef's special was Tiger-Dragon Battle. According to the waitress, it was an enormous platter of assorted snake and cat meats. At Ouyang's request, she started listing the wonderful effects of the snake. "The snake is good for blood circulation. As a medicine, it is useful in treating anemia, rheumatism, arthritis, and asthenia. Snake gall bladder proves especially effective in dissolving phlegm and improving vision."

Chen's mind was not on the chef's special. Holding the menu in his hands, he was having second thoughts about the trip. A wild goose chase? But Xie was the only lead. Giving up on her might well mean giving up the whole investigation.

Ouyang put a spoonful of the snake soup onto Chen's plate, saying, "It's definitely a must. The Tiger-Dragon Battle."

The waitress brought a bottle of wine for their inspection.

"Maotai," she said, turning it so that they could see the label.

Ouyang sipped the sample, and nodded to indicate that it was drinkable. The liquor was strong. Chen, too, drained his in one sip.

As a man of the world, Ouyang must have noticed Chen's mood, but he did not ask about it directly. It was not until after a few cups that Ouyang started to talk about his own business in Guangzhou. "Believe it or not, you're my lucky star,

Literature Star. I've just received a huge purchase order. So this is a celebration."

And it was a wonderful meal. The Tiger-Dragon Battle proved to be as fantastic as its name. Between the "dragon" and the "tiger" was a boiled egg—symbolic of a huge pearl.

"By the way, what's your business here, I mean, apart from poetry?" Ouyang asked as he placed the cat meat in Chen's saucer with his chopsticks. "If there is something you want to do in Guangzhou, I may be able to help."

"Well, nothing particular—" Chen hesitated before drinking another cup. The fourth or the fifth—it was unlike him.

"You can trust me," Ouyang said.

"Well, it's just something small, but maybe you can help me—with your local connections."

"I will do my best," Ouyang promised, putting down his chopsticks.

"I've come here to collect some material for my poetry," Chen said, "but a professor from my college years also wants me to find some information about her daughter. The daughter came to Guangzhou several months ago, but has not contacted her home to give her address and phone number here. The old professor is worried. So I promised I would try my best to find her. And here is the daughter's picture."

"Let me have a look."

"Her name is Xie Rong. When she came here about three months ago, she stayed in a hotel called the Lucky Inn for a couple of days but left without a forwarding address."

Chen was not sure that Ouyang believed his story. It was not a total invention, but he was obliged to keep the investigation confidential.

"Let me have a try," Ouyang said. "I know several madams around here."

"Madams?"

"It's an open secret. I've dealt with a number of them. Business necessities; one cannot help it. They're well informed about new girls."

Chen was more than astonished. According to regulations, he should report the madams, and even report Ouyang's connection to them. He chose not to do so. The success of his mission depended on Ouyang's help, a kind of help that was not readily available from the local authorities.

And as Ouyang promised, the snake feast was the most exotic meal Chief Inspector Chen had ever had.

Chapter 23

Detective Yu hesitated before pressing on the owl-shaped door bell as he stood on the landing overlooking an upper-class neighborhood just a few blocks north of Hongkou Park. The front door was locked, so he had come up an iron back staircase.

He was not comfortable with his share of the division of labor. Yu was to visit Jiang Wehe, an emerging artist, while Chen was away in Guangzhou. It was not that Yu had wanted to go to Guangzhou, which was most likely to be a tough trip—a wild goose chase. It was just that Detective Yu had never dealt with an artist before.

And Jiang Weihe happened to be a well-known one, and avant-garde enough to pose nude for Wu Xiaoming.

Before he placed his finger on the bell, a woman opened the door, and stared inquiringly at him. She was in her early thirties, tall, well-built, with a long graceful neck, a narrow waist and terrific legs. A nice-looking woman, with a sensual mouth, high cheekbones, and large eyes, her hair in an unruly mass of tangles. The smooth flesh beneath her eyes was smudged with black shadow. She was wearing a paint-smeared coverall drawn in at the waist by a black leather belt, and standing barefoot.

"Sorry to interrupt you at your work," Yu said, quickly taking inventory and producing his I.D. "I want to ask you a few questions."

"The police?" She put her hand up to the door frame and studied him intently without making a gesture of invitation. There was a look of confident maturity about her. Her voice was deeply pitched, bearing the trace of a Henan accent.

"Yes," he said. "Can we talk inside?"

"Am I under arrest?"

"No."

"Do you have a warrant or something?"

"No."

"If not, you've no right to push your way in here."

"Well, I've just a few questions, Comrade Jiang, about somebody you know. I cannot force you to talk, but your cooperation will be greatly appreciated."

"Then you cannot force me."

"Listen. Comrade Chief Inspector Chen Cao—you know him—is my boss. He suggested I come to you this way first. It is in our common interest."

"Chen Cao—why?"

"The situation's quite delicate, and you are well known. It would not be a good idea to draw publicity to you. Unpleasant publicity. Here's a note from him."

"I've had plenty of publicity," she said. "So why should I care?"

But she took the note and read it. Then she frowned, standing with her head slightly bowed, gazing at her bare feet, which were spotted with paint. She must have been working.

"You should have mentioned Chief Inspector Chen earlier. Come in."

The apartment was a studio but also served as a combination bedroom, dining room, and living room. Apparently she did not care much about the appearance of her room. Pictures, newspapers, tubes of paint, brushes, and clothes lay scattered all over the place. Dozens of books were shelved against the wall in different positions and at various angles. There were also several books on the nightstand, with a bottle of nail polish among them. Shoes, most of them separated from their mates, had been abandoned around the bed. The other furniture consisted of a large working table, a few rattan chairs, and an enormous mahogany bed with tall posts. On top of the table were glasses of water, a couple of containers filled with wilted flowers, and a shell ashtray containing a half-smoked cigar.

On a pedestal in the center of the room stood a half-finished sculpture.

"I'm having my second cup of coffee," she said, picking up a mug from the table. "What would you like to drink?"

"Nothing. Thank you."

She pulled over a chair for him, and another for herself which she set opposite him.

"Questions about whom?"

"Wu Xiaoming."

"Why me?"

"He has taken pictures of you."

"Well, he has taken pictures of a lot of people."

"We're talking about those—in the *Flower City*—"

"So you want to discuss the art of photography with me?" she said, sitting up in her chair.

"I'm a common cop. So I'm not interested in talking about these pictures as art, but as something else."

"That I can understand," she said with a cynical smile. "As a cop, you must have done some research work."

The shadows beneath her eyes somehow gave her a debauched look.

"Well, it's to Chief Inspector Chen's credit, I have to admit," he said.

But how Chief Inspector Chen recognized her, Detective Yu did not know.

"Really?"

"Yes. So we believe you may want to cooperate."

"What do you want to know about Wu?"

"What you know about him."

"You are asking for quite a lot," she said. "But why?"

"We believe Wu's involved in a murder. It's the case of Guan Hongying, the national model worker. There's a special investigation under way."

"Ah—I see," she said, without registering too much surprise on her face. "But why does your Chief Inspector Chen not come to interrogate me himself?"

"He is away in Guangzhou, interviewing a witness."

"So you are serious?"

"Yes, we are."

"You must know something about Wu's family background?"

"That's why we need your help."

Detective Yu believed he detected a change in the artist's tone, and also a subtle sign of it in her body language, as she slowly stirred her spoon in the coffee mug, as if measuring out something.

"You're so sure?"

"Chief Inspector Chen has made a point of excluding your name from the official file. You will be an understanding woman, he says."

"Is that a compliment?" She took a long swallow of the coffee, the cream leaving a white line along her upper lip. "By the way, how is your chief inspector? Still single?"

"He's just too busy, I think."

"He had an affair in Beijing, I've heard. It broke his heart."

"Well, that I don't know," Yu said. "He has never talked to me about it."

"Oh, I don't know much about it, either. It was such a long time ago," she said with an unfathomable smile on her lips. "So, where shall we start?"

"From the very beginning, if you please."

"First, let me make a point. The whole thing's in the past tense. I met Wu about two years ago, and we parted one year later. I want to emphasize this, not because of his possible involvement in a murder case."

"Understood," he said. "Now, how did you get to know him?"

"He came to me, saying that he wanted to take my picture. For his magazines and newspapers, of course."

"Few would turn down such an offer, I bet."

"Who would say no to have one's own picture—free and published?"

"So the pictures were published?"

"Yes, the pictures turned out to be of high quality," she said. "To be fair, Wu's a gifted photographer. He's got the eye for it, and the instinct, too. He knows when and where to get the shot. A number of magazines are eager for his work."

"What happened afterward?"

"Well, as it turned out, I was his personal rather than professional target—that's what he said to me over a lunch. Believe it or not, he posed for me, too. One thing led to another. You know what happens."

"A romantic involvement?"

"Is that a sort of euphemism?"

"Is it?"

"Are you trying to ask if we slept together?"

"Well, was it a serious relationship?"

"What do you mean by 'serious relationship'?" she said. "If it means that Wu Xiaoming proposed to me, then it wasn't, no. But we had some good times together."

"People have different definitions," he said, "but let's say, did you see each other a lot?"

"Not a lot. As a senior editor for *Red Star*, he got assignments from time to time, to go to Beijing or other cities, even abroad on one or two occasions. I am extremely busy with my work, too. But when we had time, we were together. For the first few months he came to my place quite frequently, two or three times a week."

"Days or nights?"

"Both, but he seldom stayed overnight. He had his car—his father's, you know. It was convenient for him."

"Did you ever go to his place?"

"Only a couple of times. It's a mansion. You must have been there. You know what it is like." She continued after a pause, "But when we were together, I wanted to do what we were together for. So what was the point of staying somewhere without any privacy? Even if we could shut ourselves up in one of the rooms, I wouldn't have been in the mood—with his people walking around there all the time."

"You mean his wife?"

"No, she actually stayed in her room all the time—she's bedridden. But it's his father's house. The old man was in the hospital, but his mother and sisters were there."

"So you knew he was a married man from the very beginning."

"He did not make a secret of it, but he told me that it had been a mistake. I believe it was true—to some extent."

"A mistake," he said. "Did he explain it to you?"

"For one thing, his wife's been sick for several years," she said, "too sick to have a normal sex life with him."

"Anything else?"

"Marriage in those years could have been a matter of convenience. The educated youths were lonely, and life in the countryside was extremely hard, and they were far, far away from home."

"Well, I don't know about that," he said, thinking of his years with Peiqin in Yunnan, "but you had no objection to an extra-marital relationship?"

"Come on, Comrade Detective Yu. We're in a new decade, a new time. Who lives any longer like in the Confucian books? If a marriage is a happy one, no outsider could ever destroy it," she said, scratching her ankle. "Besides, I never expected him to marry me."

Maybe he was an old-fashioned man. Yu certainly felt ancient sitting beside the artist, to whom an affair could be just like the change of her clothes. But he also felt it tempting to imagine the body under her loose coverall. Was it because he had seen it in the picture? And he also noticed the black mole on her nape.

"But if he's so unhappy with his marriage, what kept him in it?"

"I don't know." She shook her head. "I don't think a divorce would do him any good, politically, I mean. I've heard that somebody in his wife's family is still influential."

"That's true."

"I also had the feeling that he cared about her in his way."

"What made you think so?"

"He talked to me about her. She had come to him in his most miserable days—as an educable educated youth of a capitalist roader family. She took pity on him, and she took good care of him, too. But for her, he once said, he could have fallen into despair."

"She might have been a beauty in her day," he said. "We have seen some pictures of her in earlier years."

"You may not believe it, but part of the reason I came to care for him was that he showed some loyalty to his wife. He was not a man devoid of responsibility."

"Perhaps," he said. "But I've got another question about him. Does he earn a lot from these pictures—not of his wife, of course."

"As an HCC, he probably has his ways to get his money. Some people would pay him handsomely, for instance, to have a picture published in the *Red Star*. He does not have to make a living by selling the pictures. As far as I know, he spends generously on himself, and he's not mean to his friends."

"What kind of friends?"

"People of similar family background. Birds of a feather, if you want to put it that way."

"A pack of HCC," he grumbled. "So what do they do together?"

"They have parties at his place. Wild parties. It's a shame, they would say, not to have parties in such a mansion."

"Can you give me the names of his friends?"

"Only those who have given me their cards at those parties," she said, turning toward a plastic box on the shelf.

"That will be great."

"Here they are." She spread out several cards on the table.

He glanced through them. One was Guo Qiang, the man who had confirmed Wu's alibi for his whereabouts on May tenth. Several cards bore impressive titles under the names.

"Can I borrow them?"

"Sure. I don't think I'll need them."

Taking out a pack of cigarettes, he lit one after she nodded her approval. "Another question, Miss Jiang. Did you know anything about Guan Hongying while you were with Wu? For instance, did you meet her at his mansion, or did he mention her?"

"No, not that I remember," she said. "But I knew there were some other girls."

"Was that the reason why you broke things off?"

"Well, you may think so, but no," she said, taking a cigarette from his pack. "I did not really expect anything out of that relationship. He had his life, and I had mine. We had made it clear to each other. A couple of times I confronted him about his other girlfriends, but he swore that he only took pictures of them."

"So you believed him?"

"No, I didn't—but ironically, we parted because of his pictures."

"Pictures of those girls?"

"Yes, but not like those—artistic work—you have seen in magazines."

"I understand," he said, "but how did you find them?"

"By accident. During one of those parties, I was with him in his room when he had to answer a call on the telephone in his study. It was a long conversation, so I looked into his drawer. I discovered a photo album. Pictures of nude girls, you would expect, but much more than that—so obscene—and they were all in a variety of disgusting positions—even in the midst of sexual intercourse. I recognized one of the models. A well-known actress, now living abroad with an American millionaire, I've heard. She's gagged in that picture, lying on her back with her wrists handcuffed, and buried between her breasts was Wu's head. There were quite a number of such terrible pictures, I did not have the time to look at them all. Wu had printed them out like professional fashion photographs, but there was no use his protesting that they were artistic work."

"Outrageous!"

"Even more outrageous was the way he kept records on the back of those photos."

"What kind of record?"

"Well, in a Sherlock Holmes story, a sexual criminal kept pictures of the women he had conquered, along with descriptions of their positions, secrets, and preferences in bed—all the intimate details of the sexual intercourse he had with them—oh, come on, Detective Yu, you surely know the story well."

"Chief Inspector Chen has translated a few Western mysteries," Detective Yu said equivocally, having never read the story himself. "You can discuss it with him."

"Really, I thought he wrote only poems."

"Now what could Wu have wanted to do with these pictures?"

"I don't know, but he's not just a Don Juan who wants to satisfy his ego by looking over his naked conquests."

"That S.O.B.," Yu cursed, not familiar with Don Juan either.

"I could live with a Don Juan, but that kind of cold-blooded cynicism really put me off. So I decided to part with him."

"You were wise to make that decision."

"I've got my work to do," she looked down somberly. "I did not want to be involved in a scandal. Now I've told you all I know."

"That's really important information. You're helping us a lot, Comrade Jiang. We'll make sure that your name will never be mentioned in the official investigation record."

"Thank you."

She stood up, accompanying Yu toward the door. "Comrade Detective Yu."

"Yes?"

"I may have something else for you, I think," she said, "but I need to ask you a favor."

"As long as it's in my power."

"Wu and I have parted. Whatever grudge I have against him, I should not throw stones into the well where he is drowning. So I won't tell you anything I've not seen or heard myself. But I happened to know one of Wu's girls at the time we parted."

"Who is she?"

"Her name is Ning Jing. How Wu had picked her up, or what he saw in her, I've no idea at all. Perhaps just another object for his camera's eye, to be focused, shot, and pasted into his album. I'm mentioning her because she may know something about Wu and Guan. Guan could have been the next girl after her."

"Yes, that may be an important lead, Comrade Jiang. I'll definitely check it out. But what can I do for you?"

"If it is possible, please try not to involve her in any publicity. That's the favor I'm asking. I have had my share, and a column more or less in tabloid magazines does not make much difference to me. But she is different. She's going to get married soon, I've heard."

"I see," he said. "I will do my best. Do you have her address?"

"She has her name listed in the phone book," she said, taking down a directory. "Let me find it for you."

He got the name, address, and phone number.

"Thank you. I'll tell Chief Inspector Chen about all the help you've given us."

"And say hello to Chief Inspector Chen."

"I will. And good-bye."

At the foot of the stairs, Yu turned around and saw her still standing barefoot on the landing. But she wasn't looking at him. She was gazing at the distant horizon behind the multi-colored roofs.

A nice woman, though her philosophy of life was beyond him. Perhaps it was the price one pays for being an artist, Detective Yu suspected. Being different.

Just like Chief Inspector Chen—who was nonetheless a capable cop.

With Wu Xiaoming, however, it was more than being different.

Yu decided to go to Ning Jing's place immediately. It would not be a pleasant visit, nor would it be easy.

Jiang Weihe had been cooperative, but only after the combined pressure of "the hard and the soft." The threat of revealing her identity as the nude in the magazine, and the note from Chen. But with Ning, Detective Yu had nothing to use. Nothing but the scanty information from Jiang who, despite her declaration, might well have harbored a personal grudge against Ning. So the only card he could play would be that of bluff, one of the effective tactics to bring a potential witness around, especially with the possibility of a "peach-colored scandal." A phone call to her work unit from the Shanghai Police Bureau would be enough to start a wildfire of gossip, finger pointing, head shaking, saliva spitting on her back, and whatnot. It need not take a formal investigation to put her under suspicion.

Ning's apartment was on Xikang Road, close to the Gate to Joy, a nightclub that had been rehabilitated and reopened.

A young woman appeared at the door where he rang the bell. "What do you want?"

Ning wore a white T-shirt several sizes too large that completely covered her shorts. It was difficult to guess her age. The way she dressed was almost like a teenager, or else it was too fashionable for him. She had wide black eyes and a straight nose; her hair was pulled back and held in place by a kerchief. Her full lips were moist, sensuous, even somewhat wanton.

"I'm Detective Yu Guangming, of the Shanghai Police Bureau. I need to ask you a few questions."

"What have I done?"

"Not about you, but about someone you know."

"Show me your identification," she said. "I'm on my way out."

"It won't take long." He produced his I.D. "We'd appreciate your help."

"Okay, come in."

It was a small, cozy apartment, but unkempt for the home of a young single woman. A creased bedspread lay over the unmade bed. On the table was an empty but unwashed ashtray. There were no framed pictures, but a number of magazine photographs of cars and movie stars were taped to the wall. On the floor were two pairs of shoes, peeping out from under the bed. There was one thing in common between Jiang and Ning. Each had an apartment to herself.

"What do you want from me?" she said after he seated himself on a rattan chair.

"A few questions about Wu Xiaoming."

"Wu Xiaoming—why me?"

"You're his girlfriend, right?"

"No, he's just taken a few pictures of me. For his magazine."

"Really?"

"Yes, that's all."

"Then you don't have to worry about answering my questions. If you cooperate, everything you say will be kept off the record."

"Now what do you mean, Comrade Detective?"

"Wu is involved in a murder case."

"Heavens, what . . ." Her black eyes grew even wider now. "How?"

"We don't know everything yet," he said. "That's why your help would be appreciated."

"But I cannot help you. I hardly know him at all."

"You can refuse to cooperate, but then we'll have to go to your work unit," Yu said. "Huanpu Elementary School, right?"

"Go there if you want to. That is all I will say," she said, standing up and making a gesture toward the door.

She was beginning to irritate him with her attitude, so damned antagonistic. And he did not like this way of conducting the interview. There was some hard object on the rattan chair beneath him, which made him feel even more uncomfortable as he sat opposite her.

"But there is more than that, I'm afraid," Yu said. "We're not talking about your pictures in magazines, but about the ones in his album. Surely you know them better than I."

"What are you talking about?" She flinched involuntarily, but she covered it well. "Show them to me."

"We will show these pictures to your principal, every one of them." He was bluffing now. "They're by no means decent for a schoolteacher. And a number of other people will see them, too."

"You've got no right."

"Yes, we have every right. We're here in socialist China. The Party authorities are calling on the people to fight Western bourgeois decadence. These pictures will serve as a good example."

"How could you do that!"

"We can do whatever we want with them," he said, "as evidence in a criminal investigation. We also have a witness who can testify to your relationship with Wu. Since you're obstructing our inquiries, we've no choice."

She sat completely straight on the edge of the sofa, her knees tightly together. She was not only red in the face now. There were small drops of perspiration along her hairline in spite of her effort to hold herself together.

"What do you want me to do?" she finally said with a note of panic in her quivering voice.

"Tell us everything about your relationship with Wu," he added, "including all the details, like a paperback romance."

There was a bit of sarcasm he could detect in his own voice. No point, he told himself, to putting her through too much of an ordeal.

"Where shall I begin?"

"At the very beginning."

"It was about a year ago, I think. Wu came to me as a photographer from the *Red Star*. He asked if he could photograph me, claiming that I had a typical high-school teacher's face, and that he was working up a proposal for *People*."

"A typical highschool teacher's face," he repeated.

"It's not very flattering, but he had his ways of pursuing people."

"So the pictures were published?"

"Yes, but actually he had little interest in the publication, as he told me later. He just wanted to meet me."

"The same old dirty trick," he said. "And everybody fell for it."

"But he had talent and kept his word. These pictures in *People* helped my position at school. So we came to know more of each other."

"And it began to develop into an affair?"

"Yes, we started dating."

"You did not know that he was married?"

"I did not know at first, but he did not try to cover it up. On our third or fourth date, he told me about his marriage, saying he was not happy with it. I could understand why—with his sick, neurotic wife. What mattered most, he said, was the time we shared. So I believed we might work something out eventually."

"Did he take the initial step in the sexual relationship between you?"

"Do I have to answer that question?" she said, twisting her fingers.

"Yes. If you answer now, it will save you a great deal of unpleasantness later."

"Well, he invited me to a party at his place, and afterward he asked me to stay on for a while. I agreed. I was a bit drunk."

"Then he took advantage of you while you were drunk."

"No, he did not force me." She hung her head low, wringing her hands in a helpless gesture. "I was willing, hoping that sooner or later he would change his mind."

"Change his mind?"

"Yes, I hoped he would choose to marry me and divorce his wife."

"How long were you together?"

"A couple of months."

"Were you happy . . . with him?"

"At first, when things went smoothly."

"How often were you together?"

"Two or three times a week."

"What kind of man was he?" Yu asked. "Sexually, I mean."

The question came as a shock to her. She pulled at the hem of her T-shirt as she said in a whisper, "Normal."

"Weren't you afraid of becoming pregnant?"

"Yes, but I was always careful."

"Then why did you end it?"

"He chose not to divorce his wife."

"Did you discuss the issue with him?"

"Yes, but to no avail."

"You could have sued him, or approached his work unit."

"What's the point?" she said with a tear trickling down her cheek. "With his family background, who would have listened to me? Besides, I was a 'third party' to begin with."

"So you just let him get away with it?"

"I argued with him, and he did the most horrible thing. Those pictures—you have seen them, haven't you? If I continued to harass him, he threatened to show them to other people."

"That HCC bastard!" He stood up, looking over her head toward a dismal, gray sky out the window, taking a cigarette out of his pocket, lighting it, before he seated himself again on the hard rattan chair. "But how could you have let him take those photos?"

"I had posed for him on a professional level," she said sobbing. "Later on, I allowed him to take more intimate . . . . He had his own darkroom and equipment, so I was not worried. But those horrible nude photos, those were taken while I was sleeping. And he posed on top of me without my knowledge."

"Oh, I see." So those pictures were not just of Ning herself, but of her and Wu together. Yu needed some time to think about this new information. Apparently Wu had taken and kept the pictures for a purpose: to get rid of somebody when he no longer desired her.

"So that was the end of your affair?" Yu asked.

"Yes. He never contacted me again."

"Just one more question: Was Wu Xiaoming seeing somebody else when you parted with him?"

"I was not sure, but there were other girls at those parties."

"Did you know someone named Guan Hongying among them?"

"No. Guan Hongying—isn't she the national model worker? Heavens."

Yu took a picture of Guan out of his pocket. "Do you recognize her?"

"Yes, I think so. I saw her only once at Wu's place. I remember her because she clung to him all the evening, but I did not know her name at the time. Wu did not introduce her to anybody."

"Wu certainly would not have done that," he said. "Do you know anything else about her?"

"No, that's all." She fumbled in her bag and found a handkerchief.

"Contact me if you can think of anything, Comrade Ning."

"I will." She then added, "You won't tell other people?"

"I'll try my best," he said.

She accompanied him to the door, her face streaked with tears, her head hung low, no longer the hostile antagonist of an hour ago, her hands nervously pulling again at the lower edge of her oversized T-shirt.

Detective Yu had succeeded in bluffing her and getting information he had not expected. But he was not elated. Ning, too, was a victim.

He began the long walk home. The new facts, instead of diminishing the puzzle, seemed to add to its complexity.

What an HCC monster! So many women in his life. Even in his most intimate moments with a woman, Wu had not forgotten to take those horrible pictures for his ulterior purpose. But what was the point of conquering so many women if there was no future with any of them? What was the point?

There had been only one woman in Yu's life—Peiqin. But Yu was a happy man because of it.

Was there a woman in Chief Inspector Chen's life? There had been one—according to Jiang—in Beijing, years earlier. Yu had never heard anything about it, but it was said that of late there was a female often seen in Chen's company. According to the bureau housing committee, however, there was no one. Otherwise Chen would surely have tried to make a point of it when applying for an apartment.

Even Jiang seemed to have a soft spot for the chief inspector. At least she changed her attitude abruptly because of his note. The fact that Chen had recognized her in the picture also intrigued him. Nothing but her bare back showed in that photograph. Was it the black mole on the nape of her neck that had revealed her identity to him?

Could there be something between the two? Immediately Yu hoped he was wrong. He had come to think of Chen as a friend. It was time for Chen to settle down, but not with somebody as modern as Jiang.

Chapter 24

It was Chief Inspector Chen's fifth day in Guangzhou. He had awakened to find a note on the nightstand. It was just an address with a short line underneath it.

Xie Rong. 60 Xinhe Road, #543.
You will find her there. Have a wonderful day.
                                        Ouyang

Xinhe Road was not one of the main streets. Walking past a run-down Turkish bathhouse with a pasty-faced girl in the doorway and a pretentious coffee shop with several computers on the glass-topped tables beside a sign saying "Electronic Mails," Chief Inspector Chen reached a tall building at the address given him.

Old and dilapidated, the building was neither an office building, nor was it residential. Yet, there was a doorman sitting there, sorting mail at the entrance desk. He stared up at Chen over his reading glasses. When Chen showed him the address, the doorman pointed at the elevator.

Chen waited for about ten minutes without seeing any sign of the elevator coming down. He was about to climb the stairs when the elevator arrived with a thud. It appeared even more ancient than the building itself, but it carried him to the fifth floor and bobbed to a stop.

As he stepped through the squeaking door, he had a weird feeling of stepping into an old movie from the thirties. *Song Girl*—he recalled its name. There was a narrow corridor, smelling of dead cigars, lined with a number of suspiciously closed doors, as if General Yan of the movie, still wrapped in scarlet silk pajamas, would pop out of a door in the next minute to take a bouquet of roses from a flower girl. The flower girl had been played by Zhou Xuan, so breathtaking in those days.

Chief Inspector Chen knocked at the door marked 543.

"Who is it?" a young girl's voice called out.

"Chen Cao, Mr. Ouyang's friend."

"Come on in. The door is not locked."

Pushing the door open, he found himself in a room with a half drawn velvet curtain. The room contained little in the way of furniture: a double bed, a large mirror on the wall just above the head-board, a towel-covered sofa, a nightstand, and a couple of chairs.

Propped up on cushions, a young girl was reclining on the sofa, reading a paperback. She wore a blue-striped bathrobe that showed most of her thighs; her bare feet dangled over the sofa arm. On the coffee table was a crystal ashtray with lipstick-marked cigarette butts.

"So you are Chen Cao."

"Yes, has Ouyang told you about me?"

"Sure, you're special, he's told me, but it's a bit early for me, I am afraid," she said, moving to a sitting position. "My name is Xie Rong." She got to her feet, not embarrassed as she straightened her robe.

"I should have called first, but—"

"That's okay," she said. "A distinguished customer is always welcome."

"I don't know what Ouyang has told you, but let's have a talk."

"Take a seat." She gestured toward the chair beside the bed. He hesitated before sitting. The room smelled of strong spirits, cigarette smoke, cheap cosmetics, and something faintly suggestive of body odor.

Walking barefoot across the carpet, she poured some coffee from an electronic coffee pot, and handed him a cup on a Fuzhou lacquered tray.

"Thanks," he said. Chief Inspector Chen was in for something he had not expected, or not even imagined, he realized. Maybe that was why Ouyang had left the address with no explanation. A poet searching for a young girl in a large city could have appeared suspiciously "romantic"—enough for Ouyang to bring him and the girl together in a flight of best-seller fantasy. There was no use blaming Ouyang, who had meant well.

"So let's get on with it." She climbed onto the bed, sitting there, her arms folded across her knees, studying him intensely, in a posture rather suggestive of a Burmese cat. It was not a repulsive association. In a way, she reminded him of someone.

"A first-timer, eh?" she said, misreading his silence. "Don't be nervous."

"No, I've come here to—"

"What about something to relax you first? A Japanese massage—a foot massage—to start with?"

"A foot massage—" he echoed. A foot massage. He had read about it in a Japanese novel. One of Mishima's, perhaps. Something of an existentialist experience, though he had never liked Mishima. But it was a temptation. He would probably never come here again. Whether he was stepping over the line he had drawn for himself, he did not know. It was too late, however, for him to back out—unless he flashed his I.D. and started questioning her as a chief inspector.

But would that work? To Xie Rong, as well as to other ordinary Chinese people, HCC like Wu Xiaoming led an existence far above them, and above the law, too. So it was quite likely she would not dare to say anything against Wu. If she refused to answer his questions, Chief Inspector Chen could not do much in Guangzhou. One thing he had learned in the past few days was the unreliability of his local colleagues.

"Why not?" he said, flashing a few bills.

"What a generous tip! Put it on the nightstand. Let's go to the bathroom."

"No." He was still trying to draw a line somewhere. "I'll take the shower by myself."

"As you please," she said casually. "You're so different."

She scrambled down, knelt at his feet, and began to unlace his shoes.

"No," he protested again in embarrassment.

"You have to take your shoes off—that's only civil."

Before he could say or do anything, she reached out to unbutton his shirt. Feeling the heat of her breath on his shoulder, he took a step back. She then took a bathrobe from behind the door and threw it to him. He hurried into the bathroom, still wearing his clothes, the robe draped over his shoulder, thinking to himself that he must resemble some character in a movie.

The bathroom was no larger than the one at the Writers' Home; it contained an oval tiled tub with a rotatable shower head and a large towel on a stainless-steel rack. A mirror hung over a cracked blue porcelain sink. A worn rug was spread out in front of it. There was no lack of hot water, though.

He had agreed to her proposal because he needed time to think, but he knew he could not stay in the bathroom too long. With a few ideas, half-formed in the vapor of shower, he emerged wearing her scruffy flannel bathrobe, the frayed belt brushing against his bare legs.

She was waiting, sitting cross-legged on the bed, painting her toenails a bright vermilion. The window filtered the light onto the plain white coverlet. Then she thrust her legs out in front of her, flexed her toes luxuriantly, lifted one foot above the other, waggled the toes at him, and giggled.

"Ah," she said, "much better."

There was a small bikini-girl poster above the sofa, and underneath it was a line in bold characters: TIME IS MONEY! a new political slogan he had seen in Guangzhou.

"Take off your robe," she said, putting a finishing touch on her toenails with a steady hand. She then capped the polish bottle tightly, and put it aside on the nightstand. To his surprise, she lay down on her back, and waved her feet in the air as if doing synchronized swimming. Her red toenails arced in the air.

"Must I?"

"Must I help you?"

He was flabbergasted as she jumped up and helped him off with the bathrobe. Luckily, he had put his shorts back on. She guided him to the bed where he lay down, and then she turned him over. Lying on his stomach, he was very nervous as he became aware that she, too, had gotten onto the bed.

She put both her hands on a stainless-steel bar suspended from the ceiling. With the bar bearing the weight of her body like a gymnast, she started massaging his back with her toes.

It was a bizarre experience. The first two or three minutes, he was perspiring with trepidation. Any second, she could stamp down violently on his bare back, a complex of vertebrae, discs, ligaments, and nerves. But soon he started to have mixed feelings. Her bare toes and heels pressing upon him elicited sensations of ice and fire all over him. His pleasure was actually heightened by his trepidation.

She must have had some professional training. Her toes concentrated on his trouble spots, working kinks out of his back, and reducing the tension in his body. He didn't feel so bad anymore. Not about the case, nor the budget, nor the politics involved.

"You make my feet warm." She was finally finished, her face flushed with exertion, her brow beaded with sweat.

"Marvelous," he said.

"It's good exercise for me, too."

"It's the first time for me."

"I know," she said, her hand lightly touching the knot of her robe. "What about the full service now?"

That was something he could not do. A line he must not cross. This was the time to flash his I.D. Chief Inspector Chen should now take her to the police bureau and charge her with prostitution. But what about Professor Xie? He had given her his promise. News of what had become of Xie Rong would be too terrible a blow to the old intellectual who had already suffered a lot. The arrest would also incriminate his new friend Ouyang. Also, once she was taken into custody here, he was not sure if his local colleagues would help with his investigation. He was not sure that he could work out a deal for Xie in exchange for her information about Wu Xiaoming.

"You are sweating all over." He sounded more like a client so that she would not grow suspicious. "Take a good shower yourself. I'll stay here and close my eyes for five minutes."

"Yes, there is nothing like taking a short nap," she said. "I'll be back in fifteen minutes."

The moment she disappeared, he took a mini-recorder out of his briefcase and put it under the pillow. He put his shirt back on and buttoned several buttons before he closed his eyes for just a minute. In spite of himself, he dozed off. When he was awakened by the slamming of the bathroom door, it took him a few seconds to realize where he was.

She stepped out of the bathroom, naked except for a large bath towel draped around her shoulders. Fine-limbed and thin, she looked more like a high-school girl waiting for a regular checkup—except for a broad patch of black hair spreading over the lower part of her abdomen. She examined herself in the mirror, the water beading on her skin under the fluorescent light, which turned her face opalescent. Then she caught him gazing at her in the mirror. Startled, she pulled the towel down to cover her hips, but then she shook her wet hair, and gave him a long, steady look.

She started slowly toward the bed. He smelled the soap on her skin, still wet from the shower. Clean, fresh. Her body glowed.

"You are special," she said.

He was so acutely aware of her, it took all his willpower to stop her from touching him.

"Let's talk," he said.

"No," she touched a finger to his mouth, "you don't have to say anything."

"We don't know each other yet."

"Haven't we talked enough?" she said. "Unless you want to talk about money."

"Well—"

"Mr. Ouyang has paid for a whole day's service, and you've given me a handsome tip," she said. "So you can have the whole day, and the night, too. You don't have to worry about it. If you want to buy me a dinner afterward—"

"No." He sat up resolutely. It was not just all the years studying the People's Police Morals Manual that had made Chen immune to such provocation. "I want to talk to you about something else."

"What?"

"I'm a cop." He produced his official I.D. "I'm here to ask you some questions."

"You S.O.B!" She put one hand over her breasts and the other over her pubic hair.

It struck him as an absurd attempt at modesty, as if his being a cop had suddenly changed her identity, too.

"You won't get into trouble if you cooperate with me," he said. "I give you my word."

"Then why didn't you say so from start?"

"When I came to you, I was not prepared to see you like this. Ouyang had just told me that you were the one I've been looking for. I was surprised, and you did not give me a chance to say anything." He handed the bathrobe over to her. "Put it on before you get cold."

"I don't trust you," she said, taking the bathrobe. "Why should I cooperate with you?"

"I can have you arrested," he said, taking out the recorder from under the pillow. "Once you are put in jail, you'll have to talk anyway, but that's not what I want to do."

"What a treacherous sneak!"

"I'm a police officer."

"So why don't you go ahead and put me there?"

"Ouyang is my friend. Besides—"

"Why did you lie to Ouyang about being a poet?"

"No, I didn't. I am a poet."

It took him some time to ferret out his Writers' Association membership card from his wallet.

"Then what the hell do you want with me?"

"Just a few questions."

"You are so horrible." She broke down, sobbing with fear and humiliation. "When I was ready—"

He had attained authority over her with his surprise revelation of his official identity. But they were still involved in a highly dramatic scene. He, in his half-buttoned shirt and underpants; she, in a bathrobe. The knowledge of her nakedness under the robe, soft and bulging in the right places, was disturbing. He poured her a cup of tea to calm them both.

Sipping at the tea, her painted toes like fallen petals on the carpet, she regained some control.

The touch of her toes was still fresh in his memory.

"Let's go to a restaurant," he suggested. "I'm hungry."

"What?"

"You mentioned dinner afterwards."

"Why? More of your dirty tricks?"

"No. I just want to buy you a meal. What about the White Swan Hotel? It is quiet there, Ouyang's told me. As for your time—"

"Don't worry about that. Ouyang has paid for the whole day."

"So the least I can do is pay for the lunch."

He had saved enough to be able to afford this gesture, thanks to Ouyang, who had bought him so many morning teas and dinners.

"Why can't we stay here?"

"Listen, I'm a cop," he said, "but I'm a man too. If I stay here with you, just the two of us, I won't be able to help feeling distracted."

"So I'm not repulsive to you?"

"We need to have a good talk."

"Fine, if that's what you want."

She got up and went into the bathroom without closing the door. Her robe fell to the floor in a heap around her feet, her bare breasts and hips were vivid in the mirror. He turned to the window.

When she came back, she had put on a white summer dress and slung a small purse over her shoulder. She did not wear a bra, so her nipples were almost imprinted on the dress. He considered asking her to put on something else, but he held the door open for her.

On the street, he noticed she kept looking back over her shoulder, as if anxious to make sure there was no one following them. There was actually a man walking behind them at a distance, but Chief Inspector Chen did not see why they would be followed.

The White Swan Hotel was a new building on the southeastern coast of Shamian Island. It was an immense white tower, like a transplant from Hong Kong across the water. There was a dazzling waterfall in the lobby. Several Western-style restaurants were located in the eastern wing of the building, and the Chinese restaurant was tucked behind the waterfall. There was a slender hostess standing at its entrance, smiling.

He was not going to indulge himself, but he felt obliged to spend some money. He did not like the idea of having Ouyang pay for everything, even for Xie Rong's "service." And he had to admit the so-called foot massage had been an exciting experience,.

They selected a private room—the Sampan Chamber. It proved to be a cozy room shaped like the cabin of a sampan on the Pearl River and decorated like one, too. The table and chairs were made of cedar—rough, unpolished, like those he'd seen in early black-and-white movies. The soft scarlet carpet on the floor was the only difference, but it was a necessary one, to give the customer a feeling of luxury. They could talk here without fear of being overheard.

A young waitress came in. She was wearing an indigo blue homespun top and a miniskirt, barefoot, with silver bangles jingling around her ankles, exactly like a fishing girl in the southern provinces—except for the menu in her hand.

He turned the menu over to Xie. She surprised him by choosing several inexpensive dishes, and shaking her head at one of the chef's specials—fish-fragrance-sauced pigeon—recommended by the waitress.

"No, it's too expensive."

"Anything to drink?"

"Just a cup of water for me."

"Well, we'll have two iced beers then."

"You shouldn't. They charge three or four times more than they should for drinks," she added after the waitress had left, almost like a virtuous wife who wanted to save every penny. Good. Chief Inspector Chen was starting to worry about the expense.

"I thought you'd take me to the police station," she said.

"Why should I?"

"Maybe you will." She reached into the leather handbag, took out a cigarette, but did not light it immediately. "Sooner or later."

"No, whatever you do, it's not my business—not here. But I don't think it a good idea for you to stay . . . in that profession."

"You are being genteel," she said. "I do not like what you do either, but it is not so bad that I won't have lunch with you."

Smiling, she raised her glass toward him, relaxing as more dishes arrived on the table. The restaurant was known among Guangdong people for its excellent cooking.

At one point, their chopsticks crossed each other in an attempt to get hold of a large scallop on a bed of green snow beans.

"Please, you have it," she said.

"It's yours," he said, "after all your work."

The scallop looked like her big toe. White, soft, round.

She ate with relish, finishing four pancakes rolled up with roast duck and green onion, a bowl of shrimp dumplings, and almost the entire serving of beef tripe. He himself did not eat much but he put morsels in her saucer and sipped at his cup of Qingdao beer.

"Do you always eat this little?" she asked.

"I'm not hungry," he said, afraid there would not be enough food for both of them.

"You are so romantic," she said.

"Really?" That was a strange compliment, he thought, to a police officer.

There was something touching his knee under the table. As it slowly traveled up, he knew it was her bare foot. She had removed her shoes. He clasped her leg where it was thinnest, and his hand became an ankle bracelet, slipping down. The shape of her smallest toe, bending with the adjoining ones, was distracting him in a way beyond his comprehension. Gently, he put her foot down.

Confucius said, "To eat and to mate is human nature."

"What about a special dessert?" he asked.

"No, thank you."

They shared segments of a Mandarin orange and sipped at the jasmine tea—compliments of the restaurant.

"Now I'm full," she said. "You can start your questioning. But tell me first, how did you find me here?"

"Well, I had met your mother. She has no idea what you're doing in Guangzhou. She's so worried."

"She's always worried—all her life—about one thing or another."

"She's disappointed, I believe, that you did not take her path."

"Her path, indeed?" she said. "Dear Comrade Chief Inspector, how can you go about investigating people without seeing the change in society? Who's interested in literature anymore?"

"I, for one. In fact, I've read a collection of her essays."

"I do not mean you. You're so different, as Old Ouyang said."

"Another of your bogus compliments?"

"No, I think so, too," she said. "As for my mother, I love her. Her life's not been easy. She got her Ph.D. in the United States. What happened to her when she came back in the early fifties? She was declared to be a rightist, and then a counterrevolutionary in the sixties. Not until after the Cultural Revolution was she allowed to teach again."

"But she is teaching at a prestigious university."

"Well, as a full professor at Fudan University, how much can she earn in a month? Less than what I made as a tourist guide for a week."

"Money is not everything. But for a joke of fate, I might have studied comparative literature."

"Thank heaven for that joke—whatever it was."

"Life can be unfair to people—especially so for your mother's generation—but we have reasons to believe that things won't be so bad in the future."

"For you, maybe not, Comrade Chief Inspector. And thank you for your political lecture, too," she said. "I think it's time that you start asking your questions."

"Well, some may be difficult. But whatever you say will be kept confidential, I give you my word."

"I'll tell you whatever I know—after such a meal as you've just given me."

"You had worked as a tourist guide before coming to Guangzhou."

"Yes, I quit that job a couple of months ago."

"On one of the Yellow Mountain trips, you met a man named Wu Xiaoming?"

"Wu Xiaoming? Oh yes, I remember him."

"He had a girlfriend with him during the trip, hadn't he?"

"Yes," she said, "but at first I did not know it."

"When did you come to know this?"

"The second or the third day of the trip. But why, Comrade Chief Inspector? What makes me worth your trip to Guangzhou?"

"She was murdered last month."

"What?"

He produced a picture out of his briefcase. She took it over, and her fingers holding the picture trembled.

"That's her."

"She was Guan Hongying, a national model worker, and Wu Xiaoming's our suspect. So what you know about the two of them may be very important."

"Before I say anything," she said, looking into the glass in her hand, and then up at him, "I want you to answer a question."

"Go ahead."

"Are you aware of his family background?"

"Of course, I'm aware of that."

"Then why do you want to pursue the investigation?"

"It's my job."

"Come on, there are so many cops in China. You're not the only one. Why are you so dedicated?"

"I'm . . . a romantic cop, as you have said. I believe in justice. Poetic justice if you want to call it that."

"You think you can bring him down."

"We have a good chance. That's why I need your cooperation."

"Oh," she said softly, "you really are special. No wonder Old Ouyang likes you so much. Now that you have answered my questions, I will answer yours."

"What was your first impression of them?"

"I cannot remember exactly, but one of the first things I noticed about them was their assumed names."

"How could you tell?"

"Wu registered for both of them in our office. He had to change a character stroke in his signature."

"You're very observant," he said. "No one makes a mistake with his own signature."

"What's more, they registered as a couple, asking for a double room, but instead of showing their marriage license, he only provided me with a statement on official letterhead. Normally, it would be much easier to show the license."

"I see." He nodded. "Did you talk to your boss about your suspicion?"

"No, it was just an idea that crossed my mind. In the mountains, I noticed something else."

"What's that?"

"It was the second morning, I think. I happened to pass by their room. A perfect day, and everybody was having a wonderful time outside. I saw something like continuous flashing inside their room through the blinds. I felt curious—and a bit responsible too. So I peeped in. I was shocked to see Guan posing nude, on all fours, her legs wide apart, her forehead pressing against her forearms on the ground, like a kneeling dog. He was taking pictures of her. Now why should a couple come all the way to a mountain hotel room to take those pictures?"

"Um, you may have a point there," Chen said. "Did you speak?"

"Of course not. But later Wu approached me."

"How?"

"In his professional way, of course. He showed me the advanced equipment he carried in his camera bag. Imported pieces. Very expensive. There was also an album containing center-fold-size photographs of beautiful women, including a notorious actress, and some fashion models and some clippings from well-known magazines."

"Why did he want to show all that to you?"

"He said that as a professional photographer, he was hot. These women were all eager to have pictures taken by him and published. And he offered to take pictures of me."

"I see," he said. "So you accepted his offer?"

"No, not at first. It made me sick, the sight of Guan kneeling at his feet like a groveling dog. Nor did I like the idea of posing for a stranger.

"Right, you cannot be too careful nowadays. What did he do then?"

"He showed me his business card. Only then did I come to know who he was—his real name. Of course, he told me about his family background. I asked him why he had chosen a nobody like me. He said he saw in me what he had never seen before. Lost innocence or something. With his photos, he might be able to introduce me to directors."

"A trick he must have played with many people."

"He also promised I could keep all the pictures. A set of fashion pictures taken at a studio on Nanjing Road would cost a fortune, but I would not have to pay him a penny."

"Well, how was he as a photographer?"

"A real pro. He used up five rolls of film in the first hour. He kept changing the lighting and angles, and kept me changing clothes and poses, too. He said he wanted to capture my most beautiful moments."

"That sounds romantic."

"Before I knew it, he wanted me to pose with a towel around my body. He arranged the folds for me, adjusted my positions, and touched me here and there. One thing led to another, and to the bed. I think I'll spare you the details."

"So you were together quite a number of times?"

"No, only twice, if that's what you mean. During the day I was busy, meeting all the customers' requests. There were about twenty people in the group. And he could come to me only in the evening—only after Guan fell asleep."

"And what was he like in bed?"

"What do you mean?"

"Sexually."

"You really want to know?"

"Yes, details can be crucial in a case like this."

"As far as I could judge, he was just average, and me, too."

"Can you try to be a bit more specific?"

"More specific? All right, I want a man to take me up and down until I don't have anything left. He happened to be that kind. Bang, bang, bang, till the end of the world."

"Did he show any perversity?"

"No, he always had me lie on my back, with a pillow under my hips, and my legs spread wide apart. Thorough-going, no digression or deviation." She added, in a sarcastic tone, "We should have stayed in the massage room, where I could demonstrate to your satisfaction."

"No," he said, "that's not what I want. I'm a cop, so I have to ask you these questions. I'm sorry."

"No, you don't have to feel sorry. What am I? A trashy massage girl. A high-ranking police officer can do anything with me."

"A different question—" he said, catching a note of hysteria resurfacing in her voice, "how did Guan come to fight with you?"

"She must have suspected something. Wu came to my room more than once. Or maybe she had seen a Polaroid of me."

"When did it happen?"

"Two or three days after the photo session, I was alone in my room, taking a break when she burst in. She accused me of sleeping with her man. But she's not his wife. Wu had told me. It was the pot calling the kettle black."

"What did you say to her?"

"'Pee your chaste pee, and see your own reflection in it,' and she fell on me like a tigress. What a fury. She screamed and scratched, with both hands and all her fingers."

"Did the hotel security people come?"

"No, but Wu did. He took her side, trying his best to calm her down. He did not say a single kind word to me, as if I were an old piece of mop cloth discarded on the floor. And she was mad, shouting and screaming at him, too."

"Do you remember what she said?"

"No, I was devastated. Even to think about it now . . . Give me a cigarette."

She screwed her eyes shut against the smoke.

Through the smoke, he was studying her carefully, waiting.

"What did she want him to do?" he said.

"Be nice to her, I guess, like a husband—or to be her husband, I think. She was not coherent. She screamed like a jealous wife catching an unfaithful husband in the act."

"Let me ask one more question," he said. "Did the fight lead to your quitting the travel agency job?"

"No, not really. It took place behind a closed door. Even if people had overheard, it was none of their business. Guan threatened that she would approach my boss, but she did not do anything."

"She would not," he said, "not in her position."

Her napkin fell to the floor. Courteously he stooped to pick it up for her. Under the table, he saw her bare feet hooked over the bottom rung of her chair, as if cut off by the white tablecloth.

"Thanks," she said, wiping her lips with the napkin. "I think that's all I can remember, Comrade Chief Inspector."

"Thank you, Xie Rong. You've given us some very important information."

The bill was larger than Chief Inspector Chen had expected, but Xie's information was definitely worth it. The waitress walked out with them, holding the door open.

As they started back to her house, a silence fell between them. She said little until they came in sight of her building.

"You don't seem old enough to be a chief inspector," she said, slowing her steps.

"I'm older than you," Chen said. "Much older."

A ray of sunshine spilled over her loose hair, illuminating her clear profile. They stood close, her head nearly touching his shoulder.

"It's one of my mother's favorite stories. A gallant knight on a white horse comes to rescue a princess from a dungeon guarded by black demons," she said. "For her, the world's black and white."

"And for you?"

"No." She shook her head. "Nothing's ever been that simple."

"I understand," he said. "But I've promised your mother to bring her message to you. You're her only daughter, and she wants you to come home."

"That's nothing new," she said.

"If you move back, and want to find a different job, I may be able to help."

"Thank you," she said. "But I'm making money now, in my way. I'm my own boss here, and I don't have to put up with any political shit."

"You're going to make it a life-long career?"

"No, I'm still young. After I've made enough money, I will start something different, something after my own heart. I don't think you want to come to my room again."

"No, I have to leave. I have a lot of work."

"You don't have to tell me that."

"I hope we will see each other," he added, "under different circumstances."

"I was—straight—until two or three months ago," she said. "I want you to know."

"I know."

"You know that as a chief inspector?"

"No, but I also want you to know," he said, "you are an attractive woman."

"Do you think so?"

"I do, but I'm a cop. And I have been one for several years. That's the way I live."

She nodded, looking up at him, ready to say something, but she didn't.

"As for the life I lead, it is not so good either," he went on.

"I see."

"So take care of yourself," he said. "Bye." He started walking away.

The smell of rain was in the air as he boarded a bus back to the Writers' Home. The bus was packed, and he felt sick, covered with sweat all over again. The moment he got to his room, he took a shower. It was the second of the day. And the hot water ran short again. He hurried out of the bathroom. Sitting on the bed, he lit a cigarette.

That earlier shower at Xie's room was much better. He felt sorry about Xie's way of life, but he was in no position to do anything about it. It had been her choice. If the job was no more than a temporary one, as she had said, there could still be a different future for her. One thing he was supposed to do—as a cop—was to report her illegal practice to the local authorities. But he had decided not to.

Ouyang had not returned yet.

Chief Inspector Chen realized it was time for him to leave Guangzhou. His mission accomplished, he should have taken Ouyang for a farewell dinner as his treat. But it would make him feel guilty if he kept his nonpoetic identity a secret any longer from Ouyang, whom he had come to regard as a friend. So he wrote a short note, saying that he had to go back to Shanghai on urgent business, and that he would keep in touch. He also left his home phone number.

He added two lines of Li Bai to the note to him:

> *Deep as the Peach Blossom Lake can be,*
> *But not so deep as your song you sing for me.*

Then he checked out.

Chapter 25

"Chief Inspector Chen," he said, picking up his office phone. It was Chen's first morning in the office after his return from Guangzhou. He had hardly had time to make himself a cup of the Black Dragon tea which was Ouyang's gift.

"This is the office of the Shanghai Party Discipline Committee. Comrade Director Yao Liangxia wants to see you today."

It was an unexpected call, and the voice from the other end of the line was unfriendly.

"Comrade Director Yao?" he said. "What's it about?"

"That you need to discuss with Comrade Yao. You know where our office is, I believe."

"Yes, I do. I will be there shortly."

Yao Liangxia, whose late husband had been a deputy polit-buro member in the sixties, was herself an influential Party figure. Why should Director Yao want to see him?

Chen glanced out of his cubicle. Detective Yu had not come in yet. Party Secretary Li would not show up, as a rule, until after ten. He could make his Guangzhou report after coming back from the Party Discipline Committee.

The committee office was in Zhonghui Mansion, one of the impressive colonial-style buildings at the corner of Sichuan and Fuzhou Roads. He had passed the building many times, but he had not realized that there were so many institutions headquartered there—Old Men's Health Society, Women's Rights Committee, Consumers' Rights Association, Children's Rights Committee . . . He had to study the lobby directory for several minutes before locating Director Yao's office on the thirteenth floor.

The bronze elevator had been sprayed with some supposedly high-class air freshener; the air inside felt inexplicably close. He was unable to shake off the sense of being caged even as he left the elevator, which deposited him just in front of Yao's office.

The Party Discipline Committee had been founded in the early eighties, with its central office in Beijing and branch offices in all large cities. After the Cultural Revolution, it was realized that the Party, with its unlimited, uncensored power, was unable to resist corruption, which would eventually lead to its downfall. So the committee, mainly consisting of retired senior Party members, came into existence to prevent and punish Party members' abuses of power. Its main responsibility as a watchdog was to exercise a sort of censorship but the committee was not an independent institution. While it had conducted several intra-Party corruption cases, most of the time it barked rather than bit. However, the committee, which was authorized to perform background checks on Party members, was influential in the process of young cadre promotion.

Chen's knock on the office door brought out a middle-aged woman with an inquiring look. When he handed over his card, the woman, whose voice he recognized as that of the secretary on the phone, led him into an elegantly furnished reception room containing a large oyster-colored leather sofa, flanked by two mahogany chairs and a tall antique hat stand.

He had anticipated that Director Yao would keep him waiting for a while. To his surprise, Yao came out immediately and shook his hand firmly. She led him into her office and had him sit in a leather club chair in front of a huge oak desk.

Yao was an impressive-looking woman in her late sixties, squared-faced with thick eyebrows, wearing a dark suit, which was immaculate, without a single wrinkle. No jewelry. Minimal makeup. She sat straight, appearing unusually tall behind her impressive desk, perhaps due to the combined impression of her starched collar, the splendid view from the office window in back of her, as well as his seat. Sitting in a chair much lower than Yao's, almost as if he was a witness at an inquisition, he was nervous.

"Comrade Chief Inspector Chen, I'm pleased to meet you today." Yao spoke with a pronounced Shandong accent, which also fit the image of an "old Marxist woman," a notorious character in the movie *Black Cannon Incident*, in which a Marxist bureaucrat made a fool of herself by punctuating her every speech with quotations from Marx and Mao. Chen had seen it with Wang, who joked about his becoming a "young Marxist man."

"It's an honor to meet you, Comrade Director Yao."

"You're probably not surprised to learn that you are highly regarded by us old comrades, Comrade Chief Inspector Chen. I've spoken to a number of people, and they all praise you as an intelligent and dedicated young cadre. You are on the seminar list of the Central Party Institute, aren't you?"

"Yes, but I'm still young, inexperienced. So I have so much to learn from old comrades."

"And you are working hard, too, I know. You've been quite busy recently, Comrade Chief Inspector?"

"Yes, we're short-handed."

"Is there some important case you are responsible for?"

"Several. Every case is important—to us."

"Well, I have heard that you are investigating the case of Guan Hongying, the national model worker."

He didn't know whether that was a statement or a question, so he just nodded. But how could she have heard of it, he wondered.

"Is there any result so far?"

"A few promising leads, but nothing definite. A lot of questions are unanswered."

"What are they?"

"Such as evidence, motive, and witnesses." He was growing uneasy, as it was beyond the scope of Yao's office to be concerned with a homicide case. "At present, everything is just hypothetical."

"I have asked you to come here," she said with a stern quality in her Shandong-accented voice, "because I want to know how you are conducting the investigation."

"It is a homicide case. We are following routine procedure."

"You have targeted your suspect, haven't you?"

"Yes." He saw no point withholding the information. "At this stage, Wu Xiaoming is our main suspect."

"Comrade Wu Bing's son?"

"Yes."

"How could that be? Wu Bing and I were colleagues in the early fifties, in the same office, and Wu Xiaoming used to play with our kids in the same kindergarten. I haven't seen him lately, but he is doing a good job, I've learned from a cadre recommendation report from the *Red Star*. People have a very high opinion of him."

"Wu might be doing a good job at the magazine, but he had an affair with Guan. In fact, he called her on the very night of her death."

"Really!"

"Yes, we have evidence."

"What kind of evidence?"

He chose to be vague: "At present, circumstantial evidence."

"So from this circumstantial evidence you conclude," she said sharply, "that Wu Bing's son has committed the murder."

"No, we are not jumping to any conclusion. It's still under investigation."

"Still, the news would be a terrible blow to Wu Bing, and he's in such poor health."

"Comrade Wu Bing is an old comrade I have always respected. We know he is in the hospital. We know that. So we are being very careful."

"Whatever Wu Xiaoming's family background, I am not going to shelter him. Far from it. If he is found guilty, he should be punished. That's Party policy."

"Thank you for your support, Comrade Director Yao."

"But, Comrade Chief Inspector Chen, have you thought about the people's reaction to your investigation?"

Director Yao was surrounded by walls of thick, gold-edged government books. All the furniture in her office was massive. Everything bespoke the solidity of authority.

"Reaction?" he asked. "I am not clear what reaction you're talking about."

"People would say, 'What, Wu Bing's son has committed murder! Those HCC!' That will not be helpful to our Party's image."

"Comrade Director Yao, as a Party member as well as a police officer, I've always regarded it as my highest responsibility to defend the unsoiled image of our Party, but I don't see how our investigation can endanger it."

"Comrade Chief Inspector Chen," she said, sitting even more upright and crossing her hands on the desk, "our Party has made tremendous progress in economic and political reform, but during such a transitional period, there may be some problems people will complain about. And currently there is a social view opposed to high cadres' children—the so-called HCC—as if they were all capable of any wrong. Of course it's not true."

"I see your point, Comrade Director Yao," he said. "As early as elementary school, I learned what a great contribution the high cadres—the revolutionaries of the old generation—made to our country. So how can I have any prejudice against their children? Our investigation has nothing to do with any misconception about HCC. This is just a homicide case assigned to our special case group. We've made a point of keeping it from the media. I don't see how people could know anything about our investigation."

"You never know, Comrade Chief Inspector." She then changed the subject. "So you went to Guangzhou a few days ago."

"Yes, to make inquiries there."

Director Yao's knowledge of his trip disturbed him. Neither the Shanghai nor Guangzhou Public Police Bureau had to report a police officer's activity to the Party Discipline Committee. In fact, there were not too many people who knew about the trip. He had left for Guangzhou without making a report to Party Secretary Li. Commissar Zhang and Detective Yu were the only people he had informed.

"It is close to Hong Kong. The special zone. You must have seen a different spirit there—a different lifestyle."

"No. I was conducting an investigation there. Whatever the difference may have been, I did not have time to experience it. Trust me, Comrade Director Yao, I'm doing a conscientious job."

"Don't get me wrong, Comrade Chief Inspector Chen. Of course the Party trusts you. That's why I wanted you to come to my office today, I'd also like to make a suggestion to you. For a politically sensitive case like this, I think we all need to proceed with the utmost caution. It is best left in the hands of the Internal Security."

"Internal Security? It's a homicide case, Comrade Director Yao. I don't think I see the necessity."

"You will, if you think about the possible political impact."

"If Wu Xiaoming proves to be innocent, we're not going to do anything. But if he is guilty, everybody is equal before the law." He added, "Of course, Comrade Director Yao, we'll be very careful to keep your instruction in mind."

"So you're determined to go on with the investigation."

"Yes, I'm a cop."

"Well . . ." she said finally, "it is just my suggestion. You're a chief inspector, and it is up to you to decide. Still, I would appreciate it if you'd report to me when you make some progress in your investigation. It is in the Party's interests."

"That will be fine," he said, trying to be vague again. He did not think it was his responsibility to report to her. "I'm a Party member. I will do everything in accordance with bureau procedure, and in the interests of the Party, too."

"People are talking about your dedication to your work. Their praise seems to be justified," she said, rising from her desk. "You've a great future ahead of you, Comrade Chief Inspector Chen. We are old. Sooner or later we will have to entrust our socialist cause to young people like you. So I expect to see you soon."

"Thank you, Director Yao," he said. "Your advice and instructions are very important to me."

Everything she said was like a quotation from a political textbook, he reflected, nodding nonetheless.

"Also," she continued in the same serious voice, "we're concerned about your personal life."

"My personal life?"

"You are a young cadre in the process of being promoted, and it's proper and right for us to be concerned. You're in your mid-thirties, aren't you? It's time for you to settle down."

"Thank you, Comrade Director Yao. I've just been so busy."

"Yes, I know. I've read the article about your work by that *Wenhui* reporter."

She walked him to the elevator. Once more, they shook hands, formally.

Outside, the drizzle was heavier.

Director Yao's interference was ominous.

It was not just that this senior Party official knew Wu Xiaoming so well. Yao and Wu's families had moved in the same circles. An old cadre herself, her reaction to an investigation against an HCC was not too surprising. But her knowledge of the case was alarming, and she was so inquisitive about his investigation in Guangzhou, and even about his personal life, including "that *Wenhui* reporter." In her position, Yao was not supposed to be aware of these things— unless Chen himself was under investigation.

The committee was the most powerful institution determining a cadre's promotion or demotion. A week earlier, Chief Inspector Chen had told himself that he was on the way up—to serve the people.

Now he was not sure.

Chapter 26

When Chief Inspector Chen returned to the bureau, it was past twelve o'clock.

Party Secretary Li was still not in. Nor was Detective Yu. And Chen's phone was ringing off the hook. The first call came from Beijing headquarters. It was about a case solved long ago. He had no idea why Chief Inspector Qiao Daxing, his counterpart in Beijing, wanted to talk to him about it. Qiao spent twenty minutes of a long-distance call without mentioning anything new or substantial, and ended up saying that he looked forward to seeing Chen in Beijing and to treating him to Beijing roast duck on Huangfujing Avenue.

The second call was also a surprise. It came from the *Wenhui Daily*, not from Wang Feng but from an editor whom he hardly knew. A reader had written to the newspaper, asking the editor to forward her thanks to the poet for the realistic description of down-to-earth police officers. Ironic, he thought, since no one had called him "realistic" before.

The most unexpected call came from Old Hunter, Detective Yu's father.

"You recognize my voice, Chief Inspector Chen. I know you're busy, but I want to discuss something with you. Guangming, that young rascal, is going to send my gray hair into the grave."

"What! Guangming? He's the most filial son under the sun."

"Well, if you can spare me half an hour of your precious time, I will tell you all about it. Now you're having your plastic box of lunch again, I guess. No good. What about coming to the Mid-Lake Teahouse, you know the one, behind the City God's Temple. I'll buy you a cup of genuine Dragon Well green tea. It will agree with your stomach. I'm calling from a pay phone there."

It was a request to which Chen could hardly say no, and not just because of his friendship with Detective Yu. Old Hunter had served in the force for over thirty years. Though retired, the old man still considered himself an insider, with his connections in the bureau and out.

"Okay, I'll be there in about twenty minutes. Don't worry, Guangming's fine."

In the case of serious trouble between father and son, however, Chen didn't think that he was the best choice as a mediator, nor was it the right time for him to intervene. The talk he had just had at the Discipline Committee weighed heavily on his mind.

But he swallowed his plastic-box lunch, then made his way to the temple in a hurry.

The City God's Temple was said to have been built during the Southern Song dynasty in the fifteenth century. The temple had been rebuilt and refurbished a number of times, the last in 1926. The main hall had been reinforced with concrete, the clay images gilded. In the early sixties, the images had been smashed to pieces as a result of the Socialist Education Movement, and in the early eighties the temple had undergone another drastic renovation after being used as a general storage place, for it was then turned into an arts-and-crafts shopping center. The original appearance of the temple was now restored, with black-painted doors and yellow walls. Its interior presented a dazzling array of shining glass counters and stainless steel shelves. On the door was a couplet engraved in bold brush strokes: *Be an honest man so that you can enjoy a peaceful sleep,/ Do something good so that God will know about it.*

Communists, of course, did not believe in God, Oriental or Occidental, but it was nonetheless good advice to people to do something good and to have a clear conscience, especially from a cop's point of view.

So a marketplace had been made from a temple.

In front of the temple, however, he saw a group of elderly women gathering around something like a cushion. Several were kneeling on the ground. One was kowtowing before the cushion with bunches of burning incense in her hands and murmuring something almost inaudibly:

"City God . . . protect . . . family . . . stock . . ."

It was obvious that the temple was still a temple—at least to these worshippers.

Appearance and reality.

Some people said that sooner or later a temple would be made out of the market. Maybe this was a metaphor for commodity fetishism. Maybe not. He was becoming befuddled.

The surrounding bazaar consisted of numerous small shops selling a variety of local products, but what made the bazaar special was an incredible number of Chinese snack shops, bars and booths. The snacks were not expensive, but delicious in their unique flavors. In his high-school years, Chen had once invited Overseas Chinese Lu and Four-Eyed Jiang to an ambitious campaign—to sample every snack shop in one afternoon. Their tactic was to share everything. Each tried no more than one small bite. So in one afternoon they had tasted chicken and duck blood soup, radish-shred cake, shrimp and meat dumplings, beef soup noodles, fried bean curd and vermicelli. . . . They had not succeeded. Halfway through, their joint funds ran out. But that had been one of their happiest days.

Four-Eyed Jiang had thrown himself into a well during the Cultural Revolution, Overseas Chinese Lu had his restaurant now, and he, he was a police inspector.

The Mid-Lake Teahouse was a place they had not visited during that campaign, but he knew it to be a two-storied pavilion shaped like a pagoda in the middle of a man-made lake, opposite the Crane and Pine Restaurant. There was a nine-turn stone bridge with a flight of steps leading to the teahouse. He made his way across the bridge, which was full of tourists at every turn: People pointing at the lotus flowers swaying in the breeze, throwing bread crumbs to the golden carp swimming among the blossoms, or posing for pictures with the teahouse in the background.

There were only a few tea drinkers on the first floor. Chen looked around without catching sight of Old Hunter, so he walked up the vermilion-railed stairs. On the second floor there were even fewer customers, and he saw the old man sitting by the window with a teapot.

"Come and sit with me, Comrade Chief Inspector," the old man said, waving his hand, as Chen moved toward a seat beside him.

"Thank you," Chen said. "It's so elegant here."

Their table overlooked the lake filled with lotuses. The view was serene.

"On the second floor everything costs twice as much. But it's worth it. A cup of tea here is the only indulgence I've permitted myself since retirement."

Chen nodded. A cup of tea here was different from one in the crowded, stuffy room that contained the retired old man's daily life since he had relinquished the front room to his son.

There was a whisper of southern bamboo music in the teahouse, perhaps from a tape player somewhere. A silver-haired waiter carrying a heavy shining brass kettle poured the water in a graceful arc into the tiny cup before Chen. There was lore to this. In ancient China, teahouse waiters had been called Doctors of Tea, and the teahouse was a place of spiritual cultivation, as well as where people exchanged daily information.

"I know you also like good tea," Old Hunter said. "I do not know how to say this without sounding too condescending, Comrade Chief Inspector. There are not too many people I'm willing to drink tea with."

"Thank you," he said.

That's true, he thought. The old man had always been proud in his way, but nice. And helpful to him.

"I've something for you, Comrade Chief Inspector. Since I cannot get hold of Guangming, I may as well tell you."

"He's so busy," Chen said. "I have not seen him today, either."

"Working on that model worker case?"

"Yes, but what's the problem?"

"It's not really about Guangming, but about the case. Guangming has discussed it with me. I'm no outsider, you know. I have some information about it."

"Really, older ginger is spicier than young, Uncle Yu," Chen said, resorting to a cliché. "You surely have the knack of digging out information."

"A woman called Jiao Nanhua told me that Guan was having an affair shortly before her death."

"Who is Jiao Nanhua?"

"She's a dumpling vendor on Guan's street, on the corner, in front of the grocery shop. A night vendor with a miniature kitchen on her shoulder. She literally carries everything on a bamboo pole. On one end of the pole, a stove, and a pot of steaming water, and on the other, a shelf with dumpling skins, ground pork, vegetables, bowls, spoons, and chopsticks. She does her business when restaurants are closed, making dumplings then and there for the customer on the street. In three minutes, she'll have a steaming bowl in your hands."

"That's nice! I wish there was one like that in our neighborhood, too," Chen said, aware of Old Hunter's other nickname, "Suzhou Opera Singer," a reference to a popular southern dialect opera known for its performers' tactics of prolonging a story through endless digression. "So what did she say?"

"I am just coming round to it." Old Hunter was sipping at his tea with a leisured show of enjoyment. "A story must be told from the very beginning. Don't get impatient, Comrade Chief Inspector. Now on several occasions, very late in the night, Jiao saw a car pulling up across the street. Just about ten feet away. A young woman would emerge, hurrying toward the dorm building at the entrance of Qinghe Lane. The dorm was at some distance from where Jiao stood, so she could not see clearly, and she did not pay much attention at first. It was not her business. Still, she grew more and more curious. Why didn't the car pull up just in front of the lane? It's really easy to do so. It was not pleasant for a young woman to walk the distance, alone, in the depth of the night. Jiao was also a bit upset, I believe, because the mysterious woman never came over to buy a bowl of dumplings from her. One night, she moved her mini-kitchen over to the other side of the street. She was licensed to do business on Hubei Street, so it did not matter where she positioned herself. And the car appeared again—"

"Then who did she see?" Chen was growing impatient.

"Guan Hongying. None other! The well-known national model worker. Jiao immediately recognized her, having seen Guan's picture so many times in newspapers and on TV. Guan walked very fast, never looking around."

"Did she see anybody else with Guan?"

"No, except the one who drove the car."

"Did she see him?"

"Not clearly. He stayed in the car."

"What kind of a car?"

"A fancy one. White. Perhaps imported. She could not tell what make. But not a taxi. There was no taxi sign on top."

"Could there have been someone else in the car besides the driver?"

"No, she does not think so. In fact, she's quite positive there was only one person in the car."

"How can she be so positive?"

"She observed something Guan did. Every time, before heading for the dorm, Guan would lean into the window on the driver's side."

"What could that mean?"

"Guan leaned into the window for a long, passionate kiss."

"Oh, I see." It started to sound like a scene from a romantic movie, but the peddler could be right.

"She's certainly imaginative," Old Hunter chuckled. "A devilish woman."

"Excuse me, Uncle Yu. I'm just curious," Chen said. "How did she come to tell you all this?"

"Well," Old Hunter took a deliberately slow sip at his tea before reaching the climax of his story. "I'll let you in on a secret, but don't tell Guangming or anybody. And you can take the credit for discovering the witness."

"I won't tell anybody, but the credit remains yours."

"It's another long story. After my retirement, I made up my mind not to be a bore. I have seen too many retired policemen dogging their grandchildren's footsteps. I just wanted to walk around by myself, visiting various parts of the city I hadn't seen for years. Shanghai has changed such a lot. Slums have turned into parking lots, parks into factories, and a few streets have disappeared completely. But soon I had seen them all. To keep myself from being idle, I started working for the neighborhood security committee as a sort of watchdog. One of the areas I have patrolled is the food market on Fuzhou Road."

Chen knew that part of the story well. Detective Yu had told him all about it. At first, the patrolling job seemed to work out well for the old man. With the free market still regarded as politically "black"—an undesirable threat to the state market system—the work consisted of taking private peddlers' bamboo baskets and stamping on them vigorously. The job paid little, but the market patroller derived a good deal of pleasure from it, wearing a red armband, imagining himself a staunch pillar of justice whenever he drove a weeping country wench out of the market. But when times changed and the free market became a necessary complement to the socialist state market, the old man suddenly lost his purpose there.

"Are you still working there?"

"Yes. Things change so fast nowadays. Guangming and the other kids all wanted me to quit, but I'm still doing it. Not for money—just for something to do. Besides, a number of the peddlers are still up to no good, selling bad stuff and overcharging customers. And my job is to catch those guys in the act. It's not too much to do, but it's better than nothing at all. There should be somebody to keep an eye on them."

"I see," Chen said, "and I think you're right. So you patrol the market on Fuzhou Road."

"I can position myself anywhere close to the market, or the area related to it. These days peddlers no longer have to confine themselves to a market. So of late, I positioned myself close to Qinghe Lane, and I happened to catch Jiao, the peddler, in the act of stuffing her dumplings with ground pork that wasn't fresh. For something like that, she could have her license taken away. I told her that I used to be a cop, and that my son works in the bureau. That scared her out of her wits. I guessed she must have heard of Guan's death, since she does business in the neighborhood. I beat about the bush a bit, asking her to give me some information about the case. And sure enough, she did offer something in return for my not dragging her to the police station."

"You're not retired, Uncle Yu. And you're so experienced and resourceful."

"I'm glad that the information could be of some use to you. If necessary, she'll testify in court. I will see to it."

"Thank you so much. I don't know what else to say."

"You don't have to. Guess why I wanted to see you," Old Hunter said, looking into his tea, instead of at Chen. "I still have some connections, in the bureau and elsewhere. I'm a retired nobody, so people are not so guarded talking to me."

"Of course, people trust you," Chen nodded.

"I'm old. Nothing really matters that much to me now. You're still young. You are doing the right thing. An honest cop, there are not many like you left nowadays. But there are some people who do not like seeing you do the right thing. Some people high up."

So Old Hunter had called him for a reason. He had ruffled feathers at a high level. And people were talking about it. Was it possible that he had already been placed under surveillance?

"Those people can be dangerous. They'll have your phone

tapped, or your car bugged. They are not amateurs. So take care of yourself."

"Thank you, Uncle Yu. I will."

"That's all I can tell you. And I'm glad Guangming's working with you."

"I still believe justice will prevail," Chen said.

"So do I," Old Hunter said, raising his cup. "Let me drink a cup of tea to your success."

It could be his last case as a chief inspector, Chen thought somberly, as he made his way out of the crowded City God's Temple Market, if he insisted on continuing the investigation. If he buckled under the pressure, however, it might still be the last case for him. For he would not be able to call himself either an honest cop or a man with a clear conscience.

Chapter 27

When Chen reached Henan Road he thought he noticed a middle-aged man in a brown T-shirt walking behind him steadily, always at a distance, but never totally out of sight. The pressure of feeling watched, with every movement registered, every step followed, was a new experience. But when he went into a grocery store, the man in the brown T-shirt passed without slowing. Chen heaved a sigh of relief. Maybe he was too nervous. It was already past four. He was in no mood to go back to the bureau. So he decided to go to his mother's home, which was located in a small, quiet, graveled lane off Jiujiang Road.

He went out of his way to buy a pound of roast suckling pork in Heavenly Taste, a new privately run delicatessen. The suckling pork skin looked golden and crisp. She would like it. Though in her seventies, she still had good teeth. She had been out of his thoughts for days. He had even forgotten to buy anything for her in Guangzhou. He felt bad; he was her only son.

As the old house came in view, it struck him as strange, nearly unrecognizable, despite the fact that he had lived there with his mother for years, and in his own apartment for only a few months. The common cement sink by the front door was so damp he spotted green moss sprouting abundantly near the tap. The cracked walls would need extensive repairs and redecoration. The stairway was musty and dark, and the landings were piled with cardboard boxes and wicker baskets. Some might have been there for years.

His mother was silhouetted against the light falling through the curtain pulled halfway across the attic window.

"You haven't called for a few days, son."

"Sorry, Mother. I've been so busy recently," he said, "but you're always in my thoughts. And this room, too."

The familiar yet unfamiliar room. The framed photograph of his father in the forties in cap and gown stood on the cracked chest of drawers, an earnest-looking young scholar with a bright future. The photograph shone in the light. She was standing by it.

She had never really gotten over her husband's death, he reflected, though she seemed to manage, going to the food market every day, chatting with her neighbors, and doing Taiji practice in the morning. On several occasions he had tried to give her some money, but she declined. She insisted that he should save for himself.

"Don't you worry about me," she said, with the emphasis on the last word. "I've got a lot to do. I talk to your uncle on the phone almost every day, and I watch TV in the evening. There are more channels this month."

She had accepted only two things from him: the phone and the color TV.

The phone was not really his. The bureau had bought and installed it for him. When he was about to move out, he had another one set up in the new apartment. Theoretically, Chief Inspector Chen ought to have given up the old one, but he had made a point of having to talk to his mother everyday. She was in her seventies, living all by herself. Party Secretary Li had agreed with a nod; it was like being given a check for three thousand Yuan. The phone set itself was not that expensive, but with so many Shanghai people on the waiting list, installation would have cost a small fortune, not to mention all the official documents required to prove its necessity.

To her, it would be an invaluable safeguard against loneliness.

And the TV, too. He had bought it at the "state price" on sale—affordable at his salary level. He was a chief inspector, not just anybody, and the store manager knew him well, too. And why not? During the Cultural Revolution, his father's home had been ransacked by the Red Guards. In the early eighties, when his father's losses were estimated, the figure was also calculated at the state price, that of fifteen years earlier. His mother's five-karat diamond wedding ring, appraised according to the state price, had been valued at less than one-third of the cost of a color TV.

"Have some tea?" his mother asked.

"Fine."

"A dish of Suzhou sugar-frosted haw to go with the tea?"

"Fantastic."

He took the cup and saucer from his mother. In amazement, he watched her taking the jasmine blossom from her hair and putting it in her own cup. He had never seen anybody drinking jasmine tea made this way. The petals floated on the dark green water in her cup.

"At my age, I can indulge myself a little, I think. Only twenty cents for the flower."

"Fresh jasmine flower tea," he said. "What a wonderful idea!"

He was glad she had not put the flower in his teacup.

He suspected she had never stopped worrying about money. Her husband, though a well-known scholar, had left practically nothing, except the books she could not bring herself to sell. A celebrity's widow, she considered herself above peddling. But her pension would hardly cover her most basic needs. The jasmine flower, perhaps two or three days old, was about to be discarded anyway. She had made a virtue out of necessity. Next time he would bring her half a pound of genuine jasmine tea, he promised himself. The famous Cloud and Mist tea, from the Yellow Mountains.

She put down her cup and leaned back on the rocking rattan chair. "Well," she said. "Tell me how things are with you."

"Everything's fine," he said.

"What about the most important thing in your life?"

It was a question he knew too well. She referred to his dating a girl, marrying her, and having a child. He always claimed to be too busy, which happened to be true.

"There are so many things happening at the bureau, Mother."

"So you have no time even to think about it. Is that right?" she said, familiar with his answer.

He nodded, like a filial son, despite the Confucian saying, *"There are three things that make a man unfilial, and to have no off-spring is the most serious."*

"What about Wang Feng?"

"She is going to join her husband in Japan." He added, "And I'm helping her get the visa."

"Well—"she said, with no disappointment in her voice, "it might not be a bad thing for you, son. In fact, I'm glad. She is married—at least in name, I know. Not to break up someone's marriage is a worthy deed. Buddha will bless you for it. But since you parted with that girl in Beijing, Wang seemed to be the only one you really cared for."

"Let's not talk about it, okay?"

"Remember Yan Hong, the anchorwoman? She's really famous on the Oriental channel now. Everybody says how wonderful she is. A golden voice, and a golden heart, too. I ran across her in the First Department Store last week. She used to call you in the evening—I recognized her voice—but you did not return her calls. Now she's a happy mother with a chubby son, but she still called me 'aunt.'"

"Our relationship was totally professional."

"Come on," she said, sniffing at the jasmine blossom in her tea, "you've withdrawn into a shell."

"I wish I had a shell. It might protect me. For the last two weeks, I have had so many matters to deal with. Today is the first time I could steal a couple of hours," he said, trying to change the subject. "So I've come here."

"Don't worry about me," she said, "and don't change the subject either. With your current pay and position, you should not have too much difficulty finding someone."

"I give you my word, Mother," he said, "I will find a wonderful daughter-in-law for you in the near future."

"Not for me, but for yourself."

"Yes, you're right."

"You have time to have supper with me, I hope?"

"As long as you don't make anything special for me."

"No, I won't." She stood up. "I'll just need to warm up a few leftover dishes."

Not too many dishes, he suspected, looking into the small bamboo food cabinet on the wall. She could not afford a refrigerator.

The small cabinet held only one tiny dish of cabbage pickles, a bottle of fermented bean curd, and half a dish of green bean sprouts. But a bowl of watery rice porridge and pickle tasted quite palatable after a week of exotic delicacies in Ouyang's company.

"Don't worry, mother," he said, adding a tiny bit of the bean curd to his porridge. "I'm going to attend a Central Party Institute seminar in October, and after that I'll have more time for myself."

"And are you going to be a cop all your life?" she said.

He could not help staring at her. That was not a question he was prepared for. Not this evening. He was startled by its bitterness. She had not been pleased with his career, he knew. She had hoped that her son would become an academic like his father. But being a police officer had not been a matter of his choice. It surprised him that she should have brought up the subject now that he had become a chief inspector.

"I have been doing fine, really," he said, patting her thin, blue-veined hand. "Nowadays, I have my own office in the bureau, and a lot of responsibility, too."

"So it has become your career for life."

"Well, that I don't know." He added after a pause, "I have been asking myself the same question, but I have not got the answer yet."

That, at least, was truthful. Occasionally he still wondered what would have become of him had he continued his literature studies. Perhaps he would be an assistant or associate professor at a university, where he could teach and write too, a career he had once dreamed about. In the last few years, however, he had somehow come around to a different perspective. Life was not easy for most people, especially during China's transitional period between socialist politics and capitalist economics. There might be a lot of things of more importance or at least of more immediate urgency than modernist and postmodernist literary criticism.

"Son, you still yearn after the other kind of life, don't you—study, books, all that sort of thing?"

"I don't know. Last week I happened to read a critical essay, another interpretation of the poem about a butterfly flying in *The Dream of the Red Chamber*. The thirty-fifth interpretation, the author claims proudly. But what is all that to our people's life today?"

"But—but don't you want Fudan or Tongji University anymore?"

"I do, but I don't see anything wrong with what I'm doing."

"Is police work a preferable way of making a living?"

It was just one way to make a living, he thought. And literature, too, might be just another commodity, like everything else in today's market. If an academic career provided him with no more than secure tenure and a middle-class living standard, would he feel more rewarded?

"I don't mean that, Mother. Still, if I can do something in my work to prevent one human being from being abused and killed by another, that's worth doing."

He did not say anything more. There was no point elaborating on his defense, but he remembered what his father had once said to him. "A man is willing to die for the one who appreciates him, and a woman makes herself beautiful for the one who appreciates her." Another quotation from Confucius. Chen did not worship Confucius, but some of his sayings seemed to stick with him.

"You have been doing quite well in Party politics," she observed.

"Yes," he said, "so far I've been lucky."

But his luck might be changing at that very moment. It was ironic that in the defense of his career choice, he had momentarily forgotten the trouble hanging over his head. He did not want to discuss it with his mother. She had enough worries of her own.

"Still, I'd like to give you a piece of my mind."

"Go ahead."

"You've got luck, and talent, but you don't have the inner makings for such a career. You're my only son, I know. So cut your losses. Try something that really appeals to you."

"I will think about it, Mother."

He had thought about it.

If you work hard enough at something, it begins to make itself part of you, even though you do not really like it and know that part isn't real.

That was the line he had written under the poem "Miracle" to that friend far away in Beijing. It could be about poetry, but also about police work.

Chapter 28

It was already nine o'clock when Chief Inspector Chen reached his apartment.

A message light blinked on his machine. Too many messages in one day. Again he sensed a dull pounding at his temples—a new headache coming on. It could be an omen, a signal for him to stop. But he pushed down the button before he dropped his briefcase.

"Comrade Chief Inspector Chen, this is Li Guohua speaking. Please give me a call when you return. I'll be working late in the office tonight. Right now it is ten to five." It was Party Secretary Li's voice, formal and serious even when leaving a message.

He called the bureau; the phone was picked up on the first ring. Li was waiting for him.

"Come to the office, Chief Inspector Chen. We need to have a talk."

"It'll take me about thirty minutes. Will you be still there?"

"Yes, I'm waiting for you."

"Then I'm on my way."

Actually it took more than thirty minutes before he walked into the Party Secretary's fifth-floor office. Li was having instant beef-flavored noodles. The plastic bowl stood amidst the papers scattered across the mahogany desk. There was a small heap of cigarette butts in an exquisite tray of Fujian quartz with a dragon design.

"Comrade Party Secretary Li, Chief Inspector Chen Cao reporting," Chen said, observing the correct political form.

"Welcome back, Comrade Chief Inspector Chen."

"Thanks."

"How's everything?"

"Everything is fine," Chen said. "I tried to report to you this morning, but you were not available. Then I had to be out for the most of the day."

"You have been busy investigating the case, I know," Li said. "Now tell me about it."

"We've made some real progress." Chen opened his briefcase. "As Detective Yu may have reported, we targeted Wu Xiaoming as the chief suspect before my trip to Guangzhou. And now we have several other leads and they all fit together."

"New leads?"

"Well, one is the last phone call Guan received on May tenth. According to the stub book of the public phone station at Qinghe Lane, it came in around nine thirty, about three or four hours before her death. That call was made by none other than Wu Xiaoming. It's confirmed." He put a copy of the record on the desk.

"It's not just this one particular call. For more than half a year,

Wu made a considerable number of calls to her—three or four a week, on the average, some quite late at night. And Guan called him. Their relationship was apparently something more than what Wu admitted."

"That might mean something," Li said, "but Wu Xiaoming had been Guan's photographer. So he could have contacted her from time to time—in a professional way."

"No, it's much more than that. We've also got a couple of witnesses. One of them is a night peddler on the corner of Hubei Road. She said that on several occasions shortly before Guan's death, she saw Guan returning in a luxurious white car, in the company of a man, late in the night. Wu drives a white Lexus, his father's car."

"But it could have been a taxi."

"I don't think so. The peddler saw no taxi sign atop the car. She also saw Guan lean into the car and kiss the driver."

"Really!" Li said, throwing the empty plastic bowl into the trash can. "Still, other people have white cars, too. There're so many upstarts in Shanghai now."

"We've also found, among other things, that Wu made a trip to the Yellow Mountains in Guan's company last October. They used assumed names and fabricated documents, registering as a married couple so that they could share a hotel room. We have several witnesses who can testify to this."

"Wu shared the same hotel room with Guan?"

"Exactly. What's more, Wu took some nude pictures of Guan there, and then there was a violent quarrel between them."

"But in your previous report, you said Guan was not involved with anyone at the time of her death."

"That's because they kept the affair a secret."

"That is something." Li added after a pause, "But an affair does not necessarily mean a murder."

"Well, things went wrong between them. They had a violent

argument in the mountains. We have a witness to that. Guan wanted Wu to divorce his wife; Wu would not. That's what caused the fight, we believe."

"So you assume that was why Wu Xiaoming killed her and dumped her body into the canal?"

"That's right. At the beginning of our investigation, Detective Yu and I established two prerequisites for the case: the murderer's access to a car, and his familiarity with the canal. Now, as an educated youth during the seventies, Wu Xiaoming had lived for several years in a small village about fifteen minutes' walk from the canal. Wu must have hoped that her body might lie at the bottom of the canal for years, until, finally, it disappeared without a trace."

"Supposing your theory is right—hypothetically, that is—that Guan and Wu had an affair, and things went wrong between them," Li said more slowly, seeming to be weighing every word. "Why should Wu have gone that far? He could simply have refused and stopped seeing her, couldn't he?"

"He could, but Guan might have done something desperate to bring Wu down," Chen said.

"I don't see it. Guan had her own reputation, and her political career, to think about. Let's say she was desperate enough. Do you think Wu's work unit would have made a big deal about such an affair?"

"Maybe, maybe not, you never know."

"So far, your theory may explain some things, but it's flawed. I cannot see a real motive."

"That is what we are trying to find."

"What about Wu's alibi?"

"According to Guo Qiang's testimony, Wu Xiaoming stayed in his study for the whole night, developing pictures. As a professional photographer, Wu has his own darkroom and equipment; why should he have used Guo's place that night?"

"Did Wu offer any explanation?"

"Wu said that there was something wrong with his own darkroom, but that's not believable. Guo's no pro—he doesn't even have proper equipment. It did not make sense for Wu to have gone there. Guo is Wu's buddy, and he's just trying to cover up for him."

"Well, an alibi is an alibi," Li said. "What are you going to do next?"

"With a search warrant we'll be able to find further evidence."

"How can you justify proceeding further against Wu under these circumstances?"

"We do not have to issue the warrant on the murder charge. To start with, fabrication of a marriage license is more than enough. The witness I've found in Guangzhou can testify against him, not only about the false document, but also about his taking nude pictures of Guan—which amounts to a Western bourgeois decadent lifestyle."

"Western bourgeois decadent lifestyle, um, a fashionable charge." Li suddenly stood up, grinding out his half-smoked cigarette. "Comrade Chief Inspector Chen, there is a reason that I wanted you to come to my office tonight. It's not just about the case, but about something else."

"Something else?"

"To listen to a report made against you."

"A report against me?" Chen also stood up. "What have I done?"

"About your Western bourgeois decadent lifestyle—exactly the same charge—during your investigation in Guangzhou. The report claimed that during your stay in Guangzhou you were inseparable from a dubious businessman, going to all kinds of classy restaurants, three meals a day—"

"I know who you are talking about, Comrade Party Secretary. It's about Mr. Ouyang, isn't it? He is a businessman, but what's wrong with that? Nowadays our government encourages people to start their own private businesses. As for the reason that he treated me a couple of times, it is because he also writes poems."

"I've not finished yet," Li said. "The report also says that you went to a massage salon."

"Oh, the massage salon. Yes, I went there because I had to find Xie Rong, the witness I have just mentioned. She works in the salon."

"Well, a copy of the massage salon receipt says that you paid for what is called the 'full service' there. The Internal Security people have got hold of the copy, and people know what 'full service' means."

It was the second time that Internal Security had been mentioned to Chen during the day. First in Director Yao's office, now in Li's. Internal Security was a special institution, dreaded particularly by policemen—the police of the police.

"Why Internal Security?"

"Well, if you haven't done anything wrong, you don't have to worry about the devil knocking at your door in the depth of the night."

"I don't know how they could have obtained such a receipt. I did not have one myself. In fact, Mr. Ouyang had paid for me. I did not even know that it was a salon before I got there. As for the 'full service,' whatever it may mean to other people, I did not have any."

"But why approach your witness there?" Li said, lighting another cigarette for himself. "I, for one, can't see why you did not have the girl brought into the Guangzhou police bureau for questioning. It's common practice, and it produces results."

"Well—this way might be more effective, I thought."

Chief Inspector Chen had considered bringing her to the local police station, but he had made a promise to Professor Xie, and he owed a lot to Ouyang, too. Besides, it was beyond Party

Secretary Li, who lived in the high cadre residential building complex in west Huaihai Road, to understand how ordinary people like Xie Rong were intimidated by the high cadres and their children. Xie would not have dared to say anything against Wu in the Guangzhou Police Bureau.

"I stayed in Guangzhou for only five days," Chen went on. "With so many things waiting at the bureau here, I could not afford the time to investigate in a routine way, and the people in Guangzhou Police Bureau were too busy to help me. I had no choice."

"You spent over two hours in the massage room, alone with her. Afterwards, you took her to the White Swan Hotel, a private room, too. And you paid more than five hundred Yuan for the meal—more than a month's salary. You call that *investigation*, Comrade Chief Inspector Chen?"

So, Chief Inspector Chen's every step in Guangzhou had been watched. He realized what serious trouble he was in. Party Secretary Li was well informed about his trip.

"I've an explanation, Comrade Party Secretary Li."

"Do you?"

"Yes. I treated her to make sure that she would cooperate with us. The meal was expensive, but everything in Guangzhou is expensive. And I made a point of paying out of my own pocket."

"For a massage girl! You are generous indeed."

"Comrade Party Secretary Li, I was investigating a murder case there. As a detective, I decided to approach a witness in a way I thought proper and right. How come I was under surveillance every step of the way in Guangzhou?"

"What you did there may have aroused people's suspicions."

"Comrade Party Secretary Li, it was you who introduced me into the Party. If you do not trust me, what's the point of my saying anything more?"

"I trust you, Comrade Chief Inspector Chen. As a matter of fact, I've told Internal Security that all you did in Guangzhou was necessary for the investigation. I've even said that you had discussed everything with me."

"Oh, thank you, Party Secretary Li. You've done such a lot for me, ever since my first day in the bureau. I am most grateful."

"You don't have to say that to me." Li shook his head. "I know you have done good work. And on this case too."

"So we have to—" Chen came to a sudden halt, coughing with a fist against his mouth—"go on with our investigation."

"Don't even think about it," Li sighed, leaning over his desk. "They were talking about making a formal complaint against you. That's why I had to go out of my way for you, but I don't think there is any more I can do."

Chen levered himself out of the chair and then slumped back, looking up at the pictures of Li on the wall—showing the long career of a politician with other politicians. He tried to dig a crumpled pack of cigarettes out of his pocket, but Li handed him one from the case on the desk.

"I'm gone?" Chen asked.

"No, not if you are not around to goad them. Let things cool down. That's what I promised them. That you would be busy with something else."

"So I have to suspend the investigation?"

"Yes."

"It's a murder case. Why should the Internal Security people come after me, but not after the murderer?"

"This is not an ordinary murder case."

"There aren't any ordinary murders."

"Well—" The Party Secretary seemed ruffled. "You may have a point, but other people may have theirs, too, Comrade Chief Inspector."

"Yes?"

"Have you ever thought about the consequences of the case— the political consequences, I mean?"

"Well, there may be some," Chen admitted after a moment's hesitation.

"There may be a lot, some people think," Li said.

Chen waited for Li to go on.

"Timing is the heart of the matter here. In the present political climate, do you think your investigation will be helpful to the Party's image?" Li paused—for effect—before he resumed. "Who is involved in the case? A national model worker and a married HCC in an adulterous bed—if your hypothesis is correct. What would people think? Ideological bankruptcy! What is worse, people would come to see the HCC as a product of our Party system, and blame the high cadres of the old generation for every problem. And some could even use it as an excuse to slander the government. After what happened in Tiananmen Square last summer, a lot of people are still shaken in their belief in our socialist system."

"Could it be so serious?" Chen said. "With Wu's family background, our media would probably never cover the case at all. And I don't think that people would react in the way you've said."

"But it is possible, isn't it? At present, political stability is of paramount importance, Comrade Chief Inspector. So, officially the investigation will go on, and its responsibility still lies with us," the Party Secretary continued. "But if you don't stop, you can count on Internal Security making a parallel investigation. If necessary, they will block your investigation with whatever charge they can bring out against you."

"A parallel investigation, I see."

"You cannot give those people any 'queue' to grab. Or they will really tear off your scalp."

Chief Inspector Chen had enough queues, he was well aware, for others to grab. Not just the trip to Guangzhou.

The Party Secretary seemed to be doing some heavy thinking. "Besides, your hypothesis may account for some facts," Li said, "but there is no eyewitness. No weapons. No hard evidence of legal value. Nothing but circumstantial evidence in support of what is, essentially, an imaginative theory. And finally, no motive either. Why should Wu have murdered her? So at present, Comrade Chief Inspector Chen, nothing can justify the continuation of the investigation."

"Well—" Chen said bitterly, "no politics can justify it."

"Consider the case closed—at least for the time being. We don't have to declare this. Let's wait. When the political wind changes, or when you get hold of irrefutable evidence, or find the motive, we'll talk about it again."

It was always possible to wait. No one could tell, however, when that wind would change. And what irrefutable evidence could there be since the final definition of what was probative would be made somewhere else?

"But what if the weather does not change, Comrade Party Secretary?"

"You want the entire system to bend to you, Comrade Chief Inspector?" Li said, frowning. "I've made myself clear, I believe: I do not want to declare, as an official decision, that you are no longer in charge of the case. Yes, I am the one who introduced you into the Party, but as a Party member, first and foremost, I have to protect the interests of the Party. You're a Party member, too. So we are both supposed to be aware of the paramount importance of serving the Party's interests."

Any further argument would be futile, Chen concluded, and he made no further protest. "I see, Party Secretary Li," he said, rising from the table.

"I cannot see why you're so hooked on this case," the Party Secretary said as Chen left.

Nor could Chief Inspector Chen himself.

Not even back in his apartment, after thinking about it all the way home. Turning on the light, he collapsed into the chair. The room looked bare and shabby—staggeringly empty, forlorn.

A room's like a woman, he reflected. *It also possesses you. Besides, you have to spend a fortune to make it love you.*

Whether this was a metaphor he had read somewhere, or just a momentary spark of his own mind, he was unsure. Poetic images came to him, more often than not, at unexpected moments.

He could not fall asleep, he knew, but after an eventful day, it was good to lie down on the bed. As he was gazing up at the shadows flickering across the ceiling, surges of loneliness came rushing over him. Occasionally, he enjoyed a touch of solitude in the depth of night. But what struck him was more than a melancholy sense of being alone. It was as if his very existence were becoming doubtful.

Guan must have experienced those lonely moments too; as a woman she had to bear even more pressure, alone in her cell-like dorm room.

He got up, went into the bathroom, and rinsed his face with cold water. He had to make an effort to think about the case from the Party Secretary's perspective, but his thoughts moved back to Guan.

Looking out at a light in the distance, Chief Inspector Chen detected an affinity between the dead woman and himself. In their careers, both had been smooth and successful—at least in other people's eyes. They had been promoted to positions normally beyond the reach of people of their age. As Overseas Chinese Lu had observed, luck had fallen in Chen's lap. Some of his colleagues' jealousy was understandable. Jealousy could also explain Guan's unpopularity among her neighbors.

They both also happened to be, in a newly coined Chinese term, "not-too-young youths." It had carried weight with the bureau housing committee, but other than that, it was anything but pleasant, with its strong connotation that these people should have married a long time ago.

Success in a political career helped little in one's personal life. On the contrary, it could hurt. Especially in modern times, in

China. Being a Party member meant being loyal to the Party first according to the Party Constitution, which was not necessarily attractive to a potential spouse. A would-be husband would, more likely than not, prefer a wife who pledged loyalty to him first, who would take care of their family with all her heart and soul.

Being politically successful could make one's personal life difficult in a variety of ways. He knew that from his own experience: He was constantly watched—a bachelor chief inspector in his mid-thirties. He had to live up to his official role. That might have been one of the reasons that he had remained single. The same might have applied to Guan.

But it was not a night to be sentimental. Once more he tried to view matters from Li's perspective. There was something to Li's argument, Chen admitted. After all the years wasted in political movements, China was finally making great strides in economic reform. With the GNP growing annually in double digits, people were starting to have a better life. And a measure of democracy was also being introduced. At such a historical juncture, "political stability"—a popular term after the tragic summer of 1989—might be a precondition for further progress. At this moment, the unquestioned authority of the Party was more important than ever.

So rather than damage the Party's political authority, and political stability, the investigation had to be stopped.

But what about the victim?

Well, Guan Hongying had lived in the Party's interests. It appeared only logical that she should have died in the Party's interests as well. And a cover-up would be in her own interests, too—it would perpetuate her unsullied image as a role model.

It would not be the first time, nor the last, for a police officer to stop halfway in an investigation. Few would guess the real reason. So what was the big deal?

At the worst, a matter of losing face. And, possibly a matter of saving his neck.

Party Secretary Li was not alone in wondering at Chief Inspector's Chen's persistence.

Chen asked himself sleepily, why?

Chapter 29

He was awakened by the telephone ringing.

"Hello."

"It's me, Wang Feng. It's late, I know, but I have to see you."

Wang's anxious voice seemed so close, as if she were next door, but at the same time, it sounded far away, too.

"Is something wrong? Don't worry, Wang," he said. "Where are you?"

He looked at his watch. Twelve thirty. This was not a call he had expected. Not from her. Not at this hour.

"I'm at the public telephone booth just across the street."

"Where?"

"You can see it from your window."

"Then why not come up?"

There was a telephone booth standing on the street corner, a fashionable new installation, where people could insert coins or cards to make calls.

"No, you come down."

"Okay, I'll be down in one minute."

He had not seen her since that night. It was understandable

that she hesitated to come up. She must be in serious trouble.

He slid into his uniform, grabbed his briefcase, and ran down the stairs. Better business-like, alone at such a late hour, he thought, buttoning up as he rushed into the phone booth. However, there was no one there, no one on the street either.

He was confused, but decided to wait. Suddenly the public phone started ringing. For the first few seconds, he stared at it before he realized that it might be ringing for him.

"Hello," he said.

"Thank Heaven! It's me, Wang Feng," Wang said, "I was afraid you might not pick up."

"Is something wrong?"

"Yes, but not with me. This afternoon, your passport people turned down my passport application. I'm so worried about you."

"About *me*?"

He thought she was incoherent. She had been denied a passport, but that was not a reason for her to be worried about him. Could it have been such a blow that she was no longer her usual composed self?

"I mentioned your name, but the officers simply stared at me. One of them said that you've been suspended, calling you a busy-body unable to take care of your own business."

"Who said that?"

"Sergeant Liao Kaiju."

"That S.O.B.—never mind him. A small fly. He just cannot stand my being a chief inspector."

"Is it because of the Guan investigation?"

"No, we've not seen the end of it yet."

"I was so worried, Chen. I've got some connections of my own, so I made a few calls tonight. The Guan case may be more complicated than you know. Some people high up seem to be taking it as a deliberate attack on the revolutionaries of the older generation, with you as a representative of the liberal reformists."

"That's not true, you know. I'm not interested in politics. It is a homicide case, that's all."

"I know, but not everybody thinks so. Wu is busy in Beijing, I've heard. And he knows a lot of people there."

"I'm not surprised."

"Some people have even complained about your poems, collecting them, saying that they are politically incorrect, and that they are further proof of your unreliability as a Party member."

"That's outrageous. I cannot see how my poetry has anything to do with the matter!"

"A piece of advice—if you will accept it from me," she said, without waiting for his reply. "Stop beating your head against a brick wall."

"I appreciate your advice, Wang. But I will take care of my problems," he added "and yours, too."

There was a short pause. He could hear her agitated breathing from the other end of the line. And then her voice sounded different, filled with emotion.

"Chen?"

"Yes?"

"You sound so worn out. I can come over—that is, if you think it's all right."

"Oh, I'm just a bit tired," Chen said, almost automatically, "I can do with a good night's sleep. That is all I need, I think."

"You're sure?"

"Yes, thank you so much."

"Then—take care of yourself."

"You, too."

He put down the phone, but he remained standing in the booth.

The truth was that he had no idea how to take care of his problem. Let alone hers.

Two or three minutes passed. The phone did not ring again. Somehow he had been expecting it to. The silence was disappointing.

She was concerned about him. As a reporter, she was naturally sensitive to the change in people's attitudes. Officer Liao had promised to help, a promise made at the time when Chen had been considered a rising star. Chen's trouble had brought about the change. In Liao's eyes, the chief inspector's career was practically finished.

He moved out of the booth. It was no longer unbearably hot on the street; the moonlight streamed softly through the leaves. He was not in the mood to go back to his apartment. There was a lot on his mind. He found himself walking aimlessly along the deserted street, and then before he thought about it, he realized he was walking in the direction of the Bund.

At the intersection of Sichuan Road, he passed a two-story red brick building, which had once been Yaojing High School, his high-school during the Cultural Revolution. It was no longer a school now, but a restaurant called Red Mansion—subtly suggesting the luxury in *The Dream of the Red Chamber*. Perhaps its location had been too commercially valuable for a school. He resisted the temptation to go in for a cup of coffee. It was not a night for nostalgia. Silhouetted against the restaurant's neon lights, several people were exchanging currency with foreign tourists. A young girl was chasing after an elderly American couple with a bunch of Yuan in her hand. In his school days, he and other Little Red Guards had acted as traffic assistants there, chasing bikes without license plates or with illegally installed baby seats. Zealous volunteers they had been in those days.

The river came in view.

Along the Bund, a breeze blew over the parapet, bearing the tang of the river and of the docks, a characteristic Shanghai mixture familiar to him. Even at this late hour, the Bund was still dotted with young lovers sauntering along, hand in hand, or sitting still like statues in the night.

Before 1949, Shanghai had been described as a "nightless city," and the Bund "like the folds of a bright girdle furled."

He came to a stop at Waibai Bridge. The water smelled of diesel and industrial waste, though it was somewhat less black, dappled with shimmering reflections of the neon. He leaned against the railing, looking down into the silent water. There was a tugboat coming toward the arch of the bridge.

He made an attempt to sort out the thoughts crowding into his mind.

He was crushed, though he had not admitted the fact to Wang. Crushed not by the case, but by the politics behind it. An inner-Party power struggle was involved.

Deng Xiaoping, in his effort to push forward his reform, had promoted some young Party officials, so-called "reformists" through the cadre retirement policy. This did not pose a serious threat to those at the top level, but was a serious problem to most of the lower old cadres. So some had allied themselves against the reform. After the eventful summer of 1989, Deng had to appease these old cadres, retired or being retired, by restoring their influence to some extent. A subtle balance had been maintained. In the Party's newspaper, a new slogan, "political stability," became highly important.

But such a balance was unstable. The old cadres were sensitive to any move by the reformists. And the investigation directed against Wu was being interpreted as an attack on the old cadres. Wu had been propagating this interpretation to people in Beijing. With his family connections, it would not be too difficult for him to elicit the response he wanted. And the response had come. From the office of the Discipline Committee. From Party Secretary Li. From Internal Security.

An old high cadre such as Wu Bing, lying unconscious under

an oxygen mask in the hospital, must remain untouched, including his mansion, his car, and, needless to say, his children.

If Chen persisted in conducting it his way, it was going to be his last case.

Maybe he could still quit.

Maybe it was already too late.

Once on a blacklist, there was no escaping the inevitable.

How far would Party Secretary Li go to protect him?

Not far, probably, since his downfall would affect Li, too. He was sure that Li, a seasoned politician, would not choose to side with a loser.

A case had already been built up against him. A case to cover up Wu Xiaoming's case. What awaited him?

Years at a reform-through-labor camp in Qinghai Province in a dark prison cell, or even a bullet in the back of his head. Perhaps it was too dramatic to evoke these scenarios at the moment, but he was sure he would be thrown out of the bureau.

The situation was desperate. Wang had tried to warn him.

The night air was serene, sweet, along the Bund.

Behind him, across Zhongshan Road, stood the Peace Hotel with its black-and-red pinnacled roof. He had fantasized about spending an evening there in the jazz bar, in Wang's company, with the musicians doing a great job with their piano, horns, and drums, and the waiters, starched napkins over their arms, serving Bloody Marys, Manhattans, Black Russians. . . .

Now they would never have the chance.

Somehow he was not too worried about her. Attractive, young, smart, Wang had connections of her own. Eventually she would be able to get her passport and visa, and board a Japanese plane. Her decision to leave might prove to be the right one. There was no foretelling China's future.

In Tokyo, in a floating silk kimono, kneeling on a mat, and warming a cup of saki for her husband, she would make a wonderful wife. A blaze of cherry blossoms silhouetted against the snow-mantled Mount Fuji.

At night, as an occasional siren sounded in the sleepless skies, would she still think of him, across the seas, and across the mountains?

He remembered several lines by Liu Yong, written during the Song dynasty:

> *Where shall I find myself*
> *Tonight, waking from the hangover—*
> *The riverbank lined with weeping willows,*
> *The moon sinking, the dawn rising on a breeze.*
> *Year after year, I will be far,*
> *Far away from you.*
> *All the beautiful scenes are unfolding,*
> *But to no avail:*
> *Oh, to whom can I speak*
> *Of this ever enchanting landscape?*

A reversal of positions. In Liu's poem, Liu was the one leaving his love behind, but now Wang was leaving him.

As a poet, Liu was a respected name in classical Chinese literature. As a man, Liu had been down and out, drinking, dreaming, and dissipating his best years in brothels. It was even said that his romantic poems were his undoing, for he was despised by his contemporaries, who denounced him with outrage born of orthodox Confucian dignity. Liu died in dire poverty, attended only by a poor prostitute who took a fancy to his poetry, though such a deathbed companion might also have been fabricated. A sugar cube of consolation in a cup full of bitterness.

In future years, would Wang come back, a happy, prosperous woman? What would have befallen him by that time? No longer a chief inspector. As down and out as Liu. In an increasingly materialistic society, who would take notice of a bookworm capable of nothing except penning a few sentimental lines?

He shuddered when the big clock atop the Custom Mansions started chiming a new melody. He did not know it, but he liked it.

It had played a different tune in his high-school days, a melody dedicated to Chairman Mao—"The East Is Red."

Times changed.

Thousands of years earlier, Confucius said, *Time flows away like the water in the river.*

He took a deep breath of the summer night air, as if struggling out of the surging current. Then he left the Bund and walked toward the Shanghai Central Post Office.

Located at the corner of Sichuan Road and Chapu Road, the post office was open twenty-four hours a day. A doorman sat dutifully at the entrance—even at that late hour. Chen nodded at him. In the spacious hall were several oak desks where people could write, but only a couple of people were sitting there, waiting before a row of booths for long distance calls.

He chose to sit at one of these long desks, and he started writing on a piece of paper with the bureau letterhead. That was what he needed. He did not want it to appear personal. This was serious business, he thought. In the interests of the Party.

As soon as he started writing, to his surprise, the words seemed to flow from his pen. He stopped only once, to look up at a poster on the wall. The poster reminded him of one he had seen years earlier—a black bird hovering above the horizon, carrying an orange sun on its back. There were two short lines under the picture. "What will come / Will come."

Time is a bird, / It perches, and it flies.

When he had finished, he took a registered-mail envelope, and asked a yawning clerk behind the counter, "How much is a registered letter to Beijing?"

"Eight Yuan."

"Fine," Chen said. It was worth it. The letter in his hand might be his last card. He was no gambler, but he had to play it.

Although, after all these years, its value might only be in his imagination. More likely, a straw, grasped at by a drowning man, he thought.

The clock was striking two as he left the post office. He nodded again to the doorman still sitting motionless at the gate. The man did not even look up.

Around the corner, a peddler with a huge pot of tea-leaf-eggs steaming over a coal stove greeted Chen loudly. The smell did not appeal to him; he continued to walk.

At the intersection of Tianton Road and Sichuan Road, he noticed a glass-and-chrome tower rising silhouetted against a dark backdrop of alleys and *siheyuan* houses. Floodlights illuminated the construction site as the procession of trucks, heavy equipment, and handcarts carried in material for the building. Like so many other roads, Tianton had been blocked by Shanghai's effort to regain its status as the nation's commercial and industrial center. He tried to take a shortcut by turning into Ninhai Market. The market was deserted, except for a long line of baskets—plastic, bamboo, rattan—of different shapes and sizes. The line led up to a concrete counter under a wooden sign on which was chalked the words YELLOW CROAKER. The most delicious fish in Shanghai's housewives' eyes. The baskets stood for the virtuous wives who would come in an hour or two to pick them up and take their places in line, rubbing their sleepy eyes.

There was only one night-shift worker standing at the end of the market, his cotton padded collar upturned as high as his ears as he hammered at a gigantic bar of frozen fish in front of the refrigeration house.

The shortcut through the market proved to be a mistake, so he had to turn into another side street, spending even more time on his way back home.

In retrospect, many of his decisions had been mistakes, he admitted, whether serious or trivial. It was the combination of these decisions, however, that had made him what he was. At the moment, a suspended—though not officially—chief inspector, with his political future practically finished. But at least he had tried to be an honest, conscientious decision maker.

Whether sending the letter to Beijing was just another mistake, he did not yet know. He started whistling, off-key, a song he had learned years ago: *"Yesterday's dream is driven by the wind, / Yesterday's wind is still dreaming the dream . . ."*

It was maudlin, even more so than Liu Yong's poem.

Chapter 30

It was late Friday afternoon. Detective Yu was still at his desk, staring at the files of the special case squad.

Chief Inspector Chen was not in his office. He was serving as an interpreter and escort for an American writers' delegation. This had been an unexpected assignment announced by Party Secretary Li the previous day. A writer and translator in his own right, Chen had been chosen as a representative of the Chinese Writers' Association.

The announcement had come so suddenly that Yu had hardly any time to exchange information with Chen. They had missed each other on the first day of Chen's return from Guangzhou. And early the second day, when Yu had just stepped into the large office, Chen's new assignment had been made. Chen left for the airport almost immediately.

On the surface, it was not too bad a signal. It could even signify that Chief Inspector Chen was still a trusted Party member, but Yu was worried. Since that crab banquet, he had in Chen an ally, and a friend as well. Old Hunter had told him about the snag their investigation had struck, and the trouble Chen was in. And in the afternoon, Yu, too, had talked with Party Secretary Li, who assigned him to an important conference in Jiading County, to act as temporary security.

"What about the case?" Yu asked.

"What case?"

"Guan Hongying's case."

"Don't worry, Comrade Detective Yu. Comrade Chief Inspector Chen will be back in a couple of days."

"Our squad also has a lot of work."

"Finish as much as you can before reporting to the conference on Monday. Other people will take care of things here." Li added without looking at him, "Don't forget to ask the accountant about the standard meal allowance. It is possible that you will be staying there for quite a few days."

Yu had not finished much of his work by five o'clock. Files of unfinished cases were stacked high on his desk. The case of the Henan abduction ring that kidnapped girls and sold them as wives to peasants in faraway provinces, Yu thought gloomily, could be turned over to the Henan Province Bureau. As for the pilferage case at the Shanghai Number 2 Steel Plant, he did not know what to do. Factory pilferage was constant and enormous. For some workers, it was a form of additional compensation. Ordinarily, if caught, a worker would be either fined or fired. But in accordance with a recent Central Party Committee document on the damage caused by pilferage from state-run enterprises, a culprit could be sentenced to twenty years. And there were several other cases, special just because the city government wanted to make them examples to warn young people in one way or another.

Detective Yu closed the file in frustration, scattering a thin layer of cigarette ash on the desk. Justice was like colored balls in a magician's hand, changing color and shape all the time, beneath the light of politics.

A murderer was at large, while the police officers were in trouble.

In his position, however, there was nothing Detective Yu could do—except what he was told to.

At a quarter to six, the phone started ringing again.

"Detective Yu," he said, picking up the phone.

"What in heaven's name are you up to, Yu?" Peiqin's voice sounded exasperated.

"What's wrong?"

"Did you remember the parents' meeting in Qinqin's school today?"

"Oh—I forgot. I've been so busy."

"I'm not nagging, but I hate being here all by myself, and taking care of him without your help."

"I'm sorry."

"It's been a long day for me, too."

"I know. I'll come home right now."

"You don't have to come home just for my sake. It will be too late for the meeting anyway. But remember what your father said yesterday."

"Yes, I do remember."

Peiqin had been worried since Old Hunter told them about Chief Inspector Chen's trouble. So it was not just a call about his absence from the school meeting, but more about his continuing the investigation. Peiqin was too sensible to say a single word on the phone about that case.

Yu had chosen to be a cop, even though there had not been too much for him to choose from. He had not given much thought to the comfortable orthodoxy that law and order were the cornerstone of the society. He simply thought that the job was right for him, not only for his self-support, but for his self-justification, too. A capable cop, he had believed, could make a difference. Not too long after he had joined the force, however, he had few illusions left about it.

The more Yu pondered, the more upset he became about Commissar Zhang. That ancient diehard Marxist, with an always-politically-correct smile printed across his face like a postmark, must have tipped off somebody high up. Somebody who had the power to protect Wu—at any cost. Now both Chief Inspector Chen and he were practically suspended.

Outside the sun was passing behind heavy clouds. Yu hoped that he would still get a phone call from Chen. It was late, and nobody else was in the large office. He turned off the electric cup, a gift from the First Department Store, which the manager had given him in gratitude for his work on the case. At the moment, it served as an ironic reminder.

Forty-five minutes later, Yu remained sitting doggedly at his desk, with a piece of blank paper in front of him, a reflection of his mind.

The telephone started ringing. He snatched it off the hook with an uncharacteristic eagerness.

"Special case squad."

"Hello, I want to speak to Detective Yu Guangming."

It was a stranger speaking with a gurgling voice.

"Speaking. This is he."

"My name is Yang Shuhui. I work at Shanghai Number Sixty-three Gas Station in Qingpu County. I think I have some information for you."

"What kind of information?"

"The information your squad has offered a reward for."

"Hold on." Yu immediately became alert. There was only one case in which he had offered a reward. "About the corpse in the canal, right?"

"Yes, that's it. Sorry, I forget the case number."

"Listen, Comrade Yang, I happen to be on my way out, but I

would like to meet you today. Tell me where you are right now."

"At home, near the Big World, on Huangpi Road."

"Good, I have to pick up something at Jingling Market, not too far from there. There is a Hunan restaurant on the corner of Xizhuang Road. Yueyang Pavilion, that's the name, I think. If you can be there in about forty-five minutes, we will see each other."

"Is the offer of a reward still good?" Yang asked. "It's been some time. I happened to read about it in the old newspaper today."

"Yes, three hundred Yuan. Not a cent less. And your telephone number?" Yu added almost automatically. "Oh, well, don't worry. We'll meet, I'm leaving right now."

At the bureau gate, the old doorman Comrade Liang reached out to him with an envelope in his hand. "Got something for you."

"For me?"

"This morning Chief Inspector Chen received his assignment package here. There were some tickets along with the schedule. Some extra tickets, in case some others wanted to join the group at the last minute, but no one did. So he left two Beijing Opera tickets for me, and two karaoke tickets for you."

"The Shanghai Foreign Liaison Office spared no expense arranging activities for the Americans," he said. "It's very considerate of him."

"Yes, Chief Inspector Chen is a really decent man." Comrade Liang then said. "You are his assistant, and you have your work cut out for you."

"Yes, I know. Thank you, Comrade Liang."

Putting the tickets in his pocket, Yu hurried toward the restaurant.

The meeting with comrade Yang turned out to be more fruitful than Yu had expected. After interviewing this witness for more than one hour, and taping his testimony on a micro-cassette recorder, he thought of one of Old Hunter's favorite old Chinese sayings: "The god's net has large meshes, but it lets nothing through."

What would be the next step? Whatever Detective Yu was going to do, he had to contact Chief Inspector Chen. It was even more urgent as he was going to be stationed in Jiading County the following week.

Chen must have discovered something in Guangzhou, and so had he, here in his interviews with Jiang and Ning, along with the newest information he had just gotten from Yang. Only as a team could he and Chen hope to ride out the crisis.

It was not easy, however, for him to reach Chen. As an escort for the American Writers' delegation, Chen had to accompany the guests from one place to another. Besides, it was not safe for Yu to call the Jinjiang Hotel where Chen stayed with the American guests.

A case had already been rigged against Chen, according to Old Hunter. Yu's movements might be watched as well. Signs of their continuing the investigation would prompt further reaction. It was not that Detective Yu hesitated to take a risk, but they could not afford to make any mistakes.

There had to be a way to discuss the situation with Chen, a way discreet enough not to arouse any suspicion.

At the bus stop, several people were lining up along the railing. Yu stood behind them. They were talking excitedly about some new exotic show in the Meixin Theater, but he listened absent-mindedly, without really making sense of their conversation.

His mind was still a blank when he got back home.

There was no light in his room. He knew it was already past ten o'clock. Qinqin had to get up early for school. Peiqin had had a busy day all alone. At six, he had promised her he would come back immediately. He felt guilty as he closed the door behind him. He was surprised to see Peiqin still awake, waiting for him.

"Oh, you're back," she said, sitting up.

He slumped onto a bamboo stool to take off his shoes. She came over to him, barefoot. Lightly, she sank to her knees to help, bringing her head to his level.

"You've not had your supper, Yu?" she said. "I've kept something for you."

It was a steamed rice ball stuffed with minced pork and vegetables.

She sat with him at the table, watching him in silence.

"I'm late, Peiqin. I'm sorry."

"You don't have to say that to me. I should not have been so fretful this afternoon."

"No, you were right. The rice ball is so good," he said between the bites. "Where did you get the recipe?"

"Remember our days in Yunnan? Those Dai girls sang and danced the whole night. When they were hungry, they took rice balls out of their pockets."

He remembered, of course. In those long nights of Xishuangbanna, they had watched the Dai girls dancing against the rugged line of the Dai bamboo bungalows, nibbling at their rice balls at the intervals. And they had both thought that the rice balls were a good idea.

At that instant, holding the rice ball in his hand, Detective Yu had an idea.

"Have you heard of a Dai-style restaurant at the Jingjiang Hotel?" he asked. "A fabulous one, called the Xishuang Garden."

"Yes, the Xishuang Garden," she said. "I've read about it in the newspapers."

"What about going to the Xishuang Garden tomorrow evening?"

"You're kidding!"

He experienced a twinge of regret at her surprise. It was the first time he had asked her out for a date since they had Qinqin. Now he was going to do so, but with an ulterior motive.

"No, I've just got an urge to go there. You have no other plans for tomorrow night, have you? So why not go out and have fun?"

"Do you think we can afford it?"

"Here are a couple of all-inclusive tickets, covering drinking, dancing and singing-along, or karaoke. You know what it is, so fashionable nowadays. Free tickets." Yu took the tickets out of his shirt pocket. "A hundred and fifty Yuan for each, if we had to pay out of our own pocket. So it would be a shame not to go."

They were the tickets Chen had left for them. Perhaps Chen just did not want to waste the tickets. But perhaps Chen had meant for him to go there.

"Where did you get the tickets?"

"Somebody gave them to me."

"I'm no dancer," she said hesitantly. "And I've no idea how to karaoke."

"It is easy to learn, my wife."

"Easy for you to say." She was not untempted with the prospect of a special night. "We're already an old husband and wife."

"There are older people dancing and singing in People's Square everyday."

"But why are you asking me out all of a sudden?"

"Why not? We deserve a break."

"It does not sound like you, Comrade Detective Yu, to enjoy a break in the middle of an investigation."

"Well, that's exactly where we are, in the middle of it," he said. "And that's also why I want you to be there."

"What do you mean?"

"I want you to pass some information to Chief Inspector Chen. He may be there, too. It's not a good idea for us to be seen together."

"So you are not inviting me out to a party," she said, making no attempt to conceal her disappointment. "On the contrary, you are asking me to join your the investigation."

"I'm sorry, Peiqin," Yu said, reaching out to touch her hair. "I know you are worried about me, but I want to say one thing for Chief Inspector Chen—and for myself, too. This is a case that really gives meaning to our job. In fact, Chen is ready to sacrifice his career for justice."

"I understand." She took his hand. "Chief Inspector Chen shows his integrity as a police officer. So do you. Why apologize to me?"

"If it upsets you so much, forget it, Peiqin. It may just be another lousy idea of mine. Perhaps it will be my last case. I should have listened to your advice earlier."

"Oh no," she protested. "I just want to know what kind of information you want me to pass to him."

"Let me make one point clear: As soon as this case's over, I'll start looking for another job. A different job. Then I can have more time with you and Qinqin."

"Don't think like that, Guangming. You're doing a great job."

"I'll tell you about the case, and then you can tell me if it's really a great job or not."

So he started to tell her everything. When he came to the end of his account after half an hour, he reemphasized the necessity of exchanging information with Chen.

"It's a job worth your effort, and Chief Inspector Chen's, too."

"Thank you, Peiqin."

"What shall I wear?"

"Don't worry about that. It's a casual event."

"But I'll come back home first. We may be out quite late. I need to prepare supper for Qinqin."

"Well, I have to go straight from the office. Not in my uniform, of course. We'll see each other at the Xishuang Garden, but let's pretend to be strangers there. Afterward we can meet outside."

"Oh, I see," she said. "To be cautious, you should not go at all."

"No, I'd better be there, in case something unexpected happens to you, but I don't think that's likely." He added after a pause, "I'm sorry to bring you into this."

"Don't say that, Guangming," she said, "If it's for you, it's for me, too."

Chapter 31

It was the third day Chen had served as an escort to the American Writers' Delegation.

The visitors had come through an exchange program sponsored by the China–U.S. Distinguished Scholars Committee. William Rosenthal, a well-known professor, critic, and poet, was accompanied by his wife Vicky. Rosenthal's position as chairman of the American association added weight to the visit. Shanghai was the last stop on their itinerary.

At Jinjiang Hotel, Chen was assigned a room on the same floor as the Rosenthals. The American guests were staying in a luxurious suite. Chen's was much smaller, but still elegant, a world of difference from the Writers' Home in Guangzhou. Downstairs, he accompanied the American guests to choose souvenirs in the hotel gift shop.

"I'm so glad I can talk to someone like you. That's what our cultural exchange is about. Vicky, Mr. Chen has translated T. S. Eliot into Chinese," Rosenthal said, turning to his wife, who was busy examining a pearl necklace. "Including 'The Waste Land.'" Apparently Rosenthal knew of Chen's literary background, but he seemed unaware of both his mystery translations and his police position.

"In Beijing and Xi'an, the interpreters also spoke good English," Vicky said, "but they knew little about literature. When Bill started quoting something, they were lost."

"I'm learning a lot from Professor Rosenthal," Chen said, taking a schedule out of his pocket. "I'm afraid we have to leave the hotel now."

The schedule was packed full. Days before their arrival, the activities had been arranged in detail and faxed to the Foreign Liaison Office of the Shanghai Writers' Association. Chen's job was to follow the printed instructions. Morning in the City God's Temple, lunch with local writers, an afternoon's riverboat cruise, then shopping on Nanjing Road, and a Beijing opera for the evening . . . . There were several places they'd had to visit—politically necessary—such as the Red Brick House where the Chinese Communist Party had allegedly held its first meeting, the well-preserved remains of the Fangua slum under the Nationalist regime in contrast to the new building under the Communist regime, and the new development zone east of the Huangpu River, all of which they had already covered.

"Where are we going?"

"In accordance with the morning schedule, to the City God's Temple."

"A temple?" Vicky asked.

"Not really. It's a market with a temple in the center of it," Chen explained. "So some people call it City God's Temple Market. There are quite a few stores—including the temple itself—selling all kinds of local arts-and-crafts products."

"That's great."

As usual, the market around the temple was packed with people. The Rosenthals were not interested in the newly refurbished temple front with the vermilion posts and huge black gate, nor in the display of arts and crafts inside, nor even in the Yuyuan Garden behind the temple, with its glazed yellow dragons atop the white walls. The sight of various snack bars impressed the Americans more than anything else.

"Cooking must have been an integral component of Chinese civilization," Rosenthal said, "or there wouldn't be such a variety of cuisines."

"And such a variety of people," Vicky added cheerfully, "eating to their hearts' content."

According to the schedule of the foreign liaison office, they were supposed to have Coca-Cola and ice cream for their morning snack. Each activity was listed in a printout, including the place and price range. Chen would be reimbursed after turning in the receipts.

The Rosenthals came to a stop in front of the Yellow Dragon Bar, behind the window of which a young waitress was cutting up a roast duck, still steaming from its stitched rump, while an iridescent fly sucked the sauce on her bare toes. It was a dingy, crowded snack bar, but known for its variety of exquisite appetizers. For once, Chen decided to break the rules. He led them into the bar. At his recommendation, the Rosenthals had special sticky rice dumplings with mixed pork and shrimp stuffing. One dumpling had cost six cents in his elementary-school days— nowadays it was five times more. Still, he could afford to pay out of his own pocket even if he did not get reimbursed.

He was not sure whether the Americans liked it. At least he had given them a genuine taste of Shanghai.

"It's delicious," Vicky said. "You are so considerate."

"With your command of English," Rosenthal said, busy between his bites, "there is a lot you could do in the States."

"Thank you," he said.

"As English department chairperson, I would be delighted if something could be arranged for you at our university."

"And you will always be welcome at our home in Suffern, New York," Vicky added, nibbling at the transparent dumpling skin. "Try our American cuisine, and write your poems in English."

"It would be so wonderful to study at your university and to visit your home." Chen had thought about studying abroad, especially when he had first entered the force. "It's just there is such a lot to be done here."

"Things can be difficult here."

"But things are improving, though not as fast as we wish. After all, China is a large country with a history of more than two thousand years. Some of the problems cannot be solved overnight."

"Yes, there's a lot you can do here for your country," Rosenthal nodded. "You're not just a wonderful poet, I know."

Chen was annoyed, however, by his own mechanical response. Clichés—nothing but clichés from the newspapers—as if a *People's Daily* cassette was being played inside him. He did not mind occasionally saying stupid things, but it had gotten to the point where he was turning into an automatic recording.

And the Rosenthals were sincere.

"I'm not sure whether there is such a lot I can do," he said reflectively. "Lu You, a Song dynasty poet, dreamed of doing something great for the country, but he proved to be a mediocre official. Ironically, it was Lu's dream that vitalized his poems."

"Well, the same can be said of W. B. Yeats," Rosenthal said. "He was no statesman, but his passion for the Irish freedom movement informed his best poetry."

"Or his passion for Maud Gonne, the political woman Yeats loved so," Vicky cut in. "I'm very familiar with William's favorite theory."

They laughed together.

Then he caught sight of a pay phone by the door.

He excused himself, went over, and picked up a directory attached to the phone. Thumbing through the pages, he found the Four Seas Restaurant, and dialed Peiqin's number.

"Peiqin, it's Chen Cao. Sorry to call you at your work. I cannot locate Yu."

"You don't have to apologize to me, Chief Inspector Chen," she said. "We're all so concerned about you. How are things going?"

"Fine. Busy with the American delegation."

"Visiting one place after another?"

"Exactly. And dining in one restaurant after another, too. How is your husband?"

"As busy as you are. He, too, says it's difficult to reach you."

"Yes, it can be difficult. If necessary, he—or you, perhaps, if convenient—may contact a friend of mine. His name is Lu Tonghao. He runs a new restaurant called Moscow Suburb on Shanxi Road. Or he will contact you."

"That's fine. Moscow Suburb, I know where it is. It's been open for a couple of weeks, and it has made a stir already." She added, "By the way, will you be at Xishuang Garden this evening?"

"Yes, but how—" Chen cut himself short.

"It's a fantastic place," Peiqin said. "and you deserve to take a break at the karaoke party."

"Thank you."

"So take care of yourself. See you."

"The same with you. Bye."

He became suddenly alert. The way Peiqin mentioned the karaoke party disturbed him. Also, why was she anxious to end the conversation? Was her office bugged, too?

That was not likely. But the hotel might well be. That was why he had not called from there. Peiqin must have wondered. He should have mentioned that he was calling from a pay phone in the City God's Temple Market.

Then he dialed Overseas Chinese Lu.

Lu had called the office upon Chen's return from Guangzhou. In order not to drag Lu into his trouble, he had cut Lu short on the grounds of having to leave immediately. They could not speak safely on the bureau phone.

"Moscow Suburb."

"It's me, Chen Cao."

"Oh, old pal, you've really got me worried to death. I know why you hung up on me the other day."

"Don't worry. I'm still chief inspector. There's nothing to worry about."

"Where are you now? What's the noise in the background?"

"I'm calling from a pay phone in the City God's Temple Market."

"Wang has called me about your trouble. It's serious, she said."

"Wang called you?" he said. "Well, whatever she may have told you, it's not that serious. I've just had a wonderful brunch with the Americans, and we're going to enjoy a cruise on the river. First-class cabin, of course, with the American guests. But I do need to ask you a favor."

"What is it?"

"Somebody, actually my partner's wife, her name is Jin Peiqin, may contact you. She works at the Four Seas Restaurant."

"I know the place. Their shrimp noodles are excellent."

"Don't call me, either at my office or at the hotel. If there is anything urgent, call her or go to her place. You may as well have a bowl of noodles while you are there."

"Don't worry," Lu said. "I'm a well-known connoisseur. No one would say anything if I had my noodles there every day."

"One cannot be too careful."

"I understand." Lu then added, "But can you come over to my place? I want to discuss something with you. Something important."

"Really? I've been so busy the last few days," he said. "I'll check my schedule and see what I can do."

The scheduled afternoon activity was the Huangpu River cruise.

Chen was familiar with the cruise, having served as an escort on a number of occasions. He had no objection to reciting passages from official guidebooks, which he saw as an opportunity for practicing his English. It was just that the activities on the schedule became increasingly boring with repetition. He had no complaint, however, about his escort status at the booking station, where people were standing in a long line. His cruise tickets were reserved at a small ticket window marked FOR FOREIGN TOURISTS.

As they stood on the dock, breathing in the polluted air, he overheard Rosenthal muttering to Vicky about chronic carbon monoxide poisoning in the city. Another serious problem, he admitted to himself, though Shanghai had been making earnest efforts in environmental improvement. In deference to the official guidebook, he remained silent.

As always, a special room on the upper deck of the boat was assigned to foreign visitors. Their room was equipped with air conditioning and satellite TV. There was a Hong Kong kung fu movie starring Bruce Lee—another supposed privilege since Bruce Lee was not available in Shanghai movie theaters. The Rosenthals were not in the mood for the movie. It took Chen quite a long time to find the switch to turn it off.

The waiter and waitress seemed to make a point of bursting into the room, bringing drinks and fruits and snacks, smiling. Some tourists, passing by their door, also looked in curiously. Chen felt as if he were in a glass cage.

In the not-too-far distance, the Bund was alive with a colorful variety of riverfront activities. The eastern shore was catching up, changing even more rapidly with all the new construction going on.

"I'm thinking of some lines about another river," Rosenthal said. "In 'East Coker,' Eliot compares the river to a brown god."

"An ancient Chinese philosopher compared the people to river water," Chen said, "'Water can carry a boat, but it can also overturn a boat.'"

"Lost in 'The Waste Land' again?" Vicky said with mock irritation. "It would be a shame to lose the sight of the wonderful river."

They could not enjoy their conversation for long. Another knock came at the door, then a few more, persistently. "Magic show. First-class performance." A waiter was waving several tickets in his hand. "On the first floor."

Like the movie, the magic show was just another intrusion. Well meant, of course. It would not be polite for them to remain in the cabin.

There was no stage on the first floor. Just an open space partitioned off by several stanchions connected by a plastic cord, one end at the long window opening out to the deck, the other leading a small door beneath the staircase. There were already quite a number of people gathering. In the center, a magician was poking his wand vigorously into the air.

A young woman, apparently the magician's assistant, came out of the small door. A touch of the magician's wand on her shoulder, and she was immobilized, seemingly frozen in the cold blue light. As the magician approached, she collapsed into his arms. Holding her with one arm, he slowly raised her up. She lay stretched out across his forearms, her long black hair trailing to the floor, accentuating her slender neck, almost as white as a lotus root. And as lifeless. The magician then closed his eyes in concentration. To the sound of a muted drum roll, he slid his hand from beneath her, leaving her body floating in the air for a still second. Applause rose from the audience.

So that's the hypnosis of love. A metaphor for it. Spellbound. Helpless.

Had Guan Hongying also been like this? Weightless, substance-less, nothing but a prop, being played with at will in Wu's hands.

And he thought of Wang.

Everything was possible to a lover. Had he been such a lover?

He could not give himself an answer.

> The willow looming through the mist,
> I find my hair disheveled, and the cicada-shaped pin
> fallen on the bed.
> What care have I about my days afterward,
> As long as you enjoy me to the full tonight?

Another stanza by Wei Zhuang. In traditional literary criticism, it was viewed as a political analogy, but to Chen, it was simply a female's sacrifice for the magic of passion. Like Wang, who had been the more courageous, more self-sacrificing one, that night in his apartment, and then again the night in the phone booth.

And years earlier, it had been the same for Guan, who had given herself to Engineer Lai before she parted with him . . .

When the magic show was over, he could not locate the Rosenthals among the dispersing crowd. He went upstairs to find them leaning over the rail, gazing at the white waves breaking against the boat. They were not aware of him. It would be better to leave them alone. He walked downstairs to buy a pack of cigarettes.

He was surprised to see the magician's assistant sitting on a stool at the foot of the stairway. No longer in her glittering costume, she appeared years older, her face lined, her hair lusterless. The magician, too, slumped on a stool next to her. The change in him was even more striking. With his make-up removed, he was just a bald, middle-aged man with heavy bags under his eyes—his tie loosened, sleeves rolled up, and shoelaces undone. The aura of possibility that surrounded him on stage was gone. But they appeared relaxed, at ease, sharing a large cup of pink-colored drink. Probably they were a couple. They had to play their role, Chen reflected as he lit his cigarette, on whatever stage they managed to land. When the curtain fell, they stepped out of the limelight and out of their roles.

The world is a stage—or all sorts of stages.

So with everybody.

So with Guan.

She, too, had to play her role in politics, but it was little wonder that she had decided to play a different character in her private life.

His cigarette had been consumed without his awareness.

"Everything is wonderful," Rosenthal said, when they met again in the cabin.

"Were you enjoying a moment of privacy?" Vicky asked.

"Well, "privacy" is a word that is difficult to translate into Chinese."

He had stumbled over it several times. There was not a single-word equivalent to "privacy" in his language. Instead, he had to use a phrase or sentence to convey its meaning.

On their way back to the hotel, Rosenthal asked about the schedule for the evening.

"Well, there's nothing special for dinner tonight," Chen said. "It is listed as 'no activity,' so you can decide for yourselves. Around eight thirty, we're going to the Xishuang Garden in the hotel for a karaoke party."

"Great," Rosenthal said, "so it can be our turn to treat you to dinner. Choose a good Chinese restaurant."

Chen suggested Moscow Suburb.

It was not just because he had promised Overseas Chinese Lu to dine there after numerous phone invitations. There might be some new message from Peiqin. His accompanying the Americans would not appear suspicious to Internal Security, and it would bring some business to Lu. Afterward, he could even write a short article about "The Rosenthals in Shanghai," mentioning Moscow Suburb.

And Moscow Suburb proved to be as splendid as Lu had promised. With its castlelike front, golden dome, and fully landscaped sides, Lu had totally transformed the appearance of the originally shabby restaurant as if by magic. A tall, blond, Russian girl stood at the gate, greeting the customers, her slender waist supple like a young birch tree in a Russian folk song popular in the sixties.

"It seems the current economic reforms are really transforming China," Rosenthal said.

Chen nodded. Entrepreneurs like Lu were springing up, as in an old Chinese saying, "like bamboo shoots after a spring rain." One of the most popular slogans nowadays was *xiang qian kan*. A play on Chinese pronunciation, it meant: "Look to the money!" In the seventies, with the character *qian* written differently, the slogan had been "Look to the future!"

Gorgeous Russian girls were walking around in their miniskirts and the restaurant was doing a booming business. Every table was occupied. Several foreigners were dining there.

The Rosenthals and Chen were seated in a private room. The tablecloth gleamed snow white, glasses shimmered under highly polished chandeliers, and the heavy silverware could have been used by czars in the Winter Palace.

"Reserved for special guests," Lu declared proudly, opening a bottle of vodka for them.

The vodka tasted genuine. And there was caviar. The service was impeccable. The Russian waitresses were the best, attentive to the point of embarrassing them.

"Wonderful," Vicky nodded.

"To China's economic reform," Rosenthal proposed.

Everybody raised a glass.

When Overseas Chinese Lu excused himself, Chen followed him into the rest room.

"I'm so glad you could come tonight, buddy," Lu said, flushed from the vodka. "I've been so worried since I got that call from Wang."

"So you've heard."

"Yes, if everything Wang told me is true—and there is nothing else."

"Don't worry, I'm still a trusted Party member, or I would not be here tonight with the American guests."

"I know you do not want to discuss the details with me—confidential, the Party interests, a cop's responsibilities, all that crap," Lu said, "but are you going to listen to my suggestion?"

"What kind of suggestion?"

"Quit your job, and become my partner. I have discussed it with Ruru. Just guess what she said? 'Don't expect to touch me ever again if you cannot help Chief Inspector Chen.' A loyal woman, isn't she? It's not just because you managed to send us the Red Flag limousine for our wedding, or because you put in a word for her when she wanted to transfer her job. You've been such a wonderful friend to us. Not to mention the fact you gave us the biggest loan when we started Moscow Suburb. You've been part of our success, she says."

"It's very kind of her to say that, and you, too."

"Now listen, I'm thinking about opening another restaurant, an international one—with American hamburgers, Russian cabbage soup, French fries, German beer—really international, and you'll be the general manager. We'll be equal partners. Fifty-fifty. You already made your investment when you gave me the loan. If you agree, I'll have the necessary document notarized."

"I know nothing about business," Chen said. "How can I be your partner?"

"Why not?" Lu said. "You have taste. A genuine gourmet taste.

That's the most important thing in the restaurant business. And your command of English is definitely a plus."

"I appreciate your generous offer, but let's talk about it another time. The Americans are waiting for me."

"Think about it, old buddy, for my sake, too."

"I will," he said. "Now, have you had a chance to talk to Peiqin?"

"Yes. As soon as I put down the phone, I went there to have a bowl of fried eel noodles. So delicious."

"Did she tell you anything?"

"No, she seemed to be rather guarded—a detective's wife. And there were so many people in the restaurant, but she mentioned that you were going to a karaoke party tonight."

"I see," he said. He had to take the Rosenthals to the party that night. "Anything else?"

"That's about it. But another thing, Wang really cares about you. Give her a call—if you think that's okay."

"Of course I will call her."

"A nice girl. We have talked a lot."

"I know."

Chapter 32

Sitting alone at a table in the Xishuang Garden, watching the bubbles in her cup disappear, Peiqin was growing nervous.

For a second, she had almost lost herself in the magic of the night, which brought back past years. Here she was, in the elaborate dining hall with its bamboo floor, bamboo walls, and a variety of bamboo decorations. Waiters and waitresses were serving, dressed in their colorful Dai costumes. On a small bamboo stage at the end of the spacious hall, musicians played Dai melodies. During those years in Yunnan as an educated youth, Yu had often taken her to watch the Dais celebrating their festivals around the bamboo pavilions. Those girls had danced gracefully, their silver bangles shining under the moonlight, singing like larks, their long skirts blossoming like dreams. Once or twice, they had been invited into the Dai houses, where they chatted with their hosts, squatting on a bamboo balcony, and drinking from bamboo cups. As guests, however, they themselves had never danced.

Taking a small mirror out of her purse, she gazed at her reflection. Still the same image she had seen at home, but the mirror was too small. She stood up to catch a glimpse of herself in a large glass against the wall. Gathering her hair in her fingers, twisting this way and that, she tried to see different views of herself. Pleasant and presentable, she judged, though she had a strange feeling that it was somebody else staring out of the mirror—a stranger in the new dress which she had borrowed from a friend who owned a custom tailoring shop. The dress was sharply nipped in at the waist, accentuating her fine figure. The old Chinese saying was certainly right: "A clay Buddha image must be magnificently gilded, and a woman must be beautifully dressed."

But as she sat there, she realized that she was overdressed, too formal. At a table next to hers, several girls were so scantily clad that their breasts bobbed flirtatiously inside their semi-transparent blouses and low-cut T-shirts; their long legs sported threadbare jeans. One of them had a piece of cloth wrapped about her body, the way the Dai girls wrapped themselves when bathing in the river.

For Peiqin, the past and the present were being juxtaposed. Then she saw Yu coming into view, coming toward her. The entrance to the restaurant was also paved with bamboo. She imagined she detected the squeaking sound underneath Yu's feet, the same sound she'd heard on those nights long ago. Yu was wearing a black suit, a floral-patterned tie, a pair of tan-colored glasses, and a mustache. He caught sight of her, too, smiling. She was about to greet him when she saw that he was not looking in her direction. In fact, he took a seat at the other end of the hall.

She understood. He did not want to be seen in her company in case he was recognized by somebody else. She felt closer to him than ever. For it was his integrity that had tied him to the case, and tied her to him.

The music started. Yu pushed his way through to a table by the bar. He was going to buy a drink, she thought. But instead, he was making a gesture of invitation to a girl, who rose up with an air of indifference, pressing her tall body against him on the dance floor.

Yu was not a gifted dancer. That much Peiqin could see from her seat. He had attended a dancing seminar as part of the required professional curriculum, but he had never been eager to practice. The girl was almost as tall as Yu. She wore a black shift and black slippers, and danced languidly as if she had just emerged from her bedroom. In spite of his clumsiness, she fitted her body easily against his, whispering something to him, rubbing her breasts up against him. He nodded. And she began to snap her fingers and swing her hips.

"Wanton, shameless hussy," Peiqin cursed under her breath. She did not blame Yu, who could not afford to rouse suspicion by remaining idle, but it was nonetheless unpleasant for her to watch.

On the bamboo stage, somebody switched the cassette tape. Through concealed speakers came wild jungle music—all drums and flutes—and more people flocked to the floor.

At the short break before the next number, Peiqin went to

fetch a drink at the bar for herself. Yu was leaning over the table, talking to the tall girl, who smiled at him seductively, crossing her long legs, revealing a flash of her glaring white thighs.

Peiqin stood just a few steps away, staring at them. She was being childish, she knew, but she felt uncomfortable—unreasonably so.

Unexpectedly, a young man with brownish whiskers came to her out of nowhere. Bowing, muttering something like an invitation, he grabbed at her hand before she could say anything. In a nervous flurry, she followed him to the floor, moving with him, turning mechanically in time to the beat of the music, while trying to keep a distance between them.

Her partner was in his mid-twenties, tall, muscular, tanned, wearing a Polo shirt and a pair of Lee jeans, sporting a thick gold chain bracelet. Not bad looking or tough. Why would such a young man want to dance with a middle-aged woman? Peiqin was bewildered.

She could smell beer on his breath.

"It's the first time for me," she said. "I've never danced before."

"Come, there's nothing to it," he said, his hand sliding down her waist. "Just keep moving. Let your body sway with the music."

She stepped on his feet in confusion.

"You forgot to mention what to do with my feet," she said apologetically.

"You're doing fine for the first time," he said patronizingly.

As he swung her around at an increasingly quick tempo, she began to relax. In one glimpse she had over his shoulder, she saw the tall girl wrapping her bare arms around Yu's neck, like snakes.

"You're a dancer." The young man flashed a broad grin at her as the music came to a stop. "Just relax. You're doing great." He went to fetch some more drinks. She was relieved to see a girl approach him at the counter and pull at his gold bracelet.

Peiqin picked her way through the crowd back to her table, trying to make herself as inconspicuous as possible, though it would not prevent her from seeing Yu in the company of another woman.

It was at that moment she saw Chief Inspector Chen arriving with an American couple.

All of a sudden, she pictured herself as if she were in a movie she had seen years ago—Daojin, the young heroine, walking under the cover of night, posting revolutionary slogans for Lu Jiachuan, a Communist she loved. A silent alley, dogs barking all around, and sirens sounding in the distance. On that night Daojin did not understand what she was doing; neither did Peiqin this night. But it was enough to know that she was doing it for her husband, and she was doing the right thing.

The American couple were also moving onto the floor. In spite of their age, they started to zigzag gracefully. Chen remained sitting at the table, alone, in the flickering yellowish light of the small candle.

He was so different from her husband—almost his opposite in every aspect. But they had become friends.

She began to walk over to him. She saw the surprise on Chen's face, but he lost no time in standing up.

"Could I dance with you?" she said.

"I'm honored." He added in a whisper, "What has brought you here?"

"The tickets you gave Guangming. He's here, too, but he wants me to speak to you."

"But he should not have—" Chen paused before he spoke loudly, "You're marvelous."

She realized that it was meant for other ears. Smiling, she took Chen's extended hand.

Chen was not as gifted as her first partner, but it was a two-step, sensually slow, and not difficult for either of them. She put what she had just learned into practice. Immediately she found it natural to follow the beat of the music.

"Yu wants me to tell you something," she said in a low voice, her mouth nearly pressed against his ear. "He's found a witness who saw Wu Xiaoming in Qingpu County on the night of the murder."

"Qingpu County?"

"Yes, Qingpu County, about five miles from the crime scene, at a local gas station. Wu stopped there for gas. The car was a white Lexus, and the witness is a gas station attendant with a good knowledge of cars. He also has a copy of the gas ration coupon the driver used to get the gas at half-price. The coupon can be matched to a car registration."

"That is incredible."

"And something else—"

"You are so breathtaking tonight," Chen said with an engaging smile, "absolutely breathtaking."

"Thank you." She blushed despite her knowledge that the compliment was not meant for her ears. Still, it was good to be complimented. Especially by a man who had complimented her behind her back. According to Yu, Chief Inspector Chen had more than once commented on his subordinate's luck in the choice of his marriage partner.

Then she chided herself for thinking about such things. She was merely performing a task for her husband. Period. What possessed her, she wondered. She must be incorrigible—from having read *The Dream of the Red Chamber* so many times. She lowered her chin to conceal her blush. But she admitted to herself that the evening was enjoyable, finding herself more stimulated than she would have imagined by the touch of Chief Inspector Chen's hand on her waist. Earlier there had also been some element of excitement when she moved in that young man's arms.

"Yu has also interviewed Jiang Weihe and Ning Ying," she said in a hurry.

"Ning Ying—who's she?"

"Another woman involved with Wu Xiaoming. Jiang gave Ning Ying's name to Yu."

"Why?"

"Jiang did not know anything about the relationship between Guan and Wu. Ning was the one who was Wu's girlfriend after Jiang, so Jiang believed that Ning might know something about Guan."

"And did she?" He grinned broadly at a passing pair of dancers, who almost collided with them.

"Not much. But Ning met Guan at one of those parties in Wu's home."

"You're dancing so wonderfully," he said, looking over her shoulder, alertly.

"Thank you," she said, blushing again.

They were moving to a fast tune. The incessant changing of lights made the scene surreal. She could sense Chen's reluctance to hold her tight.

"And something more—"

"That's a great step."

"Oh," she said, not sure what he was referring to. "What's the next step?"

"Let me think—"

Conversation was difficult. Chen would switch topics whenever there were people near them. In the ballroom, dancers bumped against one another all the time. And she was not sure if Chen could hear her whisper amidst the blaring music.

Chen then introduced her to the elderly American gentleman who had come in with Chen.

"You are beautiful," the American said in Chinese.

"Thank you," she said in English.

She had been learning English at a night school, off and on, for several years. It was mainly for her son's benefit. She did not want to be ignorant of Qinqin's homework. She was pleased with her ability to exchange some simple sentences with her American partner.

Chief Inspector Chen also danced with someone else.

She understood that all this was necessary. It was for Yu. And for herself.

When she went back to her table, her soft drink was no longer cold. She shook her head slightly in Yu's direction. Could he see the gesture, or catch its meaning, she wondered, brushing strands of hair from her forehead with the back of her hand.

A Dai girl appeared on the stage, announcing that it was time for the sing-along, or karaoke.

Several people were moving a TV onto the stage. The big screen showed young Dai lovers frolicking in a river, singing, with a caption beneath the picture.

Peiqin was at a loss. She had no idea how she could manage to pass her remaining information to Chief Inspector Chen. She observed that a waitress was talking to him. He was listening attentively, and then he exchanged a few words with the American couple. They both nodded. To her surprise, Mr. Rosenthal came over to her table, followed by Chen, who interpreted for him.

"Would you like to sing karaoke with us in a private room?"

"What?"

"Professor Rosenthal thinks we need a partner for karaoke," Chen said. "He also says you can speak English beautifully."

"No, I have never been to a karaoke party, and I can only say a couple of the simplest sentences in English," she replied.

"Don't worry," Chen said. "I'll interpret for you. And we can talk among ourselves in the private room."

"Oh, I see."

Earlier she had noticed several bamboo huts at one side of the hall. She had thought that they were Dai-style decorations. They turned out to be "private rooms."

The one they went into was luxuriously carpeted, with a TV and VCR system set in the wall, two microphones on a table by the leather sofas, and a basket of fruit on the table.

Outside, people could select their songs on the big TV by paying a fee, but with so many people, a long wait was to be expected. There was also a lot of background noise.

"It must be very expensive, the private room and the service," Peiqin said. "Do you have to pay for it?"

"Yes, it's expensive," Chen said, "but it's a delegation activity, a government expense."

"It's the first time for us," Mr. Rosenthal said. "Karaoke is popular in Japan, we've heard, and it seems to be so popular here, too."

"Something to do with our culture," Chen said. "We would think it too assertive to sing in front of other people without some music in the background."

"Or maybe we do not sing too well," Peiqin said, waiting for Chen to interpret, "but with the background music, it does not matter that much."

"Yes, I like that better—because I do not sing like a lark," Mrs. Rosenthal said.

A waitress brought them a menu of songs in both English and Chinese, and underneath each of its name a number was indicated. All they had to do was push the number on a remote control. Chen chose several songs for the Rosenthals to sing in duet.

As Peiqin and Chen bent over the song menu, pretending to discuss their choices, she was finally able to pass to Chen a copy of the gas coupon and the tapes of Yu's interviews with Yang

Shuhui, the gas station attendant, as well as with Jiang and Ning.

Chen listened carefully to the end of her account, jotted something on a napkin, and said, "Ask Yu not to make any move during the conference. I'll take care of the case as soon as I finish this assignment."

"Yu wants you to be very cautious."

"I will," Chen said. "Don't disclose the information to anybody. Not even to Party Secretary Li."

"Anything else I can do in the meantime? Old Hunter also wants to do his part. The old man has gotten a temporary assignment—traffic control, so he is patrolling streets instead of markets."

"No, don't you do anything, neither you nor Old Hunter. It's too . . . dangerous," Chen said. "Besides, you've already done so much. I don't know how I can ever thank you enough."

"No, you don't have to," she said.

"Well, Lu will probably come to your place a lot as a gourmet customer for the noodles in your restaurant."

"We've got many regular customers. I know how to treat someone like him."

Their talk came to an abrupt end again. Mr. Rosenthal was looking at his watch. Chen said that the Americans were fully scheduled for the following day.

So they emerged from the private room.

People were leaving the large hall. Yu had left, too. Maybe it was the hour. Maybe it was not too pleasant for him to watch his wife being so popular with other men—including his boss and the elderly American.

She bid good-bye to Chief Inspector Chen and the Rosenthals.

It had been a wonderful night for her. If there was one thing she had missed, it was that Yu had not danced and sung with her.

A short man also rose from a table near the entrance, following Chen and his companions out of the hall. She might have been too suspicious, but she made sure that she was not followed before she started to look for Yu outside.

The summer night breeze was pleasant. Yu was waiting for her under a blossoming dogwood tree, still wearing his glasses and smoking a cigarette. There was a black car beside him. To her surprise, she saw Shi Qong waving to her from the car. One of their colleagues in the Yunnan years, Shi had worked as a driver at a petrochemical company since coming back to Shanghai.

It was not the only car waiting along the curb. Nor was it a luxurious one. It was a Dazhong, a product of a Shanghai and Volkswagen joint venture. It was enough, however, that a car was waiting for them. A perfect finishing touch to the night. Yu had been thoughtful to make the arrangement—so romantic.

There could be nothing more repulsive than having to squeeze into a bus—especially on such a summer night—in her borrowed dress.

The tall girl also came out, smiling at Yu with renewed interest, but she strutted away at the sight of Yu holding the door for Peiqin.

"Have you had a wonderful evening?" Shi asked.

"Yes. Thank you for your car."

"You're most welcome," Shi said. "Your husband says you've been so popular tonight. He had no choice but to wait for you outside."

"No, he just wants to smoke outside." She smiled.

On their way home, Yu did not mention the case at all. Nor did she. They talked about the songs they had sung tonight—though not together. They had to be discreet in the presence of others. She was learning fast.

Instead, she played her right hand lightly over the front of Yu's white shirt, a shirt he himself had carefully ironed for the party. Then she tilted her head to one side in a mock-serious assessment.

"Not too bad," she said, pouting her lips provocatively.

All she needed was the feeling of Yu holding her hand tightly in the backseat.

Chapter 33

Monday was Chief Inspector Chen's first day back in his office.

Nominally, Chen was still head of the special case squad. Most of his colleagues greeted him cordially, but he sensed a subtle change in the office. No one mentioned the case to him, nothing but empty, polite talk. People must have heard about the twists and turns of the investigation.

Commissar Zhang, who was not in the office, was said to be on vacation, but how long or why, no one could tell him.

Detective Yu was away on a temporary assignment—temporarily suspended—just like him.

Presently Party Secretary Li telephoned. "Comrade Chief Inspector, welcome back to the bureau. You have done an excellent job. The American guests have just sent us a fax expressing their thanks, especially for your hard work. They have a very high opinion of you."

"Thank you for telling me this."

But the Americans' praise could easily be interpreted as another indication of his affiliation with Western bourgeois culture.

"Take a break," Li said. "We'll talk about your work in a couple of days, okay?"

The Party Secretary's voice sounded smooth, but his words merely confirmed Chen's suspicion.

"Fine," he said, "but I've been away for several days already."

"Don't work too much, young man. We are actually thinking about a vacation for you."

"I don't need a vacation, Party Secretary Li. I've had enough of sightseeing and opera-watching."

"Don't worry, Comrade Chief Inspector Chen. I'll talk to you next week."

It was nothing new—the always-politically-correct Party Secretary discourse. The case had not been mentioned. There was no point in discussing it on the phone, they both understood only too well.

There was nothing he could do now in the Guan investigation, and nothing else he could really bring himself to focus on. There was some routine political paperwork on his desk, accumulated during his absence. Signing his name to the Party documents he was supposed to read was increasingly vexatious. Once more, his temples started drumming. He pulled out the drawer and found an aspirin bottle. Tapping two pills into his palm, he gulped them down. He looked out of his cubicle. Most of his colleagues had left for lunch. After locking the door, he took out the cassette of Yu's interview with Jiang. He listened to the cassette from the beginning once more.

If Jiang had discovered those pictures, so could somebody else—Guan. Jiang's reaction was that of an avant-garde artist, but what about Guan? Guan wanted Wu all for herself.

What would Guan have done?

After looking at his watch, Chen went down to the canteen, which would close in half an hour. He bought a small portion of noodles with a soy-sauce-braised steak. The canteen was crowded, but still he had a table for himself. People were distancing themselves from him, he realized. No one wanted to share his table. And he did not blame them. It was just politics.

By the time he had almost finished, however, Little Zhou come over to him with a bowl of sweet and sour pork rice. "You're not eating much," Little Zhou said.

"I've stuffed myself," Chen said, "dining with the Americans."

"Oh, those banquets," Little Zhou laughed. "But you do not look too well today."

"No, just a little headache."

"Well, go to a public bath and immerse yourself in hot water for as long as you can. When you are sweating all over, wrap yourself in a thick blanket, drink a large cup of ginger tea, and you'll be a brave new man in no time."

"Yes, that may help, especially a cup of herbal tea."

Then Little Zhou said in a whisper, leaning over as if to clean the table, "Yesterday afternoon I drove Party Secretary Li to a meeting. He got a phone call in the car."

"Yes?"

"Not too many people have Li's cellular phone number. So I was curious about it. And I heard your name mentioned a couple of times."

"Really!"

"I was driving along the Number One Overpass. The traffic was crazy there, so I did not catch all of their conversation. Li said something like—I think—'Yes, you're right. Comrade Chief Inspector Chen has been doing a great job, he's a wonderful, loyal young cadre.' Something to that effect."

"You must be kidding, Little Zhou!"

"No, I'm not. That's what I heard. Whoever made that phone call, it must be somebody in a high position. Li's tone sounded so respectful."

"What about the second time my name was mentioned?"

"I was even more alert, but I did not understand the context of their conversation. It was in connection with some young woman in Guangzhou, I guess. Anyway, it's not your problem, but hers. Again Li seemed to be putting in a word for you, or agreeing with whatever was said to him."

"Anything else about that woman?"

"Well, she seems to be in some kind of trouble—in custody or something—for illegal business practices."

"I see. Thank you so much, Little Zhou, but you should not have gone out of your way for me."

"Don't mention it, Comrade Chief Inspector." Little Zhou added earnestly, "I'm your man, and have been so ever since my first day in the bureau. Not because you're somebody, but because you're doing the right thing. Your buddy, and my buddy too, Overseas Chinese Lu swore that he would smash my car if I did not help you. You know how crazy he can be. I'll contact you if I have some more information. You just take care of yourself."

"Yes, I will. I appreciate your concern." He added in a raised voice, "In fact, I'm going to a herbal drug store during the lunch break."

Instead, after leaving the bureau, he turned into a side street, then a small lane, where there was a kiosk for a public phone station, like the one at Qinghe Lane. Looking back, he made sure that he was not being followed before he stepped into the kiosk. A disabled phone service man nodded at him, coughing with his palm against his mouth, as Chen dialed Overseas Chinese Lu's number.

"You have ruined me, Comrade Chief Inspector Chen," Lu said.

"How?"

"The fried eel noodles there are so good, the soup creamy, thick, with a handful of chopped ham and green onion, but so expensive," Lu said. "Twelve Yuan a bowl. Still, I go there every morning."

"Oh, you mean the Four Seas Restaurant." Chen sighed in relief. "Well, I'm not worried about it. Nowadays, with your pocket full of money, you can afford to enjoy yourself there like a true Overseas Chinese millionaire."

"It's worth it, buddy. And I've got some important information for you."

"What's that?"

"Old Hunter, your partner's father, has observed a white car driving around in Wu's neighborhood. A brand new Lexus, just like Wu's. As a temporary traffic patroller, the old man positions himself around Henshan Road. Wu's not in Shanghai, so the old man wonders who's been driving the car."

"Yes, that is something worth observing. Tell him to keep an eye out for the license plate number," Chen said.

"Nothing is too difficult for him. He's eager to do something, Peiqin tells me. And so is Peiqin, willing to do anything. A wonderful wife." Lu added, "Another thing. Don't forget to give Wang a call. She has made several calls to me—she's worried about you. You know why she does not contact you herself, she says."

"Yes, I know. I will call her today."

Chen telephoned Wang, but she was out on an assignment. He left no message. He felt relieved that she was not there. What could he tell her?

Then he checked his messages at home. There was only one—from Ouyang in Guangzhou:

"Sorry I cannot reach you today. How I miss our poetry discussion over morning tea! I have just bought two volumes. One is a collection of Li Shangyin.

"*When, when can we snuff the candle by the western window again,/and talk about the moment of Mount Ba in the rain?*"

"The other one is Yan Rui's. I particularly like the poem from which our great leader Chairman Mao borrowed the image: "*What will leave leaves, / What will stay stays. / When mountain flow-*

ers adorn my hair, / Don't ask where my home will be."

This was so characteristic of Ouyang, who never forgot to adorn his speech with poetic quotes. Chen listened to the message for a second time. Ouyang surely knew him well, quoting Li Shangyin—but why Yan Rui? The poem had survived in classical anthologies mainly because of a romantic story behind it. The poet was said to be a beautiful courtesan in love with General Yue Zhong. She was thrown into jail by Yue's political opponent, but she refused to incriminate her lover by admitting their relationship. The poem was said to be about her unyielding spirit in the midst of her trouble. Could that be a hint about Xie Rong to let him know she would not incriminate him?

Of course, Ouyang was wrong about one thing. There had not been anything between Xie and Chief Inspector Chen. But Ouyang's message confirmed Little Zhou's information. Xie Rong had gotten into trouble—she was in custody. Not because of her massage business, but because of him, with Internal Security behind it.

Was it possible that Ouyang had also found himself in trouble? Perhaps not. At least Ouyang was still out there, with enough money to make the long distance call, and enough composure to cite Tang and Song dynasty poetry, though the way the message was delivered suggested he was in a difficult situation.

Chief Inspector Chen decided to ask Lu to call Ouyang for him, and to cite another poem for caution's sake.

When he got back to the office, he thought of a couplet by Wang Changling: *If my folks and friends in Luoyang ask about me, / Tell them: an ice-pure heart, a crystal vase.*

That would do. He then settled down to work.

Chapter 34

At seven o'clock, Chief Inspector Chen was about to leave the bureau. The doorman, Comrade Liang, leaned out of his cubicle by the gate, saying, "Wait a minute, Comrade Chief Inspector Chen. I've got something for you."

It was a large express envelope that had been lying on the top shelf.

"It came two days ago," Liang said apologetically, "but I could not get hold of you."

Express mail from Beijing. It might be critical. Comrade Liang should have called him. There had been no message at his office; Chen had checked his voice mail everyday. Perhaps the old man, like everybody else, had heard that Chen had ruffled feathers high up. Since the chief inspector was going to be removed soon, why bother?

He signed for the envelope without saying a word.

"Comrade Chief Inspector," Comrade Liang said in a low voice, "Some people have been looking over others' mail. So I wanted to give this to you personally."

"I see," Chen said, "Thank you."

Chen took the envelope, but he did not open it. Instead, he returned to his office, closing the door after him. He had recognized the handwriting on the cover.

Inside the express packaging was a small stamped envelope, which bore the letterhead—The Central Committee of the Chinese Communist Party. The same handwriting was on this envelope.

He took out the letter.

Dear Chen Cao:
    I'm glad you have written to me.
    On receiving your letter, I went to Comrade Wen Jiezi, the

head of the Public Security Ministry. He was aware of your investigation. He said he trusted you wholeheartedly, but there were some people in high positions—not only those you have crossed in Shanghai—very much concerned about the case. Wen promised that he would do whatever possible to keep you from harm. These are his words: "don't push on with the investigation until further signal. be assured that something will be happening shortly."

I think he is right. Time can make the difference.

And time flies.

How long since we last met in the North Sea Park? Remember that afternoon, the white pagoda shimmering against the clear sky in the green water, and your poetry book getting splashed? It seems like ages.

I have remained the same. Busy, always busy, with the routine business of the library. Nowadays I work at the foreign liaison department; I think I've told you about it. In June, there will be a chance of accompanying an American library delegation to the southern provinces. Then we may see each other again.

There is a new phone installed at home—a direct line for my father. In an emergency, you can use this number: 987-5324.

Yours

Ling

P.S. I told Minister Wen I was your girlfriend because he asked about our relationship. You know why I had to tell him this.

Chen put the letter back into the envelope, and then into his briefcase. He stood up, gazing out at the traffic along Fuzhou Road. In the distance, he saw the neon Volkswagen signs shining with a halo of violet color in the night: the "violet hour." He must have read the phrase somewhere. It was the time when people hurry back home, throbbing taxis wait in the street, and the city becomes unreal.

He took out Guan's file and started writing a more detailed report, compiling all the information. He was trying to confirm the next step he was going to take. He would not turn in the report; he was making a commitment to himself.

It was not until several hours later that he left the bureau. Comrade Liang had gone, and the iron gate looked strangely deserted. It was too late for Chen to catch the last bus. There was still a light in the bureau garage, but he did not like the idea of requisitioning a bureau car to take him home while he was unofficially suspended.

A cool breath of summer night touched his face. A long leaf, heart-shaped, fell at his feet. Its shape reminded him of a bamboo divination slip which had fallen out of a bamboo container—years earlier, at Xuanmiao Temple in Suzhou. The message on the slip was mysterious. He had been curious, but he refused to pay ten Yuan for the Taoist fortuneteller to interpret it. There was no predicting the future in that way.

He did not know what would happen to the case.

Nor what would happen to him.

He knew, however, he would never be able to repay Ling.

He had written to her for help. But he had not expected that she would give him her help in this way.

He found himself walking toward the Bund again. Even at this late hour, the Bund was dotted with young lovers whispering to each other. It was there that he had thought of writing the letter to her, as the big clock atop the Customs Tower chimed. A new melody.

The present, even as you think about it, is already becoming the past.

That afternoon in the North Sea Park. *Remember that afternoon, the white pagoda shimmering against the clear sky in the green water, and your poetry book getting splashed?* He remembered, of course, but since that afternoon he had tried not to. The North Sea Park.

There he had first met Ling near the Beijing Library, and there, too, he had parted from her.

He had not known anything about her family when they first met in the Beijing Library. In the early summer of 1981, he had been in his third year at the Beijing Foreign Language Institute. That summer he chose to stay in Beijing since he could hardly concentrate in his Shanghai attic room. He was writing his thesis on T. S. Eliot. So he went to the library every day.

The library building had originally been one of the numerous imperial halls in the Forbidden City. After 1949, it had been converted into the Beijing Library. It was declared in the *People's Daily* that the Forbidden City no longer existed; now ordinary people could spend their days reading in the imperial hall. As a library, its location was excellent, adjacent to North Sea Park with the White Pagoda shimmering in the sun, and close to the Central South Sea Complex across the White Stone Bridge. It was not ideal, however, as a library. The wooden lattice windows, refitted with tinted glass, did not provide enough light. So every seat was equipped with a lamp. The library had no open-shelf system either. Readers had to write the book names on order slips, and the librarians would look for them in the basement.

She had been one of the librarians, in charge of the foreign language section, sitting with her colleagues in a recess against a bay window, separated from the rest of the room by a long curving counter. They took turns explaining the rules in whispers to new readers, handed out books, and in the interval, worked on reports. It was to her that he handed over his list of books in the morning. Waiting for her to retrieve them, he began to notice her more and more. An attractive girl in her early twenties, she had a healthy build and moved briskly in her high heels. The white blouse she wore was simple, but it looked expensive. She wore a silver charm on a thin red string. Somehow he took in a lot of details, though most of the time she sat with her back to him, speaking in a low voice with other librarians, or reading her own book. When she talked to him, smiling, her large eyes were so clear, they reminded him of the cloudless autumn sky over Beijing.

Maybe she noticed him, too. His reading list was an odd mixture: Philosophy, poetry, psychology, sociology, and mysteries. His thesis was difficult. He needed those mysteries to refresh himself. On several occasions, she had reserved books for him without his asking, including one by P.D. James. She had a tacit understanding with him. He noticed that on his order slips, which stuck out from between the pages of the books, his name was highlighted.

It was pleasant to spend the day in the library: to study under a green-shaded lamp beneath the tinted glass, to walk in the ancient courtyard lined with bronze cranes staring at the visitors, to muse while strolling along the verandah, to look at the tilted eaves of yellow dragon tiles woven with white clouds . . . Or to simply wait there, watching the lovely librarian. She, too, read with complete absorption, her head tilted slightly toward her right shoulder. Occasionally she stopped to think, looked up at the poplar tree outside the window, propped her cheek on her hand and then resumed reading.

Sometimes they would exchange pleasant words, and sometimes, equally pleasant glances. One morning, as she came toward him wearing a pink blouse and white skirt, holding the pile of his reserved books in her bare arms, he was inspired with an image of a peach blossom reaching out of a white paper fan. He even started dashing down lines but the noisy arrival of several teenage readers interrupted him. The following week, he happened to have a poem published in a well-known magazine, and he gave her the usual list together with a copy of the magazine. Blushing in her profuse thanks, she seemed to like it very much. When he returned the books in the late afternoon, he mention the uncompleted poem by way of a joke. She blushed again.

Another inconvenience was that the canteen in the adjacent building was open only to the library staff. Convenient, small, inexpensive privately-run restaurants or snack booths were nonexistent in those days. So he resorted to smuggling in steamed buns in his rucksack. One afternoon he was chewing a cold bun in the courtyard when she happened to bike past him. The next morning, she handed over his reserved books along with a suggestion: She would take him to the staff canteen, where he could buy lunch in her company. He accepted her offer. The food was far more palatable, and it saved him time, too. On several occasions, when she had to attend meetings somewhere else, she managed to bring him food in her own stainless-steel lunchbox. She seemed to be quite privileged; no one said anything about it.

Once, she even led him into the rare book section, which had been closed for restoration. It was a dust-covered room, but there were so many wonderful books. Some were in exquisite cloth cases from the Ming and Qing dynasties. He started leafing though the books, but she, too, stayed. There must have been a library rule about it, he thought. It was hot. There was no air conditioning in the room. She kicked off her shoes, and he felt a violent wonder at her bare feet beating a bolero on the filmy dust of the ancient floor.

Soon he had to resist the temptation to look at her over his books. In spite of his effort to concentrate by turning his chair sideways, his thoughts wandered away. The discovery disturbed him.

Most of the time he read till quite late and soon he found himself leaving the library with her. The first couple of times, it looked like coincidence. Then he saw that she was standing by her bike, under the ancient arch of the library gate, waiting for him.

Together, they would ride through the maze of quaint winding lanes at dusk. Past the old white and black *sihe* style houses, and an old man selling colorful paper wheels, the sound of their bike bells spilling into the tranquil air, the pigeons' whistles trailing high in the clear Beijing sky, till they reached the intersection at Xisi, where she would park her bike, and change to the subway. He would watch her turn back at the subway entrance, to wave to him. She lived quite far away.

One early morning as he was riding toward the library, he stopped at Xisi subway station, where he knew she would emerge to find her bike. He bought a ticket and went down to the platform. There were so many people milling about. Waiting there, he lost himself gazing at a mural of Uighur girl carrying grapes in her bare arms. The Uighur girl appeared to be moving toward him, the bangle on her ankle shining, infinite light steps, moving. . . Then he saw *her* moving toward him, out of the train, out of the crowd. . . .

They talked a lot. Their conversation ranged from politics to poetry and they discovered remarkable coincidences in their views, though she seemed a bit more pessimistic about the future of China. He attributed the difference to her long working hours in that ancient palace of a library.

And then came that Saturday afternoon.

The library closed early. They decided, instead of going home, to visit the North Sea Park in the Forbidden City. There they rented a sampan and started paddling on the lake. There were not many other people there.

She was leaving for Australia; she had just told him the news. It was a special arrangement between the Beijing Library and the Canberra Library. She was going there to work as a visiting librarian for six months, a rare opportunity in those years.

"We'll not see each other for six months." She put down her oar.

"Time flies," he said. "It's only half a year."

"But time can change a lot, I'm afraid."

"No, not necessarily. Have you read Qin Shaoyou's 'Bridge of Magpies'? It's based on the legend of the celestial weaving-girl and the earthly cowherd."

"I've heard of the legend, but that was such a long time ago."

"The weaving girl and the cowherd fell in love. It was against the heavenly rule—a match between the celestial and the mundane. For their punishment, they're allowed to meet only once a year, on the seventh day of the seventh month, walking over the bridge made of sympathetic magpies lining up across the River of the Milky Way. The poem is about their meeting on that night."

"Recite it for me, please."

And he did, seeing himself in her eyes: *"The varying shapes of the clouds, / The missing message of the stars, / The silent journey across the Milky Way, / In the golden autumn wind and the jade-like dew, their meeting eclipses / The countless meetings in the mundane world./ The feeling soft as water, / The time insubstantial as a dream, / how can one have the heart to go back on the bridge of magpies? / If two hearts are united forever, / What matters the separation—day after day, night after night?"*

"Fantastic. Thank you for reciting the poem to me," she said.

They did not have to say more. There was a tacit understanding between them. The reflection of the White Pagoda shimmered in the water.

"There's something else I have to tell you," she said, hesitantly.

"What's that?"

"It's about my family—"

It turned out that her father was a politburo member of the Party Central Committee, who was rising fast to the top.

For a moment, he was at a loss for words. That was not at all what he had expected.

Upon graduation, T.S. Eliot could have led an easy life by obtaining a job through the connections of his family, or those of his wife Vivien's family, but he chose not to. He took a different road. Through "The Waste Land," through his own efforts, Eliot came to be recognized as an innovative modernist poet.

Looking over her shoulder, he gazed at the red walls of the Forbidden City resplendent in the late afternoon light. Across the White Stone Bridge loomed the huge Central South Sea complex, where a group of the Party politburo members lived. Her father was going to move there soon, she had just told him.

Her family was much more powerful than Vivien's.

Such a family background could make a world of difference in China.

What could he possibly offer her? A couple of poems. Romantic enough for a Saturday afternoon. But not enough for the life of a politburo member's daughter.

Whatever she might see in him at the moment, on the North Sea Lake, he was not going to be the man for her, he concluded.

"Before I leave," she said, "shall we talk about our future plans?"

"I don't know," he said. "Maybe—since you will be back in half a year, maybe we'll see each other then—if I'm still in Beijing."

She did not say anything in response.

"I'm sorry," he added, "I did not know anything about your family background."

No future plans. He did not say it in so many words, but she understood. He promised he would keep in touch, but that, too, was no more than a varnish over their breakup. She accepted his decision without protest, as if she had anticipated it. The White Pagoda shimmered in the afternoon sunlight, in her eyes.

She, too, was proud.

Afterward, he had had his moments of doubt, but he was quick to dispel them. It was not anybody's fault. Politics in China. A decision he had to make.

After he had gotten his job in Shanghai, he became once more convinced that he had made the right decision. Her stay in Australia was extended to one year. One afternoon, on the lowest level of the bureau mail shelf, he found a letter containing a clipping from an Australian newspaper that carried a picture of her, along with a rejection of his poetry by a local magazine. He was just one of the nameless, an entry-level cop. Nor had he much hope of success with his so-called modernist writing in China.

Then, the second year, a New Year's card from Beijing told him that she had come back from Australia. They had not seen each other since that afternoon at North Sea Park.

But had they really parted? Was that why they had not said anything? She had never left him. Nor had he gotten over her. Could that be the cause of his writing to her on the night when he felt he was totally crushed?

It was the last thing he had wanted to do—to beg for her help. In the post office, he had kept telling himself that he was writing the letter in the name of justice.

She must have realized how desperate the situation was. She had gone out of her way, had thrown the weight of her family behind him. She had introduced herself to Minister Wen as his girlfriend, and now her family's influence had been put into the balance of power.

One HC's son vs. one HC's daughter.

So it would have appeared to the minister. And to the world. But what would this mean for her? A commitment. The news that she had a cop as her lover would spread fast in her circle.

She had given him so much—and at what cost to herself!

Still, she had told the minister that she was his girlfriend. And she had remained single. There must have been a lot of young men dancing around—because of her family or just for her, no one could know for sure.

An image came to him—a lady in ancient attire on a Lantern

Festival card that she had sent him, and he had kept for years—
first juxtaposed with Ling, then merged with her. It was the image
of a lonely woman standing under a weeping willow, with a
poem by Zhu Shuzheng, a brilliant female Song dynasty poet:

> At the Lantern Festival this year,
> The lanterns and the moon are the same as before,
> But where is the man I met last year?
> My spring sleeves are soaked with tears.

Ling had chosen a rice paper Lantern Festival card, the painting exquisitely reprinted, the poem in elegant calligraphy.
Without writing anything on the card herself, she simply
addressed it to him and signed her own name below.

He decided not to pursue that line of thought any further.
Whatever might have happened, or might happen yet, he was
determined to pursue the case to the end.

When he finally got back to his apartment building, it was
quite dark—like a black stamp on night's starry envelope.

He had hardly talked to any of his neighbors, but he knew that
every apartment in the building was occupied. So he unlocked
his door as quietly as he could.

He lay on his bed, staring at the ceiling.

Images at once familiar yet unfamiliar flashed by him. Some
of them had already found their way into the fragments of his
poetry, some—not as yet.

*She, at the subway entrance, carrying hyacinth in her arms, the
mural behind her of an Uighur girl walking toward him: motionless
motion, infinite, light as the summer in grateful tears; the fragrance of
the jasmine wafting in her hair, and then in his teacup, with an orange
pinwheel turning at the paper window, she holding the lunchbox under
the ancient upturned eaves against the clear Beijing sky; she unfurling
a Tang scroll in the rare book section, reading his ecstasy as empathy
with the silverfish escaping the sleepy eyes of the periods, her bare feet
beating a bolero on the filmy dust of the ancient floor; the afternoon*

light stippling her figure in the boat; she coming to him through a labyrinth of lanes on a bike creaking under the weight of books for him, a dove's whistle against a thickening sky. . . .

In the midst of his reverie he fell asleep.

Chapter 35

It had been three days since Chief Inspector Chen resumed work at the office.

Party Secretary Li had promised to talk to him, but he had not done so yet. Li had been avoiding him, Chen knew, to avoid discussion of the case. Any contact between them might be watched. Party Secretary Li was too cautious not to be aware of it. There was no telling when Detective Yu would come back from his "temporary" assignment. Commissar Zhang was still having the week off. His presence would make no difference, but his absence could.

No news from Beijing, though Chen was not really expecting any.

He should not have written the letter to Ling. And he was not going to write a second one. Nor was he going to dial that number she had given him. For the moment, he did not even want to think about it.

Maybe it was wise to wait, as she had said, to do nothing until "further signal." And there was nothing he could really do, with the knowledge that Internal Security was lurking and, ready to pounce if he made a move. Nor was there any new development except, to his surprise, he learned that Wu Xiaoming had applied for a visa for America.

Once more the news came from Overseas Chinese Lu, who had obtained it from Peiqin, and Peiqin, from Old Hunter, from his connections in Beijing. Wu was applying not for a business visa, but a personal one. It was an unusual move, considering that Wu's name was on the top-candidate list for an important position in China. If Wu was trying to get away, Chief Inspector Chen had to act promptly. Once Wu was abroad, there would be no apprehending him.

The white Lexus was Wu's; Old Hunter had identified the license plate number. In the last few days, one of the things Chen had been doing himself, which might not appear suspicious to Internal Security, was research on the regulations concerning high cadres' car service. A high cadre at Wu Bing's level was supposed to have a car exclusively, including a full-time chauffeur at the government's expense, but the cadre's family members were not entitled to use the car. With Wu Bing lying in the hospital, it was not justifiable for his family to have the chauffeur drive them around. So Wu Xiaoming, citing the necessity of visiting his father in the hospital every day, had offered to drive himself. Who had been driving it while Wu was in Beijing?

Overseas Chinese Lu had not succeeded in identifying the driver of the car. Nor had his repeated attempts to contact Ouyang in Guangzhou borne fruit. Ouyang was not at home. This could mean Ouyang had also gotten into trouble—like Xie. Internal Security was capable of anything.

The uncertainty of waiting, in light of the recent information as to Wu's application for a U.S. visa, was becoming too much for Chen. He *had* to talk to Party Secretary Li.

Despite his high rank, Li was in the habit of fetching hot water for tea from the boiler room at eleven fifteen every morning. So at eleven fifteen, Chen was also there, holding a thermos bottle. It was a place where people would come and go. Their encounter might seem natural.

Several other people were filling thermoses with water in the boiler room. Li greeted each of them warmly before he moved over to Chen. "How are you, Comrade Chief Inspector Chen?"

"I'm fine, except that I'm doing nothing."

"Take a break. You've just come back." Leaning over to pick up his thermos bottle, Li added under his breath, "Have you found what we talked about the last time?"

"What?"

"After you have found it," Li said, "come to my office."

Li had already turned toward the stairs, taking with him the filled thermos bottle and the last word.

The motive.

That was what Li had asked for the last time they met in his office. Chen had to find it. There was no point discussing anything more in the boiler room. Politics aside, justification of further investigation depended on discovery of Wu's motive.

Chen went over it again. If Wu had wanted to part with Guan, she was in no position to stop him. She was a third party—the other woman—a notorious person in China's ethical system. She would have found herself in a socially condemned position. Furthermore, revelation of an extramarital affair would have been political suicide. Even if she had been desperate enough to make such a disclosure, she probably would not have got anywhere. Wu had had an affair with her, but he wanted to end it. So what? As Party Secretary Li had pointed out, an affair would not have been considered too serious a political lapse now. With his family background and connections, Wu could have gotten away with it easily.

She could not have presented a real threat to Wu, even at a time when people were talking about Wu's promotion.

On the other hand, Guan was a national celebrity—not some provincial girl. Wu would have to have known that her disappearance would be investigated, which could lead to him, secret as their affair had been. Wu was too smart not to have realized this.

So why should he have taken such a risk?

Guan must somehow have posed a much more serious threat to him, a threat Chief Inspector Chen had not yet discovered.

And until he did, Chen could only occupy himself in reading the latest Party documents delivered to his office. One was about the ever-increasing crime rate in the country and the Central Party Committee's call on all Party members to take action. He also had various forms to fill out for the coming seminar of the Central Party Institute, though he doubted if he would be able to attend after all.

In frustration, he dug out his father's book. He had not read it since the day he had bought it. It was a difficult one, he knew. He turned to the end of the book, to an epilogue in the form of a short fable entitled, "A Jin Dynasty Goat."

Emperor Yan of the Jin Dynasty had many imperial concubines, and one favorite goat. At night, the emperor let the goat amble before him through a sea of bedrooms. When the goat stopped, the Emperor took it as a sign from Heaven to spend the night in the nearest room. More often than not, he found the goat halted in front of the three hundred and eleventh concubine's pearl-curtained door. She was wrapped in white clouds, in anticipation of the coming rain. So she bore him a son who became Emperor Xing. Emperor Xing lost the country to barbarian aggressors through his thirst for a sea harbor. It was a long, complicated story, but the three hundred and eleventh concubine's secret was simple. She sprinkled salt on her doorstep. The goat stopped there to lick the salt.

The late professor used the fable to illustrate the contingency of history. But for a chief inspector, everything about a criminal case should be certain, logical.

It was almost three. Chief Inspector Chen had skipped lunch, but he did not feel hungry. He heard a knock on the door.

"Come in," he said.

To his surprise, Dr. Xia stood in the doorway carrying a huge plastic bag in each hand.

"My shoes are wet." Dr. Xia shook his head, showing no inclination to step in. "I'm bringing you a Beijing roast duck from the Yan Cloud Restaurant. Last time you generously treated me. As Confucius says, 'It is proper and right to return other people's kindness.'"

"Thank you, Dr. Xia," Chen said, standing up, "but a whole duck is too much for me. Better bring it back to your family."

"I have another one." Dr. Xia lifted up the other plastic-wrapped duck. "To tell you the truth, a patient of mine is the number-one chef there. He insisted on giving them to me—free. Here is a small box of their special duck sauce. Only I don't know how to prepare green scallions."

"As Confucius says, 'It is not proper and right to decline a senior's gift.'" Chen tried to imitate Doctor Xia's bookish style. "So I have to accept it. Have a cup of tea in my office?"

"No, thank you, I can't stay. "But Dr. Xia remained in the doorway, fidgeting, then half turning to the main office. "But I have to ask a favor of you."

"Sure, whatever I can do," Chen said, wondering why Dr. Xia chose such a moment to approach him for a favor.

"I want you to introduce me into the Party. I'm no activist, I know. There's a long way for me to go before I can prove myself to be a worthy Party member. Still, I'm a honest Chinese intellectual with minimum conscience."

"What?" he was astonished. "But—haven't you heard the news here?"

"No, I haven't," Dr. Xia raised his voice, waving his hand, adjusting his gold-rimmed glasses. "Nor do I care. Not at all. Listen, you are a loyal Party member, that's all I know. If you are not qualified, no one else in the whole bureau is."

"I don't know what to say, Dr. Xia."

"Remember the two lines from General Yue Fei? *'I will kowtow to Heaven / when the land is set in order.'* To set our land in order, that is what you want, and what I want."

With this dramatic statement, Dr. Xia raised his head higher, as if defying an invisible audience, and walked off, not bothering to take a look at the surprised faces in the large office.

"Bye, Dr. Xia," someone said belatedly.

Chen closed the door after himself with one hand, the duck in the other.

He knew why Dr. Xia had paid him this unexpected visit. It was to show his support. The good old doctor, who had suffered such a lot during the Cultural Revolution, was far from ready to join the Party. The visit—together with the rehearsed statement and the roast duck—was a stance Dr. Xia felt impelled to take as an honest Chinese intellectual—with "minimum conscience."

And it was not just for him, Chief Inspector Chen realized.

It might be a losing battle, but Chen saw he was not alone in it. Detective Yu, Peiqin, Old Hunter, Overseas Chinese Lu, Ruru, Wang Feng, Little Zhou . . . and Dr. Xia, too.

Because of them, he was not going to quit.

He resumed reading Guan's file, making notes until it was long after office hours. Then he ate a small portion of the roast duck. The sight of its golden, crispy skin had revived his appetite. Dr. Xia had even included a couple of pancakes. The duck, rolled in the pancake with the special sauce and green onion, tasted so delicious. He stuffed the remaining duck into the refrigerator.

At about nine o'clock he left the bureau. It did not take him long to arrive at Nanjing Road. It appeared less crowded at that late hour, but the ceaseless transformation of the neon signs infused the scene with fresh vitality.

Presently the First Department Store came in view. A middle-aged man who was gazing into one of the store's windows moved away at Chen's footsteps. Chen, too, came to a stop, catching himself in front of a display of summer fashions, his own reflection faint against the glass. The lights illuminated a line of mannequins in a dazzling variety of bathing suits—skinny strap, tulip-cup neckline, brief-and-halter combination, bikini bottom, and black-and-white trim. The plastic models looked alive in the artificial light.

"A stick of ice sugar haw!"

"What?" Chen was startled.

"Sweet and sour ice sugar haw. Have one!"

An old peddler had approached with a red wheelbarrow sporting sticks of haw, sugar-glazed scarlet, shining, almost sensual. An uncommon sight on Nanjing Road. Perhaps because it was late, the peddler had been able to sneak into the area. Chen bought one. It tasted rather sour, different from those his mother had bought for him. He would have been no more than five or six, sucking at the stick, and his mother, then so youthful, was wearing her orange Qi skirt, holding a floral umbrella in one hand, and his hand in the other . . .

Things had changed so fast.

Would these models in the window age too?

A silly question. More silly than a chief inspector in his impressive uniform sucking a stick of haw, wandering along Nanjing Road.

It was nonetheless a fact that plastics could wear out. A cracked plastic flower, dust-covered, on the windowsill of an out-of-way hotel room. An image that had so touched him, inexplicably, during a trip in his college years. Probably left there by another traveler. No longer lustrous, no longer beautiful—

No longer politically attractive—in others' eyes.

Models, plastic or otherwise, would be replaced.

A model worker in the early nineties, Guan might have had more realistic worries. While on display, young, vivacious, she could admire her reflection in the ever-changing window of politics, but she must have been aware that her charm was fading. The myth of the model worker, though still honored in the Party newspapers, now appealed to few. Intellectuals got media attention. Entrepreneurs got money. TOEFL test takers got passports. HCC got positions. A model worker got less and less.

No reversing time and tide, Guan knew. The way things were going, in a few years, to be a model worker would literally be a joke.

For her, however, it had never been a joke. It had been the meaning of her life, and her life had not been an easy one. She'd had an obligation to be a model at all times: to say the right words, to do the right things, and to make the right decisions. A model—it was, and was not, a metaphor. That's where she had found her life's worth—at the moment of being admired, and emulated by others . . .

Once more his thoughts were interrupted by footsteps coming from behind him. He seemed to hear a young girl's giggle. Chief Inspector Chen must have presented a sight —a police officer gazing at the window full of glamorous mannequins in scanty swimming attire. He did not know how long he had been standing there. He took one more look as he started to move on.

Across the street, a small fruit store was still open. He was familiar with it because his mother had used it as a shortcut to a lane where one of her close friends had lived. The lane had several entrances. One, facing Nanjing Road, had at first been partially blocked by a fruit stall, which had then been converted into the fruit store, totally blocking the access. Behind those tall shelves of fruit, however, there still was a back door opening from the inside, and the store employees used it for their own convenience. He had no idea how his mother had discovered it.

Chief Inspector Chen had not used the shortcut before, though the owner greeted him warmly like an old customer. He stepped behind the first row of shelves, examining an apple like a fastidious customer. The back door was still there. He pushed at it and it opened into a half-deserted lane. He cut through the lane with quick steps. The other end led out to Guizhou Road, where he stopped a passing taxi, and gave the driver directions. "Qinghe Lane, on Hubei Road."

He made sure he was not being followed.

Chapter 36

The stick of sugar haw was as yet unfinished when the taxi pulled up at Qinghe Lane.

Chief Inspector Chen threw the stick into a trash bin. A few feet away, an idiot stood tittering all by himself, holding a plastic bag above his head like a hood. He did not see anybody else near Guan's dorm building. The Internal Security people were probably stationed under his own window.

On his way up to Guan's room he met nobody. It was a Friday night. People were watching a popular, sentimental Japanese soap opera that showed a young girl losing a battle to cancer. His mother had told him about it; everybody was enthralled.

Not Guan.

At her door, the lock remained unchanged. He still had the key. Once inside, he locked the door behind him. He did not turn on the light; instead, he took out a flashlight. He stood in the middle of the room. There was something he wanted to find. Something crucial to the conclusion of the case. If it had ever been there, it might have vanished by now. Wu might have been to the room, found it, and made away with it—hadn't one of the neighbors mentioned a man who might have come from Guan's room? Perhaps he should have searched more thougroughly, should have borrowed a forensics expert. But they were so under-staffed, and it had not seemed worthwhile. The small room could not conceal much.

If Guan had intended to hide something from Wu, where would she have put it?

Any searcher would have looked in the desk, and the drawers, tapped on the walls, turned over the bed, combed through every book and magazine . . . Chief Inspector Chen had already checked these obvious places.

He let his flashlight sweep around the room without con-sciously directing it: An effortless effort, as advocated in *Tao Te Ching*. The light finally came to a stop at the framed portrait of Comrade Deng Xiaoping hanging on the wall.

He did not know why the light had stopped there. He stared at the now illuminated portrait. It was a huge picture for the room, but such a size was not uncommon for a national leader's portrait. In fact, it was the standard size. He had a similar one in his own tiny office.

He had thought highly of Comrade Deng Xiaoping. Whatever might be said against the old man, it was undeniable that China had made great progress under Deng's guidance in economic reform and, to some extent, in political reform as well. The last decade had witnessed tremendous changes—in various aspects of people's lives.

Even in the way people hung their leader's portrait.

During Chairman Mao's time, it had been a political neces-sity to hang a huge portrait of Mao and to say morning prayers and evening prayers under it. There were those familiar lines he remembered from one of the modern Beijing operas, "Under the portrait of Chairman Mao, I am filled with new strength." So the frame had to be specially designed too. A golden frame for the godlike Mao. Not so with Deng. After his retirement, Deng had called himself an "ordinary Party member"—at least the newspapers so reported. Deng's portrait in the living room was not a political necessity. The frame in Guan's room was of a light pink color, showing some delicate embossed design. Possibly it was one originally selected for herself, but then used for Deng. He was shown sitting in an armchair, deep in thought, wearing a high-buttoned gray Mao suit, holding a cigarette, an enormous brass spittoon at his foot, a map of China behind him, his forehead deeply lined. There was no seeing through to what was going on behind the deep lines on the old man's forehead.

Chen moved a chair against the wall and climbed onto it. He removed the framed portrait from the wall, laid it on the floor, and turned it over. Several clips secured the frame to the board. They were easily bent. He removed the board cautiously.

A stack of pictures wrapped in tissue paper was revealed. He unwrapped them and spread them out on the table.

He stared at them, or they stared up at him.

The first few showed Guan in intricate poses, nude or semi-nude, her body cleverly composed to heighten various effects— her long hair covering her breasts, or her body partially wrapped in a towel, or even more shockingly, in the newspaper showing her picture as she was awarded the title of national model worker. There was one of Guan lying naked on a brown rug in front of a fireplace. The crackling fire illuminated the curves of her body, her hands handcuffed behind her back, her mouth gagged, and her legs spread wide apart. He recognized the fireplace. It was the one in Wu's living room, the green marble fireplace.

The next few were of Guan with Wu, both stark naked. The pictures must have been taken with some time-delay device. One showed Guan in Wu's lap, smiling nervously at the camera. Her arms were around his neck, and his hands on her nipples. In the next, she had turned over, showing a pair of buttocks cupped by his hands, her pubic hair T-shaped from that angle, and her bare feet enormous. The rest were of various acts of sexual intercourse: Wu entering her from behind, his part vanishing in the curve of her ass, and his free hand steadying her pear-shaped breasts; Guan arching herself up under Wu, her arms clasping his back, her face turning aside on the pillow, taut in orgasm, Wu with her legs over his shoulders, entering her . . .

To Chen's astonishment, there was also a picture of Guan with a different man on top of her, posing in a gesture of studied obscenity. This man's face was partially obscured, but it was not Wu. Guan lay spread-eagled on her back, her eyes closed, as if in ecstasy.

Then came some pictures of Wu with other women—on the bed, on the rug, in front of the fireplace, or on the floor, in various poses ranging from the erotic to the obscene. One showed Wu having sex with three women.

Chen thought he recognized one of them, a movie star who had played a talented courtesan of the Ming dynasty.

Then he noticed some small words on the back of those pictures.

"14 August. Somewhere between ecstasy and fainting out of fear. Slipping off her panties in five seconds. Entering her vaginally from behind."

"23 April. A virgin. Naive and nervous. Bleeding and screaming like a pig, and then writhing like a snake."

"A saint in the movie, but a slut off the screen."

"Passing out in her second climax, literally. Dead. Cold. Did not come back until two minutes later."

The last picture was of Guan again: wearing a mask, manacled to the wall, but otherwise stark naked, staring into the camera with a mixed expression of uneasiness and wantonness.

A model for a mask.

Or a mask for a model.

On the back of the picture was small printing: "A national model worker, three hours after she delivered a speech at the city government hall."

Chief Inspector Chen felt sick. He did not want to read any more.

He was no moralistic judge. In spite of the Neo-Confucian principles the late Professor Chen had instilled in him, he did not consider himself traditional or prudish. However, the pictures, with these comments, were too much for him. He had a sudden, vivid picture of Guan lying on the hard board bed, moaning, arching herself up to the man's thrust and writhing, beneath the framed portrait of Comrade Deng Xiaoping, who was seated, musing over the future of China.

He heard himself groaning.

There was a feeling of unreality about the whole thing. Chief Inspector Chen had finally found what he had been trying so hard to find. The motive.

Now everything was coming into perspective. Toward the end of their relationship, Guan had got hold of the pictures, which Wu had used against her, but which she had later used to threaten him. She was aware of how destructive the pictures could have been to him, especially at the moment of his potential promotion. She suspected Wu would try to get them back. That was why she had hidden them.

What she had not anticipated, however, was Wu's desperation. It cost her her life. Wu's political career was at a critical moment. With his father lying so ill, this might be his last chance to advance. A scandalous affair or a divorce, either would have damaged his chances. There was no choice left for him. To silence Guan forever would have been his only way out. Now he knew why Wu Xiaoming had committed the crime.

Chief Inspector Chen put the pictures in his pocket, hung Deng's portrait back on the wall, and turned off the flashlight.

As he looked out of the dorm building, he saw a lone man loitering, casting a long shadow across the street. He decided to take a different lane exit. It led to a side street just one block away from the Zhejiang Movie Theater.

A crowd was pouring out of the movie theater, chatting about a new documentary on the Shengzhen economic reform. People were requested to watch the movie as part of their political education. Its release was supposed to signify some dramatic turn in politics.

Chen walked amidst the crowd.

"It's not just for pleasure that Comrade Deng Xiaoping has made the second trip to Shenzhen."

"Of course not. The special economic zone is under fire from those old conservatives."

"They are saying that China is no longer on the road of socialism."

"Capitalist or socialist, that's none of our business. As long as we have three meals a day, we don't care."

"And Old Deng has made the difference in your meals, putting chicken, duck, fish and pork on your plates, right?"

"Yes, that's what it is really about. We Marxists are proudly materialists."

The difference could be seen in the way ordinary people talked about politics on the street. Comrade Deng Xiaoping became "Old Deng"; in the early seventies, people were thrown into jail for saying "Old Mao."

In the bureau, Chen had also heard of Deng's recent trip to the south. It might be a prelude to another dramatic political change, but he found it difficult to dwell on this at the moment. His thoughts were full of Guan, whose personal drama came nearer to him than all the political ones.

At the beginning of his investigation, Chen had cherished a

vision of Guan as a poor victim. An alabaster statue smashed by a violent blow. Guan *was* a victim. On May 11, 1990, she had been murdered by Wu, but even before that, she had long been victimized—by politics. And she was not an innocent, passive statue either. She was in part responsible for her own destruction.

Likewise, he, once a college student dreaming of a literary career, had turned himself into Chief Inspector Chen. He came to this realization with a shudder.

To make no choice is, in existentialist terms, in itself to make a choice.

Guan could have married Engineer Lai, or somebody else. An ordinary housewife, bargaining over a handful of green onions in the food market, searching through her husband's pockets in the morning, fighting for stove space in the common kitchen area . . . But alive, like everybody else, not too good, and not too bad. But politics had made such a personal life impossible. With all the honors heaped on her, an ordinary man was out of the question for her, not enough for her status or ambition. There was no way she could step down from the stage to pick up a man at a bus stop, or to flirt with a stranger in a café. On the other hand, what man would really desire a Party member wife delivering political lectures at home—even in bed?

And then she had came across Wu Xiaoming. In Wu, she believed she saw her answer. She also glimpsed the hope of holding on to the power through her connection with him. In politics, such a union could have worked out: A model couple in the tradition of orthodox socialist propaganda. Love based on common communist ideals. So her union with Wu appeared to be her last chance both for personal happiness—and for political ambition.

The only problem was that Wu was married, and that Wu did not want to divorce his wife to marry her.

She must have been stung by Wu's decision, the pain in proportion to her passion. She had given everything to him, at least that was what she must have felt. When everything else failed she resorted to blackmail, turning his own weapon against him. In a crisis, some people will fight back by any means, fair or foul. Chief Inspector Chen could well understand that.

Or was it possible, he wondered, that Guan finally awoke to a passion she had never known before? And surrendered to it because she had never learned how to cope with it. Having been used to wearing a mask, she had come to take the mask as her true identity. She knew how politically incorrect it was to become enamored of a married man, but that was what she had become, a helpless woman groaning behind the mask, her hands and feet bound. Had she felt for the first time an overwhelming passion that gave her life a new meaning, which she had to keep at any cost?

Chief Inspector Chen was more inclined to the second scenario: Guan Hongying, the national model worker, had been carried away by passion.

What the truth was he might never discover.

Chapter 37

Chief Inspector Chen did not expect much from meeting with Party Secretary Li the next morning, but he could not afford to wait any longer.

There was hardly any hope of pushing the investigation forward—with or without the new evidence, for in the light of the

Party's interests, even those pictures could be brushed aside as irrelevant. If it meant that his time in the force was coming to an end, he was prepared for it. He would have no regrets, and no bitterness. As a cop, he had served to the best of his ability, and as a Party member, too. When he became incapable of serving, he would leave. Or he would be asked to leave.

Perhaps it was time to turn over a new leaf. Overseas Chinese Lu had been doing well with Moscow Suburb. According to an ancient proverb, "You have to look at a man anew after three days." In a couple of months, Lu had metamorphosed into the prototypical "Overseas Chinese," confident, expansive, and ambitious, sporting a diamond ring on his finger. Now the position of manager of an international restaurant was waiting for Chen. "It's not just for you, old buddy, but for me, too. It's so difficult to find a capable, trustworthy partner."

Chief Inspector Chen had said he would think about it.

Alternatively, he could start a small business of his own. A translation or language tutoring agency. So many joint ventures had appeared in Shanghai. This could be his niche, an economics term he had learned in his college days.

But first, he had to have a talk with Party Secretary Li.

Li received him cordially, rising from his seat. "Come on in, Comrade Chief Inspector Chen."

"It's about a week since I got back from my assignment, Comrade Party Secretary," Chen said. "I need to talk to you about my work."

"Well, there is something I want to talk to you about, too."

"It's about Guan's case, I hope."

"You're still working on that case?"

"I'm still the head of the special case group, and I don't see anything wrong with doing my job. Not until my suspension is officially announced."

"You don't have to talk to me like this, Comrade Chief Inspector."

"I don't mean any disrespect to you, Comrade Party Secretary Li."

"Well, go ahead, tell me about your investigation."

"Last time we talked, you made a point about Wu's motive. A good point. It was missing, but we have found it now."

"What is it?"

Chen produced several pictures from an envelope.

"Pictures of Guan and Wu taken together—in bed. As well as of Wu with other women. They were concealed behind Comrade Deng Xiaoping's portrait in Guan's room."

"Damn!" The Party Secretary heaved a distressed sigh, but said nothing further in the face of such depravity.

"Guan got hold of the pictures—in one way or another. Then she must have used them to blackmail Wu into divorcing his wife. The timing could not be worse for Wu. He's at the top of the list for the position of acting Shanghai Culture Minister. At such a critical juncture, he could not allow any interference with his opportunity."

"I see your point," Li said.

"The committee member responsible for the promotion happens to be a comrade-in-arms of his late father-in-law's, and his mother-in-law remains active in the Central Party Discipline Committee. So he had no choice, he could not afford a divorce."

"Yes, your analysis makes sense to me, I have to admit," Li said, putting the pictures back into the envelope. "Still, Wu Xiaoming has a solid alibi, hasn't he?"

"Wu's alibi was provided by his pal Guo Qiang, to help him out."

"That is possible, but an alibi is an alibi. What can you do?"

"Bring Guo in," Chen said. "We'll make him tell the truth. At this stage, a search warrant is justified, and we may find more evidence at Wu's home."

"Under normal circumstances, yes, these are possible options. But in the present political climate, it's out of the question."

"So there's nothing we can do?"

"You've done a lot. It's just that the situation is so complicated at the moment," Li said. "Of course, that does not mean we cannot do anything. We have to proceed carefully. I will discuss it with some people."

"Yes, we are always *discussing*," Chen said, "but Wu's applying for a visa to the United States at the very moment."

"Is that true?"

"Yes," Chen said. "Wu will get away while we are still discussing and discussing."

"No he won't if he is guilty, Comrade Chief Inspector Chen," Li said slowly. "But there's something else I want to talk to you about first. It's about your new assignment."

"Another assignment?"

"There was an emergency meeting yesterday at the city government hall. About the traffic problem in Shanghai. Traffic, as Comrade Deng Xiaoping has pointed out, is one of the everyday concerns for our people. Now that more people have cars, with new construction going on everywhere and roads being blocked, the traffic situation is becoming a serious problem. Comrade Jia Wei, Director of the Shanghai Metropolitan Traffic Control Office, has been sick for a long time. We have to have someone young and energetic to fill such a position. So I recommended you."

"Me?"

"Yes, all the people agreed with me. You've been appointed temporary acting director of Shanghai Metropolitan Traffic Control. It's an important position. You will have several hundred people under your command."

Chen was confounded. It was a promotion, to all appearances. And to a position far beyond a chief inspector's level. Normally, a cadre of tenth rank would be chosen for such a post. According to an old Chinese saying, his promotion to the position was like a carp jumping over a dragon gate. And it would also be highly lucrative. The latest fashion was for people to drive their own cars, to show their wealth, success, and social status. With more vehicles adding to traffic congestion, the city government had set up strict regulations about issuing vehicle licenses. As a result, license applicants had to pay a considerable "back door" amount in addition to the regular fee. Since most of the private car owners were upstarts, they were willing to pay to get their hands on the wheel. Bribery to traffic control officers had become an open secret.

"I'm so overwhelmed," Chen said, trying to gain time by resorting to political clichés. "I'm too young for such a position of heavy responsibility. And I have no experience—none whatever in the field."

"In the nineties, we are getting experience every day. Besides, why shouldn't we use our young cadres?"

"But I am still working on the Guan case—I am still the head of the special case group—aren't I ?"

"Let me repeat it one more time: No one says that you have been suspended from your job here. The case is not closed—I give you my word as an old Bolshevik with thirty years in the Party. This is an emergency posting, Comrade Chief Inspector Chen."

Could it be a trap? It would be much easier to connect him with malfeasance in the new position. Or could it be a demotion in the disguise of promotion? Such a tactic was well known in China's politics. The new job was a temporary one, and after a while he could be justifiably relieved of it, and then of his chief inspectorship at the same time.

Anything was possible.

Outside the window, traffic was heavy along the Fuzhou Road, where a white car came rushing through the intersection recklessly.

A decision flashed through his mind. "You are right, Comrade Party Secretary," Chen said. "As long as it is the Party's decision, I accept it."

"That's the spirit," Li said, apparently pleased. "You are going to do a great job there."

"I will do my best, but I want to ask for something—a free hand. No Commissar Zhang or anybody like him. I need the authorization to do whatever I think necessary. Of course, I'll report to you, Comrade Party Secretary Li."

"You're fully authorized, Comrade Director Chen," Li said. "You don't have to go out of your way to report to me."

"When shall I start?"

"Immediately," Li said. "As a matter of fact, the people there are waiting for you."

"Immediately, then."

As he stood up, ready to walk out of the office, Party Secretary Li added casually, "By the way, you got a phone call from Beijing yesterday. It was a young woman, judging by her voice."

"She dialed your number?"

"No, she somehow had access to our bureau's direct line, so it came to my attention. It was during the lunch break. We could not find you, and then I had to attend the meeting at the city hall. Well, her message is 'Don't worry. Things are going to change. I'll contact you again. Ling.' Her phone number is 987-5324. If you want to call back, you can use our direct line."

"No, thanks," he said. "I think I know what this is about."

Chen knew the number, but he did not want to call back. Not in the company of Party Secretary Li. The Party Secretary was always politically sensitive. Ling's access to the bureau's direct line would have spoken for itself. And the phone number in Beijing, too.

She had made another effort to help—in her way.

So how could he be upset with her?

Whatever she did was done for his sake—and at cost to herself.

"So don't worry," Party Secretary Li said as Chief Inspector Chen left his office.

Chief Inspector Chen did not even have time to worry.

Downstairs, he saw a black Volkswagen waiting for him at the driveway. The driver, Little Zhou, was all smiles. Party Secretary Li was not just being dramatic about the urgency of the assignment.

"Good news!"

"I don't know," Chen said.

"Well, I know. We're off to your new office," Little Zhou said. "Party Secretary Li has just told me."

The traffic was terrible. Chen thought about it, and about his new position, as the car crawled along Yen'an Road. It took them almost an hour to reach the Square Mansion, located at the People's Square.

"What a location! And you'll have a car exclusively for yourself, and a driver, too," Little Zhou said, reaching out of the window before he drove away. "Don't forget us."

His new office was a multi-room suite in the Square Mansion in the center of Shanghai. The city government itself was located in the same building, together with a number of important organizations. Such an impressive office site was probably chosen to convince people of the serious attention being paid to traffic congestion by the city authorities, Chen reflected.

"Welcome, Director Chen." A young girl wearing a pair of silver-rimmed glasses was waiting for him. "I am Meiling, your secretary."

So he had a personal secretary working for him at a reception area in front of his spacious office. Meiling lost no time showing him the ropes. "The office is not just a department under the Shanghai police bureau. It's under the joint leadership of the city government and the bureau," Meiling said. "Even the mayor himself calls in here from time to time."

"I see," he said. "So there is a lot of work."

"Yes, we've been terribly busy. Our old director was rushed to the hospital, and we have not had any preparation for your arrival."

"Neither have I. As a matter of fact, I knew nothing about my appointment until a couple of hours ago."

"Our old director has been sick for several months," Meiling said apologetically, "There's a backlog of work."

So there was all the routine work he would have to familiarize himself with—documents to read, officers to meet, reports to review, and calls to make. Several papers were already waiting his signature.

Following Meiling, he made a tour of his office suite. There were several computers in each room, forming a network for metropolitan traffic control. In spite of the evening computer courses he had taken, he would require two or three weeks to become familiar with the system. A director's responsibilities consisted not only of dispatching traffic police officers, but also maintaining close cooperation with the public transportation bureau, the construction bureau, and the city government.

After the tour, Chen felt even more disoriented. Earlier in the morning, he had been ready to quit, believing that his career coming to an end. Now he was sitting at an impressive desk, the tall window behind him overlooking the People's Square, with the afternoon sunlight shining on his brass director's plaque.

But he did not have the time to ponder this unexpected change. Meiling handed him a copy of the department newsletter. "The latest issue, just delivered to us."

It was an edition focusing on traffic violation cases. Most of the offenders were quite young. Yet they might be seriously punished, for the report's tone sounded politically serious. Some might even get ten or fifteen years.

He leaned back in his swivel chair, feeling both exhausted and exhilarated, watching Meiling arrange the papers neatly in a pile on the desk. His first secretary. It was wonderful to have one. He was intrigued by the difference produced by a female presence in the office.

He settled down to the work.

The day turned out to be much longer than he had expected. He told Meiling to go home at six. By the time he himself was able to leave his office, it was already past eight.

Little Zhou's guess was right. Chen had a car for himself, and a driver, too, who had called his office asking when he would be needed. He declined the offer; as the director of the Shanghai Traffic Control Office, he felt obliged to learn the situation first-hand.

> With my horse galloping jubilantly in the spring wind,
> I see the flowers all over Luoyang in one day.

The decision to take the bus home instead of his car cost him another hour. The bus came to a stop in bumper-to-bumper traffic at Henan Road. The weather was hot, and the passengers cursed the stuffy air loudly. He, too, grew inexplicably exasperated—involved in the collective angst of the city. Still, it was an ethical necessity for him, he believed, to experience the traffic ordeal as one of the ordinary Shanghai people.

It was not until he had reached his apartment, and lit a cigarette, that he was able to look back at the day's events. He should have been elated by the unexpected promotion, but its very unexpectedness was disturbing to him. Why should he, of all people, have been chosen to fill such an important position?

A man, once bitten by a snake, would be nervous all his life at the shadow of a straw rope.

Yet it did not appear to be a trap. He thought about the last remark by Party Secretary Li as he left Li's office, about Ling's long distance call from Beijing. Was his promotion just due to her family? That was what he dreaded.

Chapter 38

Chief Inspector Chen—"Director Chen"—lost no time in exercising his new authority, as he sat in the leather swivel chair against a wall plastered with street and transport maps, looking down at the people moving about in the People's Square.

One of the first few instructions he had dictated to Meiling was to summon Old Hunter to the office. As the old man had been working as a temporary traffic patrol officer, it was not difficult for Meiling to page him. Old Hunter arrived at the office, as Meiling was ready to leave. Chen asked her to stay, saying, "Don't go, Meiling. Please get me the regulations regarding an adviser's position for our department. Compensation, as well as the other benefits."

"They are all in the cabinet," Meiling said. "I'll find them."

"Congratulations. Chief Inspector Chen—oh no, Director Chen," Old Hunter said as he examined the impressive office furniture. "Everybody says you are doing a wonderful job."

"Thank you, Comrade Old Yu. It's my second day here. As a new hand, I need your valuable help."

"I'll do whatever I can, Director Chen."

"You've worked as a traffic officer. So one of the problems you must have noticed, I believe, is the problem of traffic accidents. These accidents cause not only casualties, but also serious traffic jams."

"That's true," Old Hunter said, casting a curious glance at Meiling, who was kneeling on the floor, busily searching in the drawer of the tall file cabinet.

"I believe it is partially because more and more people are driving around without a license."

"You're right. Driving has become a fashion. Everybody wants to have his hands on the wheel. Driving school is way too expensive, and takes a long time, so some people go without a license."

"Yes, this is really dangerous."

"Exactly. Those young people—quite a number of them—seem to believe they're born drivers. Totally irresponsible."

"That is why I want you to do something—a sort of experiment. Choose one particular area, station yourself there, and look out for those licenseless drivers. If you have a hunch, stop the car for a checkup. Don't just give a violator a ticket, take him into custody—no matter who he may be."

"Good idea," Old Hunter said. "As that old saying goes, you have to use a strong drug for a desperate disease."

"And report to me directly."

"That's fine. Like son, like father. Where are you going to put me?"

"What about Jingan District? As for a particular street, you pick one. My suggestion is to start with Henshan Road."

"Oh, Henshan Road—yes." Old Hunter's eyes sparkled. "I see, Chief Inspector Chen—no, Director Chen."

"It's an important task," Chen said earnestly. "Only a veteran like you would be up to it. So I'd like to appoint you as our special adviser. You will have a couple of police officers under your command."

"No, you don't have to create a position for me, Director Chen. I will do my best anyway."

"Meiling," Chen said, turning to his secretary, "when you find the compensation regulation, send Adviser Yu the money in accordance with it."

"I've already got it," Meiling said, "A check can be cut right away."

"That's great. Thank you."

"No," Old Hunter protested in embarrassment. "I'd rather be a volunteer."

"No, you will be paid, and you will have your men, too. That's your authority. I just want to emphasize one point: Do whatever you are supposed to—no matter whose car it may be—with a white plate or not."

"Got you, Comrade Director Chen."

Chen believed he had made himself clear to Old Hunter—in Meiling's presence.

Old Hunter should be able to detain whoever drove the white Lexus—at least for one day. If anything went wrong, Old Hunter was no more than a traffic police officer carrying out his responsibilities. So there was one thing Chen was now able to do about Guan's' case.

The result came faster than he had expected.

On Thursday, he attended a field meeting in the morning. The mayor inspected the project connecting the banks of the Huangpu River by the Yangpu Bridge. Once it was completed, the bridge would also alleviate the traffic congestion in the area. Chen had to be there too, mixing with a group of cadres, walking back and forth along the bridge.

When he returned to the office, Meiling pointed her finger at his closed office door with a slightly puzzled expression on her face. Approaching, he could hear a high-pitched voice inside his office. "It's no good denying it, Guo Qiang!"

"It's Old Comrade Yu talking with somebody in there," Meiling said in a subdued voice. "He wanted to bring the man into your office. For an important case, he said. He's our adviser. So I had to let them in."

"You did the right thing," he assured her.

They overheard Old Hunter saying, "Why are you trying so hard to save someone else's ass, you sucker? You know our Party's policy, don't you?"

"Comrade Adviser Yu is right." Chen opened the door upon a sight he had foreseen: Old Hunter stood like a Suzhou opera singer talking dramatically to a man slumped in the chair.

The man was in his early forties, lanky, narrow-shouldered, with a suggestion of a hunchback. The photo of the stranger on top of Guan flashed through Chief Inspector Chen's mind. This was the man.

"Ah, Director Chen," Old Hunter said, "you're back just in time. This S.O.B. has not spilled the beans yet."

"He is—"

"Guo Qiang. He was driving a white Lexus—without a license."

"Guo Qiang," Chen said. "You know why you are here today?" Chen said.

"I don't know," Guo said. "Driving without a license is a minor offense. Just give me a ticket. You've no right to keep me here."

"You sound like a happily innocent man," Old Hunter said. "Whose car is it?"

"Take a good look at the white plate. It's not difficult to guess."

"Wu Xiaoming's car—or rather Wu Bing's car, right?"

"Yes. So you should let me go now."

"Well, that is the very reason why you are being held here," Chen said. "I tell you what. We have been watching you for days."

"Why—so you've purposely trapped me," Guo said. "You will regret it."

"Comrade Adviser Yu," Chen said to the old man, "thank you for bringing this suspect to us. From now on, it's no longer a traffic violation case. I'm taking it over."

"My last piece of advice to you, young man," Old Hunter said, grinding out his cigarette. "Use your brains. Don't you know who Comrade Chen Cao is? The new Metropolitan Traffic Control Director, as well as chief inspector of homicide, and head of the special case group, Shanghai Police Bureau. The game is over. You'd better come clean. A cooperative witness will be punished with leniency. Director Chen—Chief Inspector Chen—I should say—may work out a deal for you."

As Old Hunter left the office, Chen stepped out, too, walking him to the elevator. "Have the car thoroughly examined, especially the trunk," he said in a subdued voice, "for any evidence."

"Yes, that's what I'm going to do, Chief Inspector Chen."

"Do it in an official way, Comrade Adviser Yu." He held the door for the old man. "Have some other officer work together with you. Ask him to sign for anything, too."

When he moved back to the office, he said to Meiling, "It's important that we not be disturbed."

"Now," he said to Guo, closing the door, "let's have a talk."

"I've got nothing to say," Guo said, folding his arms across his chest and staring defiantly ahead.

"We are not talking about a license or speed limits. It is about Guan Hongying's case."

"I know nothing about it."

"In your testimony," Chen said, producing a file folder from the cabinet, "you said that on the night of May tenth, Wu Xiaoming drove to your home around nine thirty. Wu turned your study into a darkroom, and stayed there for the night, developing his films. On that same night, a white Lexus was seen at a gas station about five miles from the Baili Canal. It was in that very canal that Guan's body was found the following day. And it was Wu Xiaoming's car, no mistake about it. We have the receipt bearing the gas ration coupon number. So who was the driver that night?"

"Wu might have lent his car to somebody else. How can I be responsible for that?"

"According to your testimony, Wu's car was parked right in front of your home. Wu did not step out of the darkroom for one minute throughout the night. You were very emphatic. But you did not say that you yourself did not leave during the night. You had the car keys, as you do today. So you must have been the driver—unless you are providing a false alibi for Wu."

"You cannot bluff people like that, Comrade Chief Inspector. Whatever you may say, I did not drive the car that night. Period."

"You may call it a bluff, but we have a witness."

"There's nothing your witness can say against me. It's the nineties now, no longer a time when you can detain a person just as you please. If it's a case concerning Wu, don't put pressure on me."

"Don't give me that," Chen said, reaching for his briefcase. "I'm not talking about Wu, but about you. About obstruction of justice, perjury, and being an accessory to a homicide. You said in your testimony that you did not know who Guan was. False. Let me show you something."

Chen produced a picture. The picture of Guan with a man on top of her. "Take a close look," he said. "This was taken in Wu Xiaoming's mansion, wasn't it? Tell me that's not you."

"I don't know anything about the picture," Guo said doggedly, but with a hint of panic in his voice.

"You lied in your testimony, Mr. Guo Qiang," Chen said, taking a leisurely sip of his tea. "You won't get away with it."

"I did not kill her," Guo said, wiping away the sweat that had begun to bead on his forehead. "Whatever you say, you have no evidence to prove it."

"Listen, even if we cannot nail you for the murder, the picture alone is enough cause to lock you up for seven or eight years. Plus your false testimony. Fifteen years, I'd say. You will be an ancient, white-haired hunchback when you walk out again. I'll make sure you will have a wonderful time in there. You have my word on it."

"You're threatening me."

"Think about your family, too. How will your wife react when she gets hold of that picture? Will she wait for you for twenty or more years? I don't think so. You were married just last year, weren't you? Think about her, if not about yourself."

"You can't do that!"

"Of course I can. So here is your chance: Work with me. Tell us what you know about Wu and Guan, and what Wu did on May tenth. A deal may be possible."

"So you really think you can touch Wu?"

Chen understood the doubt in Guo's mind.

He opened his briefcase again. In it was the envelope of the Party Central. Ling might have purposely chosen it for others to see. He had been carrying it with him. Not for any sentimental reason. He did not want to leave the letter at home with Internal Security snooping around.

"This is a case," he said, flashing the envelope at Guo, "directly under the Central Party Committee."

"So—" Guo stammered, staring at the envelope, "it's a decision at the highest level."

"Yes, the highest level. Now, you're a clever man. Wu must have tipped you off about his maneuvers against me. What's the result? I'm still chief inspector, and metropolitan traffic control director, too. Why? Think about it."

"They are planning something against the old cadres?"

"That is your interpretation," Chen said. "But if you think Wu will help you, you are dead wrong. Wu would be only too happy to have a scapegoat."

"Are you sure you can work out a deal for me?"

"I'll do my best, but you have to tell me everything."

"Let me think—" Guo lifted his gaze from the envelope to Chen's face and slumped further into the chair, making his hunchback more pronounced. "Where shall I start?"

"How did you come to know about the relationship between Wu and Guan?"

"I came to know Guan first—as one of those party girls. A lot of them were at Wu's parties. They came of their own will. Some wanted to have fun, drinks, karaoke, and whatnot, some wanted to meet Wu, some wanted to take a look at the mansion, and some wanted to have their pictures taken . . . You have seen those pictures, haven't you?"

"Yes, every one of them. Go on."

"Wu Xiaoming has all the advanced photography equipment. His own darkroom, too. He published quite a few. Some of those hussies were just delirious about publicity. Wu's got quite a reputation among them. And a way with them, too. Not to mention the other offers he could make."

"What are the other offers?"

"Good, lucrative jobs, for instance. With Wu's connections, it was not difficult for him to arrange such things. People are willing to do things for him, you know, so someday they might ask for something in return. Also, Wu introduced several girls to modeling agencies."

"So in return, they let him take pictures—even those pictures?"

"Well, some of them fell for him anyway, with or without his offering anything. They let him pose them, totally nude, before his camera. You don't need me to tell you what happened after ward, Comrade Chief Inspector. One girl was so eager, she told me, that she was willing to sleep with him just for the pictures. 'I'll work for them,' that's exactly what she said."

"Why did Wu want to take those pictures?"

"I don't know—Wu's a man who keeps his own counsel—except for one thing he told me. He was a bit drunk that night, I think."

"What was that?"

"Those pictures could prevent the girls from getting him into trouble."

"I see. You said that you first met Guan at a party. So was she like one of those party girls?"

"Well, at first I had no idea that she was the national model worker. There were no formal introductions at these parties. There was only one thing different about her that I noticed. She appeared to be unusually stiff when I tried to dance with her."

"Had Wu told you anything about her?"

"No, not right away. But I could tell she was different. Unlike the other girls, she took it seriously."

"Seriously—what do you mean?"

"The relationship with Wu. Most of the girls were there just for fun. A one-night stand, you might say. Some are far more liberal than you can imagine, offering themselves without your asking. Guan was different."

"So Guan expected something serious out of the affair—but was she not aware that Wu was married?"

"She was well aware of it, but she believed that Wu would divorce his wife for her sake."

"Now that's really something—for a national model worker to go after a married man—what made her think she would succeed?"

"I don't know."

"But what made you think Guan wanted Wu to marry her?"

"It was so obvious. The way she clung to him in such a wifely way, and put on an air of inviolable chastity to everybody else."

"Did Wu treat her just like one of those girls?"

"No. Wu was also different."

"Can you try to be more specific here?" Chen said, handing a cup of tea to Guo after he had made another for himself.

"For one thing, Guan did not like the parties. Altogether, she was at them only three or four times, and she would withdraw into Wu's room after one or two dances. Wu stayed with her in his room, even when the party was going on like crazy outside. That was most unlike Wu."

"Staying alone with a girl in his room. That's very like Wu Xiaoming, I'd say."

"No, that's not what I mean. Wu stayed with a girl in his room after the party, but not during it. Wu was quite considerate toward Guan, going out of his way to humor her. Last year they even took a trip together. To the Yellow Mountains, I think. That was Guan's idea, too."

"They shared the hotel room as a couple," Chen said. "I'm afraid that it was not just Guan's idea."

"I don't know. Guan was okay, surely not plain, but you should have seen those actresses, more beautiful, and much younger. But Wu never made a trip with any of them except Guan."

"Well, you may be right," Chen said, nodding. "But then what happened between the two of them?"

"Wu realized that she was too serious, too demanding. It became a problem. She must have put a lot pressure on him, but it was out of the question for Wu to divorce his wife."

"Why?"

"His wife's family is powerful. You know who Wu's father-in-law was? Liang Xiangdong, the first secretary of Huadong Area."

"But Liang died during the Cultural Revolution."

"Well, there's something you may not know. Wu's father-in-law died, but his brother-in-law has become the Second Party Secretary of Anhui Province. What's more, his mother-in-law, still alive and kicking, is a member of the Central Party Discipline Committee in Beijing."

"We know that," Chen said. "All the HCC connections and nepotism. But now tell me, what was Wu Xiaoming's reaction to Guan's demand?"

"At first, Wu simply laughed, behind her back, of course. Just another of her model masks, he said, like those worn by Beijing opera players, 'different ones on different stages.' He was not too bothered with it. Perhaps he liked its novelty."

"So when did their relationship became problematic?"

"Honestly, I did not notice anything until that picture session. It was after a party last December. At the party, Guan was her usual self, as stiff as a bamboo stick, but Wu made her drink several cups of Maotai. Whether he had put something else in the wine, I don't know. Soon she passed out. Wu asked me to help her into the bedroom. And to my surprise, he started undressing her there. She was not aware of anything, as innocent as a white lamb."

"Did he tell you why he wanted you to be there?"

"No, he just started shooting pictures in my presence, those pictures, you know. He said something like—'Strip a national worker model naked, and she's just another wanton slut.' It was not something uncommon, I mean, a nude picture session for him."

"Nor uncommon for you, either?"

"Well, things like that had happened before—once or twice. With other girls, of course. Wu wanted me to take pictures, Wu and the girl together on the bed. But that night, Wu wanted me to pose with Guan, and that's the picture you have got. I swear to you that I just posed with her. I did not do anything else."

"You must have been a Liu Xiawei of the twentieth century."

"I don't know Liu Xiawei. But I was dumbfounded. Before that night, Wu had told us not to bother her. He had never made such a point about the other girls. In fact, Wu did not care at all with the other girls."

"What do you think could be the reason for Wu's sudden change that night?"

"I do not know. Perhaps Wu wanted to use those pictures to prevent her from making trouble."

"Did Wu succeed?"

"I have no idea. Afterward, they continued to see each other. What happened occurred several weeks after the photo session."

"What happened?"

"They had a fight."

"Again, you have to be more specific here," Chen said. "Did you witness the fight?"

"No, I didn't. I happened to visit him shortly afterward. Wu was simply beside himself."

"When was this?"

"At the beginning of March, I believe."

"What did he say?"

"He was drunk, talking in delirious rage. It appeared that she had taken something important from him."

"Something she could use to threaten him?"

"Right, Comrade Chief Inspector. Wu did not tell me what it was. He said something like—'The bitch thinks she can blackmail me. She'll pay for it. I'll fuck her brains out!' Yes, it was something to blackmail him with."

"Did he tell you what he was going to do about it?"

"No, he didn't. He was in such a murderous rage, cursing like mad."

"Then what happened?"

"Then one night in mid-May, he suddenly came to my place to develop pictures, saying there was something wrong with his darkroom. He stayed in my study that night. It was a Sunday, I remember, because my wife complained to me about it. We usually go to bed early on Sunday. Several days later he called me, and during our conversation, he repeated two or three times that it was the night of May tenth, the night that he came to work at my place. I did not understand his emphasis on the date until one of your men asked me about that night."

"You told Detective Yu exactly what Wu had told you to, and established an alibi for him."

"Yes, but I didn't know that I was providing an alibi for him, nor did I know that Wu had committed murder. Later I looked up the date. That Sunday was actually May thirteenth. But at the time I spoke to Detective Yu, I didn't recall that."

"Did you ask him about it afterward?"

"I called him the following day, telling him that a policeman had interviewed me. He asked me out to the JJ Bar. Between cups, he said that he was going to be promoted to be Acting Culture Minister of Shanghai, and that he would pay me back with interest."

"Did he mention Guan at all?"

"No, he didn't. He just asked what date I had told Comrade Detective Yu, and he seemed to be relieved by my answer."

"Anything else?"

"No, he did not say anything else that day, and I did not ask," Guo said. "I'm not holding anything back, Comrade Chief Inspector Chen."

The phone started ringing. "It's Comrade Adviser Yu on the line, and he says it is urgent," Meiling said. "Do you want to speak to him?"

"Yes, put him through."

"We've found something in the car trunk, Chief Inspector

Chen," Old Hunter said. "A long strand of a woman's hair."

"Send the evidence to Dr. Xia immediately," he said. "And book Guo and hold him as a material witness."

It was the time for Chief Inspector Chen to have his showdown at the bureau.

Chapter 39

Standing in a crowded bus the next morning, Chen tried to plan what he would say at the meeting with Party Secretary Li and Superintendent Zhao, but he was too distracted by a strong perfume mixed with a no less pungent body odor from a young woman passenger flattened against him. Unable to budge, he resigned himself to being like a canned sardine, brainless, almost breathless.

The bus was crawling along Yan'an Road. People kept moving in and out, elbowing and shouldering. So many possible results could come from the confrontation for which he was preparing himself, but he could not put off the meeting any longer. The chain was complete: The motive, the evidence, the witnesses. There was no missing link. No excuse to avoid a showdown.

As soon as he had received Dr. Xia's report the previous afternoon, Chen called Party Secretary Li. Li heard him out, for once not attempting to interrupt him.

"You're positive," Li finally said, "Wu Xiaoming drove the car that night?"

"Yes, I'm positive."

"You've got Dr. Xia's report?"

"Not yet, but he confirmed on the phone that it was Guan's hair found in Wu's car."

"And Guo will also testify against Wu about his false alibi?"

"Yes, Guo has to save his own neck."

"So you think it's time to conclude."

"We have motive, evidence, and a witness. And Wu's alibi is gone."

"It is not a common case," Li seemed to be lost in thought, exhaling into the phone before he continued, "and it doesn't come at an ordinary time. We will have a meeting with Superintendent Zhao tomorrow. In the meantime, do not say a single word to anybody else."

When Chen arrived at Li's office, he saw a small note taped to the office door.

COMRADE CHIEF INSPECTOR CHEN: *Please wait for us in the Number 1 conference room. Important meeting. Superintendent Zhao will be there too.*

Li.

There was no one else in the conference room. Chen took a leather-cushioned chair at the end of the long table. Waiting there, he went over his notes. He wanted his presentation to be organized, succinct, to the point. When he finished reviewing, he looked at his watch again. It was twenty minutes after the appointed time.

He was not optimistic about the meeting. Nor did he think his bosses would be looking forward to it. They would harp on the interests of the Party and dismiss him from the case. In a worst-case scenario, they would officially remove him from his position.

But Chen resolved not to retreat, even at the cost of losing his position and Party membership, too.

As a chief inspector he was supposed to seek justice by punishing the murderer, whoever it was.

As a party member, he knew what he was supposed to do. It had been the first lesson of the Party Education Program. A Party member must serve, above all things, the interests of the Party.

Here's the problem. What were the interests of the Party?

In the early fifties, for instance, Chairman Mao had called on Chinese intellectuals to find fault with the Party authorities, and Mao said that it was in the interests of the Party. When the invitation was taken literally by some, however, Mao flew into a rage and called those naive fault-finders antisocialist rightists. He sent them to jail. That, too, was done, of course, in the interests of the Party, as the Party newspapers declared, justifying Mao's earlier speech as a tactic to "lure the snake out of the cave." So, too, with a number of political movements, including the Cultural Revolution. Everything was done in the interests of the Party. After Mao's death, these disastrous movements were written off as Mao's "well-intended mistakes," which should not detract from the glorious merit of the Party; and once more, the Chinese people were taught to forget the past in the interests of the Party.

Chen had been aware of the difference between being a chief inspector and being a Party member, but he had not thought much about the possibility of his two roles coming into direct conflict. And here he was, waiting for the resolution of just such a conflict.

There was no retreating. In the worst-case scenario, Chief Inspector Chen was prepared to resign, to work in Overseas Chinese Lu's restaurant. In the Western Han dynasty, Sima Xiangru had done the same thing, opening a tiny tavern, wearing short pants, sweating, ladling wine out of a huge urn, and Wenjun had followed him, serving the wine to customers, smiling like a lotus blossom in the morning breeze, her delicate eyebrows suggesting a distant mountain range. All the details could have been the romantic imagination of Ge Hong, of course, in *The Sketches of the Western Capital*. But it would be honest work, and an easy conscience. To make a living just like others, whether or not he had a Wenjun at his side—possibly a Russian girl in a Chinese Qi skirt, with the fashionable high slits revealing her white thighs, her red hair flashing against the gray walls.

It was so absurd, he admonished himself, to be lost in such a daydream while he sat awaiting the confrontation in the Number 1 conference room.

Then he heard footsteps. Two men loomed on the threshold, Party Secretary Li and Superintendent Zhao.

Chen rose to his feet. To his surprise, several people followed the two into the conference room, including Detective Yu, Commissar Zhang, Doctor Xia, and other important members of the bureau.

Yu took a seat next to him, looking puzzled. It was the first time they had been together since Chen's return from Guangzhou.

"I was summoned back last night," Yu said simply, shaking Chen's hand.

The enlarged Bureau-Party-Committee meeting was an unusual one, for Detective Yu was not a member of it, and Dr. Xia, not even a Party member.

Standing at the head of the long table, Party Secretary Li opened with long quotations from the Party Central Committee's latest "red-character titled" document on the campaign against the influence of Western bourgeois ideology, and moved on to the topic of the bureau's recent work:

"As you may have learned, a tremendous breakthrough has been made in Chief Inspector Chen's case. It is a case speaking volumes for the necessity of our Party's new campaign. With the great economic achievement made through our Open Door Policy, we should be all the more alert against Western bourgeois influence. This case shows how serious, how disastrous such an influence can be. The criminals, though of revolutionary cadre families, fell prey to it. It is an important case, comrades. People are in support of our work. So is the Party Central Committee. We want to compliment Chief Inspector Chen on his achievement. He has overcome major difficulties conducting the investigation. Of course, both Comrade Detective Yu and Commissar Zhang have done a great job, too."

"What case are you talking about, Comrade Party Secretary Li?" Yu cut in, completely confounded.

"The case of Wu Xiaoming," Li said solemnly. "Wu Xiaoming was arrested together with Guo Qiang, last night."

It was no surprise that Yu was confused, Chen thought. One day the cops were suspended, and the very next day the criminals were arrested. The opposition had evaporated overnight. The conclusion seemed to come out of the blue. In the best scenario Chen had conceived, Wu would have escaped punishment until after Wu Bing's death. Now the son was arrested while the father was still breathing.

"How could that possibly be?" Yu stood up. "We did not know anything about it."

"Who made the arrests?" Chen asked.

"Internal Security."

"It is not their case," Yu protested. "It is ours. Chief Inspector Chen and I—with Commissar Zhang as well, of course, as our always politically-correct adviser. We have been in charge from day one."

"It's your case. No question about it. You have all done a great job. It's just because of the sensitive nature of the case that Internal Security took it over at the last stage." Party Secretary Li said, "Unusual problems require unusual remedies, comrades. A very unusual situation, indeed. The decision has been made, in fact, at a much higher level. Everything is being done in the best interests of the Party."

"So we are kept in the dark," Yu said doggedly, "in the best interests of the Party."

"Party Secretary Li has not finished yet, Comrade Detective Yu," Chen said, although he understood Yu's frustration at being deprived of the satisfaction of closing the case. After all the twists and turns, they deserved the chance to bring Wu down. Yu did not know, of course, that Internal Security had been involved with the case for a long time.

Chen decided not to say anything more at the moment. This unexpected development could signify something with enormous political dimensions.

"The special case group has made a great contribution," Party Secretary Li continued. "The Party and the people appreciate their work. We have decided to award them a first-class citation collectively. Of course, that doesn't mean our work is over. There's still a lot for us to do. Now, the superintendent will give us a speech."

"First of all," Superintendent Zhao started, "I'd like to compliment the comrades of the special case group, especially Comrade Chief Inspector Chen, for his intelligence and persistence."

"For his commitment," the Party Secretary joined in, "and the highest-level consciousness of the Party's interests."

"We have always thought highly of Comrade Chief Inspector Chen's work," the superintendent continued. "He has served well as acting director of the Shanghai Metropolitan Traffic Control Bureau. Now we can welcome him back. And in recognition of his achievement, also as embodiment of the Party's young cadre policy, we have decided that Chief Inspector Chen's going to represent us at the National Police Cadres Conference starting tomorrow at the Guoji Hotel. It is an honor he deserves after all the hard work he has put in. We also appreciate Comrade Yu's hard work. It is the Party committee's suggestion that Comrade Yu be moved to the top position in our housing committee's list.

As for Commissar Zhang, he has also made his special contributions in spite of his age, so we want to express our most sincere thanks. Finally, I want to welcome Dr. Xia to today's meeting. After the Tiananmen incident last year, some people have become shaky in their belief in our Party. Dr. Xia has chosen, however, to express to Chief Inspector Chen his intention of joining our Party. That is why we have invited him here today. Comrade Chief Inspector Chen, after the meeting, you can work out the details with Dr. Xia, and help him fill out the application form as his sponsor."

"Yes, I'm glad justice has been upheld, Comrade Chief Inspector Chen," Dr. Xia stammered, looking embarrassed rather than elated. "Congratulations on your work."

Chen turned to look in the direction of Party Secretary Li, who nodded back at him.

As soon as the meeting was over, Chen took Yu aside. His assistant could speak impulsively, as Chen had come to know during the investigation. They had just started talking under their breath, when Commissar Zhang moved over to join them, with an incomprehensible expression on his withered face.

"Everything has been done," Zhang said, "in the Party's interests."

"Everything done under the sun, or not under the sun," Yu said, "can be conveniently so explained."

"As long as we did our work with a clear conscience," Chen said, "we don't have to worry about anything."

"Bourgeois influences are everywhere, comrades," Zhang said. "Even somebody like Wu Xiaoming, a young cadre from a revolutionary family background, is not immune. So all of us have to be on our guard."

"Yes, on guard against back-biters," Yu said. "Indeed—"

Their talk was once more interrupted. This time it was Party Secretary Li who came over to take Chen aside. They moved across to the end of the conference room, overlooking the busy traffic along Fuzhou Road.

"What's all this about?" Chen asked.

"You know how complicated the situation is," Li said. "You deserve the credit, but we need to think about possible consequences."

"It is my case. Whatever the consequences, they are mine, too."

"People are all aware of Wu's family background. It is easy for some to see the case as a warning—or even as a blow—to those with a similar family background. Not as one individual case, but as a symbolic case. And you are the instrument bringing such a disgrace to the old cadres."

"I see, Comrade Party Secretary Li," Chen said, "but as I've said so many times, I have nothing against the old cadres."

"There are people and there are people. What's going through their minds, you cannot tell. Any publicity at this stage of the case won't do you any good."

"What about Detective Yu?"

"Don't worry about him. We'll conclude the case as the collective work of the bureau. Yu won't get much publicity anyway."

"I'm afraid I still don't understand this sudden conclusion."

"You will, I'm sure. You've done your job, so let others take care of the remaining problem." Party Secretary Li added after a pause, "It is not just our bureau's concern, let me tell you. Some leading comrades share our concern."

"Who?"

"You don't need me to tell you. You know—or you will know."

It would be useless to ask Li any more about it.

"I give you my word," Li promised. "Justice will be done. You will be completely occupied with the conference. We'll keep you informed."

"Thank you, Comrade Party Secretary Li," Chen said, "for everything."

For Chief Inspector Chen's future, Party Secretary Li's analysis made sense—if Chen still longed for such a future. Chen left the conference room without further protest.

He could not find Dr. Xia, who was perhaps not too eager to fill out those Party application forms after all. His search for Yu met with no success either. In his own cubicle, he found a short note saying, "I'm working with the Internal Security people now. I'll keep my mouth shut, as you have suggested, and my eyes open. Yu."

A detective could not be too cautious with Internal Security.

Later, as Chief Inspector Chen was leaving, Sergeant Liao approached him in the corridor, "Congratulations! What a wonderful job."

"Thank you."

Liao added in a whisper, "We'll make sure that Miss Wang's application for a passport is properly processed."

"Miss Wang, oh—" Chen had hardly thought of her during the last few days. But other people had. Because of him. This same Liao, who had called him "a busybody who cannot take care of his own business," was offering to take care of hers—assuming it was still his.

Now that he was back in the Party's favor, Wang would get her passport. Sergeant Liao was such a snob.

"Thank you," he said, shaking Sergeant Liao's hand energetically.

But Wang already seemed to be as far away as the woman referred to by Li Shangyin: *Master Liu regrets that Mount Peng is too far away/And I, thousands of times farther away from the mountains.*

In the ancient Chinese legend. Master Liu, a young man of the Han dynasty, ventured onto Mount Peng, where he had a wonderful time with a beautiful woman. When he returned to his village, it had changed beyond his recognition. A hundred years had passed. He never found his way back into the mountains. So the couplet was frequently read as contrition over an irrecoverable loss.

Chapter 41

It was the fourth day of the National Police Cadre Conference. The Guoji Hotel, located at the intersection betwen Nanjing Road and Huanghe Road, overlooking the central area of the city, had been the highest building in Shanghai for many years.

Chief Inspector Chen had been provided with a luxurious suite on the twenty-second floor. Looking out of the window to the east, in the first gray light of the morning, he could see the building of the First Department Store joining various stores on Nanjing Road in a colorful parade towards the Bund. But he was in no mood to enjoy the spectacular view. He hurried to put on his clothes. The last few days had been so hectic for him. Not only was he a representative of the Shanghai Police Bureau, he also had to serve as a conference host, coordinating all kinds of activities. Most of the representatives were superintendents or Party secretaries from other cities. He had to build his connections with them. For himself as well as for the bureau.

As a result, he had hardly had any time to think about the progress of the case. Still, the first thing he did that morning, as he had for the past few days, was to sneak out of the hotel to a public phone booth across the street. He had asked Yu not to phone him in his room except for an emergency. With Internal Security working in the background, they had to be extremely cautious.

At their agreed-upon time, he dialed Yu's number. "How are things going?" he asked.

"Positive. Tell you what, even Director Yao Liangxia, that Marxist Old Woman, called our office. She declared that the Party Discipline Committee stood behind us firmly."

"Was anything said by Party Secretary Li?"

"Last night, a telephone conference was held between the Bureau Party Committee and the mayor. Only Party Secretary Li and Superintendent Zhao were present. Closed-door discussion, of course. Politics, I imagine."

"Li will not say a single word about those meetings, I understand. Is there any news from other sources?"

"Well, Wang Feng has also contacted us, saying they are going to run a front-page story in the *Wenhui Daily* tomorrow."

"Why?"

"Wu's on trial today! Haven't you heard, Chief Inspector Chen?"

"What!" he said. "No, I haven't.

"That's surprising," Yu said. "I thought they would have informed you immediately."

"Will you appear in court?"

"Yes, I will be there, but Internal Security will run the show."

"How are you getting along with the Internal Security people?"

"Fine. I think they're serious. They're gathering all the documents." Yu then added. "Except they haven't really double-checked some evidence and witnesses."

"What do you mean?"

"Take Comrade Yang, the one at the gas station, for instance. I suggested that they call him in for identification, and then use him as a witness in court. But they said that it would not be necessary."

"So what do you think the result will be?"

"Wu will be punished. No question about that. Or it does not make sense to have all the fanfare going on," Yu said. "But the trial could last for days."

"Death sentence?"

"With reprieve, I bet, with the old man still in the hospital. But not anything less than that. People will not consent."

"Yes, I think that's most likely," he said. "What else has Wang told you?"

"Wang wanted me to convey her congratulations to you. And Old Hunter, too—a salute from an old Bolshevik. Old Bolshevik—that's his word. I haven't heard him say it in years."

"He's an old Bolshevik indeed. Tell him I'll treat him at the Mid-Lake Teahouse. I owe him a big one."

"Don't worry about that. He's talking about treating you. The old man does not know what to do with his adviser's allowance."

"He absolutely deserves it after his thirty years in the force," Chen said, "not to mention his contribution to the case."

"And Peiqin is preparing another meal. A better one, that much I can promise you. We have just got some Yunnan ham. Genuine stuff." Detective Yu, who should have been years beyond such overexcitement at concluding a case, kept rambling on. "What a shame. You are missing all the fun here."

"Yes, you are right," Chen said. "I've been so busy with the conference. I've almost forgotten that I'm in charge of the case."

Putting down the phone, he hurried back to the hotel. He had a presentation to make in the morning, and a group discussion to attend in the afternoon. In the evening, Minister Wen was scheduled to make an important concluding speech. Soon he was overwhelmed by the conference details.

During the lunch break, he tried to make another call to inquire about the trial but in the lobby he was stopped by Superintendent Fu, of the Beijing Police Bureau, who talked to him for half an hour. Then another director came up to him. And he had no break at all during dinner, as he had to toast all the invitees, table after table. After dinner, Minister Wen, who seemed to be especially well-disposed toward him, sought him out. Finally, after the long speeches, well after nine o'clock, Chen stole out of the hotel to another phone booth on Huanpi Road. Yu was not at home.

Then he dialed Overseas Chinese Lu. Wang Feng had called him. "She's so happy for you," Lu said. "That much I could tell. Even in her tone. A really nice girl!"

"Yes, she is," Chen said.

When Chen got back to his room, the maid had prepared everything for the night. The bed was made, the window closed, and the curtain partly drawn. There was a pack of Marlboros on the night stand. In the small refrigerator, he saw several bottles of Budweiser, an imported luxury that suited his status here. Everything signified that he was an "important cadre."

Turning on the bedside lamp, he glanced at the TV listings. The room had cable, so there were several Hong Kong martial arts movies available. He had no desire to see any of them. Once more, he looked out toward the First Department Store silhouetted against the night by the ever-changing neon lights.

Had there been an emergency, Yu would have contacted him.

After taking a shower, he put on his pajamas, opened a Budweiser and began studying the newspaper. There was not much worth reading, but he knew he could not fall asleep. He was not drunk—certainly not as drunk as Li Bai, who had written a poem about dancing with his own shadow under the Tang dynasty moon.

The he heard a light knock on the door.

He was not expecting company. He could pretend to be asleep, but he had heard of stories about hotel security checking rooms at unlikely hours.

"Okay, come in," he said with a sense of resignation.

The door opened.

Someone stepped through the doorway, barefoot, in a white robe.

He stared at the intruder for a few seconds, fitting the image against his memories before recognition came to him.

"Ling!"

"Chen!"

"Imagine seeing you—" he broke off, not knowing what else to say.

She closed the door after her.

There was no suggestion of surprise in her face. It was as if she had just come from the ancient library in the Forbidden City, carrying a bundle of books for him, the pigeons' whistles echoing in the distance in the clear Beijing sky; as if she had just come walking out of the Beijing subway mural painting, an Uighur girl carrying grapes in her arms, infinite motion, moving yet not moving, light as a summer sky, under her bangled bare feet, scraps of the golden paint flaking from the frame . . .

And Ling was the same—despite the lapse of years—except that her long hair, undone for the night, fell to her shoulders. A few loose strands curled at her cheeks, giving her a casual, intimate look. Then he noticed the tiny lines around her eyes.

"What has brought you here?"

"An American library delegation. I am serving as their escort. I told you about it."

She had touched upon the possibility of accompanying an American library delegation to southern cities, but she had not mentioned Shanghai as one of the places they were going to visit.

"Have you had your supper?" Another silly question. He was annoyed with himself.

"No," she said. "I just gotten in. I just had time to take a shower."

"You have not changed."

"Nor have you."

"Well, how did you know I was staying here?"

"I telephoned your bureau. Somebody in your office told me.

Your Party Secretary, Li Guohua, I believe. At first he was rather guarded, so I had to tell him who I am."

"Oh." *Or whose daughter*

Ling took out a cigarette. He lit it for her, cupping his hand over the lighter. Lightly, her lips brushed against his fingers.

"Thanks."

She sat in a casual posture, drawing one bare foot under her. As she tapped the cigarette into the ashtray, leaning over, her robe parted slightly. He caught a flash of her breasts. She was aware of his glance, but she did not close her robe.

They looked into each other's eyes. "Wherever you are," she said jokingly, "I can get hold of you."

She certainly knew how to get hold of him. There was no withholding information from her. As an HCC, she had her ways.

In spite of her joke, he felt tension building between them. It was illegal for man and woman to share a hotel room without a marriage license. Hotel security was authorized to break in. A loud knock at the door was to be expected at any time. "Routine checkup!" Some rooms were even equipped with secret video recorders.

"Where is your room?" he asked.

"In this same section for 'distinguished guests,' because I'm the escort to the American delegation. The security people won't check up here.

"It's so nice of you to come," he said.

"*It is difficult to meet, and also difficult to part. / The east wind listless, and flowers languid . . .*" Ling quoted the couplet about star-crossed lovers to good effect. She understood his passion for Li Shangyin.

"I've missed you," she said, her face soft under the light, though etched with travel fatigue.

"So have I."

"After all the years we've wasted," she said, dropping her eyes, "we're together tonight."

"I don't know what to say, Ling."

"You don't have to say anything."

"You've no idea how grateful I am," he said, "for all you have done for me."

"Don't say that either."

"You know, the letter I wrote, I did not mean to—"

"I knew," she said, "but that was what I wanted."

"Well—"

"Well," She looked up at him, and her eyes lost the tentative look and grew hazy. "We're here. So why not? I'm leaving tomorrow morning. No point repressing ourselves."

An almost forgotten phrase from Sigmund Freud, another Western influence in his college days. In hers, too, perhaps. He saw her moisten her lips with her tongue; then his glance fell to her bare feet, which were elegantly arched with well-formed toes.

"You're right."

He moved to turn off the light, but she stopped him with a gesture. She stood up, undid the belt, and let the robe fall to the floor. Her body gave off a porcelain glow under the light. Her breasts were small, but the nipples were erect. In a minute they were on the bed, aching for the time they had spent apart, their long wasted years. The haste was his doing as much as hers, touched with a sort of desperation that affected them both. There was no salvaging the past, except by being themselves in the present.

She groaned, wrapping her arms around his neck and her legs around his back. Moving under him, she arched herself up, her fingers long, strong, sliding down his back. The intensity of her arousal sharpened his. After a while, she changed position and lay on top of him. With her long hair cascading over his face, she was provoking sensations he had never known. He lost himself in her hair. She shuddered when she came, panting in short, quick breaths against his face. Her body suddenly grew soft, wet—insubstantial as the clouds after the rain.

They lay quietly in each other's arms, feeling themselves far above and beyond the city of Shanghai.

Perhaps due to the height of the hotel, he suddenly seemed to see the white clouds pressing through the window, pressing against her sweat-covered body in the soft moonlight.

"We're turning into clouds and rain," he said, invoking the ancient metaphor.

She whispered a throaty agreement, curling up with her head on his chest, gazing up at him, her black hair spilling.

Their feet brushed. Touching her arched sole lightly, he felt a grain of sand stuck between her toes. Sand from the city of Shanghai—not from the Central South Sea complex in the Forbidden City.

Their moment was interrupted by the footsteps moving along the corridor. He heard the sound of the hotel people producing a bunch of keys. A key turning—once, only once—at a door across the corridor. The suspense made their sensations even more intense. She nestled against him again. There was something in her features he had never seen before. So clear and serene. The autumn night sky of Beijing, across which the Cow Herd and Spinning Girl gaze at each other, a bridge woven of black magpies across the Milky Way.

They embraced again.

"It's been worth the wait," she said quietly afterward. Then she fell asleep beside him, the stars whispering quietly outside the window.

He sat up, took a pad from the nightstand and started writing, the lamplight falling like water on the paper. The stillness around them seemed to be breathing with life. Amidst the images rushing to his pen, he turned to see her peaceful face on the pillow. The innocence of her clear features, of the deep-blue night high above the lights of Shanghai, charged through him in waves of meaning.

He had a feeling that the lines were flowing to him from a superior power. He just happened to be there, with the pen in his hand. . . .

He did not know when he fell asleep.

The ring of the telephone on the night stand startled him.

As he stirred from his dream, blinking, he realized Ling was no longer beside him. The white pillows were rumpled against the headboard, still soft, cloud-like in the first morning light.

The telephone kept on ringing. Shrill and sharp, so early in the morning, like an omen. He snatched it.

"Chief Inspector Chen, it's all finished." Yu sounded edgy, as if he too had hardly slept.

"What do you mean—all finished?"

"The whole thing. The trial is over. Wu Xiaoming was sentenced to death, guilty on all the charges against him, and executed last night. About six hours ago. Period."

Chen glanced at his watch. It was just past six.

"Wu did not try to appeal?"

"It's a special case. The Party authorities put it that way. No use making any appeal. Wu was well aware of that. His attorney, too. An open secret to everybody. Appeal or no appeal, it would have made no difference."

"And he was executed last night?"

"Yes, just a few hours after the trial. But don't start asking me why, Comrade Chief Inspector."

"Well, what about Guo Qiang?"

"Also executed, at the same time and on the same execution ground."

"What?" Chen was more than shocked. "Guo had committed no murder."

"Do you know what the most serious charge against Wu and Guo was?"

"What?"

"Crime and corruption under Western bourgeois influence."

"Can you try to be a bit more specific, Yu?"

"I can, of course, but you will be able to read all the political humbug in the newspapers. Headlines in red print, I bet. It will be in the *Wenhui Daily*. Now it's part of a national campaign against 'CCB'—corruption and crime under Western bourgeois influence. A political campaign has been launched by the Party Central Committee."

"So it is a political case after all!"

"Yes, Party Secretary Li is right. It's a political case, as he said from the very beginning." Yu made no effort to conceal the bitterness in his voice. "What a great job we have done."

Chen went downstairs. He saw Ling again in the hotel lobby.

Several members of the American delegation had gathered around the front desk to admire a Suzhou embroidered silk scroll of the *Great Wall*. Ling was interpreting. She did not notice him at first. In the morning light, she appeared pale, with dark rings visible under her eyes. He did not know when she had left his room.

She was wearing a rose-colored Qi skirt, the slits revealing her slender legs. A small straw purse hung from her shoulder, and a bamboo briefcase was in her hand. An Oriental among the Occidentals. She was about to leave with the American delegation.

As he gazed at her in a flood of morning light, he was awash in gratitude.

She did not disengage herself immediately. As soon as she was free, he asked, "Will you call me when you get back to Beijing?"

"Of course I will." She added after a pause, "If that's all right with you."

"How can you ask that? You have done such a lot for me—"

"No, don't. You're under no obligation."

"Then we'll see each other in Beijing," he said, "in October. Maybe earlier."

"Remember the poem you recited for me in the North Sea Park that afternoon?"

"That afternoon, yes."

"So it's just a couple of months."

A small American woman with a slight limp came shuffling toward her.

"Are we done with what we have come for?"

"Yes, I'm done with what I came for," she said, looking at him before she turned to join the delegation members.

Outside, it was a bright, shining morning. A gray mini-van awaited the delegation on Nanjing Road. She was the last to get into the van, carrying a leather suitcase for someone. As the car started moving, she rolled down the window and waved her hand at him.

He watched as the van pulled out

I'm done with what I came here for. That was what she had said.

What had he come here for? He wished he could say the same, but he couldn't.

It had happened. It might never happen again. He did not know. He did know, however, that there was no stepping twice into the same river.

But he had to run back into the hotel. Some representatives were leaving. As the host, he had to say good-bye to them and bestow various gifts on behalf of the Shanghai Police Bureau. Smiling, shaking hands with one representative after another, he realized that his responsibilities at the Guoji Hotel had been designed to get him out of the way.

"The order of the acts has been schemed and plotted, / And nothing can avert the final curtain's fall."

By noon, he was free to go downstairs to the newspaper stand in the lobby. There were several people gathering in front of it, reading the newspaper over each other's shoulders. As he walked toward them, he saw a headline printed in red:

CORRUPTION AND CRIME UNDER WESTERN BOURGEOIS INFLUENCE

There was a full page editorial in the *People's Daily* about Wu's case.

What struck Chen as most absurd was that Guan's name was not even mentioned. She was just one of the unnamed victims. The homicide was treated as an inevitable effect of Western bourgeois influence. Chief Inspector Chen's name was not mentioned either, which was probably well-meant, as Party Secretary Li had explained. But Commissar Zhang was cited as a representative of the old high cadres determined to push through the investigation. Zhang's commitment was seen as the Party's determination.

It is not people that make interpretations, but interpretations that make people.

The editorial concluded impressively, authoritatively:

Wu Xiaoming was born of a high cadre family, but under Western bourgeois influence, Wu turned into a criminal. The lesson is clear. We must always remain alert. The case shows our Party's determination to fight corruption and crime caused by Western bourgeois influences. A criminal, of whatever family background, will be punished in our socialist society. Our Party's pure image will never be soiled.

Chief Inspector Chen did not want to read more.

There was another piece of news, shorter, but also on the front page, about the conference, with his name listed as one of the important cadres who attended it.

He became aware of other people talking in front of the newsstand. They were engaged in a heated discussion.

"How easily those HCC can make tons of money," a tall man in a white T-shirt said. "My company needs to apply for a quota for textile exports every year, but it is very difficult to get one. So my boss goes to an HCC, and that S.O.B. just picks up the phone, saying to the minister in Beijing, 'Oh, dear Uncle, we all miss you so much. My mother is always talking about your favorite dish . . . By the way, I need an export quota; please help me with it.' So this 'nephew' immediately gets his quota on a fax signed by the minister, and sells it to us for a million Yuan. You call this fair? In our company, one-third of the workers are being laid off, with only one hundred and fifty a month of so-called 'waiting for reassignment' pay—not enough to buy a moon cake for their kids at the Mid-Autumn Festival!"

"It's much more than quotas, young man," another man said. "They get those high positions like they were born to be way above us. With their connections, power, and money, what can't they do? Several well-known actresses were involved in the case, I've heard. All of them stripped naked, as white as lambs, scratching and screeching all night long. Wu has not wasted his days."

"Well, I heard that Wu Bing still is in a coma in Huadong Hospital," an elderly man cut in, apparently not comfortable with the direction of the discussion.

"Who is Wu Bing?"

"Wu Xiaoming's father."

"Good for the old man," the man in the white T-shirt said. "He will be spared the humiliation of his son's downfall."

"Who cares? The father should be responsible for his son's crime. I'm glad, for once, our government has made the right decision."

"Come on, you think they're serious? It's just like the old saying, 'Kill a chicken to scare monkeys.'"

"Whatever you say, this time the chicken is an HCC, and I would like to make a stew of it, delicious, tender, plus a pinch of MSG."

As he stood listening to the discussion, the various aspects of the case came together.

It was so politically complicated, this homicide case. In the inner-Party struggle, Wu's execution was a symbolic blow to the hard-liners, so that they would not continue to stand in the way of reform, but it was also a message modified by Wu's father being sick and away from the center, so that it would not upset those still in power to the point of shaking the "political stability." In terms of ideological propaganda, the case was conveniently presented as the consequence of Western bourgeois influence, which protected the Party's credit. And finally, to ordinary Chinese people, the case also served as a demonstration of the Party's determination to fight corruption at all levels, especially among the HCC, a dramatic gesture demanded by China's politics after the summer of 1989.

The combination of all these factors had made Wu Xiaoming the best candidate for an example. It was possible that failing Wu Xiaoming, another HCC with a similar background would have been chosen for such a purpose. It was proper and right that Wu should be punished. No question about it. But the question was: Had Wu been punished for the crime he had committed?

So Chief Inspector Chen had played right into the hands of politics.

The realization came to him as he left the hotel and walked slowly along Nanjing Road with heavy steps. The street was as crowded as ever. People were walking, shopping, talking, in high spirits. The sun cast its brilliance over the most prosperous thoroughfare of the city. He bought a copy of the *People's Daily*.

In his high-school days, he had believed in everything published in the *People's Daily*, including one particular term: *proletarian dictatorship*. It meant a sort of dictatorship logically necessary to reach the final stage of communism, thus justifying all means toward that ultimate end. The term *proletarian dictatorship* was no longer used. Instead, the term was: *the Party's interests*.

He was no longer such an unquestioning believer.

For he could hardly believe in what he himself had done.

Wu Xiaoming had been executed at the moment when he had been sleeping with Ling. What had happened between Ling and him was, by the orthodox Communist code, another instance of "Western bourgeois decadence." The same crime Wu had been accused of—"decadent lifestyle under the influence of Western bourgeois ideology."

Chief Inspector Chen could tell himself, of course, a number of convenient things—that things are complicated, that justice must be upheld, that the Party's interest is above everything else, and that the end justifies the means.

But it was more than that, he realized: the end could not but be transformed by the use of certain means.

"*Whoever fights monsters,*" Nietzsche said, "*should see to it that in the process he does not become a monster.*"

His thoughts were interrupted by a request in an Anhui accent, "Could you take a picture for me, please?" A young girl held out a small camera.

"Sure." He took the camera from her.

She began posing in front of the First Department Store. A provincial girl, new to Shanghai, she chose the glamorous models in the store window for a background. He pressed the button.

"Thank you so much!"

She could have been Guan, ten or fifteen years earlier, her eyes sparkling with hopes for the future, Chen reflected with a sinking heart.

A successful conclusion to an important case. The question for him was: How had he managed to bring the case to a triumphant close? Through his own HCC connection—and a carnal connection—with a politburo member's daughter.

What irony!

Chief Inspector Chen had sworn that he would do everything in his power to bring Wu to justice, but he had not supposed that he would have been brought to connive in such a devious way.

Detective Yu had known nothing about it. Otherwise, Chen doubted that his assistant would have collaborated. Like other ordinary Chinese people, Yu was not unjustified in his deep-rooted prejudice against the HCC.

Even though Ling might prove to be an exception. Or just an exception with him. For him.

He saw a number of similarities between Guan, the national model worker and Chen, the chief inspector. The most significant was that each had a relationship with an HCC.

There was only one difference.

Guan had been less lucky in her love, for Wu had not reciprocated her affection. Perhaps Wu had cared for her a bit. But politics and ambition had happened to be in their way.

Had Guan really loved Wu? Was it possible that she, too, was driven by politics? There could not be a definite answer—now they were both dead.

How about his own feelings toward Ling?

It was not that Chief Inspector Chen had deliberately, coldly used her. To be fair to himself, he had never allowed such an idea to come to the surface of his mind, but what about subconsciously?

Nor was he sure that there had been nothing but passion on his part last night.

Gratitude for her magnanimity?

In Beijing, they had cared for each other, but they had parted, a decision he had not really regretted. All those years, he had often thought of her, but he had also thought of others, made other friends—girlfriends, too.

When the case first came to his attention, he was dancing with Wang at his house-warming party. In the following days, it was

Wang who had accompanied him through the early stages of the investigation. In fact, he had hardly thought of Ling at all in those days. The letter written at the post office had been anything but romantic; it was inspired by a moment of desperation—by the instincts of a survivor.

He was a survivor, too ambitious to perish in ignoble silence. It was the haunting image of Liu Yong, the deplorable Song dynasty poet, who had only a prostitute to take pity on him at his deathbed, that had spurred him into desperate action. He had resolved not to end up a loser like Liu Yong. *You have to find a way out*, he'd told himself.

That's the way she came back into his life.

Maybe just for the one night.

Maybe more than that.

Now what was he supposed to do?

In spite of the difference in their family background, there ought to be some way for them to be together. They should be able to live in the world of their own discourse, not just in other people's interpretations.

Still, he could not help shuddering at the prospect before him. For it was not going to be a world of their own, but in which he would, perhaps, begin to find his life much easier, even effortless. He would never be able to shake off the feeling that nothing was accomplished through his own efforts. She did not need to go to this or that minister, claiming him as hers. He would have become an HCC himself. And people would be eager to do a lot of things for him.

There was no point going back to the bureau at the moment. He was in no mood for Party Secretary Li's recital of the *Wenhui Daily* editorial. Nor did he want to go back to his own apartment, alone, after such a night.

He found himself walking toward his mother's place.

His mother put down the newspaper she had been reading,

"Why didn't you call?"

She rose to set a cup of tea before him.

"Politics," he said bitterly, "Nothing but politics."

"Some trouble at work?" She looked puzzled.

"No, I'm all right."

"Politics. You mean the conference? Or the HCC case, today's headline? Everybody is talking about it."

He did not know how to explain to her. She had never been interested in politics. Nor did he know whether he should tell her about Ling although that was what his mother would really be interested in. So he just said, "I've been in charge of the Wu case, but it has not been concluded properly."

"Was justice served?"

"Yes. Politics aside—"

"I've talked to several neighbors. They are all very pleased with the outcome of the trial."

"I'm glad they are pleased, Mother."

"In fact, I have been doing some thinking about your work since our last talk. I still hope you will take your father's path one day, but in your position, if you believe you can do something for the country, you should persevere. It helps a little if there are a few honest policemen around, even though it may not help much."

"Thank you, Mother."

After he had his tea, she walked downstairs with him. In the hallway crowded with stoves and cooking utensils, Aunt Xi, an old neighbor, greeted them warmly, "Mrs. Chen, your son is a high cadre now, Chief Inspector Director or some high ranking position. This morning I was reading the newspaper, and his name with an important title jumped out at me."

His mother smiled without saying anything. His rank might have appealed to her a little too.

"Don't forget us in your high position," Aunt Xi continued.

"Remember, I've watched you grow up."

Out on the street, he saw a peddler frying dumplings in a gigantic wok over a wheeled gas burner, a familiar scene from his childhood, only a coal stove would have been used back then. One fried dumpling would have been a lavish treat for a child, but his mother would stuff him with two or three. A loving mother, beautiful, young, and supportive.

Time, as Buddha wrote, passes in the snapping of the fingers.

At the bus stop, he turned around and saw her still standing in front of the house. Small and shrunken and gray in the dusk. Though still supportive.

Chief Inspector Chen would not quit the police force.

The visit had strengthened his determination to go on.

She might never fully approve of his profession, but as long as he did his job conscientiously, he would not disappoint her. Also, it was his responsibility to support her. He would purchase a pound of genuine jasmine tea for her the next time he went to visit. And he would think about how to tell her about his relationship with Ling.

In the words of the poem his father had taught him, a son's return for his mother's love is always inadequate, and so is one's responsibility to the country:

> *Who says that the splendor of a grass blade returns*
> *The love of the spring that forever returns?*

The End

About the Author

Qiu Xiaolong was born in Shanghai. He was selected for membership in the Chinese Writers' Association and published poetry, translations and criticism in China. He has lived in the United States since 1989 and has an M.A. and a Ph.D. in Comparative Literature awarded by Washington University. His work has been published in *Prairie Schooner*, *New Letters*, *Present Tense*, *River Styx*, *Riverfront Times*, and in several anthologies. He has been the recipient of the Missouri Biennial Award, the *Prairie Schooner* Readers' Choice Award, a Yaddo and a Ford Foundation Fellowship. He teaches Chinese Literature at University College of Washington University and lives in St. Louis with his wife and daughter.